Taking up the Chase

Taking up the Chase

WILLIAM A. HILLMAN JR.

iUniverse, Inc.
Bloomington

Taking up the Chase

iUniverse books may be ordered through booksellers or by contacting:

iUniverse
1663 Liberty Drive
Bloomington, IN 47403
www.iuniverse.com
1-800-Authors (1-800-288-4677)

Because of the dynamic nature of the Internet, any web addresses or links contained in this book may have changed since publication and may no longer be valid. The views expressed in this work are solely those of the author and do not necessarily reflect the views of the publisher, and the publisher hereby disclaims any responsibility for them.

Any people depicted in stock imagery provided by Thinkstock are models, and such images are being used for illustrative purposes only.
Certain stock imagery © Thinkstock.

ISBN: 978-1-4620-5277-6 (sc)
ISBN: 978-1-4620-5279-0 (hc)
ISBN: 978-1-4620-5278-3 (ebk)

Printed in the United States of America

iUniverse rev. date: 08/30/2011

BOOK 1

Taking Up the Chase

Chapter 1

A young girl woke up one morning. It was an average morning, or so it seemed. On this morning she woke more by habit shortly before the alarm rung.

She closed her eyes and then rubbed them a bit. She sat up in bed and put her feet on the floor.

"Maria, it's time to get up," called the girl's mother through a closed door.

Maria Marhill shook her blonde hair out of her eyes and got up. She walked to her closet and began her usual ritual before school.

She had just put on her shirt and reached into the closet to get a coat when something happened.

She froze as something went through her that she could not describe.

The image of her mother went through her view but not her eyes. Her mother was pouring a glass of juice. Suddenly, the glass she was holding slipped from her hand. Juice went everywhere. "Oh no," she said. She reached for a towel on a roll. September 12. The date was not in her mind's eye, but she just knew it, as if it had been downloaded into her brain.

The experience stopped, and Maria looked around, frightened. *What was that?* she wondered. She walked back to her bed and sat down.

Am I sick? She pressed her hand to her forehead. *I don't feel warm.*

Maria looked at the calendar on the wall to her right. *September 16,* she thought. *That's today's date.*

"Maria, get moving," called her mother.

Maria got a sudden burst of energy at the thought of being late, and as she went downstairs, all thoughts of what had happened vanished.

Maria hurried into the kitchen after grabbing her coat off the hook. Her mother, Lois Marhill, was waiting by the table with a cup of coffee in her hand.

That's not juice, Maria thought. She sat down. *Should I tell her what happened?*

"Is something wrong, honey?" asked Lois.

Maria thought for only a moment. *I feel fine. I just want to go to school.* "No, Mom, I'm fine," she answered.

"Well, okay," said Lois. "I'll be home when you get finished with school."

"That's great," Maria said. She quickly ate her breakfast.

"See you later, Snugglebear," said Lois. Maria headed out the door.

I wonder what that was about, thought Maria, walking down the street. She soon entered the Paway High School

"Hey," called a strawberry blonde. She appeared excited as she approached Maria.

"Hey, Cindy," Maria said.

"You want to come over to my house today?" Cindy asked. "My parents will be gone, and we'll have the big screen to ourselves."

"Sure," answered Maria. She got her books from her locker. The bell rang. "See you."

Sometime later, Maria sat in class staring at the front of the room. The teacher continued to talk, but she did not pay attention. *What happened to me?* she wondered. *I saw stuff. It didn't hurt, but what if . . . I had a stroke or something? Oh no. Why didn't I tell Mom? Should I see the nurse? Maybe it's not that bad. Maybe it's something else. It could be that I was just tired. Maybe it was something I ate. No, Mom and I ate the same thing last night. What makes a person see stuff? I've never heard about anything like that before. What was with the date? It was like I just knew it. It doesn't make any sense.*

She looked at the blackboard. The teacher was still talking. *What if there's something wrong with me?* Maria wondered. She looked around. *Calm down. It's probably not that bad. Maybe I imagined it. It was probably a fluke or some other random thing that happens.*

I feel all right, right? She touched her head self-consciously. *I don't feel warm.* She looked around at the other students. The teacher continued talking.

Maria looked at him for a few minutes. *I'm not seeing anything now,* she thought. *Maybe it's nothing at all. I should probably look it up.* The bell rang and the students, including Maria, filed out of the classroom.

In the school's computer lab, Maria sat down in front of one of the machines. *Medical information sites,* she typed. A list of hits filled the screen. She clicked on the first link.

Med Know How's home page came up. *Seeing things,* she typed. A list of mental disorders and illnesses appeared.

Maria was horrified. *So now I'm crazy?* she wondered. She thought for a moment. She added */ knowing things* to her search. No hits.

Maria slumped in her chair. In some ways she felt worse than before. *So I'm either crazy or what?*

She let out a sigh. *What am I going to do?* The bell rang and she left.

Please put, As she left the classroom she saw Cindy down the hall. The look on her face seemed to be of anticipation. Sadly, Maria held up her hand and shook her head. She then ran off and left the school building.

Sometime later, after Maria ran the way home, she went in to her returned house.

"Hey there, Snugglebear," said Lois. "How was school?"

"Fine," Maria answered.

Lois went back to her magazine.

Maria put her book bag by the couch and sat on its arm. "Mom?"

"Yeah, honey?"

Maria thought for a moment. "How was your day?"

"Oh, fine," answered Lois. "Steve from accounting came in with news about a book that's coming out. He's recommending it to everyone. He really likes the author. Zercoft sales are going through the roof. Generics are doing good too."

"Anything else happen?" asked Maria. "Did anything happen here?" She was apprehensive.

"No, nothing really," Lois replied. "Just the usual chaotic moments, rushing around getting ready. I spilled some juice in all the excitement. It's a wonder I don't knock the house over. I've got to find a way to get things safely going in the morning."

It happened, Maria thought. She was not sure what she was feeling, but she tried not to show it. "When did that happen?"

"Just after you left," answered Lois.

It happened after the thing happened, she thought. "Mom, I've got to go," she said.

"Sure, honey." Maria took her notebook and left.

Before she went upstairs to her bedroom, she went into the kitchen. She opened the cupboard that held the trash can. She found a paper towel among its contents. It was stained the color of the juice.

It happened, she thought. She went up to her room.

What's going on? Maria wondered. She paced frantically around the room. *Did I have a vision of the future? I can't believe it.* Maria felt amazement rise up in her. She put her hand on her forehead and then walked to her bed, where she sat down.

She flopped her upper half down on the bed. Her legs dangled over the foot of the mattress. *This feels so unreal,* she thought. She lay there for a couple of moments.

She looked up at her computer. Without thinking she went over to it and turned it on. *Seeing the future,* she typed.

When she clicked the search button, thousands of links came up. *Seeing Ahead: Myth or Reality?* she read. *Washington University of the Paranormal, studying the unseen world for more than 20 years. Madam Roustee. The seer of your very souls. Modern Science Journal, how clairvoyance and other mental powers are impossible.*

Maria clicked on a historical link. *Practitioners from the Far East believed that knowledge of future events was possible through many sources,* she read. *From seeing how yellow sticks would fall to how stones would roll along the ground. The ones who were trained in these arts were said to be able to know about anything that would transpire in the future.*

After a few more moments, Maria stopped reading and took a deep breath. *Nothing in here is anything like what happened to me,* she thought. *This doesn't help me at all.*

She kept reading. About an hour later she stopped. *I've read everything I could find and none of it was like what happened. They don't talk about what it's like, only that they "see the future."*

She logged off. *Maybe that's not what happened to me at all.* She started to walk away.

Suddenly, it happened again.

Lois was in the kitchen. She reached to get something on the top shelf while standing on a chair. Her foot was standing on its back. It wobbled, and her foot slipped. She tried to grab the shelf, but her hands slipped. "Ahh!" she cried. She fell downward. September 12, 5:12 p.m. went through Maria's mind like the date had before.

"Mom," Maria cried. She looked around, expecting her mother to come into her room.

Maria stood there, nervous once again. *Oh my goodness,* she thought. *Is that going to happen to her?*

Maria took a deep breath. *Five twelve: that's* . . . She looked at her watch. *Now!* She darted downstairs.

"Mom," Maria cried. She reached the kitchen, where her mother was standing on a chair.

"Ahh!" Lois cried. She started to fall.

Maria grabbed her from behind. Maria fell back and they both landed on the floor.

"Oh my," Lois cried. She got off Maria. After a moment they both caught their breaths.

"I was going to get some noodles for dinner tonight," said Lois. "We were going to have spaghetti." She looked at Maria. "Thank you, Snugglebear," she said, and hugged her. "I think we'll have takeout instead." Lois went off to use the phone.

Maria went to her room. *I can't believe that happened,* she thought. She closed the door. *Who knows what would have happened if I hadn't been there.*

Maria felt anxious. *What's happening to me? Am I really seeing the future?* She threw herself onto her bed. *Is something happening to my head? Is that something going to mess me up? Am I having a stroke or something? In that movie that guy got the ability to see the future after he had an accident. He hit his head but I didn't. Did I? Maybe I did and I don't remember.*

Maria sat up. *It's possible. After all, I'm seeing the future.*

She looked around and took a deep breath. *I can't believe this is happening to me.*

"Hey, the food's here," called Lois. Maria got up and went downstairs.

She came to the table and sat down. She looked at the food.

"What's wrong, sweetie?" asked Lois. She brought a forkful of food to her mouth.

Maria thought for a moment. *What would she do if she knew?* she wondered. She felt afraid. "Nothing," she said. She ate to look occupied. *What am I going to do? Not tell her? Is that the right thing to do?*

Without thinking, she sighed. Her mother did not seem to notice. They continued eating.

Maria went into her room later that night. "Good night, sweetie," called Lois.

"Good night, Mom," said Maria. She got underneath her covers.

Lights throughout the house were turned off. Maria prepared to go to sleep. After much tossing and turning, she finally started to doze off.

Maria woke up the next morning and went about her usual routine. She tried not to think too much. *At least nothing went through my mind except some dream about butterflies,* she thought.

She put on her shirt and was reaching for a light coat when it happened again.

The teacher, Mr. Brender, got up before the class. "Now, students, I know that this is not our scheduled topic, but I found this fascinating article about Theodore Roosevelt last night in a magazine I was reading," he said. He held up a copy of the article. September 13, 8:18 a.m.

She came out of it. *Oh no,* Maria thought.

"Maria, time to get going," called Lois.

Maria arrived at the school minutes later. *Is this how it's going to be from now on?* she wondered. She waved at Cindy as she passed her. *Some people might think this was cool if it were happening to them, but I don't know what is happening to me.*

Maria got to her first class, history. *This could be only the beginning,* she thought. *This could be the symptom of some disease. Is something happening to me now?* She felt dread.

Mr. Brender came in carrying his suitcase. Maria looked at it with apprehension, not knowing whether she wanted what she had seen to happen or not. "Now, students, I know this is not our scheduled topic, but I found this fascinating article about Theodore Roosevelt last night in a magazine I was reading," he said. He held up a copy of the article.

Maria sighed, still not sure what to feel.

Later, Maria entered the cafeteria with her pack lunch in hand. She passed a brown-haired girl. "Hi, Kate," Maria said.

"Hi," Kate said.

Maria was about to sit down but then got an idea. *Maybe I can look up some more stuff and see if I can figure anything out this time.* She left the cafeteria with her lunch.

Moments later, Maria was in the computer lab doing an Internet search on *seeing the future.*

Minutes later, she sighed. *There's nothing new here since the last time,* she thought. *At least there's nothing here about people getting sick from being psychic. Psychic? Is that what I am? Is there something different about me?*

Maria looked at the clock on the wall and rubbed her eyes. *I better get my lunch now,* she thought.

She went over to a table and began to eat her lunch. As she ate, she began to feel a bit better. *Maybe it's not that bad. I mean, it's not like anyone talks about a psychic flu going around.*

Sometime later, Maria got home. "How was school, honey?" Lois asked.

"Fine," Maria answered. She went upstairs.

Maria threw herself onto her bed. She buried her face in her pillow. *It could all just be nothing,* she thought. *So I saw some things. I see fine now. I don't have a stomachache. I feel fine.*

Maria rolled onto her back. She let out a breath and felt her fear leave her.

"So, Mom, how was work today?" Maria asked. They were having dinner.

"It was fine, sweetie," answered Lois. She poked at her food. "Sales are good. People in some areas are talking about raises. Unfortunately, it looks like I'm going to have to travel again. I won't be home when you get done with school today."

"Too bad," said Maria. She looked at her food. *Maybe things won't be that different,* she thought. *I'm still talking with my mom. Still going to school.*

Still studying, reading, hanging out with Mom. I'm still doing everything I did before, only now something's different. She ate her meal.

A few hours later, Maria got into bed. *I think I can make this work,* she thought. She soon went to sleep.

Maria walked down a long hallway. It was dark, and though she reached out to her sides, she didn't touch anything. She looked around but could not see anything except something in the distance. She could not make it out, but she went toward it. She kept going to whatever it was. As she got closer, she began to hear things. She could not make them out at first. As she continued to walk, she began to make them out. She heard animal sounds that she recognized from nature shows. There were sounds made by big cats.

She went on and the sounds stopped. She was reaching the end of the hall.

Maria heard sounds overhead, but when she looked up, she could not see anything. She looked around again and finally saw dim shadows of people. They were standing off to her sides.

For some reason she continued to walk. She reached the end of the hall and saw a door. Maria reached out and opened it.

Behind it was a blinding white light that flooded the dark hall. Maria covered her eyes with one hand.

Eventually her eyes adjusted and she saw what was before her. It was a girl about her age wearing a hooded cloak. Maria realized then that she was wearing one just like it.

The girl before her looked just like her but seemed to have an intangible quality that made her seem like a vastly different person.

Suddenly, a hand touched her shoulder and she turned around to see who it was.

Maria woke up from her dream with a start. She lay there for a moment. *What a dream,* she thought. *I wonder if it has anything to do with the stuff I've been going through.*

She looked at her watch and realized that it was almost time to wake up. She got out of bed and did her morning ritual.

As she was putting her shirt on, it happened again. She had a vision.

Three men entered a building. "Give us your money, now," ordered a man carrying a baseball bat.

He slammed it on a desk. A woman behind it looked terrified, but a moment later she obeyed.

One of the men with him scooped the money into a bag.

The man with the bat and the third man herded people to one side of the room. The man with the bat knocked a name plaque off a desk. Paway First Bank, September 15, 4:12 p.m.

What? Maria wondered.

Chapter 2

What was that? wondered Maria. *Did I see a bank robbery?*

She sat on her bed. *Did I really see that? I was getting better. I never . . .* She got up and went over to her window. She took a look out and went back to her bed. *I never . . . So, I had a vision of a bank robbery. September 15, that's tomorrow.*

"Honey, it's time to get up," Lois called.

"Okay, Mom," said Maria. She left her room.

Several minutes later, Maria arrived at school. She waved at Cindy on her way to class.

What am I going to do? she wondered. *Am I going to stop it? I . . . could do that.* She sighed in dread.

Minutes later, the bell rang and the students entered the classroom. *I was just living my life and now I'm having visions of crimes that are going to happen,* Maria thought. *What am I supposed to do? Just show up and beat up the bad guys? This is too much. I'm just some girl, but I'm dealing with visions of the future and bank robberies.*

Later that day, she was in another class. "Though Darwin received much praise for his well-thought-out theories in his book *Origin of the Species,* religious leaders of the time condemned it as against God," said the teacher.

Is that why I'm getting these visions? Maria wondered. *Does God want me to stop this bank robbery? Is that why I saw something that didn't have anything to do with me?*

At lunch, the students entered the cafeteria. Maria came in and looked at the room. She got an idea and left.

Maria arrived at the computer lab and sat at the computer she had used before. *Bank robbery,* she typed. A list of links came up.

Definition: the act of stealing funds from a banking institution, she read. The rest were links to news articles about bank robberies in the past.

Maria leaned back in her chair. *You know, there's no rule that says I have to be the one to stop it,* she thought.

Maria thought for a moment and then did a search for *psychic detectives.* A series of links came up and she went through them. One talked about a detective who was suspended for requesting that a psychic be put on the case he was working on. Another one was about a police department stating officially that they did not have psychic detectives on any case. Another was an article from a skeptics' magazine arguing that psychic detectives could not be real.

Maria went through several more links. *If people who claimed to have such powers really existed, then why wouldn't federal authorities form special teams?* she read. *Since no special squads exist, it's safe to assume that so-called psychic gifts are unreliable or do not exist.*

Maria leaned back into her chair. *I better not tell anyone,* she thought.

Maria went over to a table. *Not only do I have to stop a bank robbery, but I also have to keep anyone from knowing that I get visions of the future.* She sighed.

Sometime later, a phone rang. Detective Lenny Hipar answered it. "Hello?"

"There's going to be a bank robbery tomorrow," said a hushed voice. "It's going to be at Paway First Bank at four twelve."

"Who is this?" asked Detective Hipar.

There was a pause. "Someone close to the robbers," Maria answered. "There are three of them."

"Do you know their names?" Hipar asked.

Another pause. "No."

"How do you know, then?"

"I can't say."

Detective Hipar was uncertain. "Could you please tell me how you know this bank robbery is going to happen?"

"I can't," Maria answered.

Whoever this is isn't giving me much to go on, Detective Hipar thought. "Is there a way we could meet?" he asked.

Silence. "I can't," she said.

"Is it because of your identity?" asked Detective Hipar. "Don't worry. No one will have to know. You can be a confidential informant." There was more silence. "Hello? Are you still there?"

"I'm still here," Maria answered. "I'll be there."

"Later tonight?" Hipar asked.

"How about tomorrow morning?"

The detective thought about it for a moment. "Sure. How about the corner of Peterson and Forty-second?" he asked. "At nine?"

"How about seven thirty?"

"Sure."

"What was that about?" asked Detective Jon Turner, Lenny Hipar's partner.

"I don't know," he said.

Maria stared at the pay phone. *I'm going to meet with the police to tell them about a crime,* she thought. *The closest I've ever come to that is watching a TV show.*

She started to walk away when she had a vision.

A middle-aged man with brown hair was walking through some sort of office. As he walked, he read a newspaper. His leg hit a trash can, causing him to stumble and spill the coffee he was holding in his free hand. It went all over his shirt. "Ahh!" he cried. September 15, 9:14 a.m.

The man was then sitting behind a desk reading something. A man in a policeman's uniform came up to him. "Sir," he said.

"What?" asked the first man.

"They found this man, Chuck Friees," he answered, pointing to a man wearing handcuffs standing nearby. "I believe you've been looking for him."

The first man smiled. "Chucky," he said. "How have you been?"

"Chew a worm," said Chuck. September 15, 12:45 a.m.

The man was still sitting down. A man with dark hair and a mustache came up to him. "Here's the Finney file," said the second man. He dropped the file on the desk. "Happy birthday." September 15, 2:02 p.m.

What was that? Maria wondered. *Who was that man?* She leaned against the phone booth.

Maybe it was fear or something that triggered that one, she thought. *I definitely have been feeling a lot of that lately.* She pulled her collar up to her neck and walked off.

The next morning, Maria got up and did her usual morning routine. She went downstairs.

"Hi, sweetheart," said Lois.

"Hi, Mom," Maria said. She poured a bowl of cereal and looked up at her mother as she read the paper. *It all seems so normal,* she thought. *In a little bit I'll be talking with a policeman about a bank heist.* She put a spoonful of cereal in her mouth.

"Have a good day at school," said Lois.

Maria looked up. "Sure, Mom," she said. "You have a good day at work."

A few minutes later, Maria went out the door.

"Good-bye, Snugglebear," said Lois.

"Good-bye, Mom," Maria said. She left, wishing she did not have to.

The morning light did not reach certain points of the alley by Peterson and 42nd. *I can't believe I'm going through with this,* Maria thought. She noticed a shadowed portion of the alley and went over to it. She felt uneasy.

Detective Lenny Hipar came into the alley moments later. *What's going on?* he wondered. *It would make sense if the guy giving the tip was afraid of his identity getting out, but he wouldn't give anything up. Normally a person would just say that he knew them or heard them talking, but this person was too afraid to give anything up. Something's off. I better be ready for anything.*

Maria was waiting behind a Dumpster and did not see the detective.

The detective was alert as he looked around. *Where is he?* he wondered.

Suddenly, Detective Hipar looked around the corner of the Dumpster, startling Maria. "Ahh!" she cried.

Detective Hipar went into a defensive position. "Freeze," he cried.

Maria froze in place.

"Are you the person who called for this meeting?" asked Detective Hipar.

"Yes, sir."

"Calm down," Detective Hipar said gently. "Now, come out."

Maria slowly came out from behind the Dumpster. *It looks like this didn't work,* she thought.

I wasn't expecting this, Detective Hipar thought.

As Maria saw Detective's Hipar's face in the light, she recognized him. *It's the man from my vision.*

"Are you the one who called me about the bank robbery?" he asked.

"Yes, sir," answered Maria.

"What's your name?"

"Maria Marhill," she answered. *He knows my name. What am I going to do?*

"What are you, twelve?"

"I'm fifteen," answered Maria defensively.

Detective Hipar took a deep breath and then took out his notebook. "So, Maria, you're saying there's going to be a robbery at Paway First at"—he turned a page—" four twelve."

"Yeah, there will be three guys," Maria said.

"What are their names?" asked Detective Hipar.

"I don't know."

"How do you know this is going to happen?"

Maria was silent for a moment. "I can't say," she answered.

Detective Hipar closed his notebook and put it away. "We'll put your tip on record, miss," he said. With that he turned and started to walk away.

"Wait," called Maria.

Detective Hipar stopped and turned to look at her. "Yes?"

"At 9:14 today you're going to spill coffee on yourself after hitting a trash can," she said. "At 12:45 you're going to meet a man named Chuck Friees who's going to tell you to chew a worm. At 2:02 a man with dark hair and a mustache is going to hand you a file and say happy birthday to you."

"Why would you say all that?" Detective Hipar asked.

"I can't say," she answered. She started to leave.

"Here," said Detective Hipar. He handed her his business card. "In case you want to talk."

Maria grabbed her book bag out from behind the Dumpster and darted out of the alley.

Chapter 3

Maria sat in class. *What am I going to do?* she wondered. *Once those things come true, then he'll know my secret. Then everyone will. What am I going to say or do? This isn't what was supposed to happen.*

Maria slid the business card out from beneath her book. *Detective Lenard Hipar,* she read. Beneath the name was a phone number. Looking at the card made everything seem more real. *I can't believe this is happening. My life used to be so normal. I would go to school or hang out. Now I'm getting visions and talking to detectives about stopping crimes. What's happening to me?*

Meanwhile, at the station house, Detective Hipar was walking while reading his morning paper. *That girl said I was going to spill coffee on myself around this time,* he thought. *I'm drinking coffee right now, but everyone does, and everyone spills it on themselves. It's pretty generic. Still, there's something off about that girl. I should run a check on her. How did she know I'm looking for Friees?*

Suddenly he bumped his leg on a trash can and spilled his coffee on himself. "Ahh!" he cried.

Detective Hipar quickly went to his desk. He patted himself with his newspaper, trying to soak up the coffee. *It's just like she said,* he thought. *It could just be the power of suggestion.* He looked at his watch. It read 9:14. He was unsettled. As he tried to push the whole thing from his mind, he dropped the wet newspaper into the trash.

Sometime later, Detective Hipar was sitting at his desk reading a file. A uniformed officer came up to him with a handcuffed prisoner. "Sir," said the officer.

"Yeah?" Hipar asked, looking up.

"We collared this man, Chuck Friees, today on a traffic violation," answered the officer. "I believe you were looking for him on a gun-related charge."

Detective Hipar looked at him. "Chucky," he said.

"Chew a worm," said Chuck.

Hipar sat there remembering what Maria had said. *Maybe he knows her,* he thought. He looked at his watch. It read 12:45. *How would either of them know when he'd be brought to me?* he wondered.

The officer took Chuck Friees away as Detective Hipar sat there puzzled.

Sometime later, Hipar was looking at a computer screen. *I looked through anything I could find on this Maria Marhill,* he thought. *Nothing out of the ordinary. Perfectly normal. She apparently was born a little over fifteen years ago at Our Lady of Eternal Mercy Hospital. She goes to Paway High School. No criminal record. As far as I can tell, she's never left the city. Nothing but normal.*

Just then Detective Turner came by. He put a file folder on Lenny's desk. "Here's the Finney file," he said. "Happy birthday." He started to walk away.

Detective Hipar checked his watch. It read 2:02. "Hey, what did you say?"

Turner turned to look at him. "Happy birthday," he answered. "What, upset that I didn't get you anything else?"

"Do you know any teenage girls?" Hipar asked.

"No. Why?"

"No reason."

"Are you all right?"

"I'm fine."

Detective Turner went back to his desk. Detective Hipar sat at his desk confused. *What's going on?* he wondered.

A few hours later, school got out. Maria left the building with students passing her on either side.

As she cleared school grounds, she heard a voice. "Hey."

Maria turned to see Detective Hipar standing by a plain brown car. "Get in," he said.

Maria looked around and then went across the street to him.

"How did you know those things were going to happen?" he asked.

"I can't say," said Maria.

"I need to know," Detective Hipar said. "I have to put it in my report."

"You can't put it in your report. You can't tell anyone."

"Why not?"

"Well . . . , what about me being a confidential informant?" she asked.

"Look, here's the thing," said Detective Hipar. "I need to know. This whole thing is . . ."

Maria looked at him. *He looks so unsure,* she thought. *I know how that feels.*

She took a deep breath. She started to speak but then noticed that the area they were passing through was not on the way to her house.

"Where are we going?" Maria asked.

"To Paway First."

"You're actually taking me there?"

"Hey, I want to keep an eye on you as I take these guys down."

Maria looked out the window. *Oh great,* she thought. *I'm actually going to a bank robbery! It wasn't supposed to happen this way!*

"It'll be okay," Detective Hipar said. "You'll wait in the car while I go in and defuse the situation."

Is he going to call for backup? Maria wondered. *No, I don't want anyone else involved.* She looked out the window, feeling dread as they drove.

They arrived at Paway First. Maria took a deep breath and looked around. Everything seemed quiet. Detective Hipar looked at his watch. *It's almost time,* he thought.

Suddenly, a van with a dimmed red paint job pulled up to the bank. The detective readied himself and left his vehicle. "Stay in the car and stay down," he ordered. As he darted across the street, Maria got down and locked the door.

Mom, if only you knew where I am now, Maria thought. She peeked over the bottom of the driver's window and watched as Detective Hipar jogged toward the bank. She tried to slow her breathing.

Three men got out of the van and headed to the bank. One carried a shoulder bag, and another had a baseball bat under his arm. *Uh oh,* Hipar thought. He went in after them. *Here we go.*

Chapter 4

Detective Hipar went into the bank as he heard yelling. "Give us your money now!"

The man with the bat stood in front of a teller. She looked terrified, but she put money on the counter.

Another man scooped the money into the bag. The men started herding the people to one side of the room.

"Freeze!" cried Detective Hipar. "Police!"

The men turned to him. One man came running at him, swinging his fist. Detective Hipar dodged the punch and grabbed him. He then flipped him onto the floor. As he did so, he noted the red shirt the man was wearing underneath his jacket.

One of the remaining two men started to charge at Hipar, but the man with the baseball bat stopped him. "Take it," he ordered, handing him the bag. The man took the money and headed to the rear of the bank.

Detective Hipar started going after him, but the man with the bat intercepted him. He held the bat horizontally and thrust it at the detective. Hipar grabbed the bat as it came at him. They struggled with it until the robber gave another thrust and Detective Hipar back. As he fell to the floor, he noticed that the first man had gotten up and was running past him.

He got up in a second and saw the man with the bat rushing to the back of the building. He chased after them, and as he reached the back, he saw that the rear exit was open. Hipar ran through it and into an alley. He chose a direction and ran in it.

Meanwhile, Maria was outside, waiting in the car. She saw the three robbers heading back to their van. *It's them,* she thought. *They're getting away! What happened? Did they do something to Detective Hipar?* Dread filled her. *I didn't want this to happen! I should've told more people!*

As the van roared out of the parking lot, Detective Hipar came into view. He darted to the car.

"Are you all right?" asked Maria.

"I'm fine," Hipar answered. They zoomed out of the area. Maria held on tightly as they went. *This was just supposed to be an anonymous tip,* she thought. *Is this a car chase?*

The car went down the road in a burst of speed. The van soon came into sight. "Hold on," cried Detective Hipar. *I've been doing that,* Maria thought.

They gained on the vehicle, but it turned a corner. Hipar made a wide turn after them.

"Ahh!" cried Maria. They sped after them. The van turned around another corner and they followed them. *This is a car chase,* she thought. *I'm actually in a car chase!* She gripped the dashboard and kept her eyes focused on the van before them.

The van turned yet another corner and they followed them. Suddenly, a blue car pulled out into their path. Detective Hipar made a hard turn to the left toward the street they had come from.

. Marian screamed as the car narrowly missed them, honking it horn as it went by."

Detective Hipar stopped the car in the street and looked at Maria. "Are you all right?" he asked.

"Yeah."

He started the car again and headed off in the direction the van was heading. Even after several minutes of speeding around, there was no sign of them.

Lost them, Detective Hipar thought. *I had a psychic . . . or whatever she is helping me and I still couldn't catch them.* He parked at the side of the road.

Maria felt her heart begin to slow down. She leaned back in her seat and took a breath. She had a vision. *The van went down a road as the sun began to set. It passed a few cars and then a sign that read "Chadlee, pop. 544, est. 1806." September 15, 7:13 p.m.*

"I know where they're heading," she said.

"Where?" asked Detective Hipar.

"Someplace called Chadlee."

"Then that's where we're going."

"What?"

"Don't worry—we'll be back in no time," Detective Hipar said. They went past various tall building whose reflective windows at night gave Paway its famous sparkle. As they neared the outskirts of the city, there was a small, cultivated patch of green, in the middle of which was a statue of a man with a badger next to him. Maria looked at it thinking that she had never given it much thought. She did not even know who that statue was of.

They left the city and went on to the highway. They drove off.

Meanwhile, the three men were driving down the road. One of them was looking through the bag. "Four thousand bucks," he said. "All that and only four thousand."

"Be quiet, Louis," said the man in the front. Jeff, the man who had shoved Detective Hipar, went back to looking through the bag.

"That was a nightmare," said Louis . "All that trouble and we still don't have what we need. What are we going to do now?"

The man up front took a deep breath. "I don't know, Louis," he answered. "Just let me think."

"We should've worn masks," said Louis. "We probably left fingerprints all over that joint. We all should've been armed. Nice planning, Jeff."

"Why didn't you think of that before the heist?" Jeff asked. He took a deep breath. "Look, it's all going to be okay. I know a guy back in Chadlee. We'll lie low there."

Meanwhile, Maria felt dread as they drove out of Paway. "I can't go," she said.

"But they're heading to Chadlee," said Detective Hipar.

"Yeah, but since you know that now, why don't you catch them yourself?"

"What if you have another one of those flashes? I would need to know."

"Hey, I was just going to be an confidential informant," said Maria. "I didn't think I would be along for a manhunt."

"I need your help," said Detective Hipar. "Those men are still out there and they're dangerous."

"Why don't you just call for backup?"

"I can't," said Detective Hipar. "If I do that, how do I explain how I knew that the bank was being robbed? That's why I didn't call for any when I went in."

Detective Hipar looked Maria straight in the eye. "Please, I need your help," he said. "These guys are probably going to do something like this again and then somebody's going to get hurt."

Maria was silent for a moment. "All right," she said. They drove on.

Sometime later, they were on the interstate. "So, how do you do it?" Detective Hipar asked.

Maria thought for a moment. "I've been having these visions," she answered.

"Really? Since when?"

"Since the beginning of this week. I woke up one morning and had a vision of my mom spilling a glass of juice, which came true." *It's so real now that I've said it,* she thought.

"Just like that?" asked Detective Hipar. "Do you know why?"

"No," Maria answered. *Why do I have them?* she wondered. She looked at Detective Hipar. "Why did you become a detective?"

"Family thing," he answered. Something in his tone told her not to ask.

Several minutes of silence went by. "So, what is your favorite thing to do?" asked Detective Hipar.

"Well, really, the only things I do is go to school and hang out with my mom," answered Maria.

Her mom, thought Detective Hipar. *What am I going to tell her mom after I'm finished taking her daughter along this manhunt?*

"Does your mom know about the whole vision thing?"

"No."

"Why not?"

"It's just not the right time to tell her."

"Well, okay," he said. He looked at an approaching sign. They were nearing Chadlee.

"What are you going to do once we get there?" asked Maria.

"First, I'm going to ask around," Detective Hipar answered. "A bunch of guys who just botched a robbery, they're bound to be rattled. Someone is definitely going to notice them."

"Aren't you going to call someone?" asked Maria. "Aren't you people supposed to call the local police when you come into another town? That's what they do on TV."

"I can't do that for the same reason I couldn't call for backup," Hipar replied. "I wouldn't be able to explain how I knew the crime was going to happen." *Though how am I going to take down three guys by myself?* he wondered. *I'll cross that bridge when I come to it.*

"Well, the crime's already happened," said Maria. "Also, how are you going to arrest three guys by yourself?"

Detective Hipar looked at her. "You're right," he said. "Okay, first, I'll take a quick look around. Then I'll talk with the locals."

Maria looked out the window. *What am I going to tell Mom? How's this going to end? What is she going to say?*

They entered Chadlee. They passed a row of redwoods that lined the road to their left. As they went down the streets, redwoods dotted the landscape just beyond the sidewalk. *I heard they like their redwoods up here,* thought Lenny.

Meanwhile, the three were outside an old building. Jeff was knocking at the door. "I'm coming," said a voice from inside. "Knock it off!" The door opened and a balding man appeared.

"Keith, how's it happening," Jeff said.

"How's it happening?" asked Keith. "How it's happening is that I have three deadbeats at my door and I know they want something."

"Sorry, but we need to stay at your place for a few days," said Jeff.

"What did you do?" asked Keith.

"We tried to fix our problem. It didn't go well."

Keith looked at them. "Why should I help you?"

"We have money," said Bob, the third guy.

"How much?" asked Keith.

"Enough," said Jeff.

"Okay," said Keith. "You go into the room above the garage, and no complaining about the noise if I have a customer."

They went inside.

Meanwhile, Detective Hipar parked the car near the town center. They got out. "Now what?" he asked.

"I don't know," Maria answered. "You're the detective."

"I thought you might have had another vision," said Detective Hipar.

"I haven't have one lately," Maria said.

"Oh," said Detective Hipar. He looked around. A woman was walking across a lawn carrying a bag of groceries. He went over to her and flashed his badge.

"Madam, I'm a police detective," he said. "Have you seen three men driving around in a red van?"

"No, I haven't," she replied. She looked worried. "Are they dangerous?"

"No, madam, just wanted for questioning," Detective Hipar said. *Nice going,* he told himself. *You're going to start a panic.* "Thank you," he said.

Detective Hipar went back to his car. "How did it go?" asked Maria.

"Not well."

"Are we going to the police now?"

I am the police, Lenny thought. "Not yet," he answered. "I'm going to check on the hotels. There's possibly one or two in the area."

"Not like in Paway."

"Yeah, small towns must be strange after living all your life in a big city."

"How do you know that?"

"I did a background check on you."

"Anyone else know about me?"

"No, I did it myself."

Maria still felt apprehensive.

Sometime later, Detective Hipar was questioning the clerk at the Sunny View Hotel. "You sure you haven't seen anybody matching those descriptions?"

"Definitely," answered the clerk. "We haven't had any new visitors in a while."

"Okay," said Detective Hipar. "Thanks for your time." He left and went back to his car.

"How did it go?" asked Maria.

"Still nothing. That was the only hotel in this town."

"Now do we go to the police station?"

"Yeah," Detective Hipar answered. "Let's go."

Meanwhile, the three men sat around the small room.

Bob was sitting on the bed. "What are we going to do?" he asked.

"I don't know," Jeff said. He was leaning against the wall thinking.

"You know what I think we should do?" asked Louis. "I think we should put as much distance between us and that town as possible."

"We need to settle down and think," said Jeff.

"Yeah, like when you thought of that brilliant plan of yours to rob that bank, big brother," Louis said.

"We were drowning in debt," Jeff said. "What did you expect me to do?"

"Well, armed robbery was such a great idea," said Louis.

"What other idea did you have? Win the lottery?"

"Can't we just go to sleep?" asked Bob.

"That's a good idea," said Jeff. "Louis and I will take the floor." They settled down for the night. Louis sighed before closing his eyes and going to sleep.

A few minutes later, Keith came bursting into the room. "Get out," he said. "Now."

"Why?" Jeff demanded.

"Somebody's been asking around about you," Keith answered.

"If you want our money after this, then forget it," said Louis. "We were paying for a full night."

"I don't want your money," Keith said. "I just want you gone. Now!"

Meanwhile, at the Chadlee Sheriff's Department, Detective Hipar was talking to the sheriff.

"Sheriff Connors, thank you for seeing me in person," he said, offering the sheriff his hand.

"Well, truth be told, most of my deputies are off," said Sheriff Connors. They shook. "One's sick and I think the other one's at a wedding."

"Thanks for coming," said Detective Hipar. *I hope this doesn't blow up in my face,* he thought.

"Well, not much going on," Sheriff Connors said. "Until now."

They went outside. "You said they were driving a red van?" Connors asked.

"Yeah. Sound familiar?"

"No, and I know everyone around here. They must be from out of town."

They approached his car. Maria was standing by it. "Who's that?" asked Sheriff Connors.

"My consultant," Hipar answered.

"Hi there," said Sheriff Connors.

"Hi," said Maria. *Now another guy's seen me,* she thought. *This is going to blow up in my face. I just know it.*

The sheriff turned back to Detective Hipar. "So where do you think we should start?"

"I don't know," Hipar answered. "I just think your knowledge of the area is going to come in handy. Any ideas?"

"Huh," said Sheriff Connors. He was quiet for a moment. "How do you know they're here?"

"I got a tip," answered Detective Hipar. Maria's heart skipped a beat.

Connors thought for a moment. "I think I might know a place we can try, but it might be a long shot."

"Lead the way," said Hipar. They got into their cars and drove off with the sheriff in the lead.

A short time later, they arrived at a place called Lucky's. "It's a place where people gather and have a bite to eat," Sheriff Connors said. They went inside.

Maria and Detective Hipar looked around to see a very crowded room. The sheriff had to speak up to be heard. "If they're not here, then someone here knows where they're at," he said. He went over to a man behind the counter.

"Hi, Bert," said Sheriff Connors.

"Hi, Sheriff," Bert said, wiping down a glass. "What can I get you?"

"Nothing," Connors answered. "This gentleman here is a detective from out of town who wants to know about some folks who just flew in."

"Three men," said Detective Hipar, and he gave a description of them. "They were seen driving a red van."

"Nope, haven't seen them," Bert said.

"Are you sure?" asked Detective Hipar.

"Yeah, I haven't seen a face today that I didn't know until you guys," he answered. "Sorry."

"Thanks anyway," said Detective Hipar.

Maria was looking at a man. She had a vision.

They were on a street. The three men were approaching a blue car. One fiddled with the door. In a moment he managed to open it. Another one reached inside it and opened the hood. The third man reached inside the exposed engine and did something to it. It started. They got inside and took off. September 15, 6:12 p.m., corner of Parks and Chow.

"I know where they're going," Maria said.

"How?" asked Sheriff Connors.

"I read a tip," Maria answered.

"How come you didn't say anything until now?"

"It didn't make sense until now."

"Let's get going," said Detective Hipar.

"They're going to be at the corner of Parks and Chow," said Maria. They left.

They approached a corner. As they neared their destination, a blue car darted across the intersection before them. "That's them," said Maria.

"Hang on," said Detective Hipar. He stepped on the gas and the car swung around the sheriff's.

Not again, Maria thought. She held on, feeling the force of the turn pushing her to the side. They raced down the street. As they came to another intersection, the car was a disappearing dot in their view.

Suddenly, a truck was going across their path. Detective Hipar made a sharp turn. "Ahh!" Maria cried.

The car turned turned to it's left with the trunk barely touching the truck. They remained there for a few moments.

Sheriff Connors got out of his car and went over to them. "Is everyone all right?" he asked.

"Yeah," answered Detective Hipar.

Maria took a moment before answering. "Yeah," she answered. *I can't believe that,* she thought. *I've never been in a car accident before. Did that count as a car accident? I hate car accidents.*

"You think we lost them?" asked Sheriff Connors.

"Looks like," Detective Hipar replied.

The driver of the truck stopped and got out. He was walking toward them. "Let's see if this guy's all right and then we'll go back to where they came from," said Detective Hipar. "Maybe there's a clue there."

"Good idea," said the sheriff. "Mrs. Lanners lives in the area and owns a blue car. You think they stole it?"

"Possibly," answered Hipar.

"Shame," Connors said. "She's a nice lady."

Sheriff Connors knocked on the door. Mrs. Lanners answered. "Sheriff, what is it?"

"Ma'am, you own a blue car, right?"

"Yes."

"Could you please show it to us?"

They went to a spot by the sidewalk where there was nothing. "My car, it's gone," Mrs. Lanners said. "Where is it?"

"I'll run the license and then I'm calling in all my deputies," said Sheriff Connors. He turned to the woman to calm her down and get information.

Meanwhile, the three men were driving down a street. "What are we going to do?" asked Bob.

"Everything's under control," said Jeff.

"Yeah, a growing list of crimes is always a good sign," said Louis.

"We had to get rid of the van," said Jeff. *This wasn't how it was supposed to go,* he thought. *We were just to going to take the money and then we wouldn't have to worry about them taking the land. Now, it's all spinning out of control.* They drove down the street.

Meanwhile, Detective Hipar approached Sheriff Connors as he was talking on his cell phone. "What's in that direction?" he asked, gesturing in the direction the blue car had gone.

"A lot of things," the sheriff answered. "A middle school, a warehouse, some homes, and a park."

"We should take a couple of teams and search those areas," Hipar said.

"That's a lot of area, and I've only got a couple of deputies," Connors said.

Detective Hipar went back to thinking. *Should I call in a few detectives from Paway?* he wondered.

Sheriff Connors's phone rang. "Yes?" he asked. He shot a look at the other two. "You found the van?"

Soon, they drove a short distance from where Mrs. Lanners's car was parked. They arrived by the van. A young man in uniform was next to it. "Deputy Randal?" asked Sheriff Connors. "Find anything?"

"Nothing besides the van," answered Deputy Randal. "It matched the BOLA, You know, Be On the Lookout, so I called it in."

"We will, of course, run the license number," said Sheriff Connors.

Detective Hipar went over to the van. *This is definitely the same one from the bank job,* he thought. Maria followed him.

They went around it. The van was between them and the other two. "Getting any vibrations off it?" Hipar asked.

"I don't think that's how it works," Maria answered. *Is it?*

Detective Hipar looked at the van. "I want this thing in a forensics lab immediately."

"I'm afraid we don't have a forensics lab," said Sheriff Connors.

"Then please hold it until my people can get here," Detective Hipar said.

"Does that mean you're calling in other people from Paway?" asked Maria in a whisper.

"Yeah, but don't worry," he answered. "I'll keep you out of it."

"How?" Detective Hipar was silent. *Yeah, how am I going to do that with her here?* he wondered.

What am I go to do? Maria wondered. Suddenly, she had a vision.

The three men were driving through a wooded area. They passed a huge tree that had been split in half and then made a sharp turn. They passed by a river. September 15, 7:40 p.m.

"Is there a tree split in the middle around here?" asked Maria.

"Yeah, there's one that was struck by lightning," answered Sheriff Connors. "Why?"

Maria shot a look at Detective Hipar. "I believe they were overheard talking about seeing it."

The sheriff looked uncertain. "Okay," he said. "I'm afraid I have to stay with the van, but I can give you directions." They soon got into the car and drove off.

Chapter 5

Detective Hipar looked through the trees as they drove through the woods. He tried to pierce the darkness with his eyes but still could not see anything.

Where are they going? wondered Maria. *Maybe they're on the run. That's how it goes on TV.*

Detective Hipar was looking out the passenger window. Suddenly, something came into view. He realized it was coming at them.

"Look out," he cried. He wrapped his arms around Maria before she realized what was happening.

There was an explosion of sound that seemed to fill the whole world. Time seemed to stop. Glass sprayed over her. *What's happening?* Maria wondered. She felt a jolt, and her mind and body froze as the world around her raced by. Her thoughts blurred together in a frantic outpouring of panic.

The car was pushed to the left. It came to a stop after its right side was lifted off the ground and then fell back down.

They sat there. Detective Hipar was still wrapped around Maria. He let go and looked her over. "Are you all right?" he asked.

Maria nodded. She was silent for a moment. "Yes."

Detective Hipar looked out the cracked window and saw a log suspended by two ropes that ran into the leaves of a redwood. *A trap,* he thought.

That could've . . . , Maria thought. *I didn't get a vision. I wasn't warned. Why didn't I get a vision? What's happening to my life!?*

Detective Hipar looked at Maria and noticed that she was breathing heavily. "Are you all right?" he asked.

"No," cried Maria. "I could've died!"

"Let's get you out of here," said Hipar. He opened his door and slowly led Maria out. "Anything broken? Anything hurt?"

"No," answered Maria. She appeared slightly calmer.

"Let's go over there," Hipar said, gesturing to the side of the road. Once there he looked back at the wrecked car.

"I can't believe that happened," said Maria. She was sitting on the ground. She wrapped her arms around her legs and pressed her knees to her chin.

"It's okay," said Detective Hipar. "We're okay."

Maria looked up at him. "How do you do it?"

"What?"

"Put your life on the line every day."

"I don't know. I guess it's different for everyone." He looked at the car and then at Maria. *Poor kid,* he thought.

He sat down by her. "For me, I guess, it's that I want to catch the bad guy more than I'm afraid of something happening to me."

"Has there ever been a moment when you were really afraid?"

Detective Hipar thought for a moment. "Once, when I was chasing a suspect," he answered. "I was running up a fire escape after him. The dirt bag turned and pushed me over the side. I grabbed on and was hanging as he ran away. I looked down and saw the ground a few stories below. I was terrified, but then I pulled myself together and caught up with him."

"How did you do it?" asked Maria.

"Well, I focused on the guy and how much I wanted to catch him, especially after he pushed me," he answered. "I kept my mind on that instead of the possibility of falling. What I'm saying is that you need to keep your fear in a box and keep it away from you as you're trying to do something."

Maria sighed and Detective Hipar patted her on the shoulder.

"Let's check out the car," he said.

Meanwhile, the three men were driving away from the woods. "I can't believe we did that," said Bob.

"We had to do something," said Jeff. "They were catching up with us. Some guy I talked to said they were asking questions at Lucky's. That thing will slow them down."

"That trap of yours could hurt them or worse," said Bob. "And what if someone else sprang it?"

"Don't worry," said Louis. "It probably missed them, the way big brother's plans usually turns out."

"It's fine," said Jeff. "Don't worry, it'll only rattle them, buy us some time to get away. We did what we had to do. We didn't ask for these money problems, but we have to take care of them. Everything will be fine."

"But more people are going to come after us now," said Bob.

"It's fine," said Jeff. His tone silenced the other two.

Sometime later, in a restroom of Millers Lumberyard, Jeff was looking in a mirror. He leaned against the sink. *I had to do it,* he thought. He sighed. *This is out of control. One thing leads to another. I'm robbing banks and setting traps. This isn't my life. One moment and everything is changed. Take it easy. You're doing the best you can. Robbing the bank was the best thing you could've come up with at the time. It wasn't a perfect idea, but you had to do something. There wasn't anything you could've done differently. You're doing everything you can.*

Jeff sighed and closed his eyes for a moment. *You had to do something. You were so close to losing everything. You still are. You've got to pay to win. You've got to be strong, for them.*

Jeff looked at the exit. *For them.* He left.

Soon, Jeff and his brothers sat around the break room.

"What are we going to do?" asked Bob.

"Well, you're obviously not going to be quiet," said Louis.

"Louis," Jeff said. He looked at both of them. "Everything's going be fine. Now that we have time to plan our next step, things will get better." He tried to appear confident.

"Hey, for our next step why don't we rob Fort Knox?" asked Louis.

Jeff tried to keep his anger down. "We just need to keep calm and think everything through."

Bob shifted in his chair nervously. "We can do this," Jeff said to him. "We just have to come up with a plan."

"Your last plan made us criminals," said Louis. "They're looking for us and we can never stop running"

"We just need to figure everything out," Jeff said. "Once we do that, we'll be fine." His tone silenced Louis. Bob sighed and left the room.

"You're not helping," said Jeff.

I wasn't trying to, thought Louis.

Meanwhile, Detective Hipar's cell phone rang. "Hello?"

"We traced the van through the license to a Jeff Burner," said Sheriff Connors. "Apparently, he and his two brothers, Louis and Bob, are the last members of the Burner family. I talked to a few people in town and it seems like the family business has dried up."

That would explain their need for a quick loan, thought Detective Hipar. "Did you check their last known address?"

"Yeah, they shared the family's old house and I've already sent a couple of deputies there," said Sheriff Connors. "I'm afraid it looks like they already cleared out."

"Thanks anyway. Also, we have a problem." He told the sheriff what had happened and where they were.

"Stay there," Sheriff Connors said. "I'll come get you when I can."

"Thanks again," said Detective Hipar.

Maria was looking at him. "We know who they are but not where they are," he said.

Maria looked at the log. "That must've taken a lot of work," she said. "Cutting down a tree and tying it with ropes like that."

"Yeah, hard to believe they could've done it with the short amount of time they had," said Detective Hipar. He thought for a moment and then took out his cell phone. "Sheriff, is there any place near here where someone can get lumber?"

"Yeah, the Miller Lumberyard," Connors answered. "It was one of the places that closed when the crunch hit us, like the Burners' business."

Closed down: sounds nice for a hideaway, thought Detective Hipar. He told Maria what the sheriff said. "We got them," he said.

"That was great work, Detective Hipar," said Maria.

"Call me Lenny," he said.

Soon, the three were heading to the lumberyard in the sheriff's car. "We're almost there," said the sheriff. The building started to come into view.

"When we get there, stay in the car," said Lenny.

"Sure," said Maria.

They reached the lumberyard. Lenny and Sheriff Connors got out. "I'll sneak around the back and you stay in the front," Connors said. "We'll go slowly, and if you see anyone, go back to the car and use the radio to call for backup. I've got a radio with me."

"Got you," said Lenny. They started walking toward the building.

"Lenny, be careful," Maria said to him.

"I will."

Lenny and Sheriff Connors approached the building. As they neared it, Sheriff Connors gestured that he was going around. Lenny nodded and the sheriff went around the building.

Connors reached the rear of the lumberyard and looked around. He saw nothing. He tried the doors and found that they were unlocked. He went in.

As he went deeper into the building, he could see very little in the darkness. He felt his foot touch something and backed away on instinct. Suddenly there was a creaking sound followed by a thunderous crash.

Sheriff Connors took out his flashlight. *I can't believe I forgot this,* he thought. He shined the light on the floor in the direction where the crash came from. On the floor was a collection of two-by-fours. *Another booby trap?* he wondered. He carefully went through a door.

Lenny heard the crash. *Something's going on,* he thought. He went through the front entrance.

"What was that?" asked Louis.

"Let's check it out," said Jeff. They left the break room.

The three robbers had split up and Jeff was in a room by himself. He turned on a light and found no one around. He kept looking.

Lenny went down a hall. There was light up ahead and he came to a room with the lights turned on. Out of the corner of his eye he saw something move. "Freeze," he ordered.

"Ahh!" cried Bob. "Please don't hurt me!" He covered his face with his arms.

"You're one of the robbers," said Lenny.

"You're that guy from Paway," said Bob. He lowered his arms.

"Give up?" asked Lenny.

Bob's face twisted with emotion. "I will." Lenny began to cuff him.

Meanwhile, outside, Maria went up to the front entrance. She tried to peek inside as best as she could but could see only darkness. *I can't believe I'm doing this,* she thought. *This isn't my life but they might need help.* She took a deep breath and after a moment went in.

Maria went through room after room. *I still can't believe this,* she thought. *A week ago, I was a normal girl and now I'm chasing after criminals in the dark because I had a vision of the future.* She stopped in yet another vacant room. Maria tried to look around but mostly just saw darkness. She went off to another room.

Maria leaned against a wall feeling drained. *Put your fear in a box and do what you have to do,* she told herself, and left the room.

A few minutes later, she bumped up against a man. "Who are you?" Jeff demanded.

Maria recognized him from her vision. "I was just exploring," she said.

"Exploring?"

"Yeah, I saw this place and thought it looked cool, so I was looking around," answered Maria.

Jeff looked at her. "Who are you?"

Maria felt fear shot up in her. "I've got to go," she said, and ran off.

Someone's found us, Jeff thought. He grabbed a fire ax off the wall and chased after her.

Maria turned a corner in the darkness. Jeff ran after her. He swung the ax and missed her, hitting the wall instead. He pulled it free and chased after her.

Jeff caught up with her and pushed her down to the floor. He raised the ax. "I'm only trying to make things right," he said. He swung the ax down.

Maria rolled over just as the ax hit the floor. *He's aiming at my head,* she thought.

Jeff pulled the ax free and raised it over his head. *Man with the ax,* Maria thought. She jumped to her feet and ran off. Jeff swung the ax and it barely missed her.

Maria came to a dark room. She stood there breathing heavily for a couple of moments. *Where's Lenny?* she wondered. There were numerous doors around her. She chose one and went through.

Jeff stood in another room. *I can't believe I did that,* he thought. *This isn't me! I don't chase after girls with axes! She must be with the people chasing us or she wouldn't have run. Even if she isn't, she could tell someone we're here. This wouldn't have happened if the bank hadn't foreclosed on our home! I promised my parents I would keep my brothers safe. I've got to do this!*

Jeff took a deep breath, raised the ax, and ran out of the room.

Lenny was looking around. *Someone should turn the lights on here,* he thought. *Is the power still on?*

He heard a sound. Turning toward it he saw Jeff running up at him with an ax raised. Maria came out of nowhere, swinging a two-by-four. She hit Jeff in the leg. "Ahh!" Jeff cried.

He gripped his leg as Maria raised her weapon again.

Jeff raised his ax. The piece of wood struck the ax's handle. They pressed their weapons together, struggling. Jeff gripped the two-by-four and pulled it out of Maria's hands. He threw it away and it landed by Lenny, who was running up to them.

Jeff raised the ax as Maria backed away. Lenny picked up the two-by-four and swung it at the ax. It knocked the ax off the course of its swing.

Jeff turned to Lenny. Lenny held the wood horizontally and used it to shove him against the wall. He dropped the ax.

They struggled. "Give it up," ordered Lenny. "It's over!"

"Never," cried Jeff.

"We have your brother," Lenny said.

No, thought Jeff. "It'll go easier for all of you if you give up now," said Lenny. Jeff stopped struggling. "That's good." He went behind him and took him by the arms. He pushed him out of the room with Maria following them.

They came outside with Jeff and Bob.

Soon, Sheriff Connors joined them with a cuffed Louis. "Gave up without a fight," he said.

Minutes later, they were outside the sheriff's station. Sheriff Connors was leading Maria and Lenny to a car. "Thanks for your help," said Lenny.

"Thank you," said Sheriff Connors. They shook hands. "Hope this rental car gets you home okay."

"I'm sure it will," Lenny said. They got in and drove off.

Lenny and Maria were driving down the road. "If you need me to talk to your mom, I will," said Lenny. "I won't tell her about the visions. I won't tell anybody about it."

"It's okay," said Maria. "She's working late tonight."

"What about your dad?"

"He's sick," Maria answered. From her tone Lenny decided not to ask any more about it.

They arrived outside Maria's house. She got out. "Thanks for helping me out," said Lenny. "I hope I see you again someday."

"Me too," Maria said. She turned to her house. *It's good to be home again,* she thought. Maria went inside.

BOOK 2

Wrath of the Griffin

Chapter 1

Maria Marhill sat on her bed reading a book. She went from one page to another and then, after a few minutes, put it down. She looked at the title, *Looking Into the Next World: Investigations Into Psychics. Nothing here is anything remotely like what I'm going through,* she thought.

Maria looked at her watch. *Got an hour before dinner.* She had a vision.

Two men were carrying a crate to a pile of other crates in a dark room. They put the crate on top of another one. A third man came in. "Hurry up with those DVDs," he said. "The boss wants them on the streets by tomorrow and black market or not, they better be in good shape." 120 Cricket Street, September 20, 6:49 p.m.

It happened again, Maria thought. *So I'm going to see crimes from now on?*

Maria started to leave her house. As she neared the front door, she stopped and turned to Lois. "Mom, I'm going out for a bit," she said.

"Okay, but don't be long," Lois said.

A few minutes later, Maria was at a pay phone. "Detective Hipar, please," she said.

"Hello," said Lenny.

"It's me, Maria."

"Hello. It's nice to hear from you again," said Lenny. "Did you have another vision?"

"Yeah," answered Maria and she told him what she had seen.

"Got it," said Lenny.

"See you later."

"You too."

Is this the way my life's going to be from now on? wondered Maria. *Having visions about crimes that are going to happen and calling the police with tips?*

Maria looked down a nearby alley. *When will I get my life back?* A car passed her. She was startled but it went on by. She left the alley.

Maria sat at the table having dinner with Lois. "So, I put in for a transfer," said Lois. "Maybe once I get to a new department, I won't have to work so many hours."

"Uh huh," said Maria. She was barely paying attention. She ate a forkful of green peas.

"Oh, Jennifer said hi," said Lois.

Maria kept eating. *Should I tell her?* she wondered. *No, I don't know how she would react. Then again, it could all go away. Do I want it to?*

She looked at Lois. *Of course I do,* Maria thought. *Ever since I had that first vision, I've been a nervous mess. I've gone from a normal girl to someone who has visions of the future and helps solve crimes.*

"How was your day?" asked Lois.

"Fine."

Lois took a sip of her tea. *Why is this happening to me?* Maria wondered. *Is there something wrong with me? Is this some sort of sign? Is this meant to happen and I'm supposed to do something?*

Maria sighed quietly. *I need to find out what's happening to me. Maybe if I had a CAT scan it would tell me something, give me some clues. Though if I go to the hospital and ask for a CAT scan, the doctors will ask questions. Why do you want a CAT scan? Where are your parents?*

Maria looked at her watch. *It's about time for Lenny to take care of that thing,* she thought. She started to finish her dinner.

Meanwhile, at the warehouse on Cricket Street, two men were stacking crates. A third man came and was going to say something when a uniformed officer kicked in the door. "Freeze, police," he cried.

The two men dropped the crates and started to run. Just then, two more doors in the room were kicked in. Police flooded in.

The three men were cuffed and a couple of officers pried open some of the crates. Inside were copies of Dino Warrior 2.

Lenny and his partner, Detective Jon Turner, came into the room. An older man followed them.

"Nice work, detective," said Lieutenant Steve Finn, Lenny's superior. "It looks like we got a shipment of bootlegged DVDs. How did you know where they were?"

"Anonymous tip," answered Lenny.

Meanwhile, in a dark office a phone rang. "What is it?" asked Mitch Ken.

"We've got a problem," said the voice on the other end. "The shipment on Cricket Street has been taken in by the cops."

"How?" Mitch asked.

"I don't know," answered the voice. "I'm working on it."

"Get on it," Mitch said. "The boss won't be happy." He put down the phone and took a cell phone out of his pocket. "Hello, boss," he said. "We have a problem."

The next morning, Maria got up and got dressed. She went downstairs and had breakfast.

"Have a good day, sweetie," said Lois. "I'm afraid I might have to work late for the next couple of nights." She handed Maria her lunch. Maria went out the door.

She walked down the sidewalk and looked at some clouds floating by. *It's a beautiful day,* Maria thought.

Suddenly, she had a vision.

Two men drove up to an old warehouse in a truck. One went to the warehouse while the other went to open the trunk.

A man came out from the warehouse and met the one from the truck. "You're right on time," he said.

"And we deal in quality merchandise," said the other man. He took a woman's handbag from within his jacket and handed it to the man from the building. "Can you tell it's not real?" he asked.

The other man looked it over and shook his head.

"My friend has the rest," said the man from the truck.

The second man from the truck unloaded a box from the back of the vehicle. 26 Carmel Road, September 21, 3:05 p.m.

Not again, Maria thought. She darted off in a different direction.

"Hello?" asked Lenny.

"Lenny, it's me," said Maria.

"Another one?"

"Yeah," answered Maria and she told him what she had seen. "Fake handbags—I saw something like that on TV. They're illegal, right?"

"Yeah, they are," answered Lenny. He wrote down the address.

Several minutes later, Maria walked into the school building. She just barely got into her first class before the bell rang. She sat down and let out a deep breath.

Later that day, Maria sat down in the cafeteria for lunch. *Is this what life is going to be from now on?* she wondered. *Getting visions, calling in tips, and running around? Am I some sort of psychic crime fighter now? All I need is a cape and an archenemy. Am I going to keep getting these visions? Are they only going to be about crimes from now on?*

Maria started to eat her fruit cup. *I should get a CAT scan,* she thought. *How hard would it be to get? I could just tell Mom I have a headache. No, then she would just give me an aspirin.*

Several minutes passed. *Maybe I could look up CAT scans online and see if there's some way to get one.* She looked at her watch. *No, it's too late; lunch is almost over. I'll do it when I get home. That is, if I don't have any visions before then.* She finished her lunch.

Sometime later, Lenny sat in a car watching the building on 26 Carmel Road. A truck pulled up.

Here we go, he thought. He gestured to some officers waiting in the bushes. He got out, and they circled the area.

The car stopped by the warehouse and two men got out. One man went over to the building as the other opened the trunk. A third man got out of the warehouse. "You're right on time," he said.

"And we deal in quality merchandise too," said the man from the truck. He took out a woman's handbag.

"Freeze," someone cried. Officers swarmed them, seemingly from everywhere. Lenny walked up to the men as the officers were handcuffing them.

The man who had stayed with the truck darted from an officer who was starting to cuff him. "Stop," ordered the officer.

Lenny stepped into the man's path. "Uh-uh," Lenny said. He grabbed him. "You're not going anywhere."

"There are more people inside," cried an officer who had looked through one of the warehouse's windows.

Lenny gestured toward the building and several officers went toward it. There was the sound of a door crashing down and several shouts.

Lenny turned to the man he had grabbed. "You're under arrest," he said. He then handed him over to an officer.

Sometime later, Maria arrived home. She found a note on the counter. *Hey there, Snugglebear,* she read. *Had to go to work early—sorry. Dinner's in the fridge. All you have to do is heat it up. Love, Mom.*

Maria sat on the couch and turned on the TV. "Police caught a number of people in a counterfeiting ring," said a newscaster. "There's no word yet on who's behind the operation. Now, in sports . . ." *Strange hearing about it on the news,* she thought. She turned off the TV and, after a few seconds, went up to her room.

Once in her room Maria threw her book bag onto the floor and went over to her computer. She did a search on CAT scans. *Computerized Axial Tomography,* she read. *A method for diagnosing disorders of the soft tissues of the body, especially the brain. It uses a combination of many tomographs to form an image.*

She leaned back. *I don't know what that means,* she thought.

Maria scrolled down and came to some links. *CAT scans used to diagnose new illnesses,* she read. *CAT scans, ultrasounds, and other cutting-edge technologies. Practicing medicine, the next generation.*

Maria continued to scroll down and came to links for hospitals and medical databases. She looked through them. *There's nothing here that can help me. How do I get one done? It's not like I can just go to a doctor's office and ask for them to do it.*

Maria sighed. *Well, that was a complete waste of time. I can't get a scan without Mom finding out.*

Maria had an idea. *What if I get Lenny to take me?* she wondered. *Would he do it? Isn't it illegal to take a minor to something like that if you're not their parent? Lenny's a detective. He won't do it.*

She was about to get up when on an impulse she did a search for CAT scans and psychics. A series of links came up and she clicked on the first one. *The Arizona Institute of Paranormal Studies performed CAT scans on a number of purported psychics and reported finding higher-than-normal activity in certain portions of the brain.*

High brain activity—is that what's happening to me? Maria wondered.

She kept reading. After several minutes, she closed her web browser. *Still nothing to help me,* she thought. *I still don't have a way to get one, and it's not like there's a lot of stuff about psychics.*

Maria sighed. Just then, she had a vision.

A man came up to another man in a darkened room. "Do you have it?" asked one of the men.

"Yeah, I got it," answered the other man. He gestured behind him and they went over to a trunk. They opened it and inside was a lot of money. "Can you wash it?" the man asked.

"Yeah, I can wash it," answered the first man. The Happy Tabby Cat Food Company, September 21, 9:28 p.m.

Am I going to have visions every few hours? wondered Maria. She felt helpless.

Several minutes later, Lenny answered his phone.

"I had another one," Maria said.

Again? Lenny wondered. "What was it?" Maria told him what she had seen, and the address. "With what you've been seeing lately, I'm sure that the cash wasn't for covering a movie rental fee."

Sometime later, Maria was sitting down for dinner alone. *At least with Mom gone I can call Lenny when I need to,* she thought. *Is this what my life is going to revolve around now? Before my life wasn't too exciting, but now it's more excitement than I can handle. I should watch a movie tonight, get my mind off all this.*

She looked around. *It seems so strange eating without her. Then again, it's not like it's the first time I've been alone in the house.*

Maria sat down in front of the TV. She looked over the DVDs she had in her hands. *Let's see,* she thought. *There's* Eye of Danger, Alone in Silence, Happy Clown Action, *and* Fly Far.

Maria looked at the cover of *Eye of Danger.* The hero was facing off against some stereotypical goons, and she thought about the men she had seen in her vision. *Stop thinking about that,* she told herself.

Maria put *Happy Clown Action* on. *I need a comedy.*

Meanwhile, at the abandoned cat food factory the two men came together. "Do you have it?" asked one of them.

"Freeze," someone cried. From around a corner and through a door officers came in. One officer grabbed the first man. "Hey, I think this is Jim Becker," said the officer.

Lieutenant Finn came around a corner followed by Lenny. "Ah, the great and mighty Jim Becker, career criminal," Finn said. "To what do we owe the honor of your appearance? Tax evasion? Loot from a robbery?"

"I want a lawyer," said Jim Becker.

"Sure," said Finn. He looked at the officer. "Cuff him," he ordered. The officer took him away as he read him his rights.

Finn looked at Lenny. "Nice going, detective," he said. "You're really on a streak." He then went off to supervise the crime scene.

Yeah, thought Lenny.

Jim Becker sat across from Lenny in an interrogation room. "Who do you work for?" asked Lenny.

"I'm not saying anything," Becker said. "Give me a lawyer."

"We got you on money laundering and tax evasion. You think a lawyer is going to help you with that?"

"I want a lawyer now."

Lenny got up and left the room. "He's not talking," said Lenny. Finn had been watching the interrogation through a two-way mirror.

"No, but his buddies are," Detective Turner said as he came up to them. "I overheard them one of them say 'Griffin.'"

"So, the Griffin's real?" asked Lieutenant Finn. "Apparently, the two locations of these dealings were owned by the same shell company. That could mean that they're connected." He turned to Lenny. "Keep in contact with your informant. I want you to keep up the good work."

Mitch Ken was in his office. The phone rang and he answered it. "They got Jim Becker," said the voice on the other end.

"How?" asked Mitch.

"I don't know."

"Find out now," ordered Mitch. He took out his cell phone. "Sir, they got Jim Becker," he said.

"He's one of my top guys," said Mitch's boss, the Griffin. "How?"

"I don't know, sir," answered Mitch. "We're working on it."

"Put everything on it," said the Griffin. "I want this problem solved."

"Yes, sir."

A short time later, Maria heard a knock at her door. She opened it to find Lenny outside. "Hi," he said. 'I didn't see any cars around and I remembered what you told me about your mom working late a lot, so I thought you'd be alone."

Maria was startled to see him there. "You want to come in?"

"No, I just came by to drop this off," Lenny said. He handed her a cell phone. "It's so you can call me when you get a vision."

"I've never had a cell phone before," Maria said.

"I thought all teenagers had cell phones."

"Not this one."

"Well, keep it on," said Lenny. "We don't know when these visions of yours will come." He took a quick look around. "Apparently those last two were related. They were of jobs being pulled by guys working for the Griffin."

"I don't know who that is," said Maria. *Like I would,* she thought.

"A few months ago, there was this foiled robbery," said Lenny. "Afterward, there was a rumor going around that the person behind it was also behind most of the crime in Paway. They say he calls himself the Griffin and no one knows who he is. It's rumored that he runs his orders through Mitch Ken, a known career criminal, but we've never been able to prove anything."

Sounds like a real crime boss, Maria thought. "Be careful," she said.

"I will," said Lenny.

Maria closed the door and looked at the cell phone. *This is getting too complicated,* she thought. She went to bed.

The next morning, Maria woke up. She got dressed and went downstairs.

"Hey there, Snugglebear," said Lois. "How are you doing?"

"Fine," answered Maria. She sat down for breakfast.

"How was last night?" asked Lois.

Great, except that I'm now fighting the biggest crime boss in Paway, Maria thought. "Fine," she answered. She poured herself some cereal.

"I haven't heard anything about that transfer," said Lois.

"I'm sure you'll get it," said Maria.

"Thanks, sweetie. Anyway, things have been quiet at Cure All Pharmaceuticals. Not much has been happening lately."

"Yeah, things here have been quiet too," Maria said. "Maybe something will happen in a day or two."

"I'm just worried about my transfer," said Lois. "I'm worried that they won't see any reason to move me over to that other branch."

"I'm sure it'll work out, Mom."

"Anyway, how are things at school?"

"Fine."

A few minutes later, Maria headed out the door. "See you, Snugglebear," said Lois.

"See you, Mom," said Maria. She took a few steps across a lawn and came onto the sidewalk. She headed toward school.

There was a group of men standing by a warehouse.

A truck came up to them. A man got out of it and went over to them. "Do you have it?" asked one of the men from the building.

"Yeah," answered the man from the truck.

They went to the back of the truck and opened the rear. Inside were a bunch of boxes. The man who got out of the truck opened a box and pulled out a video game with the title Alien Basher 4 *on it.*

"They looked ready to ship," said the man from the warehouse who had spoken earlier.

"Yeah, they are," said the man from the truck. 223 All's Falls Drive, September 23, 12:05 p.m.

Alien Basher 4? Maria wondered. She remembered the seemingly constant ads for it everywhere. *That's not supposed to come out until two weeks from now,* she thought. *Okay, something's not right. Better call Lenny.*

"Hello?" asked Lenny.

"I had another one," said Maria. *They just keep coming.*

"What was it?"

Maria told him the details. "It makes no sense."

"Actually, it does," said Lenny. "Last night, a shipment of the game was stolen off a truck. They must be selling them on the black market."

"Oh," said Maria. "Well, be careful getting them back."

"I will."

A couple of hours later, a truck came up to a warehouse. A man came up and walked up to a group of men waiting by the building. "Do you have it?" asked one of the men from the group.

"Yeah," answered the man from the truck.

They went to the back of the truck and opened the rear. Inside were a bunch of boxes. The man who got out of the truck opened a box and pulled out a video game with the title *Alien Basher 4* on it.

"They looked ready to ship," said the man from the warehouse who had spoken earlier.

"Yeah, they are," said the man from the truck.

"Freeze," someone yelled.

Officers flooded the area and rounded up everyone in sight.

"You're definitely on a roll," said Lieutenant Finn, walking up to the scene.

"I just have a good source," said Lenny, coming up behind Finn.

Finn looked at him. "There could be commendation in this for you," he said.

Outside the scene, a man was watching Lenny through a pair of binoculars. "Yes, sir, I have him in sight," he said into a cell phone.

A few minutes later, Maria sat down for lunch. *All the things that have been happening to me—it's hard to keep track of it all,* she thought. *I start to get visions and then they start to show crimes that are about to happen. I get involved in a chase after some crooks. Now I'm involved with stopping a crime boss, and who knows what else is going to happen? My life's out of control. At least Lenny's the one out there chasing the bad guys. I'm just giving out the tips.*

Meanwhile, at the Bell Well Phone Company's headquarters, a man walked down a corridor. He checked his nametag. *It fooled them at the front desk,* he thought. He slipped into a room.

The man sat down in front of a computer. He clicked the mouse a few times and found the client files. He did a search for the name Lenny Hipar.

At the Paway Police Station, a man approached a uniformed officer behind a desk. "What can I do for you, sir?" the officer asked.

The other man raised a badge. "I'm Detective Rowe from Internal Affairs," he said. "I need to see Detective Hipar's file."

Meanwhile, Detective John Turner was sitting at his desk. A man came up to him.

"Detective Turner?" asked the man.

"Yes?"

"Detective Hems," answered the man, holding up a badge. "Can I talk with you about your partner, Lenny Hipar?"

Detective Turner was silent for a moment. "Sure. What do you want to know?" he asked.

"Has there been anything different about him lately?"

"How so?"

"Has he been working differently?" asked Detective Hems. "Is he coming to work at a different time or doing his work differently?"

"You mean with these new arrests?" asked Detective Turner.

"Yes."

"Well, he's got an informant."

"Can you tell us anything about this informant?"

"No, I've never met him."

"What about those bank robbers he chased into Chadlee?" asked Detective Hems. "Was there anything particularly unusual about that?"

"Well, I heard that he supposedly had a consultant with him, but I never read about it in his report," Turner replied. Detective Hems wrote everything down in a notebook.

"Thanks," he said. "We'll be in touch."

Meanwhile, Maria was in class. *I wonder how that arrest is going,* she thought. *Is that all I think about now? I mean, there wasn't a lot of stuff going on in my life before but . . . I need to think about something else. Maybe if I spend more time with Cindy or Kate or maybe with new people.*

The bell rang and the students left.

Lenny was sitting in Lieutenant Finn's office. "You've been doing some great work," Finn said. "You captured those bank robbers and now these new arrests."

"Thank you, sir," said Lenny.

"Now, with this new informant of yours," Finn said. "I want to know everything he or she says. I want a report of dates and times you contact him. I want reports on meetings even if nothing happens."

"Of course, sir," said Lenny. *Oh boy,* he thought.

Sometime later, Maria arrived home. "Hi, sweetie," said Lois. "How was school?"

"It was fine," Maria answered. "I'm going to go study." She started to go upstairs.

"Okay. Dinner's going to be at six," Lois said.

Maria entered her room. *It's been a few hours and no visions,* she thought. *There's no crime, no danger, and there are no unanswerable questions. I wonder how long it'll last.*

A few hours later, Maria and Lois were eating dinner. ". . . and Jennifer said, 'Aren't you glad you didn't buy it?'" Lois said. She laughed.

"Yeah, good one," Maria said.

"Maria, is there something wrong?" Lois asked. "You seem preoccupied."

"It's nothing, Mom. I'm fine."

"All right. You know you can talk to me about anything. I may be working long hours, but I'm still here for you."

"I know that, Mom."

"Anyway, about work, it looks like that transfer isn't working out," Lois said.

"I'm sorry about that," said Maria.

Lois sighed. "It looks like I'll be still working some stiff hours. We need the money but . . . Don't worry. I'll find a way to make it up to you."

"I'm sure you will, Mom."

A few hours later, she went to bed. *Interesting day, but they have all been interesting,* she thought. *Are these visions going to keep coming or are they going to stop? Have they stopped already? Were they an accident or destiny? Why was I getting them? What do they mean?*

Maria looked out her window. The moon was visible through it. She went to sleep.

In his office, Mitch faced two men. "What do you have?" he asked.

"I managed to get his file," answered the man on his left. "Lenard Hipar, partner to Jon Turner. He seems to be a good detective. Two commendations. A lot of closed cases. At eighteen he entered the police academy and soon graduated. He had slightly better-than-average scores. Recently he interrupted a bank heist and chased the robbers into a small town called Chadlee. With the help of the local sheriff he captured them. There are the recent arrests, of course, but there's not much on file about them yet."

"About that," said the man to Mitch's right. "His partner said there was a consultant who was there. I looked up the sheriff's phone number and called him. He said the consultant was a young woman with blonde hair. She apparently looked very young."

The man took out a notebook and looked through it. "As for his phone records, it seems that recently he's been receiving calls from a prepaid cell phone," he said.

"Is there any way to track these calls, any pattern to them?" asked Mitch.

"No, sir," answered the man.

"Go then," said Mitch. "I'll call you two if I need you." They left.

Mitch brought out his cell phone. He called his boss and repeated everything they had told him. "What do you want me to do?" asked Mitch.

"Keep an eye on Detective Hipar at all times," answered the Griffin. "Ask around. See if there's a common person who's connected to all the jobs that have been stopped by the police. I also want you to create rumors of jobs that don't exist and leak them to select people. As for this consultant, send people to this town and have them ask around. Get a description."

"Yes, sir," said Mitch. "Consider it done."

Maria woke up the next morning and went downstairs. "Good morning," said Lois.

"Good morning," said Maria. She sat down for breakfast.

"I made you some pancakes."

"Thanks, Mom," Maria said. She began to eat.

A man was walking around towards the trunk of a car. He opened the trunk. There was a great deal of money inside. The man appeared to count it and then closed the trunk.

Another man came around to him. "Is that all of it?" he asked.

"Yeah, that should cover it," answered the first man. "I'm thinking that this will more than cover Jimmy's legal bills."

The second man looked at the large trunk. "Wow, that's a lot of dough," he said. *"That lawyer must be awful good." 322 Madison Avenue, September 24, 9:06 p.m.*

Oh, Maria thought. She got up.

"Is everything all right?" asked Lois.

"Yeah, I just forgot something," answered Maria. She left the kitchen.

Maria went up to her room. She took out her cell phone. *Pancakes and visions,* she thought.

Chapter 2

"Hello?" asked Lenny.

"I saw someone load money into a car," said Maria.

"Hello to you too," said Lenny. "Where was this?"

Maria told him the details of her vision. "They said it was to pay the legal bills of someone named Jimmy." You think they're talking about Jim Becker?"

"I would bet on it," Lenny replied. "The Griffin probably wants him back badly. He's apparently one of his top guys."

I help put this guy in jail, Maria thought. *Stop it. He doesn't know and there's no way for him to find out.*

"Be careful," Maria said.

"I will," said Lenny.

Lenny got up and began to walk across the squad room. Detective Turner blocked his path. "Who were you talking to?" he asked.

"Oh, just someone telling me how that last case we worked on went in court," Lenny replied. "Someone from the DA's office, I think."

"Oh, then," said Turner. He spotted the notebook in which Lenny had written the details of the vision and was holding in his hand. "You know, I haven't met your new informant yet," Turner said. "When can I?"

"I'm afraid he's a little jumpy, and I think it would be a bad idea to bring someone new to meet him this early in the relationship," said Lenny. "Excuse me," and he went past Detective Turner.

Meanwhile, Maria arrived at school. Cindy was in front of the building. She came running toward her, looking happy. "Hey, Maria," she said.

"Hey," said Maria.

"Want to go over to Pizza Place after school?" Cindy asked.

"Sure," answered Maria. They went inside.

Hours later, Maria sat down for lunch. She began to unpack her meal. *You know, I never really thought about what Lenny does,* she thought. *I'm telling him to be careful and I never really think why. He's out there dealing with Jim Becker, this Griffin guy, and all these crooks. It's his job to do that every day. I was afraid to be near Jim Becker, but Lenny is and he's going to be near people like that every day doing who knows what. I've heard being a police officer is dangerous, but I never really thought about it before. Lenny told me to put my fear in a box and keep it away from what I'm doing. Is that really what he does every day? I hope he's all right.*

After the last class had ended, Maria and the other students left the building. She saw Cindy coming up to her. *It will be nice to do something different,* she thought.

A man in a suit went up against a wall. He removed a loose brick. Behind it was a folded piece of paper. He took it and put a few bills in its place. He put the brick back. Manroes Avenue, September 24, 3:51 p.m.

Maria looked at Cindy as she was coming up to her. "Sorry, something came up," Maria said.

"Oh, that's okay," said Cindy, frowning. Maria left her.

"So that's it?" asked Lenny. He had written the details in his notebook.

"Yeah, I don't know what he's doing, but I bet it's something rotten," answered Maria. "You don't have long."

"Don't worry, we'll be there," said Lenny.

"Lenny."

"Yeah."

"Be careful."

"I will."

Maria arrived home. "Hey there, Snugglebear," said Lois. "How did your day go?"

Oh, so very boring, Maria thought sarcastically. "Fine," she answered. "I'm going to go study."

"Oh, okay," said Lois. "I'm afraid I have to work tonight."

"Okay," said Maria. She went upstairs.

Maria went into her room. She took the cell phone out of her book bag and dropped the bag on the floor. She flopped onto her bed and looked at the phone. *I can't believe this is happening to me*, she thought. *Visions, crime bosses, and I'm some secret informant to a police detective. I hope he's okay.*

The man in the suit walked up to the wall. He took out the loose brick, removed the folded piece of paper, and put the money in its place.

"Freeze," someone yelled. Officers swarmed the man. He was cuffed as one officer removed the bills.

"It looks like Roger Todd," another one said to Lenny.

"The defense attorney," said Lenny. He looked at the one who had the paper. "What does it say?"

The officer unfolded it and looked it over. "Something about Digitech Incorporated, that computer company," he answered.

"Let's hold him on suspicion and get that paper down to White Collar Crimes," said Lenny. They led Robert Todd away.

Sometime later, Maria's cell phone rang. "Yes?"

"It's me," answered Lenny.

Maria felt relieved. "How did it go?"

"Good," Lenny replied. "It was Robert Todd, a defense lawyer. Rumor has it that he was going to defend Jim Becker, but unfortunately for him, he had a side thing in dealing in insider corporate information for stock trading. He won't be representing anyone except maybe himself at trial."

"I know I've said this before, but be careful," said Maria. "This Griffin guy sounds dangerous, and he's probably going to be mad now."

"Don't worry," said Lenny. "We've dealt with dangerous people before. I've got a good partner watching my back. We'll take him down and go after the next dirt bag. It's what we do."

Meanwhile, Mitch Ken was talking on the phone with the Griffin. "Do you know who the informant is?" asked the Griffin.

"No, sir," answered Mitch.

"How could this have happened?" demanded the Griffin. "With Robert in jail things could get a lot more complicated. All because of his stupid insider trading."

"Well, he does have a gambling problem," said Mitch.

"Enough," said the Griffin. "What about those rumors you've been spreading? Have there been any bites?"

"No, sir," answered Mitch. "Not the barest nibble. Sir, there's something else."

"What?" demanded the Griffin.

"Word is that one of our guys is talking about the money we have in Hobbins," answered Mitch.

"Move it now," the Griffin said. "Also, push back that thing we were going to do with the fake credit cards. I don't want to do that until this thing is over."

"Yes, sir," said Mitch. "I'll get on that immediately."

"See that you do," said the Griffin. "And I want this informant found."

A few hours later, Maria and Lois were having dinner. Maria was poking at her food. Lois took a sip of her tea.

"How was school?" asked Lois.

"It was fine," answered Maria.

"Maria, is something wrong? It seems like you're holding something back."

"No, Mom, I'm fine," said Maria. She ate her dinner. *It's strange,* she thought. *All this weird, dangerous stuff is happening to me and I can't tell my mom about it. It's like there's this wall up. She does seem to know something's going on, though. I have to be careful.*

"Are you sure?" asked Lois.

"Mom, I'm fine," Maria said again.

Lois continued to look at her for a moment and then went back to her food.

Meanwhile, Lenny was sitting at his desk. "Hey, Lenny, you want to come with me to talk to this guy about some dough he said is stashed over at Hobbins?" asked Detective Turner.

"No, thanks," answered Lenny. "I'm going to go over some paperwork the lieutenant wants me to do."

"Okay, see you," Turner said. He left.

Maria went over to her computer. She opened her web browser and did a search for the Griffin. There were a few results, but they were about the mythical creature. She did a new search adding / *crime boss*. A few links came up and she clicked the first one that led to a story in the *Paway Planner*.

> *The Griffin, Fact or Fiction*, she read. *In recent days rumors have surfaced about a single individual who is behind most of the recent crimes that have occurred in Paway. This lone mastermind apparently controls the criminal structure of our city with an iron fist and is the planner of some of the most noteworthy acts of robbery.*
>
> *Whether this figure actually exists is the topic of great debate. Even though those who believe this mysterious crime lord exists can't name any definite suspects, their belief in his existence is no less strong.*
>
> *"You want to know if the Griffin's real?" asked Charles Loft, who comments frequently on police activities. "What about that robbery at Paway First last year or the one at Shyer Jewelry? Several guys were at both and the money was never recovered. They were both represented by the same set of lawyers who represent every bunch of guys who pull a high-end robbery and get caught, and there's no accounting for where the money to pay for the lawyers comes from. There's no doubt in my mind that there's an individual planning these jobs and covering these guys if they get caught."*
>
> *So far, the Paway Police Department has not issued a comment on the subject.*

Maria stopped reading. She went through the other links. *There's not a whole lot on this guy*, she thought. *People don't even know if he's real. Lenny thinks he is.*

Lenny came back to his desk to find that someone had placed more forms on it for him to fill out. *That's a lot of paperwork*, he thought. *There's form after form here, wanting everything from details of arrest to time of arrest to what everyone said and did. It's a wonder they don't want to know what I was wearing at the arrest.*

He took the top form off the pile and put it on his desk. He sighed and began to fill it out.

Some time passed and Lenny got up to get a drink. When he came back, there was a folded piece of paper on his desk. Written inside it was a note. *Detective Hipar,* he read. *Something's wrong. Too dangerous to use a phone. I need you to come see me. A friend.*

Maria, Lenny thought. *I need to check on her.* He bolted up from his desk and darted off.

Lenny went down some stairs that led to the parking lot. On his way he got out his cell phone. *I can't call her,* he thought. *She said she can't get to a phone, and I can't call her mother.*

Lenny put his phone away and went to his car. He checked his watch. *What time does school get out?* he wondered. Lenny drove off.

Minutes later, Maria was walking down the sidewalk. *Maybe I can just go home and forget about all this for a while,* she thought.

Suddenly, Lenny drove up. "Hi," Maria said.

He got out of the car and looked around. "Are you all right?"

"Yeah," answered Maria. "Why?" Suddenly, someone threw a sack over her.

Chapter 3

"Ahh!" cried Maria. *What's going on?* she wondered. She was lifted off the ground and heard a sliding sound.

She kicked and struggled instinctively as she seemed to be carried off. *What's going on?* she wondered again. Her heart was beating so rapidly that she could not tell one beat from another.

She was thrown against a hard surface. Fear surged through her. "Help!" Maria cried. "Help me, Lenny! Help!"

Maria heard the sound of something being slammed shut. "Quiet," ordered a voice.

Someone's doing this, she thought. She froze in fear. "Get going," ordered the voice.

It's Mitch Ken, Maria thought. *It's Jim Becker or it's the Griffin. It's somebody. Somebody has me here and Lenny can't do a thing because . . .* Awful things went through her mind. Her breathing quickened. Remembering the voice telling her to be quiet, she tried to slow it. She lay there trying to be as still and quiet as possible.

Lenny started to stir. He touched his head where they had hit him and looked around in the van they were in. He saw the three men who had abducted them in the front. They had their backs to him.

He slammed himself into the nearest man just as he turned around. The man grabbed his wrists and they struggled. Lenny swung him side to side as they wrestled. Over the man's shoulder he saw the other two men turning to them.

The man pushed Lenny back with his knee. He worked to keep himself from falling back down. The man threw a punch, which Lenny dodged. He then pushed him back. The van hit a bump and the men had to work to keep upright.

"Stop him," ordered the man in the passenger seat.

The man who had been wrestling with Lenny grabbed him and shoved him up to the roof of the van and then shoved him back.

Lenny fell next to a sack. He heard a soft cry from inside it. *Maria,* he thought. He found new energy and shot up at the man. He shoved him back, pressing him against the back of the passenger seat. The man sitting there started to sit up, but Lenny grabbed him and shoved him forward against the dashboard. He had not been wearing a seat belt.

Lenny reached over the seats and grabbed the steering wheel, yanking it from the driver. "Hey, stop," the driver cried. Lenny jerked the steering wheel to the left. The driver tried to grab the wheel back, but Lenny kept him back with his shoulder as he kept the other two away with his right hand. The van went off the road and into a tree.

The entire vehicle shook as everyone and everything was thrown about.

"Ahh!" cried Maria. For a moment cold fear suppressed all conscious thought. Images of a car accident she had been in days ago went through her mind.

Lenny was thrown to the floor. Moments later, he looked around and got up, shaking off the aches he had as he did so.

He checked the three men. The two in the driver and passenger seats were unconscious. The driver stirred. As Lenny went to him, he woke up. He tried to move, but he had put on his seat belt, and Lenny grabbed it and then pulled it back. The man was pulled back against the seat.

Lenny held him there as he searched his pockets. He found his cell phone and dialed 911. "Hello, this is Detective Hipar of the Paway Police Department. There was a kidnapping attempt. Send police and ambulances to . . . well, just follow my phone's GPS signal."

Lenny reached for the bottom of the sack and pulled it toward him. He then pulled down the top to reveal the head of a startled girl. "Are you all right?" he asked.

"What happened?" Maria asked.

"Looks like we almost got napped by the Griffin's goons."

With Lenny's help Maria got out of the sack. Lenny let go of the driver, who then slumped down in his seat. He looked down at the third man, who was unconscious.

Lenny got out of the van and then helped Maria out. "Are you feeling okay?" he asked.

"Yeah, I think so."

"Why don't you go around the corner," said Lenny. "I'll take you to the hospital after the police are finished questioning me."

Maria walked off. *Please, let her be all right,* Lenny thought.

Maria heard the sounds of sirens as she hid behind a tree.

Minutes later, Lenny came through the trees. "Let's go," he said. They walked through the wooded area. *I hope I did the right thing,* he thought.

They walked to a dark car. "I borrowed it," Lenny explained.

They drove to the hospital. Lenny walked Maria into the main lobby. "This is Jessica Smith," said Lenny to the woman behind the admittance desk. "She was in an accident, and I thought I should get her checked out."

"Does she have an insurance card?" asked the woman.

"I can't seem to find it," answered Lenny.

"Let's get those forms," said the woman. She took some forms from off a shelf and handed them to Lenny. "Please fill these out," she said. "I'll see what I can do about getting you a room.

Minutes later, Maria was in an examination room. The doctor asked a few questions and Lenny gave a few answers. Maria did not pay attention to the conversation, so she could not tell how much Lenny told the truth and how much he lied.

I guess I'll get that CAT scan after all, Maria thought blankly as she lay down. She lay there quietly as the machine made several noises.

Several minutes later, Maria was back in the examining room. "Everything looks good," said the doctor, looking at printouts of the scan.

"Everything looks normal?" asked Maria.

"Yes . . . except heightened brain activity in some areas, but nothing to worry about," he answered.

Moments later, she was discharged and they were heading to her house. "Are you all right?" asked Lenny.

"I'm okay," Maria answered. Her tone was emotionless.

He dropped her off. *This isn't right,* Lenny thought. *I shouldn't have put her through this.* She disappeared in to her house and he drove off.

"Hi, honey," said Lois. "How was school?"

"Fine," answered Maria.

Lois looked at her. "Sweetie, are you all right?"

"I'm fine, Mom," Maria said. She used the last bit of her willpower to make herself sound cheerful. She went upstairs.

Maria went into her room and lay down on her bed. She rolled into a ball and cried.

The next morning, Maria got up and got ready for school. As she looked in the mirror in the bathroom, she felt as if she did not recognize the girl staring back at her. She went downstairs.

She sat down at the table in the kitchen to have breakfast. "Are you okay?" asked Lois.

Will you please stop asking me that? thought Maria. She put a smile on her face. "Yeah, Mom, I'm okay."

"It seems like you're holding something back," said Lois. "You know, you can talk to me about anything."

Yeah, I can, but I can't tell how you'd react, Maria thought. "I know, Mom," she said.

Maria looked at her watch. "I've got to go. I must've slept in too late. See you later." She darted out the door.

"Love you," said Lois. She sat down at the table.

Maria hurried to school. *Please don't be late,* she thought. *That's all I need.*

Cindy went up to her. "Hey, you're later than usual," she said.

"Yeah," said Maria. She rushed past her and went into the building. She just made it to her first class before the bell rang.

An hour later, Maria sat in class. The teacher talked, but Maria did not hear anything. She just made some motions with her pencil. The bell rang and she went to her next class and did the same. It seemed like she just haunted the halls and classrooms, barely existing.

At lunch, Maria sat down and unwrapped her lunch. She looked at her sandwich, and emotions started to surge up. She took a deep breath to clear her mind. She then nibbled at the sandwich. It tasted different. She mechanically ate it and did the same thing with the rest of her food. The bell rang and she shuffled off like she had been doing the entire day.

"Sounds like a close call," said Lieutenant Finn. "We're really glad you're all right."

"Thanks, sir," said Lenny.

"Though why you refused medical treatment I want to know," Finn said.

"I was fine."

"Well, just don't keel over. It'll wreak havoc on our insurance."

"I won't, sir," said Lenny as Finn went over to his desk. "Are the guys who tried to abduct me talking?" he asked. *Please don't say anything about a girl,* he thought.

"No, they're not," Finn answered. "They asked for a lawyer and now they're silent."

"They were probably sent by the Griffin," said Lenny. "Makes sense with all these arrests supposedly connected to him."

"Yes, which is why you should have a protection detail."

"But sir, I've worked dangerous cases before," said Lenny. "Anyway, if I had bodyguards, it might get in the way of the investigation."

Finn appeared to be thinking. "You know, I shouldn't, but I'm going to let you do it your way on this one," he said. He picked up a pen and started filling out a form. "Like I said earlier, don't keel over—it'll be bad for our insurance."

"Thank you, sir," said Lenny. He left the office. *I hope Maria's okay,* he thought.

"I swear, sir, the assignment won't be messed up again," Mitch said.

"They shouldn't have messed it up in the first place," the Griffin said. "Now they're out there and we still don't know who the girl is. Do they know it was me?"

"I don't know, sir," Mitch answered.

"Find out," the Griffin ordered.

"Yes, sir."

"Do you have any idea who the girl was?"

"No, sir."

"Find out."

How? wondered Mitch.

"Get everyone on it and get it done now," ordered the Griffin.

The air was cold in Paway. Maria walked down the sidewalk feeling numb inside.

Lenny's car pulled up by her and she barely noticed. He got out. *Isn't he breaking the law parking here?* she wondered.

"Hi, Maria," he said.

"Hi."

He walked up by her. "How are you doing?"

I wish everyone would stop asking me that, Maria thought. "Fine," she answered. She tried to sound cheerful.

"Maria, you've been through a lot," said Lenny. "First, a kidnapping, and then a second car crash."

Not to mention everything else, she thought.

"It's okay to be scared," Lenny said.

Maria looked away from him. "I'm . . . scared all the time."

"That's perfectly normal. You've been through a lot these last few weeks. Anyone would be scared."

"There's just so much I don't know," said Maria. "I don't know what's happening to me and—this probably sounds odd from someone who gets visions—I don't know what's going to happen next."

"Yeah, that does sound odd," said Lenny.

Maria wrapped her arms around herself and looked down.

"You know, it's not all that bad," Lenny said. "You have your mother to talk to, right?"

"No," Maria answered. "I can't tell her anything."

"Why not?"

"I don't want her to know about these visions. I don't know what she'd do if she found out."

Lenny looked at her. "You have me," he said. "You can call me anytime. You have the cell phone, and I'll keep refilling the minutes."

Maria turned to look at him. She thought about the phone in her bag. "You can talk to me anytime," Lenny repeated.

Maria sighed. "What am I going to do about this?"

"Like I told you, you've got to keep the fear separate while you do what you've got to do," Lenny said. "What you've got to do is get through this one day at a time. Just focus on getting the Griffin and anything else you've got to do, and we'll worry about the other stuff later."

Well, the scan did come back fine, Maria thought. *I'm not sick. I don't think.*

"Come on," said Lenny. "I'll give you a ride back to your block."

Later, Maria threw herself onto her bed. *Well, it's been a stressful week,* she thought. *I better get ready for bed. Maybe the worst is over.*

Chapter 4

Maria walked downstairs as her mother cooked breakfast. "Morning," Lois said.

"Morning," said Maria.

Lois looked at her but said nothing. She joined Maria and they had breakfast together.

A short time later, Maria approached the school building. "Hi," said Cindy.

"Hi," said Maria. She went inside. She passed some lockers on her way to her first class. *Maybe things will be quiet now,* she thought.

Mitch looked at a man from across his desk. "Do you have everything you need, Mr. Fleece?" asked Mitch.

"Yes," answered Mr. Fleece.

"Then go." Mr. Fleece turned and left the office. After he was gone, Mitch pulled out his cell phone. "Yes, sir, I put him on it," he said.

The last bell of the day rang. *It was a better day than before,* Maria thought. She left the building with her fellow students.

She looked up at the blue sky. *It's actually a nice day,* she thought. *Maybe I can get through this.* She walked along the sidewalk.

Lenny's phone rang. "Hello."

"The girl's in trouble," said a voice.

Lenny clenched his jaw. *Maria,* he thought.

"Come to where we snatched you," said the voice. There was a click, and then silence.

Minutes later, Maria was walking around. She was actually feeling a bit better than she did before. Suddenly, she heard a car quickly approaching her.

She remembered that she was in the area where she had been kidnapped and quickly turned around. She saw Lenny's car coming toward her. *Not again,* she thought.

Lenny stopped the car and got out. "Maria, are you all right?" he asked.

Before she could answer, something flew over her head. A canister landed in front of her and green smoke poured out. *It's happening again,* Maria thought, coughing.

Lenny went into a coughing fit. "Maria, get to the . . . , " he began. He fell forward onto the ground.

Maria barely saw his form slumped down. The green smoke filled her vision. *Not again,* she thought. *No, stay awake.* She continued to cough.

Part of her wanted to keep awake, but her body seemed to act on its own. Her eyes closed and she fell over.

A trio of men watched the scene from behind some bushes. "How did you know the girl would be here?" asked one of them.

"This was where they last picked her up," answered Mr. Fleece. "Since the high school's nearby I figured this was her route from there to somewhere else."

They went over to them.

A few minutes later, Maria started to stir. She slowly opened her eyes and her mind slowly came back. She then bolted up. *Where am I?* she wondered, alarmed. She looked around, but her eyes were still adjusting.

She heard a low moan. She was stricken with fear and, after a moment, realized it was Lenny. "Lenny?" she asked.

There was some more moaning. After a few moments Lenny spoke in a groggy voice. "Yeah, I'm here."

"Where are we?" asked Maria. She brought her legs up to her body and frantically looked around.

"It's going to be okay, Maria. We just have to look around and find a way out."

There were some creaking sounds and Lenny came into view. Maria realized that some dim light was coming into the room.

Lenny came up to her. "Are you all right?"

"Yeah." Maria looked around. The light came from slits in the walls around her. She realized they were in a room of some sort. She got up and walked around. The floor creaked as if it were made of wooden boards.

Maria went up to some of the slits in the walls. *It's a boarded-up window,* she realized. "I think we're in an old house," she said.

"Me too," said Lenny.

Suddenly, there was a thunderous noise outside. Maria peeked through the spaces between the boards on the window. She could make out a yellow machine coming at them. *A bulldozer.*

"I think they're going to tear this place down with us in it," cried Maria.

Lenny went up to the boards to have a look.

No, thought Maria in terror. *No! No!* Images of the sack going over her and the car accident went through her mind. Images of her mother, school, and a bunch of other things followed, and she felt feelings of regret and loss.

Maria backed away as panic coursed through her. She nearly stumbled and had to work to keep her balance.

"Maria, keep it together," said Lenny as he came up to her. "Remember what I told you. Keep your fear in a box and focus on what you need to do. Right now, we need to get out of here. Focus on that!"

The sound of the bulldozer grew louder.

Maria followed Lenny as he went over to the window. Together they pushed and pulled at the boards covering it. *Focus,* Maria told herself. *You need to get out of here. You need to get out of here.* She felt her nervous energy give her speed for the task.

Maria took a deep breath and stepped back. She then sent out a kick. A creak from a board surprised her.

Lenny pulled at the board. Maria went up to it. She caught a glance of the bulldozer approaching them. Feeling another shot of that nervous energy she stepped back and sent out another kick.

The board came off the window. "Go," cried Lenny. He guided her to the opening she had made. She climbed out.

After her feet touched the floor, she turned to Lenny. "Go," he said again.

"No," Maria cried and she grabbed him. With the two of them working together, pushing and pulling, Lenny managed to get through the snug opening.

Then he swiftly got out of the bulldozer's way.

The machine started to stop as Maria and Lenny collapsed to the ground. They were breathing heavily.

After a few moments, they managed to sit up. "I think this construction company is a front of theirs," Lenny managed to say. "Don't worry: I don't think everyone here is a criminal, so they won't try anything in front of all these witnesses."

The crew came near them but didn't approach them. They all just exchanged puzzled glances. The two sat there for a few minutes. "But we still don't know who the Griffin is," said Lenny.

A man was on the phone. "This is Mitch," he said. "The Griffin wants you to get to the train yard. He wants some goods transported."

"Are you sure that's a good idea?" asked the voice on the other end. "With all these arrests I don't think . . . "

"The Griffin doesn't pay you to think," said Mitch. "The Griffin pays you to do, so do." 19 Millow Brook Road, September 27, 5:30 p.m.

"I think I might have something," Maria said.

Lenny entered Mitch's office. "What is this?" Mitch demanded, getting up out of his chair. Several officers came up behind Lenny.

"Your buddy Rich gave you up, and now you're going to give the Griffin up," said Lenny.

A blond man sat in a board meeting. Suddenly, Lenny and a great many officers busted into the room. "Meeting adjourned," Lenny said.

He went over to the blond man. "You're under arrest."

The blond man bolted out of his chair and ran past him. Lenny chased after him and swung his leg out. The man tripped on Lenny's leg and fell to the floor. After a moment he got to his feet. "Don't you know who I am?" demanded the man.

He swung a punch, which Lenny dodged. "Yeah," said Lenny. He grabbed the man. "You're the Griffin." He then swung him down onto the table. "You're also under arrest."

"Hello, this is Paway Evening News," said a female announcer on the Marhills' TV. "Our top story: the capture of the Griffin. Prominent businessman Sid Maxwell is said to have been leading a double life. Aside from being the CEO of Hansfield Inc., one of the area's largest companies, he is said by police to have been the head of a criminal empire that has dominated Paway for a substantial amount of time. We take you to the scene with Mike Sterner."

"Thanks, Jen," said Mike, the male announcer. The scene had shifted to outside Hansfield Inc. headquarters. "It started with the arrest of Rich Louis, a reputed career criminal, for the transportation of stolen goods. Sources close to the investigation said he very much disliked his employer and had no trouble fingering Mitch Ken, the Griffin's alleged middleman who reportedly cut a deal and identified Maxwell as the crime boss."

"I'm sure glad that unpleasantness doesn't have anything to do with us," said Lois. She and Maria were watching the broadcast.

"Police arrested Maxwell at a board meeting," said Mike. Maria picked up the remote and turned the TV off.

BOOK 3

In the Sights
of the Mastermind

Chapter 1

Maria braced for action. Her body tensed as she looked around the room.

"Again," ordered a man.

"Hiyah," she and others cried. As they yelled, they sent a punch into the air.

The man raised his hand in return. "That's enough for today," he said. He bowed, and the group before him did so too. They then broke up and went to the side of the room for their bags.

The man went up to Maria. "Congratulations on completing the course, Alisa," he said. "As always, you did well."

"Thank you, Sensei," said Maria.

"It's a shame you can't continue on."

"Thanks, but I have to do a few things, and I can't make it here anymore," Maria said. They bowed to each other. Maria then went to the girls' changing room, changed, and left.

Maria, or Alisa Jerkins as she had been known for weeks, looked around. The streets were getting dark. She crossed one and checked her watch. *Mom shouldn't be home yet,* she thought. She headed home.

Meanwhile, Lenny was finishing his paperwork. He went through various lists of events that had happened during arrests and things he had done because of police procedure. At last he put the last form down and looked at the squad-room clock.

"Hey, Lenny," said Detective Jon Turner. He came up to his desk and held up an envelope. "Something came for you."

He dropped it on Lenny's desk and walked away. Lenny picked it up.

Sleep Heavenly Hotel, Lenny read on the envelope's return address. *It must be a quest of the hotel.* He took out a piece of paper. On it appeared to be a note. *I show the time on my face. I also show a letter. Twelve appears three times.* It was signed *Mr. Mindful.*

Lenny looked at the front and the back of the note. *Must be some sort of nut,* he thought. He put the paper down. *Time to go,* Lenny thought. He got his coat and left.

Meanwhile, a man sat at a table in a dark room.

Another man came up to him. "Boss, everything's ready," said the second man.

"Good, now it's about to begin," said the first man.

"But I don't see how this is going to make us money."

It's always about money to these people, thought the man at the table. "Don't worry," he said. "This is just the first step."

The other man began to leave the room. "I'll go tell the others."

The man at the table looked at the objects spread before him: a notebook, a blueprint, and a collection of photos of people. *Soon, the rules will change,* he thought. *Then I'll unleash my craft that I have spent so long perfecting.* He smiled a sinister smile.

The next morning, Maria woke up. She looked at the clear, blue sky through her window for a moment and then got out of bed.

There was a large room. People talked quietly and walked about the plush carpet. One man went to the escalator at one wall. To the side, a man sat behind a desk. He looked at a clock on the wall.

Suddenly, there was a thunderous crash as pieces of the wall rained inward. A truck went through the wall and into the room. Sleep Heavenly Hotel. October 22, 3 p.m.

Oh no, thought Maria. She looked for the cell phone Lenny had given her. After finding it she dialed his number.

"Hello?"

"We've got a problem," said Maria.

"What is it?"

"I had a vision of a truck crashing into some place. The Sleep Heavenly Hotel at three o'clock."

The note, Lenny thought.

"This is the first time I've gotten a vision about an accident," said Maria.

"I don't think it's going to be an accident," said Lenny.

"Why?"

"Because I got an note with a return address from that place," answered Lenny. "It was some weird riddle." He recited the riddle for her. "It was signed by a Mr. Mindful. Mean anything to you?"

"No."

"Well, I'll check it out," said Lenny. "I'll also try to figure out what this weird junk means."

"Good luck," said Maria.

Maria got dressed. She went to her computer and did a search for "Mr. Mindful." There was one result:

"Please clean your room," said a mother to her son, Terrible Tommy, Maria read.

"No," said Terrible Tommy.

"You better start being mindful, mister," said his mother.

"Yada yada," said Terrible Tommy.

"That's it," said his mother. "It's time for Iron Wall Military School."

Just one hit, and somehow I don't think Terrible Tommy is trying to take out a hotel, Maria thought.

She got up and got ready for school.

Maria arrived downstairs. "Snugglebear, you're up early," said Lois.

"I slept well last night," Maria said.

Lois began to set the table. "Sorry I've been out late so much. They still want me to put a few more nights in."

"That's okay," said Maria. *Especially because it leaves me a lot of time alone to do what I need to do.*

Minutes later, Maria was out the door. "Have a good day, sweetheart," called Lois.

"You too, Mom," Maria called back.

Meanwhile, Lenny looked at the letter in his hand. *What does it mean?* he wondered.

He looked around the squad room. *I can't send anyone over to the hotel. What would I say? That a truck is going to ram into the building at three and somehow I got all that from this note? What does it mean? I show the time on my face. I also show a letter. Twelve three times. On his face. Maybe it's a guy with a clock on a headband.* Lenny sighed and leaned back in his chair.

He looked at the note again. *What does it mean? I've never been good at this stuff.*

Lenny got up and filled a cup of water at the water fountain. He sat down and drank it while looking at the note. *Numbers on my face,* he thought. *Numbers on my face. What does that mean? Tattoos? Masks? Pimples? What? This isn't how this thing usually goes. Usually, a guy commits a crime, we hear about it and go to the scene, we get clues, and then we arrest the guy.*

Lenny rubbed his eyes. *First a psychic kid, now a nut with riddles,* he thought. *This isn't what I signed up for. Is the whole thing meaningless? No, of course it's not. Don't think that. You can solve a puzzle only if you treat it like a puzzle that can be solved.*

Lenny picked up the note and ran the words through his mind yet again.

After a few moments he had a thought. *What if I run these phrases through the system.*

Lenny typed *Letter on my face* into his computer. No results were returned. He tried *time on my face* and *12 3 times*. Still nothing. *That didn't work,* he thought.

Lenny looked at his watch. Maybe Maria could get a vibe from it or something. It was almost time for her to get out of school. He got his coat and was off.

Detective Jon Turner was by the soda machine. Another detective came up to him and gestured toward Lenny across the room. "Hey, what's your partner working on?" he asked.

"I don't know," Turner answered. "Something that came in the mail, I think."

Maria was walking home from school when Lenny pulled up beside her. She looked around and got in. *I hope nobody sees me,* she thought.

"Solved the riddle?" asked Maria.

"No," answered Lenny. "I was never really any good at these things."

"Strange, with you being a detective and all. Where is it?"

"Here." He handed her the note.

Maria read it. *It's all right here,* she thought. *What does it mean?*

She thought about her vision, about the people walking around, about the man going up the escalator. She remembered hearing the ticking of the clock as the man behind the desk looked at it. *The clock. That's it!*

"There was a clock on the wall inside the hotel," Maria said. "I saw it in my vision!"

"Yeah, the surface of a clock is called a face," said Lenny.

"I've heard that."

They both thought for a bit. "He said that twelve appears three times on it, but it appears only at noon and midnight," said Lenny. He thought some more. "The twelfth letter in the alphabet is *L.*"

Maria held out her right hand in the shape of an *L.* After looking at it she held her left hand in the shape of an *L* and imagined a clock behind it. "Three o'clock," she said. "The hands of a clock make an *L* when it turns three!"

"He was telling us the time the truck was going to crash into the hotel," Lenny said. *It's fortunate that Maria's vision already told us that, because I wouldn't be able to figure it out on my own,* Lenny thought bitterly.

A few minutes later, they arrived at the hotel. "I'm Detective Hipar of the Paway Police," Lenny said to the man behind the desk. "I need to speak with the person in charge." He showed him his badge.

The man looked startled. "One moment," he said. As he went off, Maria and Lenny looked around the lobby, the room Maria had seen in her vision.

A clock, Maria thought. She looked around and saw the clock on the wall.

She went up against the wall and tried to grab it, but it was out of reach. "I need a hand," she said. Lenny went up to her and hoisted her up. She grabbed the clock off the wall.

The man who had been behind the desk reappeared, accompanied by a second man. "What are you doing here?" the second man asked.

"Police business," Lenny said. He held up his badge again.

Maria looked the clock over and turned it around. Taped to the back was a piece of paper.

She pulled it off, unfolded it, and read the note inside. "I can be seen by the naked eye," she read. "If I'm put into a bag, I will make the bag lighter. Black is the clue. I'm blacker than the galaxy. Mr. Mindful." Lenny turned to the two men. "I'm going to need you to clear this place. For everyone's safety."

Meanwhile, two men were in a truck facing the building. One man was about to put a plank between the seat and the gas pedal, but the other stopped him. He was looking at the screen of a cell phone.

"That's the signal," he said. "Our man inside saw someone get the note. Let's clear out."

Meanwhile, Maria and Lenny were looking over the area. "What's going on here?" asked Lenny. "Now we've got another riddle? Is this some sort of game?"

"Not according to what I saw," said Maria.

Yeah, but I can't tell anyone that, Lenny thought.

"You're going to call for backup?"

"What would I tell them? That someone put a note behind a clock?"

Maria looked at the paper. "What do you think it means?" She handed him the note.

I couldn't even figure out the last one, Lenny thought. "I don't know." He looked around and then at his watch. *It's 3:11 and there's no truck,* he thought.

He looked at the man from behind the desk and the man in charge. They were watching them and looking very puzzled. "Let's get out of here," Lenny said.

They got into Lenny's car. "You think these notes had anything to do with that truck?" Maria asked.

"I don't know," answered Lenny. "All I know is that a truck was supposed to hit that place but didn't. We must've done something right." They drove off.

Chapter 2

The next morning, Maria got up. She took a look out her window. The sky was still clear and blue. *It's been nice weather these last few days,* she thought. *I can't believe I'm thinking about the weather.*

> *There was a large group of people in a dark room. They were dancing while lights flashed over them. Overhead there was a large decoration consisting a ball in the middle of a dark ring surrounding by another ring with another surrounding it.*
>
> *Suddenly, the object fell toward the dancers. There were screams. 120 Caullead. October 23, 9:08.p.m.*

Oh no, thought Maria. She stood up, feeling alert. *This is your life now,* she told herself. She took a deep breath and then got out the cell phone to call Lenny.

"Hello?" asked a voice she did not know.

"I need to speak with Detective Hipar, please," said Maria.

"I'm afraid he's not in," said the voice. "Who is this?"

"Is there any way to speak with him?" Maria asked.

"I'm telling you he's not here," answered the voice.

Maria hung up. *What am I going to do?*

"Maria, you're going to be late," called Lois from downstairs.

Maria then hurried about, got dressed and ready, and went downstairs.

In the squad room, Detective Turner went to Lenny's desk. Lenny's jacket was over the chair. Turner looked around to see that no one was looking and slid Lenny's cell phone back into the jacket pocket.

Meanwhile, Lenny was sitting in Lieutenant Steve Finn's office with him and another detective. "Could you please go over it again?" asked Finn.

"Well, sir, as I said, I got this note," said Lenny. "There was a riddle in it, which I solved, and it led me to a clock in a hotel."

"Why did you go down there?" asked Detective Lofar the other detective. "Don't you have enough to do?"

"Yes, I do," answered Lenny. "It's just that something about the note struck me as off. I think this guy could be dangerous. That's why I think we should open a case. We need to find him and make sure he won't hurt anybody or do something stupid."

"All you've got is a couple of notes with riddles in them," Finn said. "I'm sorry, but that's not enough."

"But sir, what if he does something and we didn't act?" asked Lenny. "How would we look?"

Finn sighed. "I'm sorry, but we don't have the resources to go after something with so little. Try to bring us something more."

A few seconds later, Lenny came back. "Anything happen while I was gone?" he asked.

"No," Turner answered. He was leaning against his desk.

Lenny looked at his watch. "Did anyone call from the crime lab? I asked them to dust that clock for prints. *After I wiped Maria's off,* he thought.

"No."

Lenny sighed. *I hope they come back with something before this nut does something,* he thought. *I wonder if Maria will get anything.*

Meanwhile, Maria was sitting in class. *Don't worry,* she told herself. *There's plenty of time to warn Lenny.*

She tapped her pencil on her book. The teacher talked but she did not pay attention. The image of the object falling toward the dancers and their screams kept going through her mind.

A few hours later, school let out. Maria walked down the sidewalk. She then stopped and looked around. After seeing no one around she ducked behind a tree. She took out her cell phone and dialed Lenny.

"Hello."

"Good," Maria said. "I tried calling you earlier, but the man who answered said you weren't in."

"Someone answered this phone?" asked Lenny. "Who?"

"I don't know," answered Maria. "He didn't say."

Lenny felt apprehensive. "Never mind. What is it?"

"Something's going to fall from the ceiling at one twenty Caullead."

Lenny looked at his computer. He did a search for the address. "There's a club called the Black Hole."

I guess what I saw could've been a black hole, she thought. "What are we going to do?" Maria asked.

"I guess we have to go down there and check it out," answered Lenny. "I tried to get them to open a case, but they said there wasn't enough to go on."

"You know, I just thought of something," said Maria. "Can't a hole make a bag lighter?"

"Yeah," answered Lenny. "Technically, it can't be seen by the naked eye too. This probably has to do with that riddle, so we're definitely going down there."

The time I saw was 9:08—that's after Mom gets home, Maria thought. "I'm going to have to sneak out," she said.

Lenny was quiet for a moment. "Fine," he said.

That night, Maria poked her head out her window. The neighbors' lights were out, and it was very dark. *I can't believe I'm doing this,* she thought. She swung one leg out the window and then the other one.

Take a deep breath, she told herself. *Don't think about how high it is or look down.* She gripped the window ledge and lowered herself down. She tried to remember where the lower ledges and other possible holds had been when she'd looked out earlier.

Maria moved her foot around, searching for a hold. When she felt one, she pressed her weight down on it, testing it. She found that it was safe and put her full weight on it. She repeated this process several times.

She made it halfway down the house and then to the top of the first-story window. *Relax,* she told herself. *It's going to be fine. You're going to make it.* She grabbed the top of the window as she lowered a foot to the bottom. She did the same thing with the other foot. Maria then dropped to the ground.

I did it, Maria thought. She ran, feeling energized. She met up with Lenny, who was parked about a block away.

They arrived at the Black Hole a few minutes later. A bouncer tried to stop them as they went up to the door, but Lenny held up his badge. "She's with me," he said.

The inside of the club was dark. There were flashing lights like in Maria's vision. The music playing over the loudspeakers was a pounding set to a certain pattern. With the lights flashing on and off it looked like the dancers were instantaneously shifting into different positions like pictures on a TV screen whose channel was being changed.

Maria looked over the room. "There," she cried. She pointed toward the ceiling. There was a large papier-mâché black hole papier-Mache model of a black hole with the center represented by the ball with the outer edge made up of the rings. It consisted of dark purple and black rings around a large black ball.

"Let's clear the area," yelled Lenny. He and Maria then went to work trying to clear the area where the ball would fall. Maria found it much more difficult without a badge like Lenny's to show.

Suddenly, the decoration fell to the floor. It crashed down onto a spot that, fortunately, had been cleared.

The rings were sprayed about, cracked and broken. The outer shell of the ball fell away in four pieces, revealing a metal ball beneath. On the face of the ball was a digital clock counting down from fifteen, a keypad was beneath that, and a note had been taped to it.

Lenny went up to it, gesturing for Maria to stay back. He took the note off the ball. *This is a bomb,* he read. *The keypad is the only way to stop it. I'll make this one easy for you. All you have to do is put in the year that Abraham Lincoln became president. You have fifteen minutes.*

Four men wearing the dark clothes that were the uniforms of the club security came up to the scene. "We need to clear this area now," Lenny cried. He showed them his badge.

The men went off to clear the area. There were nervous murmurs as people were herded about.

Lenny went up to Maria and handed her the note. He then went back to the ball. He raised his finger about an inch from the keypad. *What's the date?* he wondered. *I know he was the sixteenth president, but that's it.*

Maria came up next to him. "I need you to get out of here," Lenny said.

"I'm staying,"

"Maria, please get out of here," said Lenny. Someone fell as he was leaving the club, and Lenny went over to pick him up,

Maria looked back to the ball. The clock was winding down and she tried to stay calm. *The year,* thought Maria. *We talked about this in Mrs. Kramer's class not that long ago. It was on a test that was multiple choice. I got it wrong but she marks the right answers.*

Lenny came back up to the ball. "I need you to get out of here now," he said.

Maria held up her hand to him. *Think,* she told herself. *What number question was it? Where was the red mark?* She tried to remember what the test had looked like when she got it back. She tried to see it in her hands.

She just barely remembered the question. *Which one was it?* she wondered. Maria remembered looking through the choices trying to figure out which one was the right answer. She tried to remember what it looked like when she got it back and which answer had a mark on it. *There was 1920,* she thought. *And 1812, 1834, 1861. That's it! It was 1861!*

She punched in the numbers. After a moment the countdown stopped at eight. Maria let out a breath. Lenny smiled and put a hand on her shoulder.

He turned and saw the remaining crowd being evacuated. "It's okay," he called. People stopped and looked at him. "We have solved the problem, but we would still like you all to leave as quickly and as calmly as possible." They began leaving again.

Lenny turned back to Maria. "Did you see it in a vision?" he asked.

"No, it was on a test."

"Well, it's a good thing you paid attention."

"Actually, I missed it, but the teacher marks the right answers."

"Good thing."

Suddenly, a small door beneath the keypad swung open. Inside was a piece of paper. Lenny put on a plastic glove from his pocket and took the paper out. *Cover in feathers of a dove while I come like the letter E in man's time.* He showed the letter to Maria. "Think about this," he said. "Wait by the car."

Maria went through a side door. "Hey," called a man's voice. She turned in time to see a man charging at her. *Think of karate class,* she told herself. She quickly tried to steady her breathing as she had practiced.

The man threw a punch and she dodged it. He tried to grab her, but she backed away. Maria swung out her leg and kicked his feet out from beneath him. He fell to the ground. He swung a punch at Maria, but she dodged it. She grabbed his wrist and put him in a wristlock.

"Ahh!" cried the man. "Let me go!"

"Get out of here," Maria ordered. She let go of him. The man got to his feet and ran off.

I can't believe how easy that was, Maria thought. *That training really worked.*

A few minutes later, the man joined another in a van a short distance away. The man who was waiting for him was talking on a cell phone. "Yeah, the bomb didn't go off," said the man. "Yeah, he probably solved the riddle. Another thing, he had a girl with him. Bert saw her leave the club alone and tried to grab her, but she fought him off." The man listened for a moment. "Yes, sir," he said. "We'll watch them both."

A little while later, Lenny came up to his car. Maria came out from a nearby alley and joined him.

"What happened?" asked Maria.

"The bomb squad went over it," said Lenny. "It was a real bomb, but you deactivated it."

Maria stood there. *It really could've exploded,* she thought.

"They want to see me in the morning," said Lenny. "I guess they believe I've really got something now."

"Well, I'm sure now that there's officially a case, this guy will be caught in no time." They got into the car and drove off.

"How are you going to get back inside?" asked Lenny.

"I'm sure my mom's asleep by now," Maria replied. "I'll just go through the front door."

First the Griffin, now Mr. Mindful, thought Lenny. *Why do all these guys have nicknames?* They drove on, not realizing that a short distance away a van was following them.

Chapter 3

Mr. Mindful sat at his table. His employees were before him. "Are you sure the detective has the clue?" he asked.

"He's got to," answered one man. "He stopped the bomb."

"This girl," Mr. Mindful said. "The file on Detective Hipar that we bought from the Griffin's former employee talked about a consultant from Chadlee who was a young woman. Bert, describe her."

"She's just like they described her in the file," said Bert. "A short blonde. Looks like a teenager."

Mr. Mindful thought for a moment. "Keep your eyes on both of them. I want to know everything about her. She might be useful."

Maria woke up the next morning. She still felt tired. *I guess that's what I get for going clubbing last night,* she thought. And then, *I can't believe I made a joke about that.*

After a moment, Maria got out of bed. She got dressed and went downstairs.

"Hi," said Lois. "How did you sleep?"

"All right," Maria answered.

Lois put breakfast in front of Maria. "I'm afraid I'm going to be working late again."

"That's okay."

"No, it's not. Also, according to my boss it won't be the last time either. With our expenses, we do need the money, but I wish I didn't have to spend so many nights away."

Maria felt sad thinking about the expenses she was talking about. *Hospital bills can be expensive,* she thought.

"Honey?" asked Lois.

"Oh, I'm fine," said Maria. "I'm sure things will get better eventually."

"I'm sure they will too," said Lois. She hugged Maria.

After Maria finished her breakfast, she went out the door.

Meanwhile, Lenny was in Lieutenant Steve Finn's office. Also in the office were some high-ranking detectives and lieutenants.

"Let's go over this again," Finn said.

"I got this note from a Mr. Mindful," said Lenny. "It was basically a riddle. I solved it and had a hunch it might mean something, so I checked it out."

"Then you solved the riddle you found at the hotel and it led you to the club where you found the bomb?" Finn asked.

"Yeah."

"What about the girl at the hotel?" asked Jon Turner. "The one who witnesses say helped you get the clock down?"

"A civilian willing to help," answered Lenny.

"They also say there was a girl at the club talking to you," Turner said. "Was this the same one?"

"I doubt it," Lenny said. "She was also just a civilian wanting to know what was going on. Of course, it was so loud and dark that I can't tell you for sure if she was the same one or not."

"Anyway, we're going over the bomb now," Finn said. "There were no fingerprints on the note or the clock. I'd like something more when we give the presentation to the rest of the squad, so let's get to work."

"What's the answer to this current riddle?" asked Detective Tow.

"I'm working on it," said Lenny.

"And the rest of us should be working on the rest of the case," Finn said. "Detective Fields, do we have anything from past cases?"

"No, sir," Fields answered. "This MO doesn't match anything on file."

"Detective Dale?" asked Finn.

"Nothing yet on the canvas, sir," Dale answered.

Finn sighed. "I'm going to the department psychologist to see about getting a profile written up," he said. "The rest of you, get to work and get me some leads." The detectives left the office.

Lenny sat at his desk. *It was Maria who solved those riddles,* he thought. He looked down at his desk, at the picture of the note. *If a fifteen-year-old can solve these things but I can't, then I'm probably a very poor detective.*

After looking at it for several minutes he leaned back in his chair. *What am I going to do? I'm used to looking at clues and evidence, not puzzles and riddles. Give me a good, not foretold, robbery.*

Lenny looked up at the ceiling. *Who is this guy?* he wondered. *Who calls himself Mr. Mindful? I think all the weirdness in this city is being drawn to me.*

He looked at his computer and did searches for parts of the riddle. Nothing came back. *Of course,* he thought.

Lenny sighed. *I hate thinking this, but maybe Maria will get something.*

Meanwhile, Maria was sitting in class. "The scandal rocked President Grant's term in office, and eventually he was forced to labor on his memoirs in his final days just to support his family," said the teacher.

Maria was not really listening. *Letter E,* she thought. *Man's time. Maybe I could look it up. It could be a poem or a historical reference.*

She looked at the clock. *I don't know what this means,* she thought. *I solved the last two only because I had visions about what was going to happen. I'm not a riddle person.*

Maria looked up at the teacher. She was still talking, apparently unaware that Maria had not been paying attention to her. Maria looked around. It seemed a few students were looking at the teacher, but many others seemed zoned out.

She shot a glance out the window. *I hope I can figure this out,* she thought. *Then again, I'll probably get a vision about this one just like the others. At least, I hope so. I hope nothing happens without me knowing about it ahead of time.*

Sometime later, Maria sat down in the computer lab. She typed *dove/ feathers/man's time.* There were no matches.

Maria looked at the screen. On a whim she typed *riddles/crimes.* Several links came up. She clicked on one. *A certain crime is punishable if attempted but not if committed,* Maria read. She clicked the answer button. *Suicide,* she read. She went through a few more. <u>There are *3,110,000 of these and not one seems to be about Mr. Mindful,*</u> Maria thought.

She tried *Crime News/Paway City*. After reading about several recent arrests, some of which she and Lenny had been involved in, she gave up. *I guess it's too soon,* she thought. *There's no mention of Mr. Mindful.*

"Boss, we're trailing the detective like you asked us to, though some of us are a little nervous about targeting a cop," said one of Mr. Mindful's men. "We also put the tracker on his car. Just in case."

"Do not worry," said Mr. Mindful. "It's just another step to your great payday."

I don't see how, thought the man. *It's not like we're pulling any real jobs.*

"Tell me what you've found out about him," said Mr. Mindful.

"Sure—he seems like a regular workaholic cop," the man said. "He goes to work and then goes home and then starts it all over."

"Where is he now?" Mr. Mindful asked.

"Last I checked, at the police station," the man replied.

No doubt he and the other law enforcement personnel are having a chat about that present I left at the club, thought Mr. Mindful. "Keep your eyes on him," he ordered. "I want to know all I can about him."

"Right," said the man. "Though I don't see how all this is going to make us money."

"Be patient," said Mr. Mindful. "You'll find out in due time." *As if mere money was my true goal.*

Maria sat at a desk in another class. She tried to pay attention, but her eyes kept going to the clock on the wall. She sighed.

A few minutes later, school let out and Maria, as well as her fellow students, left the building.

As Maria was walking down the sidewalk leaving the school grounds, Lenny's car pulled up by her. "Hi," he said. Maria got in.

"Where are we going?" she asked.

"My place."

A few minutes later, they arrived at Lenny's apartment building. It was plain in its décor and painted brown.

Lenny led Maria to a door with 2B on it and put his key in the lock. Inside was a plain room with simple, department-store furniture. File folders and papers were all spread about.

"This is kind of a big thing, inviting me to your place," said Maria.

"Well, it's a special occasion," said Lenny. "It's not every day that I almost get blown up in a nightclub." He sat in a chair and gestured for Maria to take the couch.

"Any idea who Mr. Mindful is?" asked Maria.

"None, and everyone at the station is going over some aspect of the case," Lenny answered. He tried to arrange some papers on a stand by him into a neater pile.

At the end of man's time, Maria thought. *What could that mean?*

Lenny saw that there was a pile of papers by Maria. "You can move those," he said. "They're in no special order."

Maria looked at the pile and carefully moved them aside. "I tried doing an Internet search on some of the phrases in the riddle, but I got nothing," she said.

"Well, I got nothing from the police databases," said Lenny. "Is there anything else you want to try?"

"How about the Library of Congress?"

"I think if they were there, they would've come up in your Internet search," Lenny said. He shuffled some papers on the arm of the chair. "You want anything to eat?"

"No, thank you," answered Maria. She tried thinking about it some more but could not find any new way to approach the riddle. "I'm not really a riddle person," she said.

"Neither am I," answered Lenny.

"Odd since you're a detective," Maria said. "I would think you guys would be all over puzzles."

"I'm used to dealing with crime scenes and clues," said Lenny. "This whole puzzles gimmick leaves me a little out of my depth. I'm not as smart as they think I am back at the station."

Lenny put the files from the chair on top of the pile on the stand. "There was a bomb planted in a public place, so everyone and their mother wants this case solved and done."

"Yeah, it was crazy," said Maria. "Some guy attacked me in the alley when I left."

Lenny sat up alert. "Really?" he asked. "Why didn't you tell me?"

"It was some random thing. It was either a mugger or some guy in a panic because of the bomb thing. I fought him off. I've been taking self-defense lessons."

"Since when?"

"Since after you arrested the Griffin."

"Why didn't you say anything? I could've maybe shown you something."

Maria shrugged. "It's nothing. I thought it might be something I would need."

Lenny thought for a moment. He then got up. "I better take you home."

Soon, Lenny was dropping Maria a block away from her house. *This is strange,* Maria thought. *I feel I should invite Lenny over now, but Mom would notice a police detective hanging around.*

Maria went inside. It was quiet. She went into the kitchen. It looked like Lois wasn't home yet She got an apple out of a bowel on the counter and began to eat it.

Maria went back into the living room. The light on the answering machine was blinking, so she went over to it and played the message.

"Hello, Mrs. Marhill," said a woman's voice. "This is Jen from Far Off Travel, and I'm calling to offer you the free trip of a lifetime."

I think we'll pass, thought Maria.

There was a beep and then another message played. "Hello, Mrs. Marhill. This is Fed Herman from Mercy Perks Hospital. I'm calling about the monthly bill."

Maria stopped the machine and went upstairs.

Maria entered her room and went to her bed. She looked at the ceiling for a few moments. *What if I don't get a vision?* she wondered. *I have to figure out that clue.*

She lay there thinking. *Feathers of a dove. At the end of man's time. I keep going over the same words again and again and getting nothing.*

Maria shot a look out her window. *Maybe there's another way to look at it,* she thought. She reached down into her book bag and got her math notebook. She opened it. *Maybe if I do some homework, it'll warm up my brain.* She began to do some problems.

Meanwhile, outside her house, two men waited in a car. The man behind the wheel was talking on a cell phone. "Yes, sir, she's inside," he said. "We saw the detective drop her off." He listened for a moment. "Yes, sir, we'll watch her."

The next morning, Lenny was getting ready for work. He was getting dressed when his cell phone rang. "Hello?" He almost said Maria's name.

"It's me," said Detective Turner. "We've got a lead."

"What is it?" Lenny asked.

"One of the parts from the bomb was from a company called Trenton Industries. It was formed in a town by the same name and closed about three years ago. I talked to the owner. He said they had a warehouse here in Paway and that when they closed down, they left some parts behind, including the type the forensic techs found. I think it's worth a shot."

"I'll be ready in five minutes," said Lenny.

"I'll come pick you up," said Detective Turner.

Turner drove up to the parking lot of Lenny's apartment building. Lenny was waiting outside. He picked him up and drove off.

Soon, they arrived at the warehouse. Lenny got out and looked around. "Where do you want to start?" he asked.

"I got a key and the owner's permission, so let's start inside," Turner answered.

They went up to the front doors, which were chained. Turner unlocked the padlock and they went inside.

As they looked around, Lenny thought about an old lumberyard he had visited.

They went down a hallway. Little light got through the boarded-up windows.

Suddenly Turner's foot pulled on a line that ran across a doorway a few inches off the floor.

A wall of wooden boards nailed together slammed down behind them.

"What?" Turner cried.

Lenny went to the wall as his partner watched him. "It won't budge," he said. He slammed his shoulder against it, but it would not move. "Try the window."

Turner checked some windows in a nearby room. "They're boarded up," he said.

Lenny looked down the hall before them. "Let's try up ahead." The two detectives went down the hall.

They went by a boarded-up door. Turner went up to them and tried to pry them off but to no avail. A few moments later, he went back to Lenny and they started down the hall again. They came to a pair of doors at the end of the hall that were not boarded up.

They went through the doors and heard something going through the air. An alarm went off in Lenny. He pushed the detective back through the doorway.

A two-by-four swung through the air on a pair of ropes. It swung through where they stood and hit the wall. Nails protruded from it.

"Are you all right?" Lenny asked. He took a look at the trap.

Detective Turner had fallen onto the floor. Lenny offered him a hand, but Turner got up on his own and scowled. "I'm fine," he answered. "We need to get moving."

They went under the two-by-four and went down the hall before them. There was another door. "We should be careful," said Lenny. "We don't know if there are any more traps around here."

Detective Turner darted through the door. Lenny followed him.

As they entered, they looked around and saw tables, chairs, cabinets, and a sink. "This must be the employees' break room," Turner said.

Lenny took out his cell phone and dialed the station house's number. He pressed it to his ear. "My phone's not working," he said.

Detective Turner took out his phone and tried it. "Mine's not either."

Lenny looked around. *What's going on here?* he thought.

Detective Turner went over to the cabinets and started looking through them.

"Looking for a phone?" asked Lenny.

"There's got to be something that can help us get out," answered Detective Turner. He continued looking.

After a few moments, he stopped. "There's nothing here," he said. They left the room. "What's going on?"

"Looks like whoever built that bomb wanted anyone who came looking to stay put," answered Lenny.

Turner looked around. "Did you tell anyone you were coming here?"

"No," Lenny answered. "I didn't know myself until a few minutes beforehand, and I didn't think I would have to. You?"

"No," Detective Turner answered. Suddenly he stepped on something and heard a click.

Both detectives darted back as something fell from the ceiling and crashed onto the floor.

Dust rose as they looked around. They waved away the dust and looked at the object before them. It appeared to be a bundle of two-by-fours wrapped in a plastic sheet and secured by a rope.

Lenny looked around. *How many traps are around here?* he wondered.

He went up to the bundle. "I guess we should've stayed home," he said.

Detective Turner went past Lenny. "Come on." He angrily stormed down the hall.

They came to a large room. Scattered all about were a great many boxes. "This is probably where that part came from," Turner said.

"Now all we have to do is get out so we can tell people," said Lenny.

Turner scowled and went looking through the boxes.

After a few seconds of looking he heard a click. He barely managed to duck to avoid the arrow that shot out at his head.

The arrow implanted itself into a wall and the detectives stared at it. Detective Turner tried to slow his breathing. *I can't believe that happened,* he thought.

After a few moments, Turner looked around. He saw a door across the room. He went up to it and Lenny followed.

They went through it and came to a darkened hallway. Lenny looked to his side and saw lines of dim light. He felt along them. "Hey, I think these are boarded-up windows," he said.

"This whole place must've been boarded up," Detective Turner said.

Lenny pushed on the boards. "I'm tired of walking around this bobby-trapped funhouse," he said. "Maybe we can get these boards off." He pushed forcefully and heard a bit of a creaking sound. "I think this one is broken."

He continued to push at it and Detective Turner came over. Together they pushed at the board and it creaked.

Lenny stopped and stepped back. Turner stepped aside as Lenny gave a good kick to the board. It creaked mightily. They went back to pushing it, and it broke in half.

Lenny reached through the window and grabbed the pieces. He twisted them and managed to pry them off.

Lenny looked at the gap he had made. He tried to get through it but decided that it was too small. He sent out a kick to the board above it but managed to only partly hit it. He then grabbed it and planted his feet firmly on the floor. He pushed with all his might.

Finally, it came off. Lenny let out a huge breath of air and dropped the board to the ground outside. He went through the gap and Detective Turner followed him.

Minutes later, the building was surrounded by squad cars. Lieutenant Finn was standing with Lenny and Detective Turner by his car. "We're sending in a special team," he said. "Maybe they'll find something."

About an hour later, Maria's cell phone rang. "Hello?"

"It's me," answered Lenny.

"Is everything okay?" Maria asked.

Lenny told her what had happened.

"Are you all right?" Maria asked.

"I'm fine," Lenny answered. "Maybe we'll finally have something on this guy."

Just then Lois came into her room and Maria quickly put the phone into her pocket. "Hey there, Snugglebear," she said. "How was school?"

"It was fine," answered Maria.

"I'm afraid I'm going to have to head out," said Lois. "They want me for another late shift."

"Okay, Mom."

"Dinner's in the fridge and heating instructions are taped onto the foil," said Lois. "Good-bye."

"Good-bye, Mom."

After dinner, Maria was brushing her teeth. *It's been a heck of a day,* she thought. *Thank goodness, it's over.*

Maria went in to her room and reached for the light switch. Suddenly something came over her.

Chapter 5

Maria let out a muffled cry. It took her a moment to realize that a towel had been thrown over her. *It's just like last time,* she thought. She kicked and thrashed.

Whoever had thrown the towel over her picked her up. She was carried off in one direction and then another.

She sensed that she was being carried out of her house. She was carried some distance then she heard a door opened. Maria was thrown on a hard surface and she heard the door closed.

She thrashed and struggled for several minutes as someone held her down. Suddenly, she heard the door open. She was dragged out from wherever she was and then carried off.

"Get her in here," ordered a voice after a few moments. She was thrown down somewhere and heard a door close. As they held her down. "please put" She heard an engine and felt that they were moving. She realized that they were in a car." Also, instead of "dragged from where every she was and carried off." put "dragged from the car and across the ground. She heard the sound of a door opening. She carried through it. They carried her up some stairs and in to another room. Maria fought to get out from under the towel. Maria could vaguely see by the light that came through under the door that she was in a closet.

Meanwhile, Lenny was at his apartment. He sat in his chair looking at a copy of the note from the club. *Feathers of a dove,* he thought. *Like the E in man's time. The only E in man's time is at the end and death is the end of all men's time. The dirt nap, kicking the bucket, the big snooze, eternal peace. The dove is a symbol of peace. Maybe that's how they go together.*

Lenny thought for a moment. *Doves and death,* he thought. He went over to his computer and did a search for Dove/Death/Paway.

Several hits came up. The top one was a link for the website of Sleep Peacefully Funeral Home. He went onto the website and looked it over to find that it was a local business. There was a dove on the home's logo. *I'm going to need backup,* Lenny thought.

Mr. Mindful entered the room where his henchmen had gathered to play cards. "I'm going out," he said.

"Why?" asked one of the men.

"Because I heard on the police scanner that the detective just called in backup to the funeral home," answered Mr. Mindful. "I want to watch him go in."

"Can we come?" asked one of the men.

"No."

"Why not?"

Mr. Mindful scowled. "Because there's going to be a lot of cops there. One person is less suspicious than many. Besides, I want somebody to stay here to watch the girl. She may be useful." He left the room.

Maria looked around the closet. She tried the doorknob and found it to be locked. She heard faint noises from beyond the door. *There are people out there,* she thought.

Lenny stood outside a building. There was a dove on a nearby sign. "I'm going in," he said. He walked up to the front door, which had been kicked in, and went inside.

For a few moments nothing happened. Then the building exploded. 280 Solo Drive, October 25, 9:05 p.m.

No, Maria thought. She could barely keep from screaming. *I can't let that happen.*

She stopped herself and took a deep breath. *Calm,* she told herself. *Focus on the present.* She looked around the closet and then went up to the door and listened through it.

After a few moments she got an idea. "Ahh!" cried Maria. She then threw herself on the floor, slamming it with both her fists as she did so.

There was the sound of footsteps. "What's going on in there?" someone asked.

The door opened and someone reached down toward her. She sent out a kick. A man stumbled back, grabbing his leg. She grabbed his other one and pulled it out from beneath him. He fell onto his back.

Maria quickly got to her feet and raced out of the closet. Two men darted into her way. She kicked the legs of the nearest one out from beneath him and he fell to the ground.

Maria looked at the other one. She recognized him from the alley. He tried to grab her, but she dodged him and grabbed his wrist and then flipped him to the floor behind her.

The man whose legs Maria had kicked got to his feet and charged at her. He threw a punch, but she dodged it. He threw another punch, but she blocked it. She tried to kick him, but he dodged it.

Maria sent out another kick, which he dodged as she guessed he would. She leapt out at the spot she knew he would most likely dodge to. She kicked him in the shin and swung him around. He went around and connected with the wall. Maria ran out of the room as he stumbled back, gripping his nose.

Maria left Mr. Mindful's headquarters. After running a few yards she saw a sign that said "Happy Tabby Cat Food."

Maria came to a road. A car passed her. Another car started to pass her and she noticed that it was yellow. *A taxi,* she thought.

The taxi stopped and she got in. "Please take me to two eighty Solo Drive," she said. The taxi went down the road.

Minutes later, Lenny was standing outside the Sleep Peacefully Funeral Home. He looked at the front door, which had clearly been broken into. *That's probable cause,* he thought. *Once I go in, there's no telling what I might find, though. I should probably go in alone to see if there's anything really nasty, but I won't be able to call for backup if there's another cell phone jammer like the one they found in the warehouse. I should take it slow.*

Lenny looked around at the uniformed officers standing by their squad cars. "I'm going in," he said. He started toward the building.

Maria's taxi pulled up. She saw Lenny go up to the building. *I've got to stop him,* she thought.

She scrambled out of the taxi. "Hey," cried the driver.

"I'll pay," Maria called back.

She ran up to the scene. "Lenny, stop," she called.

A nearby officer started to go up to her. "Madam, hold it right here," he said.

"It's okay," Lenny said. "I've got it." He went up to her. "Maria what are you doing here?"

"The building's going to blow up."

"What?"

Suddenly, the building blew up. The force of the explosion forced her, Lenny, and the officers to the ground. Light filled Maria's vision and she felt something she had last felt when she was in a car crash.

As everyone gathered themselves up, Mr. Mindful watched from a car. He drove off.

The next morning. Maria was talking with Lenny on the cell phone. "So you managed to get the guys working for Mr. Mindful?" Maria asked.

"Yeah, I took your description and said that it was from an anonymous source, which, technically, it was, and put bulletins out on all of them," answered Lenny. "We managed to nab them trying to get out of town together, and now they're turning against each other and ready to testify against their boss, if we ever find him."

"I'm sure you will," said Maria.

"Also don't worry," said Lenny. "I managed to put a tidbit into their deal that they don't testify about the police or agents of the police."

"Thanks."

Maria went into the living room. *Another Saturday morning,* she thought.

"I know I came in without knocking, but I don't care about being mindful about your personal space," said a voice.

Maria turned around and saw a middle-aged man. He had brown hair and average, somewhat good looks.

"Mr. Mindful," Maria said. Her heart raced, and she tried to slow it with what she had learned in her karate class. She assumed a defensive position and looked around.

"Indeed," answered Mr. Mindful.

"What are you doing here?"

"I came to see the young woman responsible for my men being in jail."

"The police are the ones who put them there."

"I think it's you who's doing the real work, not the detective. You know, you greatly interfered with my art."

"Your art?" asked Maria.

"Crime has become such a tedious thing," said Mr. Mindful. "Done by thugs in the most plain, dull ways. They do their deeds with the actual hope of not getting noticed and they do it for money, which, in the end, is meaningless."

Mr. Mindful took a step toward Maria, who stepped back. "What I plan to bring to the world is a new kind of crime," he said. "One that challenges the mind and the will. My acts will be studied well into the future by scholars of all kinds."

"There isn't any art in bombing buildings," Maria said, surprised by her outburst.

"You can't get into something without going in all the way," said Mr. Mindful. "Now, I want to know who you are and how you're working with the police."

"I . . . ," Maria started. She suddenly threw a kick at Mr. Mindful. He blocked it and then grabbed Maria by her shirt. He swung her away and she barely managed to keep her footing.

Maria turned back to Mr. Mindful. She leapt at him from one direction and then went at him from another. She grabbed his arm and put him in a wristlock.

"You've had training," said Mr. Mindful. "The detective?"

Maria did not answer. Mr. Mindful tried to swing her off. They struggled for a moment. Mr. Mindful pulled her down on to the floor and fell on top of her.

Maria let go of his arm and he got up. She swung out her leg. He managed to lift one leg to avoid her, but she hit the other one.

Mr. Mindful stumbled, trying to keep his balance. Maria jumped up and shoved him. He went flying forward and his head collided with the TV. He fell to the floor unconscious.

Maria stood there breathing heavily. She took out her cell phone. "Lenny, I've got someone here for you," she said.

Mr. Mindful sat in his cell in Paway Correctional Faculty. His rage welled up in him. *I swear I'll get the girl for doing this to me,* he thought. *I swear it!*

Meanwhile, Maria was sitting on her bed. Just then, she felt a chill go through her.

BOOK 4

A Secret in the Family

Chapter 1

Maria went into her living room. The TV was on. "The man known as Mr. Mindful was arraigned today as John Doe one-two-two-eight," said the news announcer. "Reportedly, despite the best efforts of law enforcement, his identity is still unknown. He was charged with reckless disregard to life and destruction of property for attempting to blow up the Black Hole nightclub and actually blowing up the Sleep Peacefully Funeral Home."

Maria left the living room and went into the kitchen. Lois was by the table. "Hi, sweetie," she said.

"Hi, Mom," said Maria. She sat down at the table. Breakfast was already made.

"Slept well?" asked Lois.

"Yeah." She ate the eggs and toast.

"You know, I was thinking we could go down by the park," said Lois.

"Don't you have to work?"

"I could get out of it."

"I think I have something to do."

"Oh." Maria quickly finished breakfast and left the room.

A few minutes later, Lois picked up the phone and dialed her supervisor. "Hello, Mr. Bevcock," she said. "I was wondering if there was any way I could reschedule for today."

She listened for a moment. "Yes, sir, I know," she said. "I know. It's just that I need the money."

She listened some more. "Yes, sir, I'll be in at ten."

Later that day, Maria got home and entered her room. She looked at her book bag. *Maybe I should study,* she thought. She reached inside her bag and got out some of her books. She climbed onto her bed and started going through some problems.

Maria went through her math book but was having trouble focusing on what was on the page. She kept thinking about the month she had had. *Everything's different,* she thought. *I'm different. I don't think I'm as bothered by what's going on in my life as I used to be.*

Meanwhile, Mark Jones was walking through the yard on his family's estate. He went through the front gate. He looked up at the clear blue sky but barely noticed it. He went up to the family's mailbox and took out the mail. He took a sip of orange juice from the glass he was carrying and began walking back to his home when he heard an engine.

A black van pulled up by Mark and two men got out. They headed toward him. One man grabbed his wrist and Mark swung his other arm, sending the juice through the air. The liquid hit the man's face and he stumbled backward.

Mark ran to the house and the other man chased him. A woman in a maid's uniform came out. "Mr. Jones," she cried.

"Tina," cried Mark. The first man joined the chase.

Tina went inside followed by Mark. The two men got to the house just as the door closed.

"Let's go," said one of the men.

"But we were supposed to get that guy," said the other one. He was still wiping juice off his face.

"And he could be calling the cops," said the first man. They ran back to the van and took off.

Maria was sitting on her bed going through her math book.

A man was walking to a large house. Another man came up to him.
"Hey, how's it going?" the second man asked.
"Larry, I need your help."
"Mr. Jones, they're back," cried a woman's voice.
Suddenly two men came running out from behind a tree. They grabbed the first man. "Ahh!" he cried. November 1, 10:47 p.m., Crescent Falls Drive.

Maria picked up the cell phone Lenny had given her. "Lenny, we have a problem."

Minutes later, Mark was coming up to the house. Larry came out of it and went up to him. "Hey, how it's going?" he asked.

"Larry, I need your help," said Mark.

"Mr. Jones, they're back," cried Tina. She was in his car parked not too far away.

Two men came out of some bushes nearby and ran toward Mark and Larry. Mark could see that they were the two from before.

"Hey, stop," cried Lenny. He came running up to the two men, holding up his badge. "Police."

The men stopped and ran away. "I told you he would call the cops," said one of the men.

"Hey, I didn't think he would leave his house if he did," said the other one. They went back into the bushes.

Lenny went over to Mark. "Are you all right?" he asked.

"I'm fine," Mark replied.

"Let me call this in," Lenny said. He reached for his cell phone.

"That won't be necessary. It was nothing."

"It looked like a kidnapping attempt."

"It was just a prank. Those two are old fraternity buddies."

"That's why you look so scared?"

"It's nothing," Mark said. He started to leave Lenny. "Good-bye," he said.

Tina ran up to Mark. "Are you all right?" she asked.

"I'm fine and now we're leaving," Mark answered. He escorted her back to his car.

"What was that about?" asked Lenny.

"I don't know but the Jones have always been a private family," answered Larry.

"The Jones—you mean the very wealthy family?" asked Lenny.

"Yeah."

Oh boy, thought Lenny. *Money just screams trouble.* He felt dread.

Lenny got back into his car where Maria was staying. "Did you stop them?" she asked.

"Yeah, but they got away."

"That's too bad." They drove off.

Meanwhile, the van was parked some distance away. The two men sat inside. One of them was talking on his cell phone. "We couldn't get the guy," he said.

"What happened?" asked their boss.

"A cop showed up."

Their boss scowled. "Wait a bit and then get him," he ordered.

"Yes, sir."

Chapter 2

Lenny sat at his desk. "Hello," said Detective Jon Turner, Lenny's partner.

"Hi," said Lenny. He was looking through some papers.

"What's the great detective up to now?" Turner asked.

Lenny showed him one of the papers he was looking at. It was a clipping of the local society pages featuring members of the Jones family. "Keeping up with high-class events."

Maria went down the hall to history class. "Hi, Maria," said Carly.

Maria halfheartedly waved at her. *Why wouldn't the guy want to report it?* she wondered. She went into the classroom and sat down.

"Good morning, class," said the teacher. "Today we're going to talk about Woodrow Wilson the twenty-eighth president." *I hope this is as useful as what I learned about Lincoln,* Maria thought. She sat and listened.

Sometime later, Maria was in the cafeteria. She was having lunch, barely paying attention to the sounds around her. She unwrapped her sandwich.

Mark entered a room and let out a cry of frustration. He turned to go toward a bathroom when a sack came over him. He struggled and let out a muffled cry. November 1, 8:42 p.m., Missionary Drive.

Oh no, thought Maria. She went to the restroom and got out her cell phone. "Lenny, we have another problem," she said.

A few hours later, Maria got home. "Hey there, Snugglebear," said Lois.

"Mom, you're home early," said Maria.

"I took off."

"Why?"

"I wanted to spend time with you," answered Lois. "How about we watch a DVD or play a game?"

Maria thought about her vision. "I have to study."

"Oh."

Maria went up to her room. She went over to her computer and did an Internet search for the Jones family. Several links came up. Maria noticed that a lot of them were links to the society page of the website of the local newspaper. She clicked on a biography of the family.

Fred Jones was born of family money but through hard work and ingenuity increased his fortune, Maria read. *He combined savvy marking with fresh ideas in products to make his electronics company, Neilwell Electronics, a success. His wife, Mary Jones, frequently makes the best-dressed lists of all the local events, shining in every scene. Their son, Mark Jones, is a key figure in the family's charity work. The Jones family has given money to, among other things, the Paway Police Department, the Paway Fire Department, homeless assistance programs, and local politics, including campaign contributions to the current governor of this state.*

Maria looked at the picture of the family on the screen. *They're well to do,* she thought. *The kidnappers probably want money, but why doesn't Mark Jones want anybody to know?*

Maria went over to her book bag and took out her books. *I better stand ready in case another vision comes by,* she thought. She began to read.

Hours later, Lenny's car pulled up to the Jones's house. Night had fallen.

Lenny got out. "Are you sure you can do this?" asked Maria. She had sneaked out of the house after her mother had gone to bed early.

"There's a impending crime," answered Lenny. "I have to." He went up to the fence and started to climb up. *I hope that's an excuse my lieutenant will buy,* he thought. He went over the fence.

Mark entered a room. His mom, Mary, was sitting down reading a book. "Mom, I need to talk to you."

"Yes, dear?"

"Why aren't I allowed to talk to the police about what happened?" he asked.

Mary got up. "Dear, if you do that, surely the newspapers will hear about it."

"But Mom."

"It's the downside of being wealthy," said Mary. "However, the good thing is that we have other resources at our disposal."

"Mom, we should let the police handle this."

"It's settled," said Mary. "I've made my decision and the matter's closed."

Mark turned and walked away, visibly angry. Mary sighed.

Mark entered his room. He let out a sigh of frustration. He turned to go to the bathroom. A sack came over him. He struggled as he let out muffled cries.

Lenny kicked in the door. The two kidnappers turned to look at him. The one who was not holding the sack charged at him.

Lenny swung a punch at him, but he dodged it. The man tried to hit him back, but Lenny ducked and grabbed him. He swung him around at a wall.

The other man let go of the sack and charged at Lenny. He tried to grab him, but Lenny swung a leg around, kicking his feet out from beneath him and causing him to fall to the floor.

Lenny bent down and took out his handcuffs. He turned the man around and put the cuffs on him.

Mack got out of the sack and went over to Lenny. "Thank goodness you're here," he said.

"Yeah," said Lenny. He went to the other man, who was stunned, and put a pair of handcuffs on him too. "You're under arrest," he said.

Mary came into the room. "What's going on here?"

"It's okay, madam," said Lenny. He held up his badge. "Someone tried to kidnap your son, but I managed to stop them."

Mary's expression was blank. She looked around the room and, after a moment, spoke. "Thank you, officer, but I'm afraid nothing actually happened here," she said. "It's like my son said—this is just a fraternity prank."

"But, madam . . . , " Lenny started.

"Thank you, but that will be all, officer," Mary said. "Now, if you will excuse us, the hour is late."

Mark looked worried. He looked at his mother, who returned a stern expression. Mark's face became blank.

Lenny sighed. He then uncuffed the kidnappers and they all left.

Lenny got back into his car and told Maria what had happened. "What are you going to do?" she asked.

"I know it was a kidnapping, so I'm going to dig and find out what's going on," he answered. They drove off.

Sometime later, a man sat in an office. "Your recent appointment has arrived," said a voice over an intercom.

The man pressed a button. "Thank you, Wendy," he said. "Send her in."

Mary came into the office. "Thank you for seeing me on such short notice, Mr. Tucker," she said.

"Nonsense," said Mr. Tucker. "Anytime." He got up from his desk, went over to Mary, and shook her hand.

"There's a problem," said Mary.

"What is it?"

"My son, Mark, is in trouble and I don't want the police involved."

"Has he done something?"

"No, someone wants to take him."

"I need you to tell me everything."

Meanwhile, the two kidnappers were sitting around a table in a room. One of the men was talking into his cell phone. "It didn't go well, boss," he said.

"What happened—the police?" asked their boss.

"Yeah, but then the mother came in and said nothing happened," answered the man. "They let us go."

"I see," said their boss. He was silent for a moment. "Watch him," he ordered. "Once you see an opportunity, grab him."

Lenny came into the squad room the following day. He took off his jacket and put it on his chair.

Lieutenant Steve Finn, Lenny's superior, poked his head out of his office. "Detective Hipar, I need to see you in my office," he said.

Lenny entered the office. He had a feeling he knew what the request was about. "What is it?" he asked anyway.

"You've been doing good work," said Finn. "People are talking about you, but I got a call from Mary Jones that you broke into her son's room to interrupt a fraternity prank."

"I was trying to stop a kidnapping," said Lenny.

"You didn't wait for a warrant."

"I thought I didn't have time."

"Just be more careful in the future," said Finn. "It would be a shame if your rising star fell."

"Yeah, I got you," Lenny said. *It would probably be a waste of time trying to talk to him about it,* he thought.

Meanwhile, Maria was sitting at the table having breakfast. Her mother sat down by her. "You know, I was thinking that maybe we could do something," said Lois. "Maybe go out."

Maria thought about the kidnapping attempts. "I'm afraid I've got a big project coming up," she said.

"Oh, that's okay," Lois said.

"See you later, Mom."

"See you later, honey."

On her way to school, the cell phone vibrated in her pocket. "Is there a problem?" Maria asked.

"No, I just called to tell you how things are going," answered Lenny.

"How are things going?"

"Well, the Jones are denying that anything happened. My lieutenant told me to be careful. It's cover-up city." He let out a sigh. "I ran a quiet check on their business and I found no angry ex-employees, threats, or money problems. It seems all quiet on the Jones front except for the kidnappings."

"What else can you do?" Maria asked.

"I'm going to keep digging and see if I can find out what's going on," he replied.

Lenny got up from his desk and started to leave the squad room. "Where are we going?" asked Detective Turner.

"I have to check out some leads," said Lenny. "By myself."

"Oh, okay," Turner said. Lenny left the room.

Mark sat in a room in the Jones's home. He picked up the phone and dialed a number. "Hello, Angie?"

"Hi, Mark," said Angie. "What's going on? Larry said you're acting worried."

"Something happened," said Mark. He told her what had happened.

"Why wouldn't your mom want you to tell the police about it?" Angie asked.

"I don't know," answered Mark. "Can you come over?"

"Sure."

A few minutes later, Tina led Angie into the room where Mark was sitting. "Thanks for coming," Mark said.

"It's no problem," said Angie.

"I was wondering if your father might know someone who would be able to help."

Mark and Angie sat down together. Tina brought them drinks. "Why would you think my father would know anybody who could help you with this?" Angie asked. She stirred her iced tea with a straw. "He's in the fish egg business."

"We both know your father knows some shady people," said Mark.

Angie was quiet for a moment. "Why don't we call the police?"

"Mother won't let me, and if I don't do what she tells me, then it'll probably be good-bye to the funds for the work I've been doing with the foundation," Mark replied. "All my life everything's been hush-hush. 'Money changes things,' she always said, and 'We've got to put our walls up.'"

Angie sat there looking at her tea. "All right, I'll call him."

Meanwhile, Lenny was sitting at his desk going over the notes he had made of the kidnapping attempts against Mark. He flipped through a page and came to some numbers he had jotted down. *The license numbers,* he thought. *I forgot that I wrote down the numbers of the van.*

He typed the numbers into his computer. A notice came up saying that the vehicle was stolen. *Figures.*

Meanwhile, Maria sat in class. "All right, students, I want you to do a special project," the teacher said. "I want you to get into groups and make diagrams of the branches of the government. Remember what we talked about in class and I want pictures."

Students shuffled around the classroom getting into groups. No one paid attention to Maria.

Mark was on a street corner. He walked down the sidewalk and approached a building. He had almost reached the building when someone grabbed him. 21 All Ways Street, November 3, 9:05 p.m.

Oh no, she thought. She looked around the classroom as all the other students went about and talked.

Meanwhile, the two men who had tried to kidnap Mark sat at a table at the Night Stars Club. "I'm telling you, I feel uneasy being here after what happened at the Black Hole," said one of them.

"They got the guy who did that," said the other man.

Mr. Tucker entered the room and went over to their table.

"Hey, who are you?" asked one of the men.

"I'm a guy who's interested in why you tried to snatch the Jones kid," answered Mr. Tucker.

"What are you talking about?" the other man asked.

"I asked around and heard you were the one who stole the van that was used," Mr. Tucker replied.

The man who asked what Mr. Tucker was talking about looked at him. "What van?" he asked. "What does this have to do with any kidnapping?"

"I know it was you two," Mr. Tucker said.

"How?" asked the man.

"I have my ways."

"You don't want this kind of trouble," said the other man. "Walk away. There's big people involved."

"What, organized crime?" asked Mr. Tucker. "The mob's doing kidnappings now? I thought all that sort of stuff stopped in this city when the Griffin was arrested."

"We're much bigger than the Griffin," said the man.

"A new player in town?" asked Mr. Tucker.

The man he was talking with before got up and stared him in the eyes. "Get out now."

"Sure thing," said Mr. Tucker. "Before I go, here's my card." He put his card on the table. "If there's anything you want to share off the record, call me." He left.

Lenny was at his desk looking over his papers when the phone rang. "Hello?"

"Lenny, it's me," Maria said.

"What's happening?"

Maria told him what she had seen.

"Thanks. I'll get on it."

"Do you want me to come along?"

"Thanks, but I think I've got this one."

Mr. Tucker was at his desk when his phone rang. "Hello?"

"How's it going?" asked a police officer he knew.

"Fine, Ted," answered Mr. Tucker. "Did you get what I asked for?"

"Sure," Ted replied. He looked down at the files of the two kidnappers. "I ran those pictures you took through the system and got their names. They both have been collared a number of times. They seem to be working with a group now. Word is that they're working for a guy, identity unknown, who's been active for a while. With the Griffin around he was kept down, but now he's working his way to the top."

"Thanks," said Mr. Tucker.

"You're welcome. I'll send you the information."

Meanwhile, one of the two men walked up to a hairy man in a brown jacket. He handed the hairy guy Mr. Tucker's card. "He gave us this," said the kidnapper.

The hairy man looked at the card and handed it to the man standing next to him, their boss. *James Tucker, Private Consultant,* he read. "Who is he?" asked their boss.

"We asked around, sir, and apparently, he's a guy rich people hire to solve their problems discreetly," answered the kidnapper.

Their boss thought to himself for a moment. "Okay, I'll take care of this," he said. "You just focus on getting the guy."

Minutes later, Mary's phone rang. "Hello?"

"Mary," said the boss.

"You," Mary said. "What are you doing calling or any of this?"

"Mary, I need to see him," he said.

"What are . . . ?" Mary began. "Never mind, just stop it. Stop it now!"

"Call off your attack dog," he said. "He'll only get hurt. I'm going to see Mark whether you want me to or not, but you can make it easier."

"No," Mary cried. "No!" She slammed the phone down.

Chapter 3

Maria entered her home to find Lois on the couch. "Hey, Mom," said Maria. "Aren't you supposed to be at work?"

"I'm on my lunch break," Lois answered. "Want to join me for a bite to eat?"

"I'm afraid I still have that big project to do," answered Maria. *This time I mean it,* she thought.

"Well, I guess it's lunch for one then," Lois said.

Maria headed upstairs.

She entered her room and threw her book bag on the floor. *I hope Mom's not taking it too personally that I can't spend time with her. I'm just too busy.*

Mark was on the phone. "One of my father's 'associates' called," said Angie on the other end. "He said he knows who's trying to kidnap you. He also said to meet him at twenty-one All Ways Street at nine fifteen."

"Thanks," Mark said.

"Mark, don't go. It could be dangerous. Who knows what this guy's like? I've never met him. He's just some guy who called my father."

"I've got to," said Mark. "If I don't go, then I'll be in danger all the time."

That night, Mark parked his car on the side of the street and got out. He looked around and saw a building in the distance. *That looks like the place,* he thought, and started to walk toward it.

Mark walked along the darkened street. He looked around quickly at the many patches of darkness around him. He felt nervous as his mind involuntarily imagined what might be hiding in the darkness. He pulled his jacket closer to his body.

He neared the building. *The warehouse at 21 All Ways Street,* he thought. *That's it.*

Mark had almost reached the building when he was grabbed from behind.

Feelings of fear and shock instantly went through him. He struggled against whoever was holding him, but the person was incredibly strong. He was dragged back.

"Hey," cried Lenny. He ran up to the scene. He grabbed the big man who was holding Mark and wrestled him away from the young man. The man threw Lenny off.

Lenny managed to retain his balance, but then the man tackled him. They went up against the hood of a blue car that had been waiting with its door open. The driver looked through the windshield, surprised.

Lenny struggled with the man to regain his footing. He sat up on the car's hood and kicked the man in his shin.

The man froze in pain and Lenny grabbed him. He swung him in front of the car.

The man got up. The driver backed up the car and Lenny rolled off the hood. He landed on the street by the big man. The driver then took a turn and drove off.

Lenny was watching the driver but turned to face the man as he grabbed him.

The man pulled Lenny to his feet. They struggled and Lenny swung him around so that his back faced the wall of the warehouse. Lenny then reached up and pulled out a piece of the man's hair.

The man started to reach up to touch his head, but Lenny grabbed him and pushed him to the wall. He slammed him against the wall three times. The man slumped down, stunned.

"Are you all right?" Lenny asked Mark.

"Yeah, thanks," said Mark, who was standing by the wall Lenny had shoved the man against.

"What for?" asked Lenny. "Nothing happened here, right?"

"Well, that's true, detective," said Mr. Tucker. He stepped out toward them.

"Who are you?" asked Lenny.

"I'm an employee of Mary Jones," answered Mr. Tucker. "I'm here to take this young man home."

"Whoever you are, this is a job for the police, not some hired muscle," said Lenny.

"Mrs. Jones thinks differently," Mr. Tucker said.

"The rich can't go around policing themselves."

"If you take this man into custody, the family will deny anything happened and you will just have to let him go," said Mr. Tucker. Mr. Tucker began to lead Mark away. "Good evening, detective," he said.

"What's going on here?" asked Mark.

"That's for your mother to say," said Mr. Tucker. Mark fought a rising frustration and went with him.

Lenny looked down at the man as he started to come to. "Come on," Lenny said. "Let's get you to the hospital."

A few minutes later, the boss's phone rang. "What is it?" he asked.

The person on the other end of the line gave his answer. "What?" the boss asked. "You left him there? What if he talks?"

The person talked some more. "All right, if that guy did show up, then most likely our man will be let go," the boss said. "Keep your eye on the target. Look for another chance to nab him."

The person spoke again. "The only thing that matters is that I'm the one in charge and I'm telling you to get him. So do it." He slammed the phone down.

Meanwhile, Mary's phone rang. "We've got a problem," said Mr. Tucker.

"What is it?"

"Some guys tried to snatch your son again, and there was a police detective there too."

"Is my son okay?" Mary asked.

"Yes, ma'am."

"What do the police know?"

"I don't know, but I need to know everything," Mr. Tucker said. "What's happening with Mark?"

"You don't need to know that," Mary said. "All you need to know is that I'm paying you to keep my son safe and keep the police away from this affair."

Mark came into the room just as Mary put the phone down in it's cradle. "Oh, Mark," she cried. She ran up to him and gave him a hug. "I was so worried."

"What's going on, Mother?"

Mary pulled away. "Well, we have some bad men who are trying to take you," she answered.

"No, I think it's more than that," said Mark. "I think you know what's going on."

"What do you mean?" Mary asked.

"You don't want to talk to the police about what's happening. You're hiring security. It feels like everyone knows what's happening but me."

"I'm trying to protect you," said Mary. "That's all I'm doing."

"Why won't you let me call the police?"

"When there's money involved, it's best to keep the doors closed. Don't you remember what I've been telling you since you were a child?"

"You can't keep doing this! Whatever you're doing, you can't keep doing it!" He turned and stormed off.

Mary sat in her chair and tried her hardest not to cry.

Meanwhile, Maria was woken up by a buzzing sound. She looked around and realized it was coming from her dresser. She reached in and got the cell phone, which she had set to vibrate and was making the noise.

"Hello?"

"Did I wake you?" asked Lenny.

"No. What's going on?"

Lenny told her what had happened. "I did some checking on this guy," he said. "His name's James Tucker, and he does things for those wealthy enough to afford his services. Things like destroying evidence of scandals and running background checks. I think Mary Jones is having him run interference with us and having him try to keep her son safe."

"You think the people who are trying kidnap Mark Jones are after the family's money?" asked Maria.

"No, I actually think there's something more going on that we don't know about," answered Lenny. "Anyway, thought I'd call and keep you in the loop."

"Thanks."

The next morning, one of the kidnappers neared his apartment. As he turned a corner to go around to his front door, he saw Mr. Tucker leaning against the front of the building.

"What are you doing here?" the kidnapper demanded. "I've heard of you, and I don't want to talk about what happened."

"But I want you to talk," said Mr. Tucker.

The kidnapper went over to his front door to go inside and then realized it was ajar. "You broke into my place?" he asked.

"I let myself in," answered Mr. Tucker. "I happened to find evidence of some of the other nefarious actives you've been up to."

"You can't do that without a warrant."

"That would be true if I were a member of the police force, but I'm not."

"I could have you arrested for breaking and entering."

"And I have a skilled attorney who can get me off, and while I'm fighting the charge, all your dirty secrets would become public record."

The man looked at the open door and then at Mr. Tucker. "What do you want?" he asked.

Lenny approached the police station. As he was about to go in the front door, a man came up to him. "Detective Hipar," said the man.

"How may I help you?" asked Lenny. *Come to tell me you're psychic?*

"There's something I have to tell you."

Maria was walking to school. The cell phone vibrated. "Hello?"

"It's me," Lenny said. "A friend of one of the guys who tried to kidnap Mark Jones came to me. He told me where to find the guy who hired them."

"That's great," Maria said. "Did he give you a name?"

"No, but he did say the person will be at a certain place at a certain time. He said that once I get there, I'll know who it is. Probably because I've seen all the kidnappers."

"Can I come too?" Maria asked.

Lenny thought about it for a moment. "Sure, but you have to wait in the car," he said. "Be ready by nine."

That night, Lenny drove up to a warehouse. He got out of the car. "Stay here," he said.

"I know," Maria said.

Lenny went up to the side of the house. He found some boxes stacked up by a window and climbed onto them. He looked inside.

Inside were groups of men around three tables. They seemed busy, but Lenny could not tell what they were doing.

Suddenly, Lenny heard something behind him, but before he could react, a man pulled him off the boxes.

Chapter 4

Lenny crashed to the ground. "Hey, there's someone out here," someone cried.

As Lenny got up, several men surrounded him. They grabbed him and dragged him inside.

The men brought him in front of a man standing by one of the tables. "Who is this?" asked the man.

"He was spying on us, boss," said one of the men.

Their boss looked at Lenny. "Who are you?" he demanded.

"I'm Detective Hipar of the Paway City Police."

"You're here to bust us?" asked the man before him.

"Yes, you're under arrest for kidnapping," answered Lenny. "My backup is on the way. Let go of me or you're facing a charge of assaulting an officer."

"We don't know anything about a kidnapping," said the man.

What? wondered Lenny.

Suddenly there was a loud noise outside. "You guys check it out," ordered the leader. They darted out.

Maria, Lenny thought.

Maria was honking the horn mightily but then stopped and got out of the car. She ran down an alley.

The men came out of the warehouse. "There," cried one of them. He pointed at the alley. "I saw something." They ran.

As the first man entered the alley, Maria stuck out her foot and tripped him, causing him to fall to the ground.

The second man went over the first one. It was so dark that he did not see Maria and passed her. She took a lid off a trash can to defend herself.

She smelled something pungent. She dropped the lid and picked up a heap of something she could not identify.

The man stopped and turned around and Maria threw the substance at his face "Ahh!" he cried. He stumbled back, frantically wiping at his face.

Maria turned to the third man, who came charging at her. He went over the first man as he tried to get up. Maria grabbed him and swung him around at the second man.

The third man collided with the second one. The third man got a whiff of the substance on his face and gagged. Maria swung out a leg. She tripped the man and started to fall down. As he went he hit his head against one of the walls of the alley.

The second man wiped some of the substance from his face and started to charge at her. Maria kicked him in the shin. He reached down to grab it and she kicked him in the stomach. She then grabbed him and swung him to the wall to her right. He slid down unconscious like the third man.

The first man got up and charged at Maria, grabbing her from behind. She kicked his foot. He cried out in pain and let go of her. Maria quickly reached down for the trash can lid and swung it toward the man. There was a thud and the man went down.

Meanwhile, Lenny was becoming increasingly worried. *They're going to hurt her and it's all my fault,* he thought.

Lenny broke the grip of one of the two men. He then slammed his foot on the shin of the other. As the man grabbed his leg, Lenny grabbed him and swung him at the other man.

Lenny darted to the door. "Stop him," ordered the leader.

Lenny ran out of the building followed by the men. He turned around a corner and stopped.

As the first of three men came around, he grabbed him and swung him around to the wall. The man fell to the ground as Lenny spun to face the next one.

The man threw a punch at Lenny, which he blocked. He grabbed the man and flipped him to the ground.

Lenny then turned and faced the third man. The man threw a punch, which Lenny blocked. He punched the man, and the man went down.

The man on the ground got up. Lenny backed away, bracing himself for the attack. The man threw a punch, which Lenny dodged. He grabbed his arm and then his wrist. Lenny put him in a wristlock. "Ahh!" cried the man.

"Give up?" asked Lenny.

"Yeah," the man said. Lenny then brought him to a lamppost and cuffed his arms around it.

Sometime later, Maria was hiding in an alley. *What am I going to do?* she wondered. *I should use the phone to call the police, but won't they trace it to Lenny? He said it was disposable.*

Suddenly, Lenny's car went past the alley. It passed a light. *Lenny,* Maria thought.

She waved the car down. "Are you all right?" asked Lenny.

"Yeah, I took care of the guys who were chasing me."

Lenny looked at her for a moment. "I see," he said. They drove off.

"What was going on?" Maria asked. "Did you find out who's trying to kidnap Mark Jones?"

"It had nothing to do with that. This was just some gang running a racketeering ring. I called the guys down at the station. They're all booked."

"Are you all right?"

"Yeah. Thanks for honking the horn. That's not the first time you've saved me."

"No problem."

A short time later, after Lenny dropped Maria off, Lenny knocked on the door of the man who had given him the tip.

"You," said the man. "How did you find me?"

"I followed you to your car and got your license," answered Lenny. "I then ran it through the DMV. You're not as sneaky as you think." Lenny stared at the man. "Why did you set me up?" he demanded. "Tell me or you're going to have a cop after you."

The man looked frightened. "It wasn't anything personal," he said. "Some guy paid me to do it."

"Describe him," Lenny ordered.

"Middle aged, dark-blond hair, your height."

Tucker, Lenny thought.

A short time later, Tina was showing Lenny to a room in the Jones's home. Mary was sitting but stood up when they came in. "Detective," she said. "How may we help you?"

I hope I don't regret this, Lenny thought. "You're rich, but that doesn't mean you can just play around with the law," he said.

"I'm afraid I don't know what you mean."

"People could've been hurt by your guy's little prank," said Lenny. *Maria could've been hurt,* he thought.

Mary tried not to let her surprise show. "I still don't know what you mean."

"From now on I'm not only looking at the people after your son but at you too," Lenny said. He stormed out of the room.

Mary called Mr. Tucker. "Did you do something to the police detective who's trying to investigate the kidnappings?" she asked.

"I sent him on a wild goose chase," answered Mr. Tucker.

"Now that you've done that, things are a thousand times worse," Mary cried. "He said he's going to keep his eye on me as well! I can't have that!"

"It'll be fine," said Mr. Tucker. "He can't look too deeply into you without attracting attention, and your friends in the police department won't allow it."

"What if someone had been hurt?"

"It turned out fine. I'm a professional. Just let me do my job."

Mr. Tucker looked at his computer screen. There was a dot marking a spot on a map. *The GPS tracker's working,* he thought.

The next morning, Maria lay on her bed reading a book. *No visions for a while,* she thought. *Maybe things are finally settling down.*

She flipped a page. *I should get started on that project,* she thought. *Maybe in a few minutes.*

She checked her watch: it was 10:23 a.m. *I've got a full day ahead of me. Wonder what I'll do. Then again, I might have a vision after all. There's no way of telling with this thing. It comes and goes and I have no way of controlling it.*

Maria looked at the closed door and thought about her mother. *I thought Mom had to work to pay the bills and everything. Now she's taking time off work to try to spend time with me, but I have to do all this stuff with these visions. I used to stay home just to spend time with her. Is it wrong that I'm saying no?*

Maria sighed and put the book down.

Soon, she was working on her project. She had books lying open on her bed and was drawing lines on a piece of cardboard with markers. She had already printed out several pictures. *I should have this done in no time at all,* Maria thought.

Mark was brought before a man. "Is this him?" demanded the man.

"Yeah, boss," answered one of the men behind Mark. He was one of the men who have been trying to abduct him. 128 Gilway Drive, November 5, 4:05 p.m.

Not again, thought Maria. She went over to her dresser to get the cell phone.

Around that same time, Lieutenant Finn called Lenny into his office. Detective Turner watched him go in.

As Lenny entered the office, he saw Mary sitting in a chair. *Uh oh,* he thought. She got up as he entered.

"Detective Hipar, Mrs. Jones has told me that you came into her home and caused a disturbance," Lieutenant Finn said.

"I was working on a case," said Lenny.

"You are not to go near the Jones family again."

"But, sir, new evidence has come up."

"You ran none of this by me."

"I felt that the situation warranted a quick response."

"Well, it ends now," Lieutenant Finn said. He looked at Mary. "Madam, rest assured that he won't bother you or your family again."

"Thank you, Lieutenant," said Mary.

Finn turned to Lenny. "You're dismissed."

Lenny left the office. *This is going to be tough to work around,* he thought.

Meanwhile, Mark was standing in a room. Tina announced Angie. Angie came into the room and quickly went over to Mark. "I'm so sorry about what happened," she said. "Someone along the line of people my father called sold you out. He never meant for it to happen. Please believe that."

"It's okay," Mark said. "Do you think the people your father knows are the ones trying to kidnap me?"

"I don't know," Angie answered. "I really don't know a lot about my father's business."

Mark sighed. "If only I could call the police."

"Why don't you?"

"Like I told you, if I do that, then Mother could cut off the funds for the charity."

"Then get another job," Angie said. "My father could help you find something."

Mark thought for a moment. "You know, all my life my mother has drilled into me this need for secrecy. Maybe it just had a greater hold on me than I realized."

Suddenly they heard the sound of glass breaking from another room.

Meanwhile, Lieutenant Finn was on the phone with Mary. "Yes, Madame, I'm sorry that he bothered you," he said. "As soon as he gets back I'll take to him. There will be consequences for this."

"Thank you, Lieutenant," said Mary from her car phone. She looked out her window at the passing scenery. *One problem solved,* she thought.

Suddenly, her phone rang. "Hello?"

The person on the other end talked. "Tina, what's wrong?" Mary asked.

There was more talking. *Oh no,* thought Mary. *Oh no. This is what I was afraid of.*

She put the phone against her chest. *What do I do?* she wondered. *I've got to call Mr. Tucker, but what can he do? I could call the police. Should I?*

Mary looked at the phone. *Of course I should,* she thought. *He's my son.* She dialed a number.

"Yes?" Lieutenant Finn answered.

"They've got my son," Mary said.

Meanwhile, a group of men took Mark into a dark room and dumped him on the floor. He got to his feet and looked around. "Where am I?" he asked.

The men grabbed him and forced him forward. Mark was brought before a man. "Is this him?" demanded the man.

"Yeah, boss," answered one of the men behind Mark who had been trying to abduct him.

"Who are you?" asked Mark.

The man moved into the light. "I'm your father," he answered.

Chapter 5

"What?" asked Mark. His mind raced.

"I'm your father," asked the man. "My name's Peter Coldstein."

"My father is Fred Jones," said Mark.

"No, he's not," said Peter. "I am. Years ago, you mother and I met at a party thrown by the Chaltons, friends of your mother and her husband."

Angie's parents, Mark thought.

"The Chaltons had friends who, like me, were in the business," said Peter. "We saw each other for several months, and when she learned that you were about to come along, she broke it off. She said she didn't want to be with a 'low-life criminal' and a 'bottom feeder' anymore. I just went back to doing what I do."

"What is it that you do?" asked Mark.

"I'm in the services industry."

Criminal services, Mark thought. *It can't be true. Can it?* Mark's heart raced and he fought several emotions.

Mark looked Peter in the eye. "Why now?"

"I wanted to see you," Peter replied. "Twenty-six years is a long time to go without seeing your only child. Now that my problems with the Griffin are over, I thought it would be a good time to see you."

Mark tried to take it all in. *My father, my real father is a criminal,* he thought. *My mother's been lying to me my whole life.* "When money's involved, it's best to keep the doors closed." *It was all so she could lie to me.*

Memories of his life and of his time with his parents went through his mind. *That can't all be lies,* thought Mark. *Can they? What I feel for them, what I know they feel for me—it's real.*

Peter approached him. "Keep away from me," Mark cried. The men behind him started to approach him, but Peter waved them off.

"I know this is a lot to take in," said Peter.

"I want to leave now," Mark said.

"Not yet."

"Why not?"

"We have to wait for the heat to be off," answered Peter. "Right now, a lot of people are in a frenzy over what happened to you."

Meanwhile, in the squad room, everyone was running about. "I want squad cars at the scene," said Lieutenant Finn. "I want squad cars cutting off the whole block!"

Lenny's phone rang. "Hello?"

"It's me," Maria said. "I tried calling you, but your cell phone was off. They're going to get him again."

"They already have."

"I think I know where they took him."

"Okay, tell me where and I'll pick you up on the way," said Lenny. Maria told him what she had seen.

Lenny looked around and then sneaked out of the room.

A few minutes later, Lieutenant Finn looked around. "Where's Detective Hipar?" he asked.

A short time later, they arrived at the address Maria had seen. "I can't believe I brought you along," said Lenny.

"I can handle myself," Maria said.

Lenny was quiet for a moment. "I know." *I just hope no one sees you,* he thought.

He was about to get out when he saw a black car parked around the corner. "Get down," he ordered. Maria slouched down in her seat.

Lenny got out of his car and darted to the other one, trying not to be seen. Mr. Tucker got out of the car as Lenny approached it. "You," he said. His anger rose. "What are you doing here? This is police business."

"I'm here for my client," said Mr. Tucker.

"Did Mary Jones send you?" asked Lenny.

"She doesn't know I'm here. I found this place because I placed a GPS device on the car of one of the kidnappers."

Mr. Tucker went up to the building. "This is a police matter," said Lenny.

"It doesn't look like you called for backup."

Lenny thought for a moment. He sighed. "Okay, but you tell no one about certain things you see."

"Discretion is a big part of my business," Mr. Tucker said.

He started to go up to the building, but Lenny darted in front of him. "Another thing: if Mark Jones gets hurt, I'm requesting an arrest warrant for James Tucker for reckless endangerment," he said.

"Okay," said Mr. Tucker. He walked past Lenny.

"Go around the side and see what you can see," Lenny said. "If you don't see anything, come back up front and we'll figure something out."

Mr. Tucker started to go around, but suddenly there were footsteps. "Someone's here," a voice cried.

Maria, Lenny thought. He shot a look at the car.

They grabbed the men and dragged them inside. Maria watched from the car. *Lenny,* she thought.

The men brought Lenny and Mr. Tucker to Peter. "Boss, these guys were spying on us," said one of the men.

"Is that so?" asked Peter. He went up to Lenny. "Who are you?"

"We're just a couple of guys going door to door selling cookies," Lenny answered.

Peter started to say something, but then Maria busted into the room. *Oh no,* thought Lenny.

A man charged at her, but she knocked his feet from underneath him with a side kick. She then flipped off the lights.

Good girl, Lenny thought. He swung wide around him.

Maria quickly looked around. *Keep calm,* she told herself. *Remember your training.* Suddenly she heard someone coming at her. She sent out a probing kick and felt someone close.

She reached out and grabbed the person. They struggled and then Maria managed to flip the person to the ground.

Lenny made several grabs into the air. He touched someone and they gave a cry. *That doesn't sound like Tucker,* he thought. He grabbed the person and threw him onto the ground.

Lenny turned around and started to walk away when someone grabbed at him. Lenny pulled away. The figure in the darkness tried to grab him again, but Lenny broke his grip. Lenny tried to grab him, but he broke his grip. They repeated this again and again, their struggle almost becoming like a slap fight. Lenny reached out and grabbed what felt like wrists. They wrestled briefly. Lenny kicked out and heard a man cry out in pain. Lenny then set out a punch and hit something, and he heard someone fall.

Mr. Tucker stood there. He could hear sounds all around him. He rotated his arms and bounced around on the balls of his feet, never really stopping moving. He would strike out every now and then but hit only empty air. He looked around, but his eyes could not pierce the darkness. Mr. Tucker was on constant alert.

"Somebody turn the lights back on," ordered Peter.

Mark was in another room. He heard sounds in the distance. After a moment of thinking it over, he got up from the chair he was sitting in and went up to the door. He knocked on it.

"What do you want?" demanded a voice. The door opened and a man poked his head in.

Mark shoved him back and went for his chair. As the man stumbled back into the hall, Mark came at him. He swung the chair and the man went down.

Mark heard footsteps and turned his head. A man was running in his direction. Mark threw the chair at his feet. The man tripped on it and fell to the ground. Mark ran in the direction of the noise.

In the darkness, everyone moved around as carefully as they could. "I said, turn on the light," said Peter.

"Here," said Mark. He turned on the light.

"Atta boy."

Everyone's eyes started to adjust to the light.

Mr. Tucker could see two men by him. They charged at him. He tripped one and he fell to the ground. The other threw a punch, but he caught it and put the man in a wristlock. Another man came rushing at him, and he shoved the man he was holding down to the ground. Mr. Tucker grabbed the man coming at him and threw him onto the man he had tripped. Another man came at him and Mr. Tucker flipped him.

Lenny was facing off with a man who threw a punch at him. Lenny blocked the punch and then flipped him onto the ground. Lenny stepped down hard, and the man clenched his stomach as the wind went out of him.

Peter went up to Mark. "We've got to get out of here, son."

"I'm not your son." He swung a punch and the crime boss went down to the floor.

Minutes later, the police had surrounded the building. "Mark," cried Mary. He went up to her.

They hugged and about a minute later they broke it up. "Why didn't you tell me?" asked Mark.

Realization went across Mary's face. "I thought it didn't matter," she answered. "Also, I hoped no one would find out because I was ashamed. When I met him, he was charming. What he did for a living was thrilling when I allowed myself to acknowledge it. It's been so long."

"Where's Dad?"

A kind of relief went over Mary's face. "He's back home. I managed to keep him from hearing about what happened."

"Is this why you always taught me to be secretive?"

"Yes. I was always afraid that everyone would find out. I was especially afraid you would. I was afraid you'd be ashamed of me."

"I could never be ashamed of you," said Mark. They hugged. "Let's go home."

"Nice working with you," said Mr. Tucker to Lenny. Lenny watched him walk off and then left the scene himself.

Lenny went up to his car. Maria sat up in the seat. "It turns out that Peter Coldstein was Paway's second-biggest crime boss," said Lenny. "The Griffin had kept him under control all this time, but with him gone he thought he would connect with his long-lost son."

"Paway's not going to have crime bosses for long if this keeps up," said Maria.

"Let's hope so," said Lenny. "How about I drive you home?" He got into the car and they drove off.

BOOK 5

Hunter and Prey

Chapter 1

Maria woke up. She got up and went through her usual routine, and then went downstairs. "Hi, Mom," she said.

"Hi, sweetie," said Lois. Breakfast was on the table. "I called my supervisor, and I'm back to normal hours."

"Oh," said Maria.

"How did your project go?"

"Fine."

Lois went over to the stove. "Jane was talking about her daughter yesterday," she said. "She's taking an art class, and I wondered if you would like to take one too."

"No, thank you," said Maria. She finished her breakfast.

"I'll see you later, sweetie," said Lois. She put a frying pan in the sink.

"See you, Mom," said Maria. She went off to school.

A few hours later, at Mercy Perks Hospital, a man lay in a bed. There was a series of beeps from the machine he was connected to. The beeps came one after another in a simple pattern. The whole room had the stillness of a picture.

Suddenly, there was a beep followed by another more quickly than usual. Another beep came, then another, and then another almost immediately.

Doctors and nurses came into the room. As they neared him, the man opened his eyes and sat up. They held on to his arms as he thrashed.

"Someone call the neurologist," someone said. "Jeff Marhill is awake."

Maria came home. "Mom, I'm home," she said. She went into the living room. Her mother was sitting on the couch. She had a strange look on her face. "Mom?" Maria asked.

"It's your father," Lois said. "He's awake."

Maria stood there. All sorts of emotions went through her, many she could not identify. *He's awake,* she thought. Maria remembered the last time she had seen him years ago. It had been in the hospital, and he had been unconscious.

"He's awake," said Lois. "They say it happened about two hours ago."

Maria stood there as contrasting images of her father went through her mind. In some he was active and moving around, and in others he was lying in the hospital bed. Emotions she had not felt in a while came flooding back. *He's alive.*

"Do you want to go see him?" asked Lois.

"Yes." They got into the car and drove to the hospital.

Maria and Lois were escorted into a room. Maria noted that it was a different room from the last one she'd seen him in.

Jeff Marhill was lying in a bed. "Hello," he whispered.

"Oh, honey," Lois said, overcome with emotion. She went up to him and wrapped her arms around him. He, however, could give her only a light hug.

"Be careful," said the doctor.

"Of course," said Lois. She released him from her hug.

Jeff looked at Maria. "Hi," he whispered.

"Hi," said Maria.

"There's something we need to talk about," said the doctor.

"Yes, of course," said Lois. "Maria, why don't you wait outside?"

"Yeah," Maria said. She went outside.

Maria sat in a chair. As she waited, images of her father went through her mind: before he was in the coma, as he was unconscious, and just then, now that he was awake. She felt confused.

A man was running through a field. There were the numbers 1237 on his gray shirt.

He came up to a fence and climbed over it. He then ran a little more and came to a gas station. The sign read "Joe's Filler-Ups." He went up to a car and did something to the door. He got in and, after a few moments, drove off. 12 Mace Drive, November 9, 4:11 p.m.

Not now, Maria thought. She went outside and got out the cell phone Lenny had given her.

"Hello?"

"I had a vision," Maria said. She told Lenny what she had seen.

"Okay, let's see what we've got," said Lenny. He typed the numbers into the police database. "It seems that there's a Teddy Foreman whose prisoner number matches that one. I'll check it out and call you back." *Those visions come often,* he thought.

"Thanks," said Maria. She went back into the hospital.

Soon, Maria and Lois arrived at home. "That was something," Lois said. She took off her coat.

"Yeah," said Maria.

"Maria, there's something we need to discuss."

"What?"

"Your father is going to need some long-term care. There's a facility called the Peaceful Field Rehabilitation Center. It's where your father is going to be for a while. I'm going to check it out, but I'll be gone most of the weekend."

"Oh."

"Are you going to be all right by yourself?"

"Yeah, I'll be fine."

A look of worry came over Lois's face. "I'll give you a number to call in case anything happens," she said.

Maria went to her room and called Lenny. "Did you get him?" she asked.

"We just missed him."

"Oh, well, in case I see anything, I'll call you."

"Thanks."

Maria lay down on the bed. She looked up at the ceiling, and an image of her father went through her mind. *He's back,* she thought. A multitude of emotions went through her, causing her to feel both confused and upset. She looked out the window. The day seemed so normal outside. She went back to looking at the ceiling.

Her father's face was in her mind as she felt things she did not understand and could not act on. *What am I going to do?* she wondered. Shame went through her. *Don't think that.*

Teddy Foreman was driving down a road in the car he had stolen. He kept checking the rearview mirror, but there was no one in view. He passed some fields. He then went past a sign that read "Which Falls, pop. 478." Buildings came into view. November 9, 6:09 p.m.

Maria picked up the phone and dialed Lenny. "What is it?" he asked.

"I know where he's going," answered Maria. She told him what she had seen.

"Okay, I'll go get him."

"Can I come too?"

"It's going to take a while," said Lenny. "What about your mother?"

"She's going to be gone for the weekend. Can I come?"

"Sure." Maria went to get some stuff to take with her.

Chapter 2

Maria left the house. She walked two blocks and found the car. "Hi," she said.

"Hi," said Lenny. "Did your mother see you?"

"No, she's long gone," answered Maria. She got in. "How long until we get to Which Falls?"

"About half an hour."

I should have packed more music, Maria thought. They drove off.

They drove on winding roads. The signs they passed were not new to Maria, but driving around without her mother knowing where she was gave them a new look.

I wonder what my dad would say if he knew I have visions, Maria thought. She watched the signs and scenery pass by outside.

Lenny thought about what he was doing. *I'm taking a minor out of town. That's custodial interference. Not that that's much worse than the other things I've done.*

Time passed. They soon passed a sign that read "Which Falls, 20 miles." Maria sat up in her seat and blinked. She had almost fallen asleep.

"Getting any visions?" asked Lenny.

"No."

"I'm thinking that we check in with the local law enforcement and then maybe look around town."

"What do you want me to do? Hide in the car?"

Lenny thought for a moment. "No. I can tell them you're a consultant."

"You know, one of these days people are going to ask what I consult on."

And one of these days those reports of a young blonde woman at crime scenes are going to add up, Lenny thought.

They arrived at Which Falls. Small mountains in the background made the scene before them look like a picture. Lenny stopped next to a woman walking her dog and asked for directions to the police station.

Minutes later, Lenny was at the sheriff's department holding up his badge. "I'm Detective Hipar of the Paway Police Department," he said. "I'm looking for this man, Teddy Foreman, a fugitive." He held up a photo.

"You think he's here?" asked the sheriff.

"Yeah, I have a consultant who believes so," answered Lenny. "I was hoping you could help me in a search."

"Sure," said the sheriff. "My name's Fred Bo and this is my deputy, Chad Stevens." Lenny shook their hands.

The three men left the building. "What kind of consultant gave you this advice?" asked Deputy Stevens.

Think, Lenny told himself. "Well, she's a behaviorist," he answered. "She's good at predicting subjects' future behavior."

They reached the car. "There she is," said Lenny.

"She looks young," said Sheriff Bo.

"She's a bit of an overachiever." Lenny gestured to Maria to come out. "This is Janet Flenn," he said. "She's the behaviorist I told you about."

The sheriff and the deputy shook Maria's hand.

"Any place you think this guy would go?" asked Lenny.

"There's a low-budget motel in town," Stevens answered.

"Let's try that." They got into their cars and drove off. The sheriff and the deputy led the way in their police cruiser.

"So I'm a behaviorist?" Maria asked.

"I had to tell them something," Lenny said.

Soon they reached the motel. "We're looking for this man," Bo said to the clerk, holding up the picture of the fugitive.

"I haven't seen him," the clerk said.

"Mind if we look around?" Bo asked.

"Not at all," answered the clerk.

They went over to the building that contained the rooms. Maria looked around. *Not exactly the place you dream of taking a vacation in,* she thought.

Lenny looked at the windows. They all had their curtains closed, but he could see light coming through some of them. *We should probably start with the rooms that are occupied, but then, he could've just left the light off,* he thought. *Maybe we should check with the clerk and see which rooms have registered visitors so we can check for an "unregistered guest."*

"I think I'm going to go back to the car," said Maria.

"Why don't you give home a call?" asked Lenny.

Maria went to the parking lot. As she walked, she glimpsed at one of the mountains. A man dashed across the lot before her. It took her a second to realize that it was Teddy Foreman.

Teddy looked at her and saw her alarmed expression. Maria turned around and started to jog back. "Hey," he cried. He chased after her.

Teddy grabbed Maria's arm. She broke his grip and kicked his legs out from beneath him. He fell to the ground.

Maria ran off and Teddy got up and chased after her again. He threw a punch, which Maria dodged. She grabbed him and flipped him onto the ground. Teddy got up, but instead of chasing after her he ran away.

Maria ran back to the three men. "I found him," she cried. "He's by the parking lot!" She led the way.

They arrived just as a car was speeding out. "That could be him," said Lenny. "He's known to steal cars."

"Maybe we can catch him," Sheriff Bo said. He and his deputy got into the cruiser as Maria and Lenny got into his car. They drove off after him.

"He's got his taillights off," Lenny said. He could barely make out the car in the darkness.

Suddenly, the car ahead made a sharp turn, which Lenny followed.

Lenny kept looking at the fleeing car. He realized that it was heading toward the interstate. *That can't happen,* he thought.

Lenny sped up, as did Maria's heart rate. He started to approach the car's right, but as he almost touched its bumper, it pulled over, blocking his way.

Lenny slowed down a bit. He tried to approach its left side, but it moved over and blocked his way. *So, it's going to be like that,* he thought.

The car passed a sign that said it was nearly at the interstate. It swerved to avoid hitting a man. Lenny avoided him too, and tried to catch up with the car.

The car shot around a corner and Lenny duplicated the maneuver. Maria held on as he did so.

Lenny's car spun out of control and he had to stop. The sheriff's cruiser came up with its sirens blaring.

The sheriff and his deputy got out. "Is he gone?" asked Sheriff Bo.

Lenny looked out his back window. There was no sign of the car. "Yeah," he answered. He sighed.

The sheriff and his deputy went back to their car. Lenny looked at Maria. "Are you all right?" he asked.

"I'm fine."

A short time later, they drove up to Which Falls's other motel, which had a crude picture of mountains on its sign. Lenny led her to a room. "It's getting late," he said. "We're going to stay here until the sheriff hears something. I got you your own room."

"Thanks," said Maria.

Lenny unlocked the door for her. As she went in, he handed her the key. "Good night," he said.

"Good night," said Maria. She closed the door behind her.

Maria looked around. *This feels so strange,* she thought. *I've never been this far from home before with out Mom knowing about it.*

She threw herself onto the bed and looked at the ceiling. After a few minutes, she got up. Maria got some pajamas from the book bag she had brought with her, changed, and went to bed.

Chapter 3

Maria woke and looked up at the ceiling. She reached for her cell phone and held it up. *Maybe I should call her,* she thought. *Nah, I'm sure things are going all right.*

As soon as she finished dressing, there was a knock on the door. She opened it to find Lenny.

"Good morning," he said. He held up a bag that said Burger Palace on it. "I got you a breakfast sandwich."

"Thanks."

"How did you sleep?"

"Good, how about you?"

"Good, but I'll sleep better when we get this guy."

Lenny went over to a chair as Maria ate her breakfast. He looked at the TV. "Did you get anything last night?" he asked.

"No."

Lenny sighed. *How are we going to find him?* he wondered.

Teddy went into a house. A man was sitting in the living room eating cereal. The man looked up with a surprised look on his face.

"Charlie, you've got to help me out," said Teddy.

"Why should I?" asked Charlie.

"Because we're cousins," answered Teddy. 20 Fish Avenue, November 10, 10:09 a.m.

"I know where he is," said Maria. She told Lenny what she had seen.

"Of course—he has relatives in the area," Lenny said. "That's one of the first things I should've checked."

"It's okay," said Maria. "You were in a hurry."

"No time to make me fell better now" Lenny said. "Let's go." They left the room.

Maria and Lenny arrived at the house on Fish Avenue. The sheriff, whom Lenny had called on his cell phone, arrived with his deputy minutes later.

"How do you think we should do this?" Sheriff Bo asked.

"How about you guys go around back and I go through the front?" asked Lenny. "Some guys in sheriff's department uniforms will look less suspicious sneaking around the backyard than a plainclothes detective." They split up.

It was quiet in the living room. Lenny darted in, followed by Sheriff Bo and Deputy Stevens. "Freeze!" he cried.

Charlie threw his hands up into the air. "I didn't do anything."

"Where is Teddy?" demanded Lenny.

"How would I know?" Charlie asked.

"We know you helped him."

"He took the car. He said he was heading to Con Tree."

Sheriff Bo looked at his deputy. "Check the house to make sure," he said.

A couple of minutes later, Lenny came back to the car and told Maria what had happened. "So, we're going to Con Tree?" she asked.

"Yeah," answered Lenny. "I already said good-bye to the guys for you."

They drove down the interstate. About an hour later, Maria started to doze off.

Maria was in a large room. She suddenly saw her father before her, but then he vanished. "Dad," she cried.

Suddenly there was a sound she did not recognize, like a chain being rattled.

She turned around and saw a clown but could not clearly see what he was wearing. He raised a knife and brought it down at her. Maria dodged the knife and sent out a kick, but he was gone. "You need to be mindful of others," someone said.

Maria woke up. "Are you all right?" asked Lenny.

"I'm fine," Maria answered.

"I thought you slept well last night."

"Probably not as well as I thought. Are we there yet?"

"Almost."

"So, we're going to check in with the local police same as before?" Maria asked.

"Yeah," answered Lenny.

"Where do you think he'll go?"

"I don't know. You're the psychic."

Maria looked out the window at the passing scenery. "This is like the first case we did with each other," she said. *Case,* Maria thought. *I sound like a detective.* She sighed. "Chasing crooks to another town. A lot has happened since then."

"Yes, a lot has happened," said Lenny. "You've been through a lot, but you got through it. You're very brave."

"All that is just a part of my life now," Maria said.

"Yeah, so is helping others and putting away the bad guys."

After a period of silence Maria spoke. "My dad was in a coma and now he's awake."

"That's great," said Lenny. He looked at her face. "Isn't it?"

"I don't know." A look of horror came over Maria's face. "I can't believe I said that." She put a hand over her face.

"Hey, this can be a lot to take in," said Lenny. "With everything that's been happening to you, it's no wonder you're overwhelmed." He took one hand off the steering wheel and put it on Maria's shoulder.

"It's everything," said Maria. "It's like everything's coming at me." She leaned against the passenger's-side door.

"All the stuff with the visions can be a lot," Lenny said.

"It's not just the visions. It's everything." Lenny looked at her, worried.

"When I was eleven, my dad got in an accident," she said. "He went into a coma. After that I thought one of the best things I could do for my mom was be there for her. I didn't have friends or join clubs. I tried to be home as much as I could, but she had to get that job and worked a bunch of hours. My entire life then was pretty much existing at home when I wasn't at school, hoping that Mom might need me. It was just the same routine day after day. Then I started to get the visions. I was afraid I was sick, but after the visions came true and I was out stopping one crime after another, it just became my new routine. Now my dad's awake and once again everything's different. I just don't know what I'm going to do."

Maria sighed. Lenny let silence fill the air for about a minute before speaking. "My dad died when I was young," he said. "I still remember the police officers who came to inform my mom and me. They were always in my memory as years went by. They're a big reason why I became a cop myself."

Maria slowly looked up at him. "Do you think I'm horrible for feeling this way?" she asked.

"No," answered Lenny. "Like you said, your life just drastically changed and then changed again just as you were getting used to it. It's natural to be overwhelmed."

They came up to a sign that said "Welcome to Con Tree" and had a picture of a tree above the letters. A large building was visible on the horizon with a sign that read "Conrich Inc." on it. "Let's catch this guy and then we'll talk about everything," Lenny said.

"Okay," said Maria.

A short time later, Lenny entered a motel with Sheriff Potter and Deputy Kern. "Have you seen this man?" he asked holding a picture of Teddy up to the clerk.

"Yeah," answered the clerk. "He checked in a while ago and then left. He left a message for anyone who came looking for him. He will be at the Fallen Tree Club."

"That's where people around here like to gather," said Sheriff Potter. The three men left.

They arrived at the club and went through a door under a sign with a tree that raced downward at an angle. Lenny looked around at his noisy surroundings. When he spoke, he did so loudly to be heard. "I wonder who he left the message for," he said. "Maybe he's going to meet someone."

"When we catch him, you can ask him," the sheriff said.

Suddenly, Lenny was grabbed and pulled away from the others. He vaguely realized he was being dragged to the back door. He broke free from the grip, but then he was grabbed from the other side and swung around. He went through the door.

Lenny stumbled and fell on his back onto the ground in an alley. He looked up and saw a young man with short hair coming at him.

The young man lifted a foot and brought it down. Lenny managed to dodge the foot and tried to punch him. The man blocked the punch and grabbed him. He pulled him up and slammed him against a wall.

Sheriff Potter and Deputy Kern darted into the alley and the man took off. The three gave chase after him.

The three reached the end of the alley, but as they got there, garbage that had been stacked up fell down toward them. Lenny managed to clear it, but the other two were buried. Lenny saw the man against a wall. *He must've pushed over the trash,* he thought. The man ran and Lenny chased after him.

They ran into the street. The man stopped and turned around. He charged at Lenny.

Suddenly a figure came out at the man. Maria got between the man and Lenny. The man threw a punch, which Maria blocked. She kicked him in the shin, and as he paused in pain, she grabbed his wrist and then flipped him. After he was on the ground, Maria brought his arm around his back and put him in a wristlock.

"Ahh!" cried the man. "Okay, I give up!"

Lenny came up to them. "Thanks for the help," he said. He looked down at the man. "You're under arrest," he said. Sheriff Potter and Deputy Kern came up to them.

"You think this is the guy Teddy Foreman was going to meet?" Potter asked.

"Only one way to find out," Lenny said. He reached down and cuffed the man, and then lifted him to his feet. He led him away, followed by the sheriff and his deputy.

A few minutes later, Lenny went over to the car where Maria was waiting. "His name's Jonah Taylor," he said. "Basically, he's just some guy who works at the mill. He's a local strongman Teddy Foreman hired to rough up anyone who came looking for him. He left instructions for Jonah to watch the motel for anyone who came with the police. Apparently the message was a trap. He seems to have thought the crowd would be the perfect spot for an ambush."

"Any idea where he's gone now?" asked Maria.

"None," answered Lenny. "We're going back to the motel to check for clues."

About an hour later, Maria and Lenny checked into a motel. "I can't believe this guy didn't leave any clues," said Lenny. "Either this guy's very lucky or he's very good." He sighed. "I'm going to make a few calls back home."

A few minutes later, Lenny was on his cell phone while Maria was watching TV. She looked at the cell phone in her hand. *What if Mom calls home?* she wondered. *I can't believe I didn't think of that. I could call and check the messages. She'll want to know why I didn't answer. I could say I was in the shower or something.*

"Thanks," Lenny saidto his friend on the phone then he hung up He sighed and looked at Maria. "No luck. He has no family or obvious friends in the area. Of course, he has no credit card records or other financials to follow."

Maria was sitting on the bed. "What about the car?" she asked.

"He dumped it a few blocks from the club," Lenny answered. "I'll go back to the sheriff and see if he's got anything." He put on his jacket. "You want anything?"

"No, thank you."

"There's a vending machine down the hall in case you get hungry."

Maria went back to watching the TV. A man walked up to another man in a metallic room surrounded by computer consoles. "The wrap shields are going out," he said. "We might not get through this hyper-portal." Maria turned the channel.

"In other news, Sid Maxwell , also known as the Griffin, made a deal with D.A. Shane Roberts today," said a female news announcer. "Apparently the former leading crime boss of Paway will give up the names of his leading associates in exchange for less jail time." Maria turned the channel.

"It's delicious, it's cold, it's the best soda ever sold," said the voice of a computer-generated dancing can. "It's Fizz Cola." Maria turned the TV off.

Maria went into the hallway and went over to the vending machine.

Teddy drove a car down a road. He passed a sign that said "Welcome to Whisper Field." Teddy saw the lights of a plane going through the sky and smiled. After a few minutes he stopped at a large sign with a map on it. Teddy looked around the map and pointed at the spot labeled "Whisper Field Airport." He smiled. November 10, 6:04 p.m.

Maria went back to her room. She called Lenny on the cell phone. "I had a vision," she said. She told him what she had seen.

Maria and Lenny were in the car. "We have to hurry," he said. "It won't be long before he gets to Whisper Field."

"So he's taking a plane?" asked Maria.

"Yeah, and even with those smaller planes he could go far. Plus, there's no telling where he'll go from there."

A moment passed by. "It was a good thing you had that vision," Lenny said.

"Just being useful," said Maria.

"You do that a lot. And it's not just the visions."

"Just doing my duty as a citizen."

"You do more than report crimes. If it weren't for you, things would be different for me."

"How so?" asked Maria.

"Well, I would have a lot more open cases," Lenny answered. "Who knows what else? You saved my rear end a few times." He sighed. "I'm a detective who's trained to think things through, but I'm dealing with things no one at the academy ever talked about. I've got a psychic coming to me with visions and I'm solving crimes that haven't even happened yet. I dealing with all kinds of stuff that's off the wall and I'm chasing a man I wouldn't even have known about if it hadn't been for you."

"Well, if it weren't for you, the guys who commit those crimes wouldn't be behind bars," said Maria. "If I could've put them away myself, I wouldn't have gone looking for a detective."

"You may not have been able to stop them yourself when you first got the visions, but you've changed," said Lenny. "Remember that guy in the alley?"

They entered Whisper Field. Maria looked around at the buildings. *Everything's so close together,* she thought. *I've heard this town's famous for that gorge behind it. I wonder if we'll be able to see it before we leave.* Lenny drove the car past City Hall and they were soon in Sheriff Hymer's office.

"These are my deputies Lee and Steiner," he said, gesturing to the two men at his left.

"Nice to meet you," said Lenny. He shook their hands.

"So, you think there's a fugitive in the area," Sheriff Hymer said.

"Yeah, his name's Teddy Foreman," said Lenny. He held up Teddy's picture.

Sheriff Hymer looked the picture over. "You also think he's heading to the airport?" he asked.

"Yes, and I also think we should head there now," answered Lenny. He showed the picture to the deputies.

"Then let's go."

They soon arrived at Whisper Field Airport, which was a short distance away from the gorge. This allowed planes to fly over it at the beginning of their flights to give their passengers a visual treat. The four men left their cars. "Stay in the car," Lenny said to Maria. They went inside.

They made their way through a small crowd of people. The sheriff, Lenny, and the two deputies looked through the crowd. The sheriff and his men compared the people's faces with copies of the photograph Lenny had brought with him.

Lenny looked around. Because Whisper Field was a small town, it had a small airport, and looking out a window he saw just a few planes. It seemed busier than he would have thought. He could see no sign of Teddy.

A man in glasses came up to them. "Sheriff, is everything all right?" he asked.

"Everything's all right," Hymer answered loudly enough for everyone to hear him. "Go about your usual business." The man went back behind a counter, but several people in the crowd were still looking at the group.

Sheriff Hymer looked at Lenny. "It doesn't look like he's here," he said.

"He's got to be," said Lenny. *Where is he?* he wondered.

Meanwhile, Maria was in the car, watching an airplane take off.

Teddy came out of a room dressed in a pilot's uniform. He closed the door behind him. On the door was a sign that read "Pilots' Locker Room."

He walked a few feet and went out through a door.

He was outside and went over to a plane. He got in. "Hi, everyone," *he said to the passengers. "I'm going to be your pilot today." Whisper Field* *Airport, November 10, 6:44 p.m.*

He's getting on the plane, Maria thought.

Chapter 4

Maria went into the airport. She looked for Lenny and found him. "What are you doing here?" he asked.

"I had a vision," whispered Maria. "Teddy's going to get a pilot's uniform and get on a plane." She explained what she had seen.

Lenny thought for a moment. "I'll send the sheriff and the deputies to the lockers," he said.

"I could help."

"You already have, and as I said, you helped a lot, but I don't want these guys getting curious about why a 'behaviorist' is doing so much," Lenny said. "Go back to the car."

Maria went back to the car as Lenny went over to the men.

"Is your witness sure?" asked Sheriff Hymer.

"He looked sure, and I can't ask him again," said Lenny. "He took off. He had to catch a plane."

"He better hope it's not the plane this guy's trying to hijack," said Sheriff Hymer. He looked around. "Lee and I will check the lockers while you and Steiner go to the control tower to get check-ins from all the pilots. They're bound to know all the regulars' voices, so anyone new will get spotted."

"Right," said Lenny. They took off for their destinations.

Soon, Sheriff Hymer and his deputy entered the control room. Lenny and Deputy Steiner were standing by the air traffic controller.

"We found one of the pilots tied up in the locker room," said the sheriff. "A Roger Johnson."

"He was scheduled to fly flight twelve, and that's the only one who hasn't responded to my request for a check-in," said the air traffic controller.

"It's him," said Lenny.

There was a beeping on a screen. "It looks like he's about to take off," said the controller.

"No, he's not," Lenny said. He ran out, followed by the three men.

They ran onto the tarmac and Lenny pointed at a plane that was moving toward the end of the runway, which was a couple of yards from the edge of the gorge. They chased after it.

Out of nowhere Maria darted toward the plane. She leapt onto the wing of the Cessna 402 and went up against the door. She grabbed the handle and opened it. Teddy kicked at her, but she dodged his foot and grabbed his leg. She pulled on it, but she could not pull him out because he was wearing a seat belt.

Maria let go of Teddy, who brought his legs inside the plane. Maria grabbed the door and the wing, trying to hang on. Teddy grabbed the door and tried to close it, but Maria held on to it. "Suit yourself," said Teddy. He increased the plane's speed.

Maria held on as the wind pressing against her increased. She could see Lenny and the others coming up to the plane, but it passed them. Maria tried to hang on as she was pushed back by the wind and the plane's motion. She could see the gorge coming up to her but pushed down her fright.

Maria let go of the wing and reached out to Teddy. She quickly unfastened his seat belt. He grabbed her wrist, but she broke his grip and then grabbed his legs with both of her hands.

Maria was pushed back, but she held on to Teddy's legs. He was ripped from the plane. He tried to hold on to the frame of the door, but he lost his grip and they both fell off the plane.

They landed on the ground and Lenny, with the other men, rushed to them.

Sheriff Hymer quickly went after the plane, which had been steered to the right by the struggle between Maria and Teddy. He jumped onto the wing and climbed inside. He brought the plane to a halt. "It's going to be all right, everyone," he said to the passengers.

Lenny lifted Teddy up. "You're under arrest," he said.

He led Teddy over to the sheriff, who was walking toward them.

"Here he is," said Lenny. "I'm sure you've got a cell to hold him until we arrange for transport."

"Sure," said Sheriff Hymer.

"Thanks for all your help, guys," Lenny said. He handed him to the sheriff, who then cuffed him.

Maria, Lenny, and Sheriff Hymer went to the front of the airport. "My men will take him to the station," Hymer said. "They'll want you to make a statement."

"Of course," said Lenny.

Will they want that from me too? wondered Maria.

Lenny gestured for Maria to go back to the car. From there she saw Lenny talking with Sheriff Hymer. After a few minutes, Lenny went to the car. It's too late to go back to Paway and since I don't want to drive all the way back to the motel in Con Tree let's get a room," he said. "They'll take my statement tonight."

"What about me?" Maria asked.

"Don't worry," said Lenny. "I informed them that as part of Paway Police departmental procedures your statement will be taken back home."

Relief washed over Maria. *It's over,* she thought.

The deputies were driving toward the station with Teddy in the backseat. Suddenly, Teddy leaned forward. "I'm going to be sick," he cried.

Deputy Lee pulled the car over. "I'll watch him," said Deputy Steiner. He got out and started to escort Teddy out to the side of the road.

They got a few inches, but Teddy dragged his feet. "Oh no, you're going to be sick, do it away from the car," Deputy Steiner said. Deputy Lee got out to help him.

The deputies held on to Teddy from both sides. "Let's go," said Deputy Steiner. Suddenly, Teddy kicked out at his shin. He grabbed his leg. As Deputy Lee reached over to him, Teddy stomped his foot. Deputy Lee grabbed his foot and Teddy turned around and rammed his back into him. As they went down, he grabbed his belt.

They hit the ground and Teddy undid his belt. He sprang up, pulling the belt from his pants as he did so.

"Get him," Deputy Steiner cried. They chased after him and he went around a house as he did so. He fumbled around on the belt for the keys to the handcuffs.

As they went around the corner, he was gone. "Call this in," said Deputy Steiner.

Meanwhile, Maria and Lenny were in a motel room. "Seems like a lot of money to spend for something we're not going to use for long," she said.

"It's not that expensive for one day," said Lenny. "You know, that phone I gave you isn't just so you can call about your visions. If you ever need to talk, call me."

"I'll be fine," said Maria.

"Just call," said Lenny.

Maria sighed. "Speaking of calling people, I think there's another call I have to make."

Lois's phone rang. "Hello?"

"Hi," said Maria. "How are you doing?"

"Maria, I'm doing fine," answered Lois. "It's good to hear from you."

"How's Dad?"

"He's doing fine. Everything's going well."

"That's good."

"How well did your project do? Was it an A?"

"It was about a B," answered Maria. "Anyway, I just called to see how you're doing."

"I'm doing fine," said Lois. "Thanks for calling."

"Love you."

"Love you too."

"How are things?" asked Lenny.

"Good," answered Maria.

Lenny's phone rang. "Hello?" A distressed look came over his face. "He's out? I'll get down there right away."

"What's wrong?" asked Maria.

"Teddy Foreman's escaped," answered Lenny. "I'm going down to the station. I want you to stay here."

I wonder why I didn't get a vision, Maria thought. Lenny left the room. Maria looked down at her phone. *I hope we solve the case before Mom gets home.*

Minutes later, Lenny entered the station. "What happened?" he asked.

Sheriff Hymer turned to look at him. "He faked being sick to get my deputies to stop the cruiser," he answered.

Lenny sighed. "Any idea where he might be now?" he asked.

"No," answered Sheriff Hymer. "He has no friends or family in the area, no connection. We don't know why he even came here."

"Probably for your airport," said Lenny.

"Yeah, I heard that the planes in our airport have desinations are farther away than the airports in the area," said Sheriff Hymer.

"Where was the plane he hijacked going?" asked Lenny.

Sheriff Hymer took a piece of paper off the desk. "Campbell," he answered.

Lenny thought for a moment. "Is there another way to get to Campbell from here?" he asked. "A bus or a truck transporting something there?"

"I don't know," the sheriff answered. "I'd have to call around."

"My brother's in shipping," said Deputy Steiner. "I'll call him."

"And I'll check with my expert," Lenny said.

Maria's cell phone rang.

"It's me," Lenny said when she answered.

"Did you catch him yet?" Maria asked.

"No. Have you seen anything about him?"

"No, I would call if I did."

"Just checking," said Lenny. Maria looked at her watch. *When does Mom get home?* she wondered.

Lenny went over to the sheriff, who was sorting paper and talking on the telephone. "Anything?" Lenny asked.

"Not yet," answered Sheriff Hymer.

Deputy Steiner came into the room. "I've got something," he said. "There's a company called Farfields, which is based in Whisper Field that's shipping some gasoline for a gas station chain. There's a shipment heading toward Green Ridge, which is by Campbell, it's leaving in less than an hour."

Sheriff Hymer looked at Lenny. "You want us to look into his record and see if there's a connection between him and Campbell?" he asked. "Most likely it was because that was the farthest any of the planes were going, but we could check just in case."

"No time," answered Lenny. "Let's get down to where they're shipping it out."

"We should set up surveillance," said Sheriff Hymer. "That way we won't scare him off. You want us to get your behaviorist?"

"I think we can get this guy ourselves," answered Lenny.

"She could show us how he might approach the scene," said Sheriff Hymer.

Or she could have a vision, thought Lenny. "Okay," he said. "I'll go back to the motel and pick her up."

Minutes later, Lenny was parked around the corner from the warehouse where the truck making the delivery was going to leave from.

"How long until this guy shows?" asked Maria.

"You're the psychic," said Lenny. "You tell me."

"I hope this ends soon," said Maria.

"It will," said Lenny. "The shipment is leaving in a few minutes. If he's going with that truck then he'll have to get on it soon."

"Good, because I want to get home before my mom does," said Maria. "I don't know how much longer she's going to be away."

Lenny was silent for a moment. "Maria, what you said before," he said.

"It's not important," said Maria.

"It is," said Lenny. "The thing is, it'll just take time. Soon, you'll be feeling happy that your dad's back, but in the meantime, if you have problems, you can always call me. I'll be there."

Maria sighed. "You think there's something wrong with me?"

"No, you're just human."

Maria looked at him. "Thanks."

"No problem," said Lenny. "Just hang in there and all this stuff will pass over."

Really? wondered Maria.

Lenny continued to watch the warehouse. No one was in sight. *Where is he? How is he going to get in? If I knew that, then watching this place would be a lot easier.*

"It seems that stakeouts are actually just waiting a long time," said Maria.

"Yeah, it's a part of police work that they don't show on TV," Lenny said. "Everyone sees high-speed car chases and interrogating suspects, but what people don't think about is that one of the most important things a detective needs is patience. Puzzles or mysteries don't unravel or show an important clue on your schedule. They do it on theirs. You have to wait it out."

Lenny leaned back in his seat. *Where is he?*

Maria looked at her cell phone and then back up at the warehouse. She saw movement. "Lenny."

Lenny sat up and saw a small figure move across the loading dock. The truck started to move. *He's going to try to get onto the truck as it starts to leave,* he thought. He raised the walkie-talkie the sheriff had given him to his mouth. "He's on the move," Lenny said. "He's approaching the truck from the west."

"All right, we'll try to get from the front," said Sheriff Hymer.

Lenny started his car. "Get ready," he said.

The truck started to leave the area and the figure was blocked from their view. When the truck went down the street, the figure was gone. "He's on the truck," Lenny said into the walkie-talkie.

"We're on it," Sheriff Hymer said.

Lenny drove onto the street and pulled up behind the truck.

"There he is," said Maria. Teddy was holding on to the back of the truck. He was bent down and seemed to be doing something to the doors.

"I think he's trying to force the doors open," said Lenny.

There was the sound of sirens, and the truck stopped. "They formed the roadblock," Lenny said. He stopped the car and got out. He ran over to the truck. "Freeze!"

Teddy forced the doors open. He scrambled inside and then poked the upper half of his body out. He raised a barrel and threw it.

The barrel hit Lenny's car. *Maria,* Lenny thought. He stopped and turned to the car.

Teddy threw another barrel and Lenny turned back barely in time to dodge it.

Lenny darted over to the truck. Teddy swung another barrel at him. He dodged it, but then Teddy tackled him. They both went down to the ground. Teddy quickly got up and ran away.

The sheriff and his deputies chased after him as he ducked into the alley. At the end of the alley was a chain-link fence, which Teddy climbed over.

Sheriff Hymer reached the fence and started to climb up it. As he reached the top, Teddy threw a garbage can at him. He ducked and it missed him. He looked up and could not see Teddy. He climbed over and exited the alley. He looked around but could not see the fugitive anywhere.

A few minutes later, Lenny joined Sheriff Hymer and his deputies. "Where is he?" Lenny asked. He looked around the dark street.

"We lost him," said Sheriff Hymer.

Lenny let out a cry of frustration. "How many times is this going to happen?" he asked.

The four men returned to the truck. "I'll get the driver's statement," said Sheriff Hymer. He looked at the deputies. "You guys corner off the nearby roads. Maybe we'll get lucky." The deputies darted off. *Won't help,* thought Lenny. *He's on foot.*

Lenny returned to the car. Maria poked her head out the window. "Are you all right?" he asked.

"I'm fine," she answered.

Lenny got inside the car and sighed. "We'll catch him," said Maria.

"Have you had any more visions?" he asked.

"No."

Lenny sighed again. "Well, I guess we wait for another lead." He looked out the windshield. "Maybe I'll just take you home."

"No, we're going to stay and find this guy," Maria said. "I have plenty of time."

"Feels like all I do is lose him," Lenny said.

"We just have to find him again."

Lenny thought for a moment. "How about I take you back to the motel and I'll come back here and see if these guys have found anything."

"Are you sure?"

"Sure—you can rest up and call if you get anything, and I'll see if there are any clues at the scene." Lenny went out to the scene and told the sheriff his plan. Then he got back into his car and drove off.

They arrived at the motel parking lot. "You did good," said Maria.

"He got away," said Lenny.

"You tried your best and you're going to do even better the next time."

"Like you," said Lenny. "You're doing your best with all this crazy stuff you have to deal with. Most people, including me, would've gone crazy dealing with it, but you're doing a good job. I'm sure if you father knew, he'd be proud of you."

Maria looked at him. "Thanks," she said, and got out of the car.

Maria entered their room. She sat on the bed feeling tired. She pulled out her cell phone. *Should I call her?* she wondered. *Nah, too soon.* She flopped herself onto the bed and looked up at the ceiling. After several moments she looked at the cell phone and then put it away.

Meanwhile, Sheriff Hymer and his deputies were looking around. There was no sign of Teddy or any obvious clue as to where he had gone. *Maybe we need to call in officers from neighboring towns,* Hymer thought. *This is getting tricky to do with just four guys.*

Deputy Lee came up to him. "Anything?" Hymer asked.

"No, sir," Lee answered.

"Keep looking."

"Sir, I think we've looked everywhere in the immediate area."

"Where could he have gone?" Sheriff Hymer asked. "He was on foot."

Deputy Steiner came up to them. He smelled unpleasant. "What's that smell?" the sheriff asked.

"I was checking a Dumpster. I thought it would be a good place to hide."

Lenny pulled up to the scene and got out. "Find anything?" he asked.

"No, but now we're going over places where he could've hidden himself," Hymer answered. He turned back to his deputy. "Good idea. I want you and Lee to check in any Dumpsters you find. The detective and I will check for any other hiding spots."

"Got you," Steiner said. He and Lee got into a cruiser and left.

"You want to take my car or yours?" Sheriff Hymer asked.

"Yours has a radio tuned to the local police band," Lenny said. "Let's go."

They got into the car and drove off. "Where do you think we should start?" asked Sheriff Hymer.

"How about the main roads," Lenny replied. "After that we can try any parking lots or places where he can get to a car."

"I think I might know of a place," the sheriff said. He took a right.

Meanwhile, Maria was sitting in the motel room.

Teddy was limping along a dark street. He looked around. There was not a single person in view.

Suddenly, a car came down the street. It slowed down and then stopped. The man rolled down his window. "Are you all right?" he asked.

Teddy darted over to the car. He grabbed the man and quickly reached for the door handle. He opened the door and swung the person onto the ground. Teddy got into the car and took off. Trout Street, November 10, 10:03 p.m.

Lenny's cell phone rang.

"I had a vision," Maria said. *So much for detective work,* thought Lenny. Maria told him what she had seen.

"I'll be there," he said.

"What is it?" asked Sheriff Hymer.

"Someone I know got a tip."

Minutes later, they arrived at Trout Street. They stopped at the corner and waited.

Teddy suddenly limped into view. A car slowed down and stopped next to him.

"Let's go," said Sheriff Hymer. They got out of the car.

"Are you all right?" asked the driver. Teddy grabbed him and reached for the door handle.

"Freeze," ordered Lenny. He and Sheriff Hymer ran onto the scene.

Teddy let go of the man and started to run off. Lenny chased after him.

Teddy stopped and turned around. He threw a punch, which Lenny blocked. Lenny grabbed him and swung him to the ground. He held on to him as he struggled. Teddy pushed himself up, pushing Lenny back.

Teddy managed to get out from beneath Lenny. He started to run, but Lenny grabbed him by the back of his shirt. Teddy turned around and kicked at him. Lenny grabbed the foot before it hit him and pulled it down. Teddy went down onto the street.

Lenny put his foot on Teddy's back as he wrestled for his hands. He cuffed Teddy. Lenny pulled him up. "I said, you're under arrest, and this time it's going to stick." He led Teddy to the approaching officers.

"Don't worry," said Sheriff Hymer. "It will." They took him from Lenny's custody. "I want double guards on him at all times and no more falling for any 'sickness,'" he told his deputies.

"Thanks for your help," said Lenny.

Sheriff Hymer turned to Lenny. "You're more than welcome."

There was a knock at the motel room's door. Maria opened it to find Lenny. "We got him," he said. "Let's go home."

The next morning, Maria went downstairs. Lois was sitting at the table.

"Hi, Mom," Maria said. "How's Dad?"

"He's doing well," Lois answered. "He just needs time to recover."

Just like me, thought Maria.

Lois looked off into the distance. "They say that at most, it'll be a few months before he'll be back to full mobility," she said. "We'll just have to see."

"I'm sure he'll get better in no time."

"Maybe," said Lois. "After all, no one can tell the future." Maria sighed.

BOOK 6

Return of
the Mastermind

Chapter 1

In the Paway Correctional Facility the man known as John Doe 1228 lay on the floor of his cell. His arms and legs were all spread out and one of his arms was on his bed.

A guard went by. He stopped when he saw the man on the floor. "Are you hurt?" he asked.

The man gave no answer.

The guard stood there for a moment and then unlocked the door. He went in and was about to radio his supervisor when the man sprang up. He threw a punch at the guard's stomach. As the man clutched his stomach, the man grabbed him and slammed him down onto the side of the bed.

The man left the cell dressed in the guard's uniform. The guard was unconscious beneath the bed, bound and gagged by torn strips of sheets.

The man went through several long hallways and came to a door with a sign that read "Alarm Will Sound If Opened." He felt along the side of the door and took out a sharpened piece of metal. He cut some wires along the door's frame. He then took out a piece of wire and picked the lock with it.

The man went through the door and came outside. *I'm free,* he thought. *Mr. Mindful is free to show the world a new kind of crime!*

Two weeks later, Maria Marhill was in her room doing some karate exercises. She did her last stance and exhaled.

"Maria, time for breakfast," called Lois. Maria hurried downstairs.

Maria entered the kitchen. "Hi, sweetie," said Lois. "How are you doing?"

"Fine. Why do you ask?"

"Well, you've been a bit off ever since your father woke up."

Actually, I've been off ever since I started to see the future, thought Maria. "I'm fine," she said. "How's Dad?"

"Great. He's doing really well at the rehab center." Lois looked at Maria. "Is there anything you want to talk to me about? You know you can talk to me about anything, right?"

"I'm fine, Mom," Maria said. She finished her cereal and started to head toward the door. "Good-bye."

"See you later, sweetie."

Meanwhile, a man sat in an office. He was visited by another man. "Hi, Stu," said the visitor.

"Hi, Roger."

"How was the movie last night?"

"I didn't go."

Roger put a cup of coffee on Stu's desk. "I got you a cup," he said. He raised his own cup in a toast.

"Thank you," said Stu. He did not look up.

Roger looked out the window. "How about we go to a movie tonight?"

"No, thanks." He continued to do paperwork.

Roger looked out the window again and then left the room.

Maria entered the school and went to her first class. "Hello, everyone," said the teacher. "Please take out your textbooks. We have a lot to go over if we want to keep up with the schedule."

The students took out their books. "Remember to keep studying," said the teacher. "You never know when there will be a surprise quiz in your future."

The future, Maria thought. She flipped through the pages of her textbook.

Roger was on his cell phone. "I'm trying to talk to him," he said. He paused for a moment, listening to the person on the other end. "I know how important it is," he said. "What can I do? He won't have anything to do with me." He paused again. "Yes, I understand."

The next day, Lenny was at his desk. "Detective Hipar, please come into my office," Lieutenant Steve Finn said poking his head out of his office.

Lenny got up and went across the squad room. *Uh oh,* he thought. His heart started to beat rapidly. Detective Jon Turner looked at him as he went.

Lenny entered the office. "Sit down," Finn said.

Lenny sat down. "What is it, sir?"

"There's going to be a gathering of guys from upstairs and you've been invited," Finn answered.

Am I being invited to a party? Lenny wondered. "Sir, are you inviting me to a party?"

"It's just a few people getting together," said the lieutenant. He looked at Lenny for a moment. "Truth is, the guys from upstairs want to get a look at you. You've been making a lot of high-profile busts lately, and word is that you're going places."

Lenny sat there surprised. *Going places?* he wondered.

"It's at my place at nine," Finn said.

That night Lenny arrived at Lieutenant Finn's home. He felt nervous. *Oh boy,* he thought. He sighed and then knocked on the door.

Finn answered the door in casual wear. Seeing him like that surprised Lenny, though he had known that was how he would be. "Sir, I'm happy that you've invited me," he said.

Come in, Lenny," said Finn. He was smiling.

"Yes, sir."

"Call me Steve," said Finn. "This is just an informal gathering." He led him down a hall.

Steve and Lenny came to a large room. Lenny looked around at the group of people before him. *Whoa,* he thought. He recognized most of the guests.

"There are some people who want to meet you," said Steve. He led him to a group of people. "This is Captain Hartman."

"Call me George here," the man said. Lenny reached out and shook his hand.

"It's a pleasure, sir," said Lenny. George shot him a look. "George," Lenny said quickly.

"We've been hearing good things about you," said George.

"Really?" asked Lenny. He was not sure how to feel about that.

"Yeah, catching the Griffin and Peter Coldstein and that 'Mr. Mindful' guy," said George. "Also, the fact that you did it all single-handedly. Impressive."

"Yeah," said Lenny.

"You're going places," said George. "They're talking."

"Excuse me, but there are some people who want to talk to this man," said Steve. He led George to a group of men nearby.

"Making friends?" asked a voice from behind Lenny.

Lenny turned around and was stunned to find that it belonged to the chief of detectives. "Sir," he said.

"Call me Paul," he said. He gave Lenny a great big smile.

"Yes, of course," Lenny said. He returned the smile but still felt uneasy.

Paul gestured to George. "You know, that guy really likes fish," he said. "They say that's how Steve got his job. You know, his last name being Finn and all."

Lenny laughed weakly as Paul gave a small chuckle.

Steve came over to them. "Hey, Lenny," he said. "There are some people you've got to meet." He led Lenny across the room.

A few hours later, Lenny returned to his apartment. He threw himself down into his chair and sighed. The images of all the high-ranking people went through his mind. *I can't believe what happened,* he thought. He was not nervous anymore, but the event had taken its toll on him.

Early the next evening, Maria and Lois were in their living room. Maria got up and was about to leave. "Honey, can I talk with you?" asked Lois.

"Sure, Mom."

"You know you can talk to me about anything, right?"

"Yeah, I know," Maria answered. Her guard went up.

"With your father coming out of his coma you must be going through a lot," said Lois. "You can talk to me about how you're feeling or anything else."

"Mom, I'm okay." Maria smiled. "I'm happy that Dad's awake. Things are going to be great."

Lois looked at Maria. "Just in case, you know you can talk to me, right?"

"Right," answered Maria. She went upstairs.

Maria entered her room. She tried to control what she was feeling.

A man tapped at a window. He then pushed at it as he worked its edges with a tool. The window gave way and he put it on the ground. He climbed into the building and was followed by another man. They looked around what appeared to be a dimly lit store. Tella Whiz Electronics, 30 Maple Lane, November 28, 9:23 p.m.

That's tomorrow, Maria thought. She got out her cell phone and called Lenny.

"Hello?"

Maria told him what she had seen. "Okay, I'll pick you up tomorrow night," he said. Then he was silent.

"Lenny, is there something wrong?" Maria asked.

"It's nothing," Lenny answered. "It's just that something happened tonight."

"What happened?"

"I attended a party."

"Excuse me?" Maria asked. Lenny told her what had happened to him.

"Wow, I guess you're moving up in the world," said Maria.

"Yeah," said Lenny. *I would just be another guy if not for your visions,* he thought. "Anyway, I better get going. Got to hit the sack early with what's going to happen tomorrow."

"Okay. See you."

The next day, Lenny entered the squad room. He passed by Detective Turner. "Good morning," he said.

"Hi," Detective Turner said. "I've heard you've been going places."

Lenny simply shrugged. He sat down.

"The lieutenant must think you're pretty special to show you off to the brass," Turner said.

"Maybe it's my personality."

"Yeah, that must be it."

Lieutenant Finn poked his head out of his office. "Detective Hipar," he called.

Lenny went across the squad room and went into the office. "Yes, sir?"

"Have a good time, Lenny?"

Lenny was taken by surprise but recovered. "Yes, sir," he said. *Does he want me to call him Steve?* he wondered.

"Good to hear that," Finn said. He sat down at his desk. "That'll be all."

Lenny went back to his desk. *I never thought I'd be glad to be doing paperwork,* he thought.

That night, Maria went out her window and climbed down the side of her house. She was less fearful because she had done it before.

She darted across her neighbors' lawns and came up to Lenny's car. She got in and they drove off.

They arrived at the store. "Now we wait," said Lenny.

A few minutes later, he spotted a van parked nearby. An alarm went off in him. "Wait here," he said. "I'm going to check out that van."

Lenny left the car and went over to the van while Maria watched.

He quickly peeked through the driver's-side window. The van was empty. *I should call this in,* he thought, but the memory of the previous night's party went through his mind.

Lenny hurried up to the building and then slowly went around it. He was on constant alert.

He came across an opened window. He went around to the front and kicked in the front door.

As he entered, he saw the dim outlines of two men. "Freeze," he ordered. "Police!"

One of the men ran up to him. Lenny grabbed the man and flipped him. As the one man landed on the floor, the other came up to Lenny. He grabbed him and tossed him over a counter. "Let's go," cried the man. His partner got up and they ran to the door.

Across the street, Maria watched the two men run toward the van. *Lenny,* she thought. She got out of the car and went over to the store.

As she approached the store, the van tore down the street, missing her by inches.

Maria pushed down the fright coursing through her and started again toward the store.

Lenny came out of the building. "Lenny, are you all right?" asked Maria.

"I'm fine. How about you?"

"I'm okay."

Lenny sighed and took out his cell phone. "I'm going to have to call this in," he said. "You know what to do."

About an hour later, Lenny stood with two officers as they surveyed the taped-off scene. "You think they came back to get a look?" asked one of the officers. They were looking at the small crowd that had formed.

"I wouldn't be able to tell if they did," said Lenny. "I didn't get that great a look at them. Take their statements and I'll go over them tomorrow." He made his way through the crowd.

Lenny drove around the block and then stopped. Maria got out from behind a tree and got into the car. "How did it go?" she asked.

"Fine," answered Lenny. *Some hotshot I turned out to be,* he thought. "Let's get you home."

Meanwhile, the two would-be robbers approached a man behind a desk. "I see you haven't come back with anything," said the man.

"I'm sorry, boss, but we were interrupted by a cop," said one of the men. "It was a fluke."

"Fools," said the man. "We needed that equipment for the job."

"Hey, we can the stuff from another place," said the other man. "There's no need to be like that, Mr. Mindful."

"We're just lucky we didn't hit that girl or we would've drawn some serious attention," said the first man.

"What girl?" demanded Mr. Mindful.

"As we were taking off, we almost hit a kid," said the second man. "Some blonde."

It couldn't be, thought Mr. Mindful. He turned away from the men. *Could it be her?*

Chapter 2

Maria woke up the next morning and got ready for school. Lois knocked and came into her room. "Hi, Mom," said Maria.

"Hey there, Snugglebear," said Lois. "I thought this weekend we could get together and maybe catch a movie."

"I'm afraid I can't," said Maria.

"How about we do something else then?" Lois asked. "Like get a bite to eat or maybe go down to the park?"

"I'm afraid I've got a lot of stuff to do for school."

"You can still do it," Lois said. "I just want a chance for else to get together."

Maria tried not to sigh. "Okay." She followed her mother downstairs.

Maria was soon walking to school. *I actually would like to go with her,* she thought. *It would be nice for things, for a while at least, not to be so crazy, but I never know when I'll have a vision. It seems to be pretty much a twenty-four-hour thing.*

Maria approached the school building. *Maybe I can call Lenny if I see anything,* she thought.

Maria passed a girl she knew named Cindy. Cindy did not even bother to look up. Maria went on to class.

Meanwhile, in Stu's office, Roger was sneaking around. He shuffled through some of his papers and looked through his day planner. *4:00 p.m. lunch, Pernard's,* he read.

Outside the office Roger spoke into his cell phone. "It's me," he said. "I know where he's going to be."

Meanwhile, in the squad room, Lenny was typing his report. Detective Turner came over to him.

"Hey, I heard about what happened last night," he said.

"Yeah," said Lenny.

"So, a robbery at an electronics store," said Detective Turner. "Those guys got one over on you, huh?"

"Well, it was dark."

"You know, if I had been there, we would've gotten those guys," Turner said. "If we had been together, things would've ended differently."

"I'm sure."

Detective Turner went back to his desk. *Is he angry at me?* Lenny wondered.

Meanwhile, Stu was walking down the street. Suddenly, two men darted in front of him.

What the . . . , thought Stu. One of the men had the hood of his jacket up and the other one had a bandana wrapped around his face.

"Give us your money," demanded the man in the hood.

Stu frantically fumbled for his wallet.

"Hey," said Roger, running up to them. He kicked at the man in the hood, who went back. He then grabbed the man in the bandana and shoved him against the wall. The man slumped down.

"Get out of here," ordered Roger. The two men got up and ran off.

Stu looked at Roger. "Thank you," he said.

A short distance away, the men stopped in an alley. One of them got out a cell phone. "Sir, it went according to plan," he said.

The next night, Maria and Lois came out of the movie theater. Lois threw away an empty cup. "What did you think of the movie?" she asked.

"It was good," answered Maria.

"I'm glad we're finally spending time together."

"Me too."

"You know, I just had a snack attack so I'm going to go back inside get us some snacks for the road," said Lois. "I'll be right back." She went inside as Maria stood on the sidewalk.

That was kind of nice, thought Maria. *It was a quiet evening without visions or danger. It was just me and Mom. I can't remember the last time it was like that. It's been such a long time.*

Lois came back out. Maria looked at her face. *Should I tell her about the visions?* she wondered. *I didn't tell her before because I was worried about how she would react. Are things different now? Then again, with Dad awake she's got enough on her mind.*

They got into their car and drove off. *I can keep the secret,* Maria thought. *After all, I've been doing it for this long.*

An hour later, Lenny was sitting in his apartment going over some old files. His cell phone rang.

"It's me," said Maria.

"What is it?" asked Lenny. "Did you have a vision?"

"No, it's not like that. I just want to talk."

"Is everything all right?"

"Sure. Everything's fine. In fact, my mom just took me to see a movie."

"What did you see?"

"*Marcy's Day Off.* She's been wanting to spend time with me a lot lately."

"She just wants to make sure you're all right," said Lenny. "With everything that's been happening to you it's only natural."

"And she doesn't even know half of what's been happening to me," said Maria. "The thing is, I keep worrying about what happens if I have a vision."

"Well, then you call me. It's not like she has some way of telling if you have a vision, right? You have them by me like when the one with that tree strucked by lighting and that one about Mitch Ken and I can't tell."

"No," answered Maria.

"Then it'll be fine," said Lenny.

"Thanks for listening."

"No problem. I'm always here if you need to talk."

"How's your new high-ranking social life?"

"It's going fine."

A few days later, Roger came into Stu's office. Stu smiled. "Roger, nice to see you," he said.

"Stu, we've got a problem," said Roger.

The smile disappeared from Stu's face. Roger handed him a piece of paper. "You know the Olsen account?"

"Yeah, that's the account I'm in charge of," Stu answered.

"Well, according to this, Jim Culler is about to transfer a lot money out of it," Roger said. "I don't know why, but it looks like the account's in danger."

There's almost two million dollars in that account, thought Stu. "Where did you get this?" he asked.

"I'm afraid I can't say. Do you trust me?"

"After what you did for me, yeah."

"I think you should take the funds and convert them into something that can't be as easily transferred as cash," said Roger. "Something like gold. I know a guy who could handle it."

"I don't know. I could get into trouble."

"You could also be a hero," said Roger. "You could be the guy who saved the Olsen account. Come on, time is of the essence."

"Okay," said Stu.

A short time later, one of the men who worked for Mr. Mindful was looking at the screen of a laptop computer. He spoke into a cell phone. "I've got it," he said. "The spy program Roger put into Stu's computer gave me the transfer information. We know where it's going to be."

"Good," said Mr. Mindful.

Another man came into the room. "I traded surveillance off to Bill," he said. "To be honest, I'm kinda nervous about spying on a cop."

"What are his movements?" asked Mr. Mindful.

"Nothing spectacular," answered the man. "Really, we got nothing you didn't already know."

I need to get ahold of his phone records, thought Mr. Mindful.

The next day, Lenny was sitting at his desk when Lieutenant Finn came over to him.

"Hi, Lenny," he said.

"Sir, about me losing those burglars," Lenny said.

"Never mind that. There's something we need to discuss."

"What, sir?"

"It seems that there was a bureaucratic mess-up, which is why you weren't informed even though you were the arresting officer," Finn answered. "That guy known as Mr. Mindful escaped."

About an hour later, Maria was walking home when her cell phone vibrated. "Hello?"

"We have a problem," said Lenny.

"What is it?"

"Don't worry, but Mr. Mindful has escaped."

Mom, thought Maria. "He knows where I live."

"Don't worry," said Lenny. "He's been out for a few weeks now. If he was going to come around, he would've done so by now."

"Why are you calling now if he's been out for so long?"

"There was a mess-up and I've only heard about it now," answered Lenny. "Don't worry, we're going to get this guy."

Maria arrived home. She tried to act as normal as possible. She looked around but saw nothing. *Is he watching me?* she wondered. *He wouldn't wait this long. Would he?*

Maria entered the house. Lois was sitting on the couch. "Aren't you supposed to be at work?" asked Maria.

"I got off early," answered Lois.

"You can do that with the bills?"

"It'll be all right. I wanted to be here to make sure you're okay."

"I'm fine," said Maria. She started to go up to her room.

Meanwhile, Lenny was sitting at his desk talking on the phone. "Are you sure he didn't say anything before he broke out?" he asked. "Anything that might be a clue?"

"No, he kept to himself," answered the voice of a corrections officer. "Everyone I talked with thinks he thought he was better than everybody else."

"How's the guard he roughed up?" asked Lenny.

"Fine," answered the officer. "His statement is being shipped over to you."

"Thanks."

"No luck?" asked Detective Turner.

"We didn't found anything," answered Lenny. He looked over the reports and forms on his desk. "No real name, known friends, known active accomplices," he said. "There's no hint at what he's planning."

"If I were him, I would hightail it out of the area," Detective Turner said.

Lenny was silent. *Maria said that when he was in her house, he made a speech about being more than a common criminal. If a person wanted to prove they were some sort of master criminal, what would they do?*

Meanwhile, Mr. Mindful was sitting behind his desk when one of his men came in. "Sir, I got the phone records," he said.

"That was quick," said Mr. Mindful.

"The guy we bribed at the phone company got right to it. It seems that this guy has made a lot of calls to a prepaid cell."

The man handed Mr. Mindful a piece of paper. Mr. Mindful looked at the number appearing multiple times. *Is that the girl's number?* he wondered. He put the paper down on the desk. *It doesn't matter.* "We've got to get rid of him," he said.

Chapter 3

Lenny's phone rang.

"Is this the detective in charge of the Mr. Mindful investigation?" asked a man's voice. His tone was fearful.

"Yes, how may I help you?" asked Lenny.

"I saw him," said the caller. "I recognized him from the paper, but I couldn't believe it."

"Where?"

"Forty-nine Ball Wheel Street."

"Who is this?" asked Lenny.

"I can't say," answered the caller. He hung up.

Lenny looked around and then left the squad room.

"Thanks for the help, Mom," said Maria. She finished her math assignment.

"Anytime, sweetie," said Lois. "All you have to do is ask." She left the room.

Maria closed her book. She went over to the window and looked outside. She saw no one, but she still wondered if anyone was watching her. *I guess if there were anybody watching me, I wouldn't see them. If there were somebody, then why haven't they done anything by now? Mr. Mindful has been out for so long. I hope Lenny catches this guy soon, but then what would happen to anybody who is watching me? If they tried anything, I should see it coming with the visions, but then again I've been surprised before.*

Maria backed away from the window and sat on her bed.

Lenny was outside a building. Detective Turner was next to him. Lenny went through the front door. His partner remained outside.

Lenny went through a hallway and came to another door. He opened the door and went through it. His foot went through a laser that ran along the floor. The building exploded. 49 Ball Wheel Street, December 1, 5:07 p.m.

Lenny, thought Maria. She quickly went over to her book bag and got her cell phone.

Lenny and Detective Turner were outside the building. He started to go toward it when his phone rang. Lenny thought for a moment and then answered it.

"Lenny, are you at Forty-one Ball Wheel Street?" asked Maria.

"Yeah," answered Lenny. "Why?" Maria told him about her vision.

About an hour later a member of the bomb squad came out of the building. He went up to the two detectives. "We defused the bomb," he said.

"Thanks," said Lenny. The man turned around and went over to the other members of the squad as they came out of the building.

"How did you know?" asked Detective Turner.

"That call I got was from an informant tipping me off," Lenny replied.

"You think the bomb was from this Mr. Mindful guy?" asked Detective Turner.

"Yeah," answered Lenny. "Let's hope there's something we can trace to him."

"I'll talk to the bomb squad," said Detective Turner. "See if they can find any signature common between this one and the ones he's used in the past." As Turner left, Lenny took out his cell phone.

"Are you all right?" asked Maria.

"Yeah, thanks to you," answered Lenny. He looked at the building. "We think it was a booby trap Mr. Mindful set to get me off his trail."

"He's still out there," said Maria. "I thought he might've left town."

"It looks like he's still here."

"You think he's planning something?"

"I don't know."

"What about my mom? Do you think she's in danger?"

"No. If he was going to make a move against you guys, he would've done it by now," answered Lenny. "Just be careful, though."

There was a knock on the door. Maria quickly put the cell phone behind her.

Lois poked her head into the room.

"Hey there, Snugglebear," she said. "I was making some popcorn and wondered if you wanted any."

"Sure, Mom," said Maria.

Snugglebear? Lenny thought.

Meanwhile, one of Mr. Mindful's men came up to him. "I just came back from the building," he said. "There's a bunch of cops around the place and it hasn't exploded."

Mr. Mindful scowled. "We still go on with the plan," he said.

"But boss, are you sure that's a good idea with this cop still around?"

"We need the money," said Mr. Mindful. "What happened was then, and this is now. He won't stop me." *Nor will the girl,* he thought. *Though I wonder how she fits into everything.*

The next morning, Maria came downstairs for breakfast.

"Hi, Mom," said Maria.

"Hi, sweetie," said Lois. She put a plate of pancakes on the table and sat down. "Honey, I want you to know that I'm here for you," she said. "Ever since your father woke up, no, before that even, there's been some distance between us."

"Mom, I'm fine, really," Maria said. "It's been a lot to deal with since Dad woke up, but I'm dealing with it."

"It just seems like there's more going on," said Lois. "Is there something you're not talking about?"

Uh oh, thought Maria. "It's just that I have a lot going on at school. That's all."

"Uh-huh," said Lois. "You know, I meant what I said. Anything, anytime."

"Thanks, Mom," said Maria. She finished her breakfast and went to school.

Lenny was sitting at his desk looking over the bomb squad's report. *No substance was found that could be individualized,* he read. He sighed.

"Anything?" asked Detective Turner.

"Nothing," answered Lenny. "You?"

Detective Turner was silent for a moment. "Nothing," he answered.

"What are we missing?" asked Lenny. "This guy can't be that good."

"Well, he does consider himself a 'master criminal,'" said Detective Turner. Lenny rubbed his eyes. "Getting tired?"

"I just need a new lead," said Lenny. "Anything you can think of?"

"Maybe you should just go home. I'll take over."

"No, I got it," Lenny said. *I can't go home while Maria's in danger,* he thought. Lenny's mind flashed back to when he first met Maria. *That seems like a lifetime ago.*

"Go home," said Detective Turner.

"No, I got it. I'll go over it again."

"Okay," Turner said. He went back to his desk.

Lenny looked through the reports on his desk. *There's got to be something here,* he thought.

Maria was in class. The teacher spoke, but Maria did not follow. She had trouble focusing. *How am I supposed to concentrate when there's a "master criminal" running around?* she wondered.

She tried again in vain to keep her attention on the lesson. *Lenny's out there running around, tracking this guy down, but maybe there's something I can do.*

A couple of hours later, Maria was in the computer lab. She opened her notebook, where she had written "Thinks himself a 'master criminal,' doesn't want to commit 'boring' crimes, big ego, intelligent, and identity unknown" on a page.

I've gone over every news article I could find about Mr. Mindful, Maria thought. *There's no clue of who he could be. I've done Internet searches on Mr. Mindful, new kinds of crime, and criminal genius, and there's nothing. What am I missing?*

She sat there for several minutes until she noticed the clock on the wall. *It's almost time to go,* Maria thought. She quickly gathered her things and left as the bell rang. *I haven't even gotten anything done.*

That night, Maria got ready for bed. *Hours of searches on the web and nothing,* she thought. *I did learn a lot about criminology. I just hope that website was accurate. I could always ask Lenny.*

A truck came up to a building. Mr. Mindful got off it as some men jumped off and went past him. They went up to the building. Two men went up to a collection of wires on the side of the building. They placed a metal box on the wires.

One of the men was standing by Mr. Mindful. "I told you I could get the equipment," said the man.

"Just get the job done," said Mr. Mindful.

Sparks flew from the metal box. "Security disabled," said one of the men.

Another man took a pair of lock cutters to the door. They opened the doors and inside was a table with a stack of gold bars on it. "Load it up," said Mr. Mindful. 25 Pole Avenue, December 2, 9:24 p.m.

He's back, thought Maria.

A few minutes later, a truck came up to U-Store Storage. Mr. Mindful was driving and next to him was Roger. They stopped in front of the building.

Mr. Mindful and Roger got out. The back of the truck opened and three men got out.

Two of the man put a metal box on a collection of wires. "I told you I could get the equipment," said the man who stayed by Mr. Mindful.

"Just get the job done," said Mr. Mindful.

Sparks flew from the metal box. "Security disabled," said one of the men.

Another man took a pair of lock cutters to the door. They opened the doors. Inside was a table with a stack of gold bars on it. "Load it up," said Mr. Mindful.

"Freeze," ordered Lenny. He and a dozen officers came out of the darkness toward them.

Roger raised his hands in fright, but another man charged at an officer. The officer grabbed the man and swung him to the ground.

Another man darted by Detective Turner. An officer stuck out a foot and tripped him. The man fell to the ground and the officers grabbed him and held him down as he cuffed him.

Mr. Mindful looked around. He grabbed the nearest one of his men and threw him against the nearest officer. He then ran off.

"Hey, stop him," cried an officer.

Mr. Mindful ran around a corner and then down the length of a building. He darted into an alley and came up to Maria.

"You," cried Mr. Mindful. "Maria isn't it? Who are you?"

"You know my name," said Maria.

"I meant who are you really?" demanded Mr. Mindful. "Why are you working with the detective? What do you do for him?"

Maria kicked out at him. He dodged the blow. Maria threw a punch, which he blocked, but she grabbed the arm he had used to block her and flipped him onto the ground. She tried to stomp him, but he grabbed her foot.

Mr. Mindful pushed her away. He jumped up swinging. She grabbed him and shoved him against the wall of the nearby building. "You stay away from my family," she said.

Lenny came up to them. "I got him," he said. He grabbed him and shoved him against the building face-first. He then cuffed him. Lenny looked at Maria. "Go," he said.

Minutes later, Lenny met Maria behind a nearby tree. "They got everybody?" asked Maria.

"Yeah, the whole crew's been rolled up."

"Do you guys know who this guy is?"

"He didn't tell us last time, and he isn't telling us now."

"I don't understand why he doesn't tell anyone about me," Maria said.

"Who knows?" asked Lenny. "I don't think he's all there." He looked around. "Why did you come here?"

"I wanted to look him in the eyes and get him to keep away from my mom."

"Let me finish up here and then I'll take you home," Lenny said.

"Okay," said Maria.

"Thanks for your help."

". . . and he said that the gold would be safer than cash and he had a friend who could handle it," Stu said. He was giving an officer his statement.

"How are things going?" asked Lenny.

"We're wrapping it up," Detective Turner replied.

"Good, because I'm going home," said Lenny. "Why don't you handle things here?"

"Sure," said Detective Turner. He went over to the squad car where Mr. Mindful was being held.

Lenny drove over to the tree. Maria went up to him. "Let's go," he said. They got into his car and they drove off.

BOOK 7

A Dangerous Hobby

Chapter 1

Lou Duffy sat at his desk and looked at the cell phone in his hand. *I've got to do this,* he thought. He dialed a number.

"Hello?" said a voice on the other end.

"Remember that loan I made to you?" asked Lou. "Well, it's time for payback. I want to know where Bill Manning is right now."

There was silence on the line. "He's at the Happy Mug," the man answered. "Don't call here again."

After looking up the location of the club, Lou went down there. He scanned the crowd and recognized Bill from his picture.

He went up to him. "Bill Manning?"

Bill looked up from his drink. "Who wants to know? "

"The man who's going to make you rich," answered Lou. "I've got big plans for Paway."

The next morning, Maria woke up and got ready for school. After she got dressed, she did a number of push-ups and then some karate exercises. She then headed downstairs, where Lois was at the table.

"Hey there, Snugglebear," Lois said. "Sleep well?"

"Yeah, thanks," answered Maria. She sat down for breakfast.

A few minutes later, Maria was darting to the front door. "See you, Mom."

Maria soon arrived at school. She went inside and down a hall. People were talking. "Cindy's party was really something," someone said.

Party? Maria wondered. She saw Cindy and went up to her. "You had a party?" she asked.

"Yeah," answered Cindy.

"Why didn't I hear about it?"

"I'm sorry, but we haven't been as close as we used to be," said Cindy. "I hope I didn't hurt your feelings."

"No, it's fine," said Maria. "I was just curious, that's all." She went off to class.

"Why should I help you?" asked Bill.

"Because you can become filthy rich," answered Lou.

"You're crazy."

"It's the perfect time. The Griffin's gone and the game's wide open."

"Why me?" asked Bill.

"I need someone who knows the players, who knows how things work," answered Lou.

Which means you don't, thought Bill. "No, thanks," he said. He turned and started to walk away.

"Wait," said Lou. He darted in front of Bill. "Don't you want to move up in the world? Be in some nicer clubs than the Happy Mug? Be a big man who's on top of it all, with everything in his pocket?"

Bill listened to him. He thought about it for a moment. *What can I lose?* he wondered. "Okay." They shook hands.

A few hours later, Lou was back home. He called Bill. "Have you assembled the gang?" he asked.

"Yeah, I've got the best guys," Bill answered.

"And they don't know who I am?"

What do you think? wondered Bill. "I didn't tell them."

"The guy's going to be out of the house tonight and you've got the code for the security system," said Lou. "You know what to do."

"Yeah," said Bill. "By the way, how did you get it?"

I heard my dad tell him that it's a bad idea to use one's birth date, but he said there was no way for anyone to know, thought Lou. "I have a source."

"Well, it shouldn't take too long," said Bill. "About that art stuff, we're going to need a buyer if we're going to turn it into cash."

"I have a buyer," said Lou. *He's a disgruntled employee at my mom's favorite art gallery who knows someone who wants to buy it from him.*

"We're going to have to put some of the money we get from this job away for future costs if you seriously want to be a major player," Bill said. "You've got to spend money to make money. Paying the guys, equipment, and stuff."

"Sure," said Lou.

In the computer lab, Maria sat at a table having lunch. *Both Mom and Cindy think I'm distant,* she thought. *It's not my fault. I've been busy. Every day it seems like there's some new guy running around committing crimes, and I get a vision. It's always hectic. Will it slow down? I need a break. I should just do something calm and peaceful. If I get a vision, I'll just call Lenny. What should I do? Should I go to the movies, the mall, or maybe the new rec center? I should probably just buy a book. Just have a good read. No visions, crimes, criminal masterminds, moms, parties, or dads waking up from comas. I hear that the new Treachery in the Night book is coming out. I should get that and then spend the rest of the day reading it.* The bell rang and she left.

The next afternoon, Maria was walking home. She had stopped at the bookstore and was carrying a bag. *Only a few copies left,* she thought. *Boy, do these books go fast.*

Maria entered her house and was about to go up to her room when Lois came into the living room. "Maria, could I see you in the kitchen, please?"

Maria followed her into the kitchen and sat down at the table. She was alarmed. *Does she know about what I do with Lenny?* she wondered. Lois sat down at the table as well.

"What is it, Mom?" asked Maria.

"Ever since your father woke up, he's been in physical therapy," said Lois. "The reason I've never taken you to see him is because the therapy has been hard and he never wanted you to see him in the condition he was in, but now he's gotten better. He's gaining weight, among other things, and they say he's reaching the next level of his progress. I was thinking that tomorrow you and I could go see him."

Oh, thought Maria. "Sure, Mom," she said. "I would love to."

Lois smiled. "That's good," she said. "He'd love that too."

They hugged and Maria went up to her room. *So much for reading,* she thought. *What am I going to say or do?*

Lenny was typing at his computer when Lieutenant Steve Finn came over to him. "Lenny, I need to speak with you," he said.

"Yes, sir?"

"It's nothing serious," said Finn. "I just wanted to say you've been doing a great job with all the arrests you've been making recently."

"Thank you, sir."

"I also wanted to know if you would like to go fishing with me and George this weekend."

I can't say no, thought Lenny. *That might wreck my career.* "Sure," he said.

"That's great. I'll pick you up."

As Lenny watched him walk off, he sighed. His cell phone rang. "Hello?"

"It's me," said Maria.

"What's wrong?"

"It's not like I had a vision. It's just that something's come up. Do you have a minute?"

"Sure," answered Lenny. "What is it?"

"As you know, my dad's awake," Maria said. "Mom wants to take me to see him."

"And you don't want to go?"

"It's not like that. It's just that this is big and it's yet another thing coming at me. I just wish I could take a break."

I know how you feel, thought Lenny. "Well, maybe you can tell your mom that you want to go another time."

"But I have to go," Maria said. "I said yes."

I know how that feels too, Lenny thought. "This may not sound like great advice, but maybe you should just go and get it over with. It probably won't be that bad once you do it."

"Yeah," said Maria. She did not sound convinced.

"Tell you what, you tell me the time you're meeting him and call me after," Lenny said. "I want to know the time so I can clear my schedule. We can talk about whatever you need to."

"Thanks."

"You're welcome."

Meanwhile, Lou and Bill were talking over the phone again. "Combine what you say we can get for the art and all the stuff we got from the house and we made nearly two hundred thousand from the job," said Bill. "We can use a big part of it to do the bank job. I've got a guy who planned it for the Griffin but never got to use it."

"Good," said Lou. "I approve." Bill rolled his eyes.

"Once we're done with that, we can expand into other areas," Bill said. "I know a guy who's into smuggling. He can help us get our reach a lot farther than Paway."

"My reach, Bill," said Lou. "It's my reach and my money. You've been a great help, but always remember that or the consequences could be dire."

Bill hung up. *Yeah, yeah,* he thought. *Airbag.* He left the room to talk to one of the guys.

Meanwhile, Lou was in his family's study. A voice called from outside the door.

"Lou," said Mindy Burk, Lou's mother. "Come out and say hi to our friends. It's your party too."

"Coming, Mom," said Lou. *Tonight I might be just another rich kid, but soon I'll be the crime lord of Paway.*

The next day, Maria and Lois stood outside the Peaceful Field Rehabilitation Facility. They were led to Jeff's room. *All right, here we go,* thought Maria. They went in.

Chapter 2

Maria looked at the man in the bed. *Oh my . . . ,* she thought. A wave of emotions crashed through her.

Jeff lay in the bed. His skin was very pale, but most of the color of his brown hair was still there. "Hi, kiddo," he said. His voice was low.

"Dad," said Maria. "How are you?"

"Better now," answered Jeff. Maria went over and hugged him. *Oh, Daddy,* she thought. Memories of the past raced through her mind.

"How's your therapy coming?" asked Lois.

"It's coming along," Jeff said. "I can walk for short bits, but I tire easily and I can't talk loudly yet. The doctors say it'll get better."

"It will," said Lois.

"I'm sure too," said Jeff.

Maria let him go. "How are you feeling?" she asked.

"At first a little out there but now I'm fine," Jeff answered. He looked at Maria. "How are you doing?"

"Fine," answered Maria. She felt anxious. *I'm just having visions of the future and fighting crime, that's all,* she thought. "I'm getting a B average in school. I also just completed a big project. Not much to talk about."

Jeff looked at Lois. "How are things at the office?" he asked.

"The same as always," she answered. "It's actually quite boring."

"The same as around here," said Jeff. "The same thing day after day. At least you're not eating hospital food." He touched his throat.

"Honey, are you all right?" Lois asked.

"My throat's just a little sore that's all," Jeff answered. "How's Carl?"

"I haven't talked with him in a while," said Lois. "We've both been busy."

Lois looked out a window. "Anyway, what have the doctors been saying about your progress?" *Should I have asked that with Maria here?*

"They say it's been going well," answered Jeff. "I could be getting out of here in a couple of weeks."

Different emotions surged in Maria. "That's good," said Lois.

A nurse came into the room. "I'm sorry but I'm afraid you're going to have to leave now," she said. "He needs his rest."

"Sure," said Lois. She turned to Jeff. "I love you, sweetie," she said.

"Love you, Dad," said Maria.

"Love you too, guys," said Jeff.

Maria and Lois went out to their car. *I wish Dad could come home with us now,* Maria thought.

Maria got home and went up to her room. She got her cell phone and dialed Lenny's number.

"Hello?"

"It's me," said Maria.

"How did it go?"

Maria was silent for a moment. "It went better than I thought. I looked at him and . . . memories came back. It was different from last time and I don't know why, but everything's much better now." She lay on her bed smiling.

"Good to hear that," said Lenny.

"It's just that he's my dad," said Maria. "I don't know why I was so worried about meeting him before."

"Well, with everything that's been happening it's only natural for you to be overwhelmed."

"I just looked at him and wanted to be with him. Everything I'd been feeling is just gone."

"That's great," Lenny said. "With everything you've been going through it's good that you have something positive going on."

"Yeah," said Maria. "I just wanted you to know how it went."

"I'm glad you called. This could be the start of things looking up for you."

"I hope so."

Maria lay on the bed for several minutes. She then got up and went over to her computer. She did an Internet search on people who wake up from comas. A series of articles came up, including a review of a book by a man who had woken up from a coma.

There are two scans used to gauge consciousness during a coma, she read. *The Glasgow coma scale and the Ranchos Los Amigos scale.*

Dad's already up, thought Maria. She went to another article. *Comas rarely last more than two to five weeks,* she read. *Terry Wallis and Jan Grzebski both woke up after nineteen years. The most common cause of death during a coma is infection.*

Maria shuddered and went back to her bed. *Thank God Dad's awake.*

Meanwhile, in the skylight of a bank a motorized saw cut through the glass. It cut a rectangular shape, and then two men lifted the shape out of the window and put it down on the roof. "Are you sure the security's off?" asked one of the men.

"Yeah, let's go," answered the other man, sounding annoyed.

Ropes descended into the darkened room. Four men slid down along them to the floor. They went to a wall before them and strapped a box to it.

They went over to the other side of the room and one of the men pushed a button on a remote.

The box exploded, and the men covered their faces as plaster flew everywhere.

In a few seconds the dust settled and the men went over to the hole the bomb had made. They went through it and entered a vault. On tables surrounding them were stacks of money. They filled their bags with the money and left. They went back to the ropes and climbed out of the bank, pulling the ropes up after them.

"It went as planned," said Bill an hour later.

"Good, how much money?" Lou asked.

"About two million dollars."

"Good—call the guy."

"Already have," said Bill. "He'll meet us Thursday."

"I won't be meeting him," Lou said. "You go. I can't have my face known by anybody but you."

Maybe that's not such a bad idea, thought Bill.

The next day, Maria entered her school. She saw a girl she knew named Kate. She went up to her. "Hey," Maria said. "You want to do something after school?"

"I'm afraid I can't," said Kate. "I've got plans."

"Okay," Maria said. She went on to class.

Later, in the computer lab, Maria sat down at a table and ate lunch. *With everything that's been happening it's been a while since I talked to anyone here at school.*

Meanwhile, Lou was sitting at a table having lunch with his parents. "Did you hear what happened to Fred?" asked Mr. Burk.

"Yes, it's terrible," Mrs. Burk answered. "First the Johnsons' house gets robbed and now Fred's bank. It's not safe in this city anymore."

"How did they know where the money was?" Lou asked. "Didn't you guys tell me Fred said he transferred the money to a new site and almost no one knew where it was?"

"I don't know," Mr. Burk replied. "I guess that's for the police to figure out."

"It's terrible," said Mrs. Burk.

"Yeah, it's terrible," said Lou. He suppressed a snicker.

A few days later, Bill met with a man. "Are you Sloan?" he asked.

"I am," answered Sloan.

"Word on the street is that you're the guy to go to when you need something moved," said Bill.

Sloan looked around. "Maybe."

Bill took out a stack of bills. "I have money. There's someone who's willing to pay you good money to help us move stuff out of the city on a regular basis."

"Who?"

"Doesn't matter," Bill said. He held up the money to Sloan's face. After a moment Sloan took the money.

A man walked by a newspaper stand and looked at the collection of papers and magazines. He spotted one paper. *This looks good, but I don't have the money,* he thought. He looked around and then slid the paper under his jacket.

"Hey," called a voice. The man turned around and saw that it was a police officer.

The man ran and the officer chased after him. A few blocks away he caught up to him and grabbed him. He shoved him down to the ground. "You're under arrest," the officer said.

Chapter 3

The man who stole from the newsstand sat in an interrogation room in the police station. Two detectives stood in front of him. "They say you claim to have info on a job that went down," said one of the detectives.

"Yeah, the bank that got robbed," said the man.

"Well, Mel, we've been talking with some people and they say that you're not exactly big time," said the detective. "That's a little over your head, isn't it?"

"Well, I've changed, moved up in the world," said Mel. "A guy recruited me for the job. I've never done anything like that before. We went in through the ceiling and blew a hole in a wall to get into the vault.

"What kind of explosive did you use?" asked the other detective.

"I don't know," answered Mel. "I wasn't the one who blew it. I just went in, got some of the money, and then got out." He looked at the two detectives nervously. "Look, I know about a robbery that's going to happen. Cut me a deal and I'll tell you."

"If you just finished a job, then why did you swipe that paper?" asked the first detective.

"I lost all the money I'd made," answered Mel. He paused before speaking again. "At the track." The two men left the room.

"Lenny, Detective Turner, get in here," said Lieutenant Finn. They got up from behind their desks and went into his office.

"A couple of detectives just got a lead on the recent bank robbery," Finn said. "I'm handing it over to you. They got a statement from some guy who claimed to be a part of it. Here's the statement." He handed Lenny a file.

"Are you sure that's necessary?" asked Lenny. "I'm sure these guys are good detectives."

"Well, with your track record for bank robberies I thought you might be able to handle this," Finn answered. "I'll call the D.A. and let him know."

"A lot of money involved?" asked Detective Turner.

"That and it belonged to a lot of wealthy people," Finn replied. "Apparently there's a banker named Fredric Hayer who had a circle of well-to-do clients. He moved all their funds to another place, which these guys robbed. Apparently only a few people knew where the money was."

Lenny was looking through the file. "So, we're thinking that it was an inside job?" he asked.

"Looks like," Finn said. "Why don't you start there?"

"On it," said Lenny. He and his partner left.

Meanwhile, Lou and Bill were in an empty warehouse. "I'm thinking that we can use this place for planning jobs and other things," Bill said. "It's more secure than the last place, and it'll be where we take the men before and after the jobs. It used to belong to the Griffin. I made a deal with some guy who used to work for him."

Bill went over to a table next to a stack of boxes. "I have another place for storing the loot," he said. "I'll keep that place a secret so no one gets greedy."

Lou looked around. *All I'm getting is scraps from the Griffin. Not for long.* "It'll do for a start," he said. "Get the place ready. We're going into business."

The next day, Maria went up to Kate. "Hi," she said. "You want to do something tomorrow?" Kate was silent, as if she were thinking about it. "It'll be fun," Maria said.

"Okay," answered Kate. They then went off to their classes.

Meanwhile, Mel entered an abandoned warehouse, where a group of men was hanging around. "Where have you been?" asked one of them.

"I got caught up in some business, Al," answered Mel.

"Just remember that this is your business," said Bill. He turned to the rest of the men. "All right, listen up. Our next spot is the garment factory at one forty-eight Elm Street. They're transporting a lump of cash for their employees' yearly bonus. I know a guy who can help turn those checks into cash."

"Did your friend help with the last job?" asked Mel. His nervousness was showing as Bill eyed him.

"That's none of your business," Bill said.

Take it easy, thought Lenny. He and Detective Turner listened in on the other end of Mel's wire in a van parked a few blocks away.

"The details we'll go over the next time we meet," said Bill. "You know the time."

The men started to leave. Mel went up to Bill. "Hey, Bill, I was thinking of bringing a guy into the group," he said.

"That's not your call to make," said Bill.

"Well, he's really good."

"Good?"

"Yeah, he's very good at breaking into places. Apparently he's done some stuff out West, but I don't know where."

Don't push too hard, Lenny thought.

Bill thought for a moment. "Okay, bring him in," he said. "I'll see what he can do."

Both Lenny and Mel sighed.

The next morning, Maria went downstairs. "Honey, how are you doing?" Lois asked.

"Fine," answered Maria. She sat down for breakfast.

"It's just that seeing your father must be a lot for you," said Lois.

"I'm fine," said Maria. She was telling the truth.

A short time later, Lenny and Mel sat down before Bill at Bee Bee's Diner. "So you're a talented guy," said Bill.

"I have a few tricks," said Lenny.

"What's your name?" Bill asked.

"Don Sharp," Mel answered. Lenny shot him a look.

"I don't think I've heard of you," Bill said.

"I just got into town," Lenny said.

"Where are you from?"

"Why do you want to know?"

"I want to check out your references."

"What is this, an internship at a law firm?"

"I want to know who you are," said Bill. "Either you tell me or you don't work for me."

Lenny appeared to think for a moment. "Okay, there's this guy in Rueport, Joe Shuein." He gave him a phone number.

"I'll check this out and then call you," said Bill. He looked him over and then left.

The next day, a prepaid telephone rang. "Hello?" asked Lenny.

"It's me," said Bill. "You got the job."

"Good. When do I start?"

"Today at three thirty," answered Bill. He gave him the address of the warehouse.

Later, Maria was sitting in a classroom. The students were doing their assignments. Maria tried to concentrate but was having trouble doing so. She felt anticipation for the movie she was planning to see.

The bell rang and the students got up and left.

As Maria left the building, she saw Kate nearby. She began to go up to her.

Lenny went up to a man. "So, Bill, what do I do?" he asked.

"Now that you've checked out, we're going to give you a job to start with," Bill answered. *Another man came up to Lenny and handed him a small stack of papers. "Here's what you're going to do," said Bill. "First . . ."*

"Hey," cried a new voice. Yet another man came up to them. "He's not who he says he is. He's Detective Hipar—police!"

Two men charged out from nowhere at Lenny. 129 Tucker Lane, December 17, 3:48 p.m.

Oh no, thought Maria.

She ran up to Kate. "I'm afraid we're going to have to do this another time," she said. "Something's happened."

"Okay," said Kate. Maria ran off.

A short time later, Lenny was standing in front of Bill with a few men surrounding them. "So, Bill, what do I do?" he asked.

"Now that you checked out, we're going to give you a job to start out," Bill answered. Another man came up to Lenny and handed him a small stack of papers. "Here's what you're going to do," said Bill. "First . . ."

"Hey," cried a new voice. Yet another man came up to them.

He began to say something when Maria charged into the room. She side-kicked his legs out from beneath him. *Maria?* wondered Lenny.

Maria looked at him. "Go," she cried. Bill and the other men looked at Lenny. He darted toward the door, as did Maria.

"Stop them," ordered Bill. The men took off after them.

A man grabbed Lenny. He spun around and put the man's hand in a wristlock. The man cringed in pain and Lenny let him go before darting again toward the door.

The men stood there holding his wrist. Two men came up behind him, and one pushed him aside as they chased after Maria and Lenny.

The fleeing two had almost reached the door when a man jumped out at Maria from her left. She grabbed him and put him in a wristlock, and then swung him at a wall. He was momentarily stunned but recovered and came at her again. She kicked him in the shin, and as he clutched his leg, she followed Lenny as he went for the door.

They went through the door followed by the two in pursuit. Maria and Lenny went around an alley. Lenny stopped and waited by the corner. As one of the men came around, he sent out a clothesline. The man went down.

He looked at Maria as she watched. "Go on," he said.

"Not without you," she said.

The other man came into the alley. Lenny grabbed the lid off a garbage can and swung it. The man went down. Maria and Lenny took off.

After gaining a great deal of distance they stopped. "What happened?" asked Lenny. "Why were you there?"

"I had a vision that they found out that you were a police detective and they attacked you," answered Maria.

"Thanks, but I'm afraid you're going to have to find your own way home," said Lenny. "I hate to do this to you, but there are other detectives nearby. They're waiting for me, and they would notice if I went off without them to take you back."

"It's okay," Maria said. "See you." She ran off.

Lenny returned to the van where Detective Turner and the others were waiting. "What happened?" Turner asked.

"I got made," answered Lenny. "Apparently one of the guys knew me."

Lenny climbed into the van. "Who was the female voice?" asked Turner.

"I don't know," Lenny answered. "Just some woman who wandered onto the scene."

"Is she all right?" asked one of the other detectives.

"She ran off so I wouldn't be able to tell you," Lenny said.

"Well, the operation's blown," said another one of the detectives. "We'll get Mel into protective custody."

"There's got to be something more we can do," Lenny said.

"We had two officers go in for 'calls of a disturbance' after the shouting, and the place is empty," the detective said. "We'll figure out our next move back at the station." They drove off. *I hope Maria's okay,* thought Lenny.

"We've been found out," Bill said into his phone. He was in the place where he planned to store their loot.

"What do you mean, found out?" demanded Lou.

"I was getting a new guy, but he was an undercover detective," Bill said.

"This is on you," Lou said. "Why should my business suffer for your carelessness?"

"Hey, don't put this on me. Stuff like this happens!"

"What are we going to do?"

"It's not 'we' out there," said Bill. "It's usually me."

"What?"

"Nothing. You stay where you are. I'll handle this."

That little punk, thought Lou. *Without my start-up money he would be just another street thug.*

Lou gripped his cell phone. He started to throw it but stopped. He thought about Bill the thug who probably smashed anything he got his hands on. He then tossed it onto the pillow on his bed and sighed angrily.

Maria came home. "Hi, sweetie," said Lois. "How was the movie?"

"Something came up," Maria said. She went upstairs.

Maria entered her room and took out the cell phone.

"It's me," Maria said when Lenny answered

"Are you all right?" asked Lenny.

"Yeah, I got home all right."

"I'm sorry to do that to you, but with those other detectives there I couldn't bring you home."

"It's all right."

"Thanks for the save, but I hope you'll call in the future if you get any more visions."

"I tried but your phone was off."

Oh, thought Lenny.

Meanwhile, Bill dialed a phone number. "What?" asked the voice on the other end.

"We're pulling one last job," Bill said. "We need money to get out of town."

"What about the boss?" asked the voice.

"He's unreliable," Bill said. "Get everyone together, because we're hitting the other bank."

The next morning, Maria woke up.

A black van pulled up to a building. The van had a red flower in a blue circle on its side. Beneath the symbol was written "Algous Flowers."

A group of masked men got out. They went into the bank.

"Nobody move," cried one of the men. "This is a robbery!" Paway First Bank, December 18, 12:14 p.m.

That's the bank where I had my first vision about a crime, thought Maria.

She reached into her book bag and got the cell phone. She then called Lenny.

A few hours later, a black van pulled up in front of Paway First Bank. A group of masked men got out and went into the building.

"Nobody . . . , " began one of the men. He stopped when he saw that the place was empty. *What . . . ,* he thought.

"Freeze," ordered Lenny. About a dozen officers came out from behind pillars and desks. "Nobody move."

The man who shouted—Bill—looked around. *Oh no,* he thought.

Two officers came at him. He shoved the nearest one. The officer went back, and as he tried to regain his balance, Bill grabbed him and swung him at the other officer. They collided and went down to the floor. Bill made a break for it.

Several other men tried to follow him, but officers came upon them. One officer tackled a man and they went down to the floor.

Another man looked at an officer coming at him and threw out a type of kick he had seen in an action movie. The officer easily dodged it and grabbed the leg. The officer pulled and the man became off balance and fell to the floor.

The two remaining men looked around at their partners being cuffed. They turned around and tried to run deeper into the bank but came up against a wall of officers. One of the men held up his fists as he had seen a martial artist do on TV, but the man next to him held up his hands in surrender. The man looked at his partner and then put up his hands too. Two officers went up to them and cuffed them.

Lenny looked around at the men being unmasked and read them their rights. "Where's the guy who got out of the bank?" he asked into his radio.

"He gave us the slip," answered one of the officers posted outside. "He was last seen heading west on foot."

Lenny scowled.

Maria waited on her bed for news on how the trap worked. Her phone vibrated.

"Good news and bad news," said Lenny. "We stopped the robbery and got the gang, but apparently the guy directly under the boss got away."

Maria groaned. "What now?"

"Now we try to find another lead," answered Lenny. "Don't worry. The way these guys are talking we're sure to come up with something. We'll get these guys."

A short time later, Maria had a vision.

Two men were in a dark room. "Do you have it?" asked one of the men. He looked ragged.

"Yeah, I got it," answered the other man. He was cleaner and dressed more neatly than the other man. He tossed the first man an envelope.

The ragged man opened the envelope and counted the money inside. "We never see each other again," he said. 18 Pine Drive, December 18, 4:12 p.m.

Maria called Lenny. "I've got something," she said.

Two men were in a dark room. "Do you have it?" asked one of the men. He looked ragged.

"Yeah, I got it," answered the other man. He was cleaner and dressed more neatly than the other man. He tossed him an envelope.

The ragged man opened the envelope and counted the money inside. "We never see each other again," he said.

"Freeze," shouted Lenny. Officers swarmed in with him and grabbed and cuffed the two.

Lenny went up to one of the men. "Hey, I've seen you in the paper," he said. "You're Lou Burk. You're also under arrest for aiding a fugitive."

"It was all his idea," said Bill. "Getting the gang together, pulling the jobs, and everything. He wanted to play big-time crime boss and asked me how. I'll give you details if you cut me a deal."

"Why you," said Lou. He tried to go after him, but the officer who cuffed him held him back.

Lenny went up to him. "Why?" he asked. "Your dad owns a huge company and after he's gone, you'll get it and be worth millions."

Lou looked at him. "All that excitement," he said. "I thought it would be a good hobby." The officer read him his rights and took him away with Bill.

Lenny went out to his car. "Did you get them?" Maria asked. She came up to him.

"You shouldn't have come, but yeah, we got them," Lenny answered.

"Was that really Lou Burk?" asked Maria.

"Yeah."

"Another rich guy busted," said Maria.

"Thanks for your help," Lenny said. He looked at the scene that the officers had taped off. The two had met at an empty town house owned by one of the Burks' friends. "I couldn't have done it without you."

"It's nothing," said Maria. "We're partners."

Lenny looked over at Detective Turner, who was talking on his cell phone. "Come on, I'll drive you home," he said.

They got into his car and drove off.

BOOK 8

Attack of the Pack

Chapter 1

Maria went into the apartment building and went up to one of the doors. She knocked on it.

Lenny opened the door. "Whoa," said Maria.

"Do you like it?" Lenny asked. He ran a hand over his newly grown mustache.

"I leave you alone for a few days and this is what happens," asked Maria. She went inside the apartment.

"I though it might be good for a change." Lenny closed the door and went over to the counter and picked up a DVD.

Maria sat down. "You're sure this movie's good?" she asked.

"That's what Paul said," Lenny said. He went over to the TV and put it in.

Maria watched the TV screen as the opening credits rolled by and the main characters came into view.

There was a bearded man. He went into a convenience store followed by a group of men.

"Can I help you?" asked an old man behind the counter.

"Yeah," answered the bearded man. "Give us your money."

"What?" asked the old man.

The bearded man grabbed him. "Give us your money and you won't be hurt," he said. The two struggled.

"Joseph," cried an old woman over to them. The men continued to struggle and the bearded man shoved Joseph back. 120 Rollmore Avenue, Super Savings Store, December 20, 4:09 p.m.

"We've got trouble," said Maria.

Outside the Super Savings Store, the bearded man approached with the others. As they got near it, Lenny pulled up in his car and got out.

"Get out of our way," ordered the bearded man.

"Guys, I'm Detective Hipar with the Paway City Police," Lenny said. He waved around his badge. "I'm just here to make sure nothing illegal is going on."

"I said get out of our way," said the bearded man. He started to go toward him but stopped.

I hope you're making the call, Maria, thought Lenny.

A short distance away, Maria watched the scene from around a corner and dialed 911 on her cell phone. "Yeah, I'm at one twenty Rollmore Avenue and see a bunch of guys surrounding a man. They look very threatening."

Lenny stared down the bearded man. He looked at him and the others, memorizing details of their features.

"I don't know about this, Sam," said a man with an earring. "This is a cop."

"Doesn't matter," answered Sam. "We're getting what we came here for."

"What's that?" asked Lenny. Sam shot him a sharp look. "Now, take it easy," Lenny said. "This doesn't have to be anything. You just turn around and go back and it's just another day."

Sam shot a look at a man with spiked hair. "Grab him," he ordered.

"What?" asked the man.

The man with the earring grabbed Sam's shoulder. "Sam, we need to go," he said. Sam was silent for a moment.

Just then, a patrol car came on the scene and two officers got out.

A short time later, Maria and Lenny returned to the apartment. "Sorry the movie got blown," said Lenny.

"That's okay," said Maria. She looked at the cover of the box. "So, you had to let those guys go?"

"Yeah, there wasn't enough to hold them," answered Lenny. "It's not like we can enter your vision as evidence. I hope those guys will stay out of trouble."

"This just stinks," said Sam. He and the others entered an apartment. Sam went over to a couch and sat down, and the other men surrounded him.

"It's not too bad, boss," said the man with the earring. "At least we didn't get nailed by the cops."

"But we didn't get any money," said Sam. He picked up a candy dish from the coffee table and threw it against a wall. It hit with a loud thud but did not break.

"Boss, I don't want to lose the security deposit on this place," said a man in sunglasses.

"Be quiet," ordered Sam. The man with the earring went over to him as the man in sunglasses went over to the spot where the candy dish hit.

"We'll get the money, boss," said the man with the earring. "We just have to lie low and wait."

"Forget that," said Sam. "If we don't get it because we backed down, then we lose our respect on the streets." He got up and walked around. "This is only the beginning. This town is wide open, and we're going clean up, because everyone will pay if they know what's good for them."

A few hours later, Joseph was preparing to close the store. The phone rang and he answered it. "Yes?"

"Hi," said Sam. "You owe us money."

"What?" asked Joseph. "Who is this?"

"The guy who's going to come by tomorrow at three, so you'd better be ready," Sam said.

The next day, Lenny went over to his desk and sat down. He looked up and saw Lieutenant Finn coming up to him. "Sir, what is it?" Lenny asked.

"Oh, it's nothing," Finn answered. "It's just that yesterday with that incident there have been some concerns raised over you."

"Concerns, sir?" asked Lenny. "I just stopped a group of men who were acting suspiciously, and when I approached them, they became hostile."

"I know but they made a complaint," said Finn. "I want you to take it easy if you see them again. I would hate for you to have problems when you've shown such promise." He walked away.

What does he mean, "promise"? wondered Lenny. He started to look at the forms that had been placed on his desk. He spotted Detective Turner, at his desk talking on his cell phone.

A few minutes later, Turner finished his call and went over to Lenny, who was filling out a form. "Who were you talking to?" asked Lenny.

"Oh, no one," Turner answered. "Just trying to get something from records for a case."

"Oh," said Lenny.

"Hey, I heard you had a run-in yesterday," Turner said. "You ended up getting saved by some anonymous caller. I also heard they traced the call to a prepaid cell."

"Well, all I know is that I saw some suspicious characters and decided to talk to them and then things almost got rough," said Lenny. "The caller was probably some passerby."

"Yeah," the detective said. "Well, see you later. There's something I've got to do." He returned to his desk to get his coat and then left.

Sometime later, Maria was in art class. She was cutting construction paper.

Sam and the others went into a store. Sam shoved some tools off a shelf. "Hey," said a guy from behind a counter. He came running up toward them. "What do you think you're doing?"

"Getting the money you owe me," answered Sam, "like I told you over the phone. Give it to me now or we'll bring this whole place down."

Steve picked up a can of motor oil and threw it at a glass case. It made a low crash. "Give me my money now." Ralph's Hardware Store, 21 Timber Lane, December 19, 2:14 p.m.

Maria raised her hand. "Yes, Maria?" asked Mrs. Hardash.

"May I be excused to go to the bathroom?"

"Yes, you may," answered Mrs. Hardash. Maria got up and left the classroom. She hurried to the restroom.

Maria went into a stall and got out her cell phone. She turned it on and dialed Lenny.

"Lenny, it's me," she said when he answered. She told him what she had seen.

"Twenty-one Timber Lane," Lenny repeated. He wrote down the address. *The lieutenant said to take it easy around these guys, but it sounds like they are going to cause some real trouble.* "Don't worry, Maria," said Lenny. "I'll handle it."

"Be careful."

"Don't worry, I will."

"I don't know about this," said Detective Turner as he and Lenny sat in Lenny's car. They were parked outside Ralph's Hardware Store.

"I got a tip that they plan to rough this place up," said Lenny. "If I don't do anything, someone could get hurt."

"It's not like I'm saying let people get hurt. It's just that you have to step carefully," said Detective Turner.

"I will," said Lenny. He got out of the car, followed by Detective Turner. "Just cover my back, okay?"

"I will," Turner answered.

Suddenly the gang appeared around the corner. Detective Turner felt nervous as he watched Lenny go up to them.

The man pointed at Lenny as he approached. "It's that guy," he said. "The cop."

"Gentlemen," Lenny said.

"What are you doing here?" asked Sam.

"Just making sure everybody's acting friendly."

Sam got angry and balled up his fists. He looked ready to hit Lenny.

"Hey," cried Detective Turner. He went up to them.

"Let's go, Sam," said the man with the earring. He and the others looked at the detectives warily, though Steve seemed unmoved.

Lenny and his partner were tensed up, ready to go on the defensive.

"Sam, let's get out of here," said the man with the earring. This time his tone was more forceful.

Sam slowly backed away from the detectives, and the rest of the gang followed. Detective Turner sighed in relief.

"I thought I told you to stay away from them," said Lieutenant Finn.

"I know, sir, but I got a tip that they were going to try something at the hardware store," said Lenny. "It sounded like they were really going to mess the place up."

"They filed another complaint," said Finn. "Now we're going to have to take this seriously."

"But, sir, I didn't do anything to them," Lenny said.

"They say you've been following them around, harassing them." Lenny kept himself from scowling. "I know you wouldn't want to stand by and let crimes happen, but next time give the tip to another detective," Finn said.

Finn went back to his office and Lenny went back to his desk. Turner came up to him. "He really told you, didn't he?" he said.

"No, but he did say this was getting serious," Lenny said.

Turner put a stack of files on the desk. "Well, I got something," he said. "The boys upstairs were so busy circling wagons that no one bothered to check your new friends, who all have records."

Lenny went through the files and saw that one contained a picture of the whole group. "I talked to Gang Intelligence and they saw that these guys form a charming social group known as the Pack," said Detective Turner.

Turner held up the file with Sam's picture paper-clipped to it. "Sam Foss, aka 'the Lion.' Apparently they all have nicknames based on animals. He's the supposed brains of the group. He has a temper, and he once took a swing at an officer."

The detective then pointed to the file with the picture of the man with an earring on it. "Joe 'the Tiger' Paris. Supposedly the second in command. One CI, or as the Das called them; Confidential Informant, said that he sometimes keeps Sam cool—sometimes."

Turner pointed at the file with the picture of the man with spiked hair. "Carl 'the Jaguar' Cramer. Rumored to have started shoplifting at twelve. Once they searched him and found five hundred dollars in jewelry and watches on him."

He then pointed at the picture of someone Lenny thought looked like the man in sunglasses. "Tony 'the Puma' Steward. Rumored to be an expert forger, but he's never been caught making fake anything. The only charges he was collared on were burglary. He also apparently lets the gang use his home as their headquarters. In fact, that was where Sam took that swing at an officer."

Detective Turner then pointed to a muscular man Lenny had seen with the group. "Tom Roberts, also known as 'the Panther.' The group's strongman. Arrested for assault and started lifting weights in prison, where, they say, he worked up to six hundred pounds. This was juvenile detention."

Lenny picked up the top folder. "These guys are all small time, but be careful," Turner said.

"I will," Lenny said. He began to look through the file.

The next day, Maria was in her room lying on her stomach, trying to read a book. "Maria, there's someone on the phone for you," Lois called up the stairs.

Lenny? Maria wondered. She went downstairs.

As she entered the kitchen, Lois was cradling the phone and had an unusual look on her face. "Maria, it's your father. They say he's well enough to talk on the phone."

Dad, Maria thought. Excitement filled her as she took the phone. "Dad?"

"Yes, it's me, sweetie," said Jeff. "How are you doing?"

"Great," answered Maria. "How are you doing? How's your therapy going?"

"It's going well. The doctors say I'm making good progress. How's school? Are you keeping those grades up?"

"I got a ninety-seven on my last chem test."

"Great," said Jeff. "Anything else interesting going on?"

Maria was silent for a moment. "Not really."

"Well, anyway, I love you," said Jeff.

"I love you too, Dad."

"Can I talk to your mother now?"

"Sure," answered Maria, and she handed the phone to Lois. Maria walked away feeling happy. *He sounds better.*

"Are you sure?" Lois said into the phone after Maria left the room.

That night, Sam and the rest of the Pack gathered around Tony's apartment. "What are we going to do?" Tony asked.

"I have a plan," said Sam.

"What is it?"

"You'll find out when I'm ready." Sam sat back in his chair looking angry.

"It'll be fine," said Joe.

"If it hadn't been for that cop, we could've shook down that place for who knows how much money," said Sam. "Just a few days ago I saw a guy buy two hundred pounds of lumber from that place." The Pack listened to Sam make angry mutterings.

Sam threw the TV remote at the wall and Tony cringed. "We're going to do something about that cop. I've got plans. We're going to own this town."

The next day, Maria went to school. She entered the building and went to her first class.

As she waited for class to begin, she saw a girl that she knew and remembered spending time with her a year ago before she had visions. She remembered even further back to how different things were before her father's accident . *That girl hasn't talked to me in months,* Maria thought. She felt sad and looked up at the wall clock. *Maybe Lenny will want to do something today.* The bell rang and class began.

After school, Maria was on her way home when Lenny's car pulled up next to her. "Lenny," she said. She got in. "Something wrong?"

"No, I just got some new facts about the gang we keep meeting up with and I thought I'd share them with you in person," answered Lenny. He told her about the Pack.

"So they're a street gang," said Maria. "I thought they were just a group of guys who got together."

"Well, we've taken on organized crime," Lenny said. "Ideally, this won't be any harder."

"I hope not."

"Don't worry. These guys will go down like all the others."

They came within a block of her home and Lenny dropped her off before turning around.

Lenny parked a block from Tony's apartment. *Maybe they'll do something now that they're at their place.*

Lenny looked at Sam's file, which he was holding. *It shouldn't take too long with a hothead like that.*

Inside, Sam sat on a chair surrounded by the other members of the Pack. He looked at Tony. "Did you do it?" he asked.

"Yeah, it's done," answered Tony. "The kid's work has been sent in."

"Good," said Sam.

"Though why are you having me do some kid's homework?" Tony asked.

The smile on Sam's face faded. "Because I told you to, that's why."

"Yeah, sure, boss."

After a few tense moments Sam looked up at the ceiling and sighed. *The first part's complete.* He sat up and looked around at the others. "It's going to take a few days, but we're going to pull a big score. Once we do that, we're on our way to bigger and better things."

"What's the big score?" asked Carl.

"You'll know that when you need to," Sam replied.

"Yeah, right, boss," Carl said.

"Don't worry," said Joe. "It'll work without a hitch. It's a solid plan."

Carl and Tony looked at each other but said nothing. Joe was looking at Sam nervously as he looked around at them all. *I'm going to be the new crime lord of Paway and then I'm going to spread out even farther,* Sam thought. *I'm going to control everything.*

Just then Tom came into the room. "Did you get the stuff?" Joe asked.

Tom held up a grocery bag. "Yeah, it's here. I got everything, but I think we have a problem. There's a car parked outside, and I think whoever's in it is watching us."

"What?" demanded Sam. He got up and went toward the door. *Nothing's getting in the way of my plan,* he thought.

"Boss, it could be nothing," said Joe.

"I'm going outside and you're coming with me," said Sam. "Nothing is getting in the way of my payday."

Lenny was sitting in his car reading Sam's file. When he looked up, he saw the Pack coming toward him. *Uh oh,* he thought.

Lenny started the car and quickly fumbled with the drive. He stepped on the gas and the car sped away backward. *I have it in reverse,* he thought. He came to a corner and did a sharp turn, righting himself. He sped away as the Pack ran down the street.

"What was that?" asked Carl.

Trouble, thought Joe. "Nothing," sneered Sam. "It was a nothing." He went back into the house and the rest of them followed.

Lenny arrived at his apartment and threw himself onto his couch. He sat in the darkness. *Well, that was something,* he thought. *So much for being careful.*

After a moment he got out his cell phone and called Maria.

"Hello?"

"Hey, I thought tomorrow we would take another shot at seeing that movie," said Lenny.

"Sounds good," said Maria.

"I'll pick you up."

The next day, the bell rang and Maria and her fellow students left the school building. Maria walked quickly down the sidewalk.

About a block away, Lenny's car pulled up. "Hey," he said.

"Hey," Maria said. She got in the car.

They drove off. As they went, Lenny had an idea. *Maybe I should check out the area and see if they're up to anything,* he thought. He made a left.

"Where are we going?" asked Maria.

"I'm going by the one guy's house to see if they're there."

Soon they were a block from the apartment. Suddenly, as they stopped at an intersection a car sped past them and Lenny spotted the license plate. "I know that car," he said.

"Really?" asked Maria.

"Yeah, I remember reading that license number in one of the files."

The light turned green and Lenny followed the car.

Soon, they arrived at Happy Greens Park. Lenny got out. "Stay in the car," he said. "I'll check this out." He went into the park.

Meanwhile, the members of Pack were at the playground. Tony was throwing eggs at a slide. "So, this is what you mean by relaxing," he said. "Smashing this stuff."

"Yeah," said Sam. He was striking a seesaw with an ax. *This is what I call recreation,* he thought. "Have at it, boys. Yeah!"

Carl was spraying graffiti on the side of the slide while Tom was taking a crowbar to the chains that held the swings up. "This is why you had me get the eggs and paint," said Tom.

"Yeah, this is a treat I had planned for all of us," Sam said. He gave another whack to the seesaw.

Joe was not doing anything. His body was tensed and he was on the defensive and was looking around. *Don't do anything,* he told himself. *Just keep an eye out for trouble.*

Lenny sneaked through a bush. He moved a branch and looked out at the group. *There they are. No gray area this time. It's time to take them down.* He felt in his pocket for his cell phone but could not find it. *I must've left it in the car.*

Lenny looked at them and thought for a moment. He then quickly got out of the bush. "Freeze," he cried. "Police!"

They all turned around and looked at him for a moment and Sam smiled wickedly. "It looks like you're all alone, cop," he said. Lenny braced himself.

"Get him," ordered Sam. He charged at him, waving his ax, and was joined by all the others except Joe, who stayed back.

Lenny dodged the ax and grabbed it by the handle. He tried to pull it from Sam's hands, but Sam held on. Lenny then used the ax to flip him onto the ground.

As Sam landed, Lenny turned to see Carl coming up to him. Carl threw a punch, which Lenny blocked by using the ax's handle. "Aughh," went Carl. He stumbled back, holding his hand.

Sam got up and came up behind Lenny. He put him in a bear hug. "Get him," ordered Sam.

Tom came up to them swinging the crowbar. Lenny bent forward, pulling Sam down with him. Tom swung the crowbar and there was a thud as Sam let go.

Lenny grabbed Tom's wrist and bent it back, causing him to drop the weapon. Tom grabbed him by the shoulder, but Lenny broke his grip. Tom swung a punch at Lenny, who dodged it. Lenny kicked at one of Tom's legs as he lost his balance and Tom fell to the ground.

Carl darted at Lenny. He threw a punch, which Lenny blocked. Lenny kicked out at one of his shins. "Ow," said Carl, stumbling back.

Lenny's eyes shot to Tom, who was getting up. He then looked around, trying to see where everyone was. He noticed that Joe had not joined the fight yet.

Sam was still stunned. "Get him," he said groggily. "Get him."

Carl and Tom went back to Lenny. They started lashing out at him. He dodged their blows and backed up against a tree. Sam got up and looked around. Tony then came into view. "Sorry I'm late," he said.

Sam pointed at Lenny. "Never mind—just get him," he said. Tony and Sam joined the other two. Joe still continued to stay back.

Lenny looked at the four coming up to him looking like hungry animals. Alarm rose up in him as he looked around and realized that he did not have an exit. His heart raced as he raised his fists and went into a defensive position.

Tom raised the crowbar. "Give me that," said Sam. He grabbed it from him. He then looked at Lenny with a smile on his face. "We've got you now, copper," he said. They all advanced toward him.

Suddenly, there was the sound of an engine and Lenny's car came through the bushes. They were blinded as the car's lights washed over them. "What the . . . , " began Sam. The car headed straight for them.

"Run," cried Tony. The members of the Pack took off except Sam and Joe.

"Boss, we got to get out of here," Joe shouted.

"No," Sam cried. Joe pulled on Sam, and as the car neared, he finally followed Joe as they took off.

The car stopped before Lenny and the Pack were gone. Lenny blinked as he stared ahead into the light. *What . . . ,* he wondered. In a moment, his eyes adjusted and he went around to the side of the car.

Maria was crouched low in the driver's seat. "Thanks," said Lenny.

Lenny got in as Maria scooted over. "How did you know I was in trouble?" he asked. "Had a vision?"

"No," answered Maria. "After you were gone for a bit, I went to the edge of the playground and saw that you were in trouble so I went back into the car and drove here. By the way, that was my first time driving."

"You did very well," said Lenny. They drove out of the park.

In an alley, Sam and Joe came to a stop to rest. "That car," Sam said. "That's the same car that was watching us."

"How can you be so sure?" asked Joe. "It was so bright."

"It has to be," said Sam. "Whoever it is has got to be working with that cop."

"What can we do about it? It's not like we can file a complaint that says we were walking in the park when they started harassing us. The damage is there and they'd know that we did it."

Sam scowled. "We're going to do something else," he said. He swung out a fist and knocked some trash cans over.

Chapter 2

The next morning, Lenny woke up in his apartment. He got dressed and ready for work. As he opened the door to leave, he saw words painted on it: "We're going to get you."

They know where I live, thought Lenny. He inspected the spray paint. *At least I struck a nerve.*

Lenny went outside. As he came to his car, he stopped. *What if they tampered with my brakes?* He bent down to look under the car and saw that the tires had been slashed. *I guess I'm getting a ride.*

Minutes later, Detective Turner picked him up. "I'm glad I was finally able to get ahold of you," Lenny said. "It took forever to get through, it seemed."

"I was calling for a doctor's appointment," Detective Turner said. A few minutes of silence passed. "So, what's the deal with you and this gang?"

"Just doing my job," answered Lenny. "I guess they don't get my charm."

"Yeah, but you seemed to be going the extra mile. Is there something else?"

"No, just getting a few tips and following them. This gang is planning on doing a lot of damage."

"I'm just saying you're putting a lot on the line for these tips," Turner said. "You're going to lose what the boys upstairs are grooming you for if you go too far off the rez, so they must be from a good source."

"I have to do what I have to do," said Lenny. "My job's catching criminals."

"Anyway, the person who's apparently helping you stay ahead of these guys, he wouldn't happen to be the person who's been giving you the other tips, would he?"

"You know I can't say," said Lenny. "Like I told you, if I bring a new person in, then the people I talk to get spooked."

"Yeah, sure. I was just asking."

"Anyway, thanks for the ride."

"Sure," said Detective Turner.

Minutes later, they arrived at the station house. "Are you sure you don't want to check them out?" Turner asked. "We know where they hang out."

"I already tried that and they spotted me," said Lenny.

"Well, they wouldn't recognize my car," the detective said.

"Detectives, what are you doing?" Lieutenant Finn asked. He walked up to them. "You usually get here earlier."

"We're going to the warehouse on Percy Street to do the stakeout for the Johnson case," Detective Turner replied.

"Just do your paperwork," Finn said.

They drove off. "Thanks," said Lenny.

Later, they were a block from Tony's apartment, parked in a different direction from the building than Lenny had been. They waited and watched.

"You think they'll do something?" asked Detective Turner.

"Well, they haven't been quiet so far," Lenny said.

They watched for several minutes. "So you really don't want to go up the ladder?" Turner asked.

"That's not my goal."

Detective Turner repressed a scowl. "So this informant—you trust him?"

"I told you I can't tell you about that," said Lenny.

"Hey, I'm your partner. I'm going in with you on this. I have to be able to trust the info, and I have to be able to trust you."

"You don't trust me?"

"No, that's not what I'm saying," Detective Turner replied. "Remember the Randal bust? Before all these tips and the moving-up stuff? I trusted you then because we were partners. Are we still partners? I want to know."

Lenny sat there. *Partners,* he thought. He thought about Maria. *What should I do? Should I tell him? How would that affect Maria? She doesn't want anyone to know and I don't blame her. What if I ask her about it? What if he wants to know now? He is taking a big chance here, but if I tell him, it could seriously affect Maria's life.*

"I do trust you," said Lenny.

"Don't change the subject," said Detective Turner. "If you trust me, then why do I feel like I'm getting only half the story? What are you hiding?"

"I'm not hiding anything."

"It doesn't feel that way," Turner said.

Suddenly there was movement outside the building. "What's that?" asked Lenny.

"Don't go changing the subject again."

"I'm not," said Lenny. "I see movement."

Detective Turner turned to look at the building as Lenny got out of the car. He darted over to a bush. Detective Turner got out and joined him, and then the two of them slowly went over to the building.

They reached the bush where Lenny had seen the movement. He slowly looked into it. Suddenly there was a flash of motion. "Ahh!" cried Lenny and he crouched down and raised his arms to guard his face.

A cat darted across the yard and then went across the street. "Nice going, detective," said Turner.

Lenny straightened himself up and dusted himself off. He looked around. *There's no one around. The group must've split.*

Lenny went up to the house. He examined the door and then pressed his hand against it. "It's open," he said.

"We need a warrant first," said Detective Turner. Lenny looked at the open door and thought for a moment.

Suddenly, there was a noise. "That came from out back," Lenny said. He started to go around the house.

"Don't we need a warrant to go over there too?" Turner asked.

"Exigent circumstances," said Lenny. He went along the side of the building, followed by Detective Turner.

They reached the backyard, which was fenced off. Lenny went up to the fence and looked around, and then went over it. Turner followed him.

The detective went across the backyard, looking around as they went.

Turner was about to say something when there was a growl. They turned their heads and saw a dog baring his teeth at them. *I guess that's what made the noise,* Lenny thought.

The two men turned and ran off with the dog chasing them and barking as he went. They reached the fence as the canine gained on them. Detective Turner leapt onto the fence and Lenny pushed him up. Turner climbed over the fence as Lenny started to climb up it. The dog came up to the fence as Lenny quickly climbed over it. It took a big bite, barely missing his leg.

Lenny got down on the ground next to Detective Turner. The dog continued to bark and the two men ran off.

They turned around the corner and reached the car. They stopped as they saw it. "What?" asked Detective Turner. *Oh great,* Lenny thought.

On the driver's side door was painted "ha ha," and on the hood was painted "dork." The windows were all broken and there were scratches all over the vehicle. The tires had all been slashed.

"My car," Detective Turner said.

"Oh no," said Lenny. *They must've sneaked around when we went out back. They might've made the noise themselves.* He put a hand on Detective Turner's shoulder. "Sorry," he said.

An hour later, Lenny arrived at his apartment and flopped onto the couch. *I guess neither one of us is going to be driving for a while. I've been going at these guys with everything I've got, but it just seems to backfire. First, those complaints against me in my file and then my car and now Jon Turner's. I just want to give up, but if cops did that, then the crooks would win—and then what would happen?*

In an office, a phone rang and a man answered it. "Hello?"

"Arthur Truman?" asked Sam.

"Yes, that's me," answered Arthur.

"Look in your incoming mail," said Sam.

Arthur looked through the mail on his desk and found an envelope with no return address. Inside was a CD. "What is this?" he asked.

"Play it," said Sam.

Arthur put the CD into a slot in his computer. An audio file played. "So, is this it?" asked the voice of Phil, Arthur's son.

"Yeah, this is the paper for that Mrs. Kelp's class," Tony answered. "You sure you want to buy this paper for the final?"

"Sure—it beats doing the work," Phil answered.

"What is this?" Arthur asked Sam.

"I've got proof that he cheated while attending that fancy private school you sent him to," Sam said. "I know about all the programs and schools you got him into. You have him on the path to become some big-time doctor or scientist, but if I give this to the right people, it all goes away. What you got is only a copy."

"How did you know about his cheating when I didn't?" Arthur asked.

"I've got friends who write papers for a living. Phil told him everything when he complained about all that preparation and work you and he do to see him on the path of the learning elite."

"What do you want?" asked Arthur.

"You're in charge of money transfers for your bank, right? Well, I want you to change one of these transfer's designation."

"I can't," said Arthur. "I'll lose my job and possibly go to jail."

"You can say it was just a mistake. It's only going to be some small amount. It'll be insured, but think of your kid's future."

Arthur thought for a moment and then sighed. "Okay, I'll do it."

The next day, Maria was walking home. *Where's Lenny?* she wondered. *I guess we're not watching that movie after all.* She walked home.

Later, Maria dialed Lenny's number. "Hello?"

"Hi," Maria said. "How are you doing?"

"Not good," he answered, and then he told her what had happened.

Oh no, thought Maria. "And both of your cars are wrecked?"

"Yeah, but no one was hurt," said Lenny.

A man with shiny black hair and glasses watched as two men took bags from a truck and brought them to him. "What's going on?" he asked.

"We're here with the transfer," answered one of the men.

"There's no transfer scheduled today," the man in glasses said.

Suddenly someone jumped out from behind a corner and swung a club at the man.

He went down in front of the two men from the truck. They looked around as two more figures darted at them. They swung clubs and the men went down.

Another truck pulled up to the scene and Sam got out. "Load the money up," he ordered. Tony, Tom, and Carl got to work. Sweet Savings Bank, 14 Creston Way, December 23, 5:14 p.m.

"We've got a problem," Maria said.

A few hours later, a truck pulled up to the van. The man with shiny black hair watched two men get out. Suddenly police cars pulled up to the scene. Lenny got out of one, holding his badge up. "Paway Police," he cried. "We've got a situation!"

What the . . . , thought Sam. He was watching from the truck. *Him again?* he wondered. Joe was sitting next to him. "Boss, what are we going to do?" he asked.

Sam snarled and gunned the engine. He charged at Lenny. "Boss, wait!" Joe cried.

The truck sped toward Lenny, but there was a car in the way. The truck hit the car, breaking glass and bending metal. The car was pushed away and the truck stopped. Sam got out of the truck. "Get him," he ordered.

Carl and Tony came around the corner and looked around. *Enough of this,* thought Tony. *I'm out of here.* He and Carl took off.

"There they go," cried Lenny.

Three officers ran over to them and blocked their path. They raised their hands in surrender.

Tom was around the corner thinking about what he should do. "Where do you think you're going?" asked Detective Turner. Tom turned to see the detective standing next to him. He raised his hands above his head.

Sam charged at Lenny, darting around the damaged police car. He threw a punch at him that Lenny dodged, and then he threw a round punch, which Lenny also dodged. His face twisted in a mask of fury as he threw yet another punch. Lenny just stood there as the blow went past him. *That's what I call blind rage,* thought Lenny. "Aughh," cried Sam. He threw another punch. Lenny dodged it and grabbed Sam while he still had his arm out.

Lenny swung him around toward the side of the damaged police car. There was a thud and he went down.

"It's over," said Lenny.

A few minutes later, the gang members were all in cuffs. "It looks like the Pack's caged," Lenny said. He left the officer and went over to Sam, who was being led to a car.

"May I?" asked Lenny. He took ahold of Sam's arm and looked over at Detective Turner, who was on his cell phone.

Lenny put Sam into the back of the patrol car. "I'm going to get you for this," said Sam.

"Yeah, yeah," Lenny said. He closed the door.

BOOK 9

Rise of the New Power

Chapter 1

A man sat at a desk. *It's finally mine,* he thought. *The power's mine. No more following orders. Now I'm giving them.*

The man pressed a button on an intercom on the desk. "Come in," he ordered.

Another man came into the room. "Yeah, boss," the man said.

"Tell all the lieutenants to meet me at the house," the boss answered. "We go over the first part of the plan tonight."

"You got it," said the man, and left.

Soon, thought the boss. *Soon this town will be mine.*

Meanwhile, Maria sat in class. "I hope everyone is having a Black History month ," said the teacher. "Please remember those trailerbrazers that paved the way in black history but don't forget that the projects are due two weeks from now. I want them to cover the basics of your topics. I don't want them to be novel long, but I want them to have some meat." The bell rang and the class left.

Maria was walking home and talking on her cell phone. "So, you want to catch another movie?"

"Yeah, but I can't," answered Lenny. "The lieutenant has me working overtime."

"That's too bad. Well, see you later."

"You too."

Maria walked through her front door. "Hi, Mom," she said.

"Hey there, Snugglebear," said Lois. "I've got some big news."

Apprehension went through Maria. "What is it?"

"It's your father. We're bringing him home today."

"What?" asked Maria. *You'd think I would have seen this coming,* she thought, *being clairvoyant and all.* "When are we leaving?"

"Right now."

Nothing like plenty of notice, thought Maria. She threw her book bag onto the couch and followed her mother as she left the house.

At Peaceful Field Rehabilitation Faculty Maria and Lois were helping Jeff into the car. "It's okay," said Jeff. "I'm better. I don't need the help."

"The doctor said to take it easy," said Lois.

"He didn't say 'Don't move,'" said Jeff.

Maria went around the car ahead of them and opened the door. Lois guided Jeff in.

"This isn't necessary," he said. Lois tried to buckle his seat belt for him, but he grabbed it and did it first.

Maria got in the back as Lois got into the driver's seat next to Jeff, and they drove off.

Minutes later, they arrived home. "Just like I remember it," said Jeff. He quickly unbuckled his seat belt and started to get out. Lois got out of the car and darted around it. By the time she reached the other side, he was already out.

Jeff started to walk to the house. Lois walked by him and Maria followed.

They got inside. "Here, let me," said Lois. She took Jeff's coat as he got it off his shoulders. She handed it to Maria. "Please hang this up, honey."

Maria went over to the coat rack.

Two men went up to a window, and after a few creaking noises it opened. They climbed in. They went through the darkness up to a door. Maria found it hard to see them, but she could make out a few motions. There was a click and the door opened.

One of the men shined a light into the room. "Let's get on with it," he said. Sherman's Electronics, February 3, 9:15 p.m.

That's tonight, Maria thought.

"Maria, could you get the luggage out of the car?" asked Lois.

I guess I'll have to wait to call, Maria thought. She hung up the coat and went outside to the car.

About an hour later, Maria went into her room.

"Dinner's almost ready," Lois called.

"I'll be down in a minute," Maria said. *Taking Dad's suitcase upstairs, unpacking, and spending time with Mom and Dad took a lot longer than I thought it would.* She went over to her bed and reached under it. She got her cell phone and dialed Lenny.

"Hello?"

"Lenny, it's me," said Maria.

"How're you doing?"

"We have a situation." She told him what she had seen. "I would've called you earlier, but, well, I'll tell you later."

That evening, Lenny pulled up to a corner a few feet from Sherman's Electronics. His partner, Detective Jon Turner, was in the passenger's seat.

"So, this is another tip, eh?" Turner asked.

"Yeah," Lenny answered. He got out of the car. "You go around back and I'll take the front." They went across the street toward the store.

Detective Turner went along the side of the building. Halfway along, his cell phone rang. "What?" he asked.

He listened to the person on the other end. "I can't talk now," he whispered. "I'm investigating a robbery that's supposed to happen."

He listened some more. "Yeah, another one of his 'tips.' Look, I'll call you back."

Meanwhile, Lenny was in the front of the store. He looked through a window, and after his eyes adjusted to the darkness, he saw that a door in the back was open. *Uh-oh,* he thought. *They're already inside.* He looked around but could see no one.

Where's Joe? Lenny wondered. *They might've gotten him.* He took out a flashlight and kicked in the door. He went inside.

Lenny slowly went through the store and waved his flashlight about as he scanned the area.

Suddenly, a man in a ski mask came out at Lenny. Lenny grabbed the man and swung him to the floor. He turned back from the maneuver just in time to see something come at him. He raised his arm and then a personal computer system hit him. He went down under its weight.

The man on the floor got up and went over to Lenny. Lenny shined his flashlight in his eyes. "Ahh!" he cried. As he was blinded, Lenny swung his leg around, tripping him, and he fell to the floor.

As Lenny got up, another man in a ski mask came at him. Lenny swung his flashlight at him, but he grabbed his wrist. They struggled for a few moments. In their struggles they knocked over a stand of small electronics and then fell to the floor.

Lenny pushed the man off him and got to his feet. The man lay there and Lenny came upon him. He grabbed him and then rolled him onto his stomach. He forced his hands behind his back and cuffed them. "Don't move," he ordered. "You're under arrest."

Detective Turner came into the room and shined his flashlight around as he looked over the scene. "Get the other guy," said Lenny.

Minutes later, squad cars surrounded the store. "You guys did a great job," said Officer Bucole.

"Thanks," said Lenny. He grabbed Detective Turner by the arm. "Excuse us."

They walked a short distance away. "What happened?" Lenny asked. "I was all alone in there."

"I had trouble getting in the back," answered Detective Turner.

Lenny looked him over. "Were you on the phone?"

"No."

"Relax, I was only kidding. It's just that I'm out there with you and I want to trust you."

"How can you talk about trust with all the secrets you keep?" Turner asked.

"Hey, no need to get defensive," Lenny said. "Also, I always have your back, though I can't tell you everything. You know, if you don't trust me, then have one of the officers give you a ride." He walked off.

Meanwhile, a man came into the office. "Sir," he said.

"Yes, Louis?" asked the man at the desk.

"The job at Sherman's Electronics—the police caught them," said Louis.

The man sat there feeling angry. *No,* he thought. *This happened to the Griffin. It's not supposed to happen to me. I'm supposed to be the man!*

The man thought for a moment. "Was Detective Hipar involved?"

"I don't know but I can find out," Louis said.

"Do, and get the boys down from Harper," the man ordered.

Louis left the room. *This can't be happening,* thought the man. *I'm so close and I'm more careful than he ever was. I will succeed!*

The next morning, Lenny dialed Maria's number. It rang several times. *No answer,* he thought. *Oh well.* He left the apartment.

Lenny walked into the squad room. He started to go to his desk but was stopped by Lieutenant Finn. "Nice work last night," he said.

"Thank you, sir, but it wasn't just me," Lenny said. "My partner was also there."

"Anyway, my place, tomorrow at eight," Finn said. He walked off.

Lenny went over to his desk and began to fill out the report about the previous night's robbery attempt. He looked over at Detective Turner, who gave him a cold look. *So that's how he's going to be,* Lenny thought. *What's his deal? He's the one who dropped the ball. Is it really about my keeping secrets?*

He looked over at Turner again. He was hunched down over his own paperwork. *What am I going to do?* Lenny wondered.

Meanwhile, Maria and Lois were listening to Jeff as the three of them sat around the kitchen table. ". . . and your grandfather asked, 'You bought that with ballerina money?' and I said, 'There's no shame in working at a dance studio.' He then said, 'You're a boy,' and I asked, 'Why can't you just enjoy your gift?'"

Maria and Lois listened intently even though they had heard the story before.

That afternoon, Maria arrived home from school. "Hi, Dad," she said.

Jeff was watching TV but turned it off when Maria got home. "Hi, honey," he said. "How was school?"

Maria took off her book bag. "Good. I turned my project in early and got it back. I got a B."

"That's great," said Jeff. "It's good to see you doing well."

"Yeah, things have been going well," said Maria. She sat down by Jeff. "How are you doing?"

"Good," he answered. *Besides the fact that I threw myself into bed last night because I pushed myself so hard yesterday.* "Anyway, I never got to ask you, have you been doing any extracurricular activities?"

Fighting crime, Maria thought. "No, right now I'm focusing on my essay for history and my upcoming math tests," she answered.

"Ah, it's good to hear that you're keeping up with your schoolwork. Are you still a big reader?"

"Kind of," Maria answered. "It's been a while, but the last book I read was about a guy who gets lost during a canoe trip and has to find his way home. It's called . . . *Jim's Way.*"

"Sounds interesting."

"You should read it if you have the time."

"Yeah," said Jeff. *I have lots of time,* he thought.

Maria started to go toward the stairs. "I should get started on my homework."

"Okay, see you," Jeff said. He watched her go upstairs.

Maria entered her room and sat on her bed. She went through her book bag and took out her cell phone.

"Hey, Lenny, it's me," she said when he answered.

"Where have you been?" asked Lenny. He told her what had happened.

"Sorry I didn't answer—it's just that I've been so busy lately," said Maria.

"You want to talk about it?"

"I'm afraid I can't right now. Mom said she's going to be making dinner early. How about later?"

"Sure."

The next morning, a limousine was parked in a deserted parking lot. It was before dawn, and the vehicle was nearly invisible in the darkness. A van pulled up by it and a man got out.

He entered it by the rear passenger side. He looked at the other side, where his boss sat.

"You ready to begin?" asked his boss.

Yeah, I had a nice flight, the man thought. *Thanks for asking.* "Yeah."

"Good," the boss said. He handed the man a file folder. "Here's all the information we have gathered on Detective Lenard Hipar. He was instrumental in my predecessor's downfall, and we have just learned that he was the one who ruined a job we tried to pull. What happened to my predecessor cannot happen to me. Take care of him immediately. Got that, Elliot?"

Elliot nodded and his boss waved, signaling him to leave, which he did.

Chapter 2

Maria sat in a classroom, her mind wandering as her teacher talked about polynomials. *First I could barely get away to make a call to Lenny, and now I couldn't take his,* she thought. *I hope everything that's going on with Dad doesn't keep interfering with my vision stuff.*

Maria tried to concentrate on what the teacher was saying, but her mind wandered again. *Maybe it won't be so bad. Maybe once everything settles down it'll all fit together and then things will be . . . normal?*

Several minutes passed and Maria somewhat managed to pay attention to what was being said.

Lenny was in front of his apartment. He had a bag in one hand and was unlocking his front door with the other. He opened the door. The building shook as an explosion filled the hallway. Costeasy Apartments, Copper Way. February 5, 12:09 p.m.

Oh no, Maria thought. She had to stop herself from bolting upright from her chair. *Lenny!* Maria looked at her watch. *That's sixteen minutes from now.*

"Mr. Hecker, may I go to the bathroom?" Maria asked.

"Now? But it's so close to the end of the period," Mr. Hecker said.

"Please, it's an emergency."

"Okay."

Maria quickly left the classroom and scurried to the restroom. She took out her cell phone before even getting into a stall. *Come on,* she thought as the phone rang. She slammed the stall's door behind her.

Maria anxiously waited as the ringing sound filled her ears and seemed deafening. Her heart raced as she looked at her watch. She did not hear the bell as she tried to keep herself from thinking horrible thoughts. *Please,* she thought. *Please answer.*

"Hello," said Lenny. *Thank goodness for speed dial,* Maria thought. She finally let out a breath.

"Lenny, there's something I've got to tell you," she said. She explained about her vision.

About an hour later, men in padded suits came out of Lenny's apartment carrying a steel box.

Lenny and Lieutenant Finn watched them from a distance. "We had to evacuate everybody in the building," Finn said. "I'm afraid we won't be able to keep this out of the news. Sorry."

"That's okay," said Lenny.

The lieutenant looked at the bomb squad members working. "I'm afraid stuff like this comes with being big time."

"You're saying I'm big time, sir?" asked Lenny.

"With the way you've been going, you're heading there."

They looked at the crew again. "So, they were able to disable the bomb?" Lenny asked.

"Yeah, and they're going to take it back to headquarters using every precaution," Finn answered. He looked at Lenny. "Are you all right?"

"I'm fine."

Hours later, Maria hurried away from school. As she got a block away from the school building, she took out her cell phone.

"Yes?"

"Lenny, are you all right?" Maria asked.

"I'm fine," answered Lenny. "You might hear them talk about the bomb on the news. What do you know? I'm a TV star."

Maria gave a little grin. "That's a relief."

"You warned me in time, so don't worry."

"I was afraid something else might've happened to you," said Maria. "Not many people have gone all the way to your apartment to get to you. Any idea who's behind it?"

"No, but the guys back at the station house believe it has something to do with one of my cases."

"What are you going to do?"

"Detective Turner and I are going to go through my old files and see if there's anyone who might've done this," Lenny replied. "Don't worry—we're going to get this guy."

"Good luck," said Maria.

Maria arrived home. Jeff was sitting on the couch watching the television. "Police are said to have no clues about who planted the bomb, but sources say that the investigation is under way," said a male news announcer. "Once again, it is believed that a Paway police detective was the target of the bombing attempt."

Maria looked at the image of Lenny's apartment building on the screen and felt uneasy. "I'm going to do my homework," she said.

"Okay. just remember that your mother said she'll have dinner ready early again," said Jeff. Maria went upstairs.

Meanwhile, the boss watched the news on a big-screen TV. The failed bombing attempt was the featured story.

"We don't know what went wrong, sir," said Louis. "He shouldn't have had any way of knowing about the bomb."

"Have surveillance put on him," ordered the boss.

"Are you sure that's wise?" Louis asked. "With what happened the police will be on alert. They could spot the surveillance."

"Just do it."

"Yes, sir."

"We continue as usual. Get me Elliot on the phone."

Steve Finn called Lenny into his office. He came in and saw Detective Turner sitting by the desk.

"Lenny, we need to talk," Finn said.

"Yes, sir?" asked Lenny. He felt alarmed.

"With the attempt on your life we need to take every precaution," said the lieutenant. "You're off active duty, effective immediately."

"Sir, is that necessary?"

"Lenny, we don't want anything to happen to you."

We, meaning the boys upstairs, thought Lenny.

"Detective Turner will handle the investigation from here on out," said Lieutenant Finn.

Detective Turner stood up and took out his notebook. "Lenny, since they think this bombing attempt might be connected to one of your old cases, I'm going to need to see your notes and the names of all your CIs, otherwise known as Confidential Informants."

"I'm afraid I can't do that," said Lenny. "If I do that, they'll stop talking to me."

"I'm your partner and I'm the one investigating your case," Turner said.

"There's no need to rouse every CI Lenny has," said Finn. "I'm sure you'll have all you need to solve the case."

Turner looked at Lenny. "Yes, sir," he said. He left the room.

Finn turned to Lenny. "As for you, I'm afraid you're on desk duty," he said.

"But sir . . . , " began Lenny.

"That's final," said Lieutenant Finn.

"Yes, sir."

A few hours later, Maria called Lenny. "Hey, did you ever get those messages I left?" Lenny asked.

"Yeah, sorry I didn't call back sooner," she answered.

"It's all right," said Lenny. "It's been a crazy day."

"How's the investigation going?"

"They've taken me off active duty. They're putting me on a desk. It's for my 'protection.'"

"What are you going to do?"

"I don't know. I think I'm going check on a few things by myself."

"If I see anything else, I'll call," said Maria. "Also, if you need help, I'm here for you."

"Thanks," Lenny said. "Maybe I'll come across something."

"How are you going to get any evidence if you're not allowed to work on the case?"

"I'll think of something. After all, I work with a consultant no one can ever see. Besides, if I find anything, then they probably won't care that I was off active duty."

Meanwhile, Detective Turner was walking down the street. Around a corner, a figure was poking his head out, watching him. *What am I going to do if I can't get at his information?* Turner wondered. The figure watched as he went down the street. After a few moments the figure slowly followed.

The detective did not notice the man following him. The man looked around but didn't see anyone else on the street. He continued to follow him.

There has to be another way to get the information, Detective Turner thought. *Maybe there's a reference in one of his old cases. It could be someone he knows. Maybe it's somewhere else. I could look at his day planner or something. Does he have a day planner? How do I not know this? Well, the phone records won't help.*

The figure watched him and started to go after him when suddenly, there was a creaking noise. The man turned his head and saw a stack of crates falling toward him. They crashed onto him.

Detective Turner heard the noise and turned around. He saw the man beneath the crates and rushed over to him. He began to pick one crate off him and then another.

Turner's phone rang. He paused for a moment and then answered it. "Hello?"

He listened to the voice on the other end. "You did what?" he asked.

The voice talked some more. "He was doing what?" Turner asked. He looked down at the unconscious man. "He could still be hurt. I have to call this in."

Meanwhile, the boss got a call at his desk. "What is it?"

"Sir, there's a problem with Kyle," answered a man on the other end of the line.

"The guy we have on surveillance? What is it?"

"We had him watching Detective Hipar's partner when apparently he was attacked."

"How?" asked the boss. "I thought he was supposed to stay out of sight."

"Apparently someone spotted him and hit him with some crates or something," the man replied. "I don't have the whole story."

"Post some more surveillance on the partner and hit the streets," ordered the boss. "Find out who's protecting him."

"I thought it might be the police."

"If it had been the police, they would've arrested him, not hit him with crates." He slammed the phone down into its cradle.

A few minutes later, a phone rang and Elliot answered it. "Yeah?"

"It's time," said the man on the other end of the line. "You botched the bombing, but you're being given another chance. Start the plan we discussed."

Elliot looked over at the other man in the motel room. "What is it?" asked the man.

"It's time, Tom," answered Elliot. "Get the boys together." Tom left the room.

The next day, Maria was sitting at the table with her parents. *This thing with trying to fit Dad and my vision stuff together—I should tell Lenny about it,* she thought. *He needs to know why I haven't been doing that well. I think the reason I haven't told him is that I want to keep these parts of my life separate.*

Lois saw Maria fiddling with her cereal. "Are you all right, Snugglebear?" she asked.

"I'm fine," answered Maria.

Lois was still worried.

Maria got up. "I've got to go," she said. "See you, Mom, Dad." She left.

As she left, Lois looked at Jeff. *Should I tell him that Maria seems off?* she wondered. *No, he has enough to deal with.*

Hours later, Lenny heard a knock on his door and opened it to find Maria.

"Hi, there," said Lenny. "How was school?"

"It was good," Maria answered. "We have to talk." She went inside.

Maria went into Lenny's living room and threw herself onto the couch. "Lenny, something's been going on in my life and you need to know about it, because it's affecting my helping you," she said.

"Is everything all right?"

"Everything's fine. It's just that Dad's home now."

"Oh. Well, you've gone through a lot with everything that's happened."

"I'm over that. It's just that it's hard to keep this secret with two other people in the house. That's why I didn't get your call and everything. Things have been so busy with him coming back that I have had trouble getting away."

Lenny sat on the arm of the couch. "I'm sure we can think of something," he said. "Undercovers have to conceal their identities from criminals and people around them at all times. Let me talk with some I know. Maybe they'll know something that can help you."

"Thanks."

"No problem."

Suddenly, the door was kicked in. Something flew through the air and landed before Maria realized what was happening.

There was a flash of light. "Flash bomb," cried Lenny. Maria waved her arms wildly through the air.

Suddenly she heard footsteps approaching, and then someone grabbed her.

Chapter 3

Maria broke the grip of whoever was holding her. "Grab her," someone ordered.

Maria struck out blindly and felt her fist connect with something. There was a cry of pain. She sent a kick to where she'd heard the sound come from and could see a dim form fall back.

"Get her," someone cried.

Maria thought she heard someone come up to her. She sent her fists into the air, but they struck nothing.

"Don't just stand there," shouted a voice.

"But Elliot . . . ," started another voice.

Lenny's vision started to adjust. He looked at the blurred figure holding one of his arms and grabbed it and then flipped it to the floor.

"Elliot," someone cried.

Lenny turned and looked at the blurred figures before him. He sent out a punch and a kick but did not hit anything. *Just stall for time,* he thought. He was as alert as he could be to his surroundings. *Wait for your vision to recover.*

Lenny saw two figures dart at him. He swung out his fists and they appeared to back away.

Maria's vision started to recover fully and she sent a kick at one of the men advancing on Lenny. She struck him and sent him toward the other man. As they fumbled, she kicked a leg out from under one of the men and they fell to the floor.

A figure on the floor by Lenny got up and darted for the wrecked door. It went through it and was gone.

"Did you see his face?" asked Lenny.

"No, my vision's not all the way back," Maria answered.

"Mine either." Lenny slowly made his way back to the couch and sat down. "Why don't you get out of here while I report this. Stay nearby, though; we don't know if there are any more of those guys around."

Soon after, Lenny watched as the officers took the cuffed men away. Lieutenant Finn came over to him. "The work you've been doing is phenomenal," he said.

"I just did what any trained cop would've done," said Lenny.

"You took on four men by yourself and managed to collar three of them," Finn said. "Most guys would've been overwhelmed."

Images of Maria punching and kicking men went through Lenny's mind. "Thanks," he said. Finn went back to the officers.

"What do you mean it all fell apart?" demanded the boss. He was talking on his phone, which was set to speaker. "He was there and you were supposed to get him."

"He and somebody else fought us off," said Elliot.

"Who?"

"I don't know—some young woman," answered Elliot. "We could try again."

"No, this failure was quite enough," the boss said. "They got three of my best men now and you can't tell me why."

Elliot was silent. *They won't talk,* thought the boss, though he felt a twinge of doubt.

Louis was standing by the desk. "I'll get them all lawyers," he said.

"Yeah, and run the legal bills through the dummy corporation," said the boss. He sat there in silence for a moment and then said, "Bring him in."

A man entered the room. "Joe, is it?" the boss asked.

"Joe Paris, sir," answered Joe. He put a file folder on the desk. "Our guys in Weatherton have got the shoes."

The boss opened the file and look through it. "Rocket Jumps—they're the hottest new sneakers on the market," Joe said. "All the kids want them and we've got more than four dozen of them. I had a friend who forged the shipment forms and everything else we need to move them. While the cops are looking in Weatherton for the stolen shoes, they'll be on the black market here in Paway. The truck that's carrying them is due here tomorrow night."

"Good," said the boss. "With the money I'll make I'll be able to do bigger things and really be the boss of this town."

Maria was sitting on her bed.

A man with sideburns was walking to his car when he saw something on his windshield. It was a ticket placed under a wiper blade. He pulled it out and went into his car. He opened his glove box where there was a large collection of tickets and tossed the newest one in. 20 Trout Lane, February 6, 8:46 p.m.

That's different, thought Maria. *I don't usually get a lot of visions about traffic tickets.* She called Lenny and told him what she had seen.

"Okay, I'll send someone to check it out," he said.

Chapter 4

Louis was walking to his car when he saw something on his windshield. It was a ticket placed under his wiper blade. He pulled it out and entered his car. He opened his glove box.

"Sir, I'm going to have to ask you to step out of the car," said a voice. Louis looked up and saw that it belonged to a police officer.

He got out of the car. "Can I help you, officer?" he asked.

"Yes. I have reason to believe you have multiple unpaid parking tickets," answered the officer.

Louis's heart quickened. "Really?"

The officer looked into the car and saw the opened glove box and the collection of tickets inside. He looked back at Louis. "I'm going to have to ask you to come with me." He led Louis away.

In the boss's office the phone rang. "Yes?" Moments later a look of anger came over his face. "What?" *We're going to bring in the largest shipment of stolen merchandise in years and he gets collared for a traffic violation?* The boss slammed the phone down in its cradle. "Ahh!" he cried.

He sat there seething in anger and worry. *Don't worry,* he told himself. *He won't rat on you, but you're going to have to handle the shipment yourself. I won't stop when I am this close to being top dog.*

The next afternoon, Maria went up to Jeff, who was sitting on the couch. "How's it going, Dad?" asked Maria.

"A lot better, actually," answered Jeff. *Yeah, you're looking and walking better,* thought Maria.

"Yeah, you're making a lot of progress," said Lois. "Dr. Romp will be quite pleased."

"I'm quite pleased," said Jeff. He smiled, and both Maria and Lois laughed.

"Hey, why don't we play that game Bango?" asked Jeff. "Just like old times."

"Sure," answered Lois.

A truck came up behind a warehouse. The area was dark. A few feet away a group of men stood ready. "Let's get this stuff moved," their leader said.

About half a dozen men went up to the truck. Two men opened the trailer door, and soon they were unloading crates. "Let's get going," ordered the leader. 120 Alvear Way, February 9, 9:13 p.m.

That's tonight, Maria thought.

"Maria, don't you want to play?" asked Jeff. Lois was setting up the board. They both looked at her with smiles on their faces.

"Sure," she answered.

Soon after, Maria rolled the dice. "Seven," cried Lois. *It won't hurt to wait before calling Lenny,* Maria thought. *It's still a couple of hours away.* Both Jeff and Lois counted as she moved her game piece seven spaces on the board.

A few minutes later, Jeff was shaking the dice. "Come on, lucky seven," he said.

"Isn't that a different game?" Lois said, smiling. Jeff threw the dice. "Snake eyes," cried Lois. She laughed.

"Isn't that a different game?" Jeff asked. He smiled and then they both laughed. Maria checked her watch.

Minutes later, Maria picked up a card from a deck on the game board. "Skip ahead two spaces," she read.

She moved her piece. *It can't be that much longer,* Maria thought. She stole a look at her watch.

"Is everything all right?" asked Lois.

"Sure," Maria answered. She handed Jeff the dice and he rolled a five.

Minutes later, Lois was bringing her game piece around the board. Maria was only a few moves away from going completely around it. *Finally,* she thought. She looked at her watch and found that they'd been playing for almost an hour.

Soon, she went up to her room, dialed Lenny, and told him what she had seen. "We're on it," he said.

"Sir, I have a hot tip about someone shipping illegal items into town," said Lenny. He was in Lieutenant Finn's office.

"Another one of your informants?" Finn asked.

"Yes, sir," answered Lenny. *Does he have a problem with it now?*

"Let's go."

They left the office and went through the squad room. Finn ordered several detectives to come with them, including Detective Jon Turner.

The boss sat in the back of the car. *This is it,* he thought. His heart raced. *I'm going to be somebody. No more watching somebody else get all the money and respect.*

The car stopped. "Sir, we're here," said the driver.

Sir, thought the boss with relish. He got out of the car.

A truck came up behind a warehouse. The area was dark. A few feet away a group of men stood ready. "Let's get this stuff moved," the leader said.

About half a dozen men went up to the truck. Two men opened the trailer door, and soon they were unloading crates. They put the crates on a forklift and used it to bring them to a van. "Let's get going," cried the leader. They continued the process.

"It won't be long now, sir," said the leader. He was standing next to the boss.

"Good," said the boss. "I want them loaded up as soon as possible."

Suddenly, police cars raced onto the scene. They stopped and officers came out. Lenny came out with a bullhorn. "Police!" he cried. "Everybody freeze!"

"Everyone scatter!" someone shouted. All the men ran about. *No,* thought the boss. *This isn't what is supposed to happen!*

He looked around frantically, seemingly at a loss about what to do. "Boss, we've got to go," said the leader of the group of men.

All around them officers came out of the shadows, grabbing every man in sight.

One man swung a punch at an officer. He ducked it, grabbed the man, and then swung him into the side of the truck. The man fell down, stunned. "You're under arrest," said the officer.

Hands grabbed the boss. "No," he cried. He swung out wildly, twisting himself about, but it did not seem to matter. The hands grabbed him and then swung him onto his car. "You're under arrest," said Lenny.

The boss struggled as handcuffs were placed on him. "No," he cried. "This was my moment! My moment!"

Lenny turned him around. "I know you."

He looked at Detective Turner, who was wrestling with another man. "Look who we have here," Lenny said. "It's Robert Flinch. He was one of the Griffin's lieutenants, back in the day."

Turner held up the man he was struggling with. "Yeah, well, we also have Steve 'the Lion' Foss here," he said. "It's like a reunion." He pulled the struggling man away. *To be reduced to some guy loading merchandise for someone else,* Steve thought. *I'll get you for this, Hipar.* Detective Turner helped Steve into a squad car.

"No," cried Robert. "This was supposed to be my day!"

"Your day's over," said Lenny. He took him over to a squad car and put him in.

An hour later, Lenny was talking to Maria on the phone. "Anyway, that's what happened," he said. "Everyone's beaming over this." *There's even talk about promoting me.* "Thanks for your help. Good night."

Jeff poked his head into Maria's room and she quickly hid her phone. "Hi, honey," he said. "What's going on?"

"Nothing, Dad. Nothing at all."

BOOK 10

Revenge of
the Mastermind

Chapter 1

Maria was in a darkened room. She had a vague feeling of wondering where she was. Suddenly, there were figures clad in shadows moving all around her. She braced herself for an attack, but none came.

Maria turned around and saw the figures go through a door. She could not see what was beyond the doorway. As soon as the last figure was through the door, bars came down. The doorway looked like a prison cell.

Maria then realized that she was suddenly wearing medieval armor. She looked all over herself, wondering how that had happened.

She felt someone behind her and turned around. There was another figure, this one holding a mirror. Maria looked into the mirror and saw a young woman who, though she wore the same armor, looked completely different. She did not recognize the woman. A hand raised something above the mirror, and Maria saw that it was a knife.

It swung down at her and she braced for it, but it never touched her. She looked around, but the knife had disappeared. Somehow, she just knew that she had become the woman she saw in the mirror.

She looked up at the figure. The mirror was gone and it just stood there. She reached and grabbed the figure. She pulled something off and looked at her hand to see what she was holding, but it was gone. She looked up and the figure was gone too.

Maria looked around and realized that she was now in a tunnel. She heard a train coming and saw a bright light coming toward her. The sound of the train became deafening and the light blinding. Maria held up her hands, unable to scream.

"Ahh!" cried Maria. She bolted up and looked around, breathing heavily. She was in her room. *What a horrible dream,* she thought. She put a hand to her forehead. *As if I don't already have enough going on in my head.*

Maria checked her clock and saw that it was nearly time for her to get up, so she got out of bed and got ready for the day.

Maria went downstairs to the kitchen where her parents were sitting at the table. Jeff was reading a newspaper. Lois was eating pancakes.

"Good morning," said Maria.

"Good morning," her parents said together.

Maria sat down at the table and helped herself to pancakes.

"Sleep well, kiddo?" asked Jeff.

"Yeah," answered Maria.

"Well, I guess you won't be a kiddo for much longer with your birthday just a few days away," Jeff said.

That's right, Maria thought. *I forgot!*

"You're going to be sixteen years old," said Lois.

"Sweet sixteen," said Jeff.

"Yes—then you'll be getting a driver's license, getting your own car and soon going to college," said Lois. She smiled.

"Oh no, college tuition," said Jeff in mock horror. "I guess I chose the wrong time to come out of a coma."

"Speaking of long periods of sleep, I have a meeting at work," said Lois. "Once that's over, how about I come home and maybe we could watch a movie."

"How about we go out to dinner afterward?" asked Jeff.

"Now, dear, we're already planning a party for her and we wouldn't want her to become spoiled now, would we?" Lois asked. She was smiling throughout the whole sentence, which she said in a light tone to show that she was kidding.

"We're having a party?" asked Maria.

"Well, a girl turns sixteen only once," Lois said. "What kind of cake do you want?"

"Chocolate," answered Maria. Her parents laughed.

It's been a while since I've felt like this, Maria thought. *It was before the accident. This feeling—it's back and it's going to stay.*

Meanwhile, at Paway Correctional Facility, a man was being escorted to the gate by two guards. "See you later, John Doe," said one of the guards. He had a smirk on his face.

They led him to a prison transportation van and handed him off to the two guards standing by. One of the guards by the van handed a prison guard some papers. He quickly looked through them. "He's all set," said the prison guard. "Prisoner John Doe one two two eight is now in your custody."

"Also known as the fearsome Mr. Mindful," said the other guard. They both gave poorly repressed snickers. *You're on the list,* thought Mr. Mindful.

He was loaded onto the van, and one of the guards got in with him in the backseat. The other guard climbed into the front next to a man behind the wheel. They drove off.

A few minutes later, the man who was sitting in the front passenger seat turned around to look at Mr. Mindful. "So, boss, you think they bought it?" he asked.

"If they hadn't, they wouldn't have let us go, Josh," said Mr. Mindful. His tone was forceful. He looked at the man next to him and held out his cuffed hands. "Tim, take these things off me now," he ordered.

Tim took out a lock pick and began to work on the cuffs.

"I was worried that the trusty we bribed to get you into the warden's office so we could get those transfer forms would blab," said Josh.

"He won't if he knows what's good for him," said Mr. Mindful. *They all will get what's coming to them: those guards, the warden, the detective, and that girl. Who does she think she is? A little girl daring to challenge the will of a criminal mastermind.*

"Did you prepare everything like I told you?" asked Mr. Mindful.

"Don't worry—reception was good on that cell phone we smuggled to you," Josh replied. "We heard all your instructions. Isn't that right, Ken?"

"Yeah," answered the driver. "We just want to know what you want to do now, boss."

"Now I'm going to get my revenge," answered Mr. Mindful.

Chapter 2

Later that day, Lieutenant Steve Finn came up to Lenny's desk. Lenny looked up. "Sir?" he asked.

"Lenny, we have a problem," the lieutenant said.

"What is it, sir?"

"That guy, the one who thinks he's a criminal mastermind, who calls himself Mr. Mindful, has escaped."

Oh no, thought Lenny. *Maria!* "When?"

"A few hours ago," Finn said. "You and Detective Turner are to go to the prison and talk with the warden."

"Got you, sir," said Lenny. Finn headed off.

Lenny saw his partner Detective Jon Turner come up to him. "I heard," he said. "Let's go." Lenny put on his jacket and they left.

"I don't know how this could've happened," said Warden Downer. "They had the papers and everything."

Lenny was taking notes. "What about the computer message about the transfer?" he asked.

"According to our head technician our system's been hacked," the warden said.

Maybe Computer Crimes can find out who broke in, thought Lenny. "And the guards who handed him off?"

"They're with the sketch artist you sent over, describing the men they gave him to," answered the warden.

"Sir, is there anything you think could be connected to how he escaped the last time?" Lenny asked.

"No, of course not," Downer replied. "His metal shop privileges were revoked so he wouldn't be able to make any more tools like he did before, and we took every precaution with handling him."

Lenny continued writing. "We have to ask, sir," he said. "Was he close to any other prisoner?"

"No, not really," answered Downer. "Everyone I talked to thought he was kind of a snob."

Lenny closed his notebook. "Thanks for cooperating, sir," he said. "Don't forget, call if you remember anything."

Lenny left the warden's office and went into the cellblock where Mr. Mindful had been kept. He saw that Detective Turner was kneeling in front of the cell. "Found something?" he asked.

Detective Turner bolted up and turned around. "Oh, it's you," he said.

"Did you think another prisoner had gotten out?" asked Lenny.

"Just jumpy with all these crooks around," Turner answered.

"Find anything?"

"No. I was going to talk with this guard." He went across the cellblock. Lenny followed him but stopped when his cell phone rang.

Maria? Lenny wondered. "Hello?"

"It's me," said Lieutenant Finn.

"Sir?"

"How's the case going?"

"We're just collecting preliminary statements now, sir."

"Good to see that you're on the case," Finn said. "Everyone upstairs is nervous about this guy because of what he's done, but we know you can bring him in again. You've been hitting home runs for months now."

Lenny felt uneasy. "Thank you, sir."

"In fact, once this case is finished, we're going to talk to you about your future," said the lieutenant.

Lenny's unease grew. "Thank you, sir," he said.

Lenny looked into the cell that had held Mr. Mindful. It was empty, and there was no sign that anything out of the ordinary had happened there. He walked away from it, and halfway along the cellblock saw Detective Turner coming toward him. Lenny thought he saw him put something in his coat.

"Anything useful?" Lenny asked.

"Huh?" asked Detective Turner.

"Did the guy know anything useful?"

"Oh, no," Turner answered. "He didn't." They left the prison.

Meanwhile, in a room in an abandoned building Mr. Mindful sat behind a desk surrounded by his henchmen.

"So, you understand the plan?" he asked.

The men nodded, though Ken looked doubtful. "I don't know, boss," he said. "Isn't this going too far?"

Mr. Mindful gave him a sharp look. "She tried to restrain me," he said. "She needs to pay."

Chapter 3

Come on, thought Lenny. *Come on.*

Maria's cell phone was still ringing but she was not answering it. Lenny had been trying for a while.

He hung up. *No answer. Where is she?*

Later, Lenny was in the squad room. "What have you got?" Lieutenant Finn asked.

"We managed to identify one of the men who picked up John Doe," answered Lenny. "A Josh Manning. He was picked up for petty thief and burglary and was released about a year ago. His last known address is in another city, and we asked the department there to talk with his known associates. We're also trying to track down where they got the van. One of the guards got a partial number."

"Good," said Finn. "We know we can count on you."

As Finn went over to his office, Detective Turner came up to Lenny. "Hey, I got a tip from one of my informants," he said. He handed Lenny a piece of paper. "Said he saw the guy going into this address. Said he remembered him from the TV."

"Let's go," said Lenny. He started to reach for his coat.

"I'm afraid I can't," said Turner. "There's something I've got to do. Cover for me?"

"Sure," answered Lenny. He put on his coat and left.

"So Charlie said, 'I didn't get those pads there,'" said Lois. She and the other Marhills were sitting around a table in a restaurant. They were all smiling. "'I can't see anything without my glasses and I lost them.' Then Mr. Brady picks them off the top of his head and hands them to him and says, 'Here they are.'"

All three of them broke out laughing. Lois took a sip of her drink. "Not much happens at work, but when it does, I swear . . . , " she began.

Maria was still laughing when Jeff took a bite out of a breadstick. "A lot's been happening since I've been gone, huh?" he asked.

"Not really," said Lois.

"So, Maria, what do you want for your birthday?" asked Jeff.

"I haven't really thought about it," answered Maria.

"Come on, this close and you haven't been thinking about it?" Jeff asked.

"I've had other things on my mind."

Jeff waved a waiter over and ordered more breadsticks. "Well, you still have some time to think about it," said Lois. "It's all in the future."

The future, Maria thought.

A few hours later, Maria was lying on her bed reading.

A man with blond hair was walking through a grocery store. He paused at a shelf with different types of candy on it. After looking around he picked up a candy bar and put it into his pocket. Henry's Grocery Mart February 24, 2:19 p.m.

That's tomorrow, Maria thought. She got out her cell phone and dialed Lenny. After a few moments she heard the message for his call waiting service. *Where is he?* Maria wondered. She left a message saying what she had seen.

"Hey," said Jeff. He came into the room just as she put away her phone. "Your mom wants me to pick up some milk. You want to come?"

"At Henry's Farmer's Market?" asked Maria.

"That's usually where we buy our groceries," answered Jeff.

It'll be weird being there, thought Maria. "Sure," she said. She followed Jeff out of the room.

Josh and Tim watched Maria and Jeff leave their home. They were parked around a corner and Josh had a pair of binoculars. "There she is," he said.

Tim was on a cell phone. "We see her, boss," he said.

"Do it," Mr. Mindful said. Tim hung up and started the car.

Maria felt happy as they drove down the street. She looked out the window at the neighborhood, her home.

"You know, I'm sure things haven't been easy for you," said Jeff. "With everything that's happened I'm sure you had to go through a lot. Now that I'm here, though, I'll help you any way that you need."

"I know, Dad," said Maria.

"Things have been rocky but everything's going to work out."

Suddenly the car shook. *What . . . ,* wondered Maria.

Jeff looked in the rearview mirror. "Someone's hitting us."

The truck that the two henchmen were driving pulled back and raced forward again. They came to a curve in the road as the truck struck the car. It was thrust forward through the curve and flew up and into the far side of a ditch with a crash.

Lois heard the crash through the neighborhood and came out. She saw the truck pull away. She went over to the curve as people started to come out of their homes. She saw the car and cried out.

Chapter 4

Lenny looked around the large empty room inside the warehouse. *No one's here,* he thought. *I searched this place from top to bottom.*

He held up his cell phone. *Still no reception. I don't get it.*

He looked around once again. *Maybe the guy was wrong. They could be in another building. Problem is, this is the warehouse district and there are dozens of abandoned buildings.*

A few minutes later, he came out. Lenny started to go to his car when he noticed that his tires were flat. He looked closer and realized that they had been slashed. *Bad neighborhood,* he thought.

Lenny got up and sighed. *Nearest bus stop is a ways away.* He looked up at the twilight sky. *I don't think they run this late. It looks like I'm walking.*

As he walked away, Ken watched him from around a corner. He was talking on a cell phone. "Yeah, boss, he didn't call for a ride," he said. "The cell phone jammer must've worked."

About an hour later, Lenny entered the squad room. "Where have you been?" asked Detective Lowe.

"I was out and had car trouble," Lenny said. He made his way to his desk and sat down. He rubbed his eyes and sat there for a moment.

"Where's your partner?" Lowe asked.

"Out doing something," Lenny answered. He started to look through the papers on his desk.

"Well, I've got to go out and watch a scene while they tow a wreck away," said Lowe. "It's a real block of scrap metal."

"You're transferring to Traffic Division?" asked Lenny.

"No, but they're shorthanded," Lowe answered. "You know the overflow from the lake on the outskirts of town? It froze and has become a real hazardous patch. There have been several accidents there."

"That's where you're heading?" asked Lenny.

"No, the place where I'm going is on Maple Street," answered Detective Lowe.

Lenny paused. *That's the street Maria lives on,* he thought. "Yeah, some father and daughter got forced off the road," Lowe said.

Maria? wondered Lenny. "Do you have their names?"

"Just the family's name, Marhill. Why?"

Lenny's heart raced and it took all of his self-control to remain visibly calm. "Nothing," he answered. "I've got to go do something." He got up and went to another detective in the room. "Paul, can I borrow your car?"

Minutes later, Lenny was briskly walking down the halls of Brothers in Peace Paway Hospital. He looked around quickly.

Finally he found Lois sitting in a waiting room. He had done a background check on Maria when they first met and recognized Lois from a photo.

Oh no, he thought. Until then he had held on to some hope that it was all a mistake.

Lenny calmed himself and carefully went up to her. "Ma'am" he asked.

Lois looked up, her eyes moist. "Has there been any word?" she asked. "Do they know anything?"

"Madam, I'm sorry but I'm not a doctor," said Lenny. He took out his badge and showed it to her. "I would like to ask you some questions."

"I already talked to the police," said Lois.

"I know, I just want to ask you for a few more." He hated himself for what he was putting her through.

Lois sighed and breathed back the tears. "It's like I said," she said. "I heard a crash and went out to see what had happened. All I saw was the truck driving away."

"Did you catch any part of the license plate?" asked Lenny.

"No," cried Lois. She turned away and slammed her fist against the wall. "Ahh!" she sobbed.

Lois turned back to Lenny, tears running down her face. "Why is this happening again?"

The father, thought Lenny.

Lois put her hand on her forehead. "Why?" she seemed to ask of no one in particular. "Why?" She looked at Lenny. "Why is this happening twice? This sort of thing isn't supposed to happen twice. What's going on?"

Lenny thought about Maria and felt a pang of guilt. *We never told her,* he thought. *I never told her and I'm the adult. I'm supposed to be the one with the clear head, right?*

A man in hospital scrubs came up to them. "Mrs. Marhill?" he asked.

Lois got up. "Yes?" As she looked at the man, she felt many emotions.

"I'm sorry," said the doctor. "Your husband's gone."

"No," cried Lois. She closed her eyes as tears ran down her cheeks. Lenny went up to her and held her. It seemed that he was the only thing keeping her upright.

She opened her eyes and regained a small amount of composure. "What about my daughter?" Fear gripped her heart.

"She's been stabilized," answered the doctor. "You'll be able to see her in a little while. I'm sorry." The doctor turned and walked away.

Lois began to weep fully now and once again seemed to lose the ability to stand on her own. Lenny held her and helped her to a seat. "Oh God, I'm a mess," Lois said.

"It's okay," said Lenny.

"No, it's not okay," Lois said. "I work with numbers all day long and I can't remember anything from that license. When my family actually needs me to be good at numbers, I can't, but with stupid cold medicine on a spreadsheet at work I'm a whiz."

Lois shut her eyes for a moment. "Oh God, I was the one who got them out. I wanted milk for breakfast tomorrow."

"It's not your fault," said Lenny. He put his hands on her shoulders and looked her squarely in the eyes. "It's not your fault. We'll find out whose fault it is, I swear."

"I just don't know how I'm going to be strong for my daughter."

"You don't want your daughter to be without anyone, right?"

"Right."

"Make that your main emotion, not the pain you're feeling," said Lenny. "Deal with the pain, but when you need to, focus on your desire for her not to be alone rather than the loss you're feeling. Focus on one thing over the other."

A woman came into the waiting room. She seemed to be a bit older than Lois. Lois saw her. "Excuse me, that's my sister," she said. Lois got up and went over to the woman and they hugged.

What happened? wondered Lenny. *Why didn't Maria's visions warn her?*

Lenny looked around the waiting room and noticed that no one seemed to be paying attention to him. He leaned forward, putting his face into his hands.

Lenny remembered meeting Maria. *I thought she was crazy, and really I didn't know what to think when those things she told me started to come true. Next thing I know she's riding in the car with me as we leave town chasing after bank robbers. I remember how scared she was after that booby trap was set for my car. Why did I take her along? Why didn't I tell anybody? If I had told a few people, I could've put protection on her.*

Lenny looked at a picture that hung on the wall across from him. He looked at the coloring of the paint. The bright tones, however, failed to quell the feelings inside him. *I didn't tell anyone because I didn't want to think I was crazy for getting advice from a psychic. I didn't want to be put on leave like that last guy who suggested using a psychic, but that didn't stop me from accepting all that attention from the boys upstairs, did it?*

Lenny got up and paced around. He angrily kicked a trash can. It went skidding across the floor. Lenny looked around, but no one seemed to notice what he had done.

Lenny thought about Maria being in the car when it was hit by the booby trap, being kidnapped, being put in a house as it was being bulldozed, and all the fights she had been in.

I kept putting her in danger, thought Lenny. *Some cop or even adult I turned out to be.*

Lenny punched the wall in anger. He went back to the chair and sat down. He dropped his face into his hands. *What am I going to do? There's no psychic teenager to drop the answer into my lap.*

He leaned back in his chair and looked up at the ceiling. *I've got to do something. I should've been doing more since this stuff happened. I've got to solve this case on my own. The only thing is, how am I going to do that when there are other detectives assigned to it? In fact, how much longer can I stay here until someone notices me?*

Lenny reached into his pocket. *They probably already called me.* He looked around and saw a sign that said the hospital did not allow cell phones to be used inside.

He got up and headed out. He passed Lois, who was being comforted by her sister. "You know this is where they took Jeff when he had his first accident," she said, and broke out in a new wave of tears.

Once outside, Lenny checked his messages. There was only one. "Hey, Lenny," said Maria's voice. Lenny's throat tightened as he heard the rest of the message.

Great, thought Lenny. *A candy bar. She gets runs down and whoever or whatever sends her these things warns her about a single, worthless piece of sugar!*

In an outburst of rage Lenny had to resist throwing his cell phone.

He went over to a tree and hit it several times. Once he was finished, he screamed, getting looks from several people. He then went back to the parking and got into his car.

I have half a mind to ignore this candy thing, but Maria left me this message and I'm going to follow through on it. Besides, I need to do something. After I'm done with this, whoever's responsible for this better start praying. He started to drive off.

The next morning, Lenny was walking down the aisle in the store. He had in his hands a tabloid that he pretended to read. *A stakeout for a candy bar,* he thought. He tried to keep his anger down.

When he had woken up that morning, he had had to remind himself that it had not been a dream. He did not go to work but came right to the store.

This is what I'm doing, Lenny thought. *No tracking down evidence, no talking to suspects, just looking out for a candy bar. I thought this at least would be doing something, but now I'm not so sure.*

Frustration welled up in him. *That's it,* he thought. *I'm gone.*

Suddenly a blond man came into his view. He matched Maria's description and caught Lenny's attention. The man looked around and then took a candy bar off the shelf and put it in his pocket.

Lenny went over to him. "Sir," he said.

The man looked up in surprise. "You're that detective," he said.

He must've seen me on TV, Lenny thought.

"How did you find me?" asked the man. "Look, I was only doing what they told me to."

Lenny thought for a moment. "You think the D.A. is just going to buy that?" he asked. He took out his handcuffs. "You're going to have to spill the whole thing if you expect any breaks."

The man sighed. "I'm sorry," he said. "It wasn't anything personal. I didn't want to run the girl over. It was his idea."

Lenny stood there and for a moment could not understand what he was hearing. "What?"

The man looked unsure of the question. "Running the girl off the road," he answered. "Like I said, it was his idea. I didn't have any choice."

It was like a switch had been flipped in Lenny. "Who?" His voice was quiet.

The man was silent and Lenny grabbed him. He shoved him against the shelves. "Who told you to do it?" he asked. "Who?" His voice was rising and he was nearly screaming. People all around looked at them. Lenny was gripping the man by his jacket, going through to his shoulders.

The man had a look of fear and shock on his face. He seemed unable to speak. "Mr. Mindful," he cried out finally.

Mr. Mindful, thought Lenny. *I should've known!* "Where is he?" He was pressing the man so hard against the shelves that they nearly tipped over.

"I can't tell you."

"Oh, you'll tell me," cried Lenny. Lois's face and the things he felt went through his mind. He then stopped himself and took a very deep breath.

Lenny looked at the man. "You're under arrest for being a despicable life form," he said. He forcefully spun him around and cuffed him. "You have the right to remain silent because anything you say will definitely be used against you. If you can't afford a lawyer, then one will be provided for you. Do you understand these rights?"

He walked the man toward the exit and a frightened stock boy came up to them. "I'm police," Lenny said. He got out his badge and held it up. He waved it around for the crowd of frightened people who were watching him.

Several minutes later, Lenny was walking down a hallway in the station house.

Lieutenant Finn came up to him. "What's going on?"

"I'll tell you later, sir," Lenny answered. He passed him and came up to a door then went inside.

Inside the interrogation room, Lenny looked down at the man sitting at the table.

"Tim Miler, that's your name?" asked Lenny.

"Yeah," answered Tim.

"Why did you steal that candy bar when you're working for a big-time criminal like Mr. Mindful?"

"I forgot my money and thought, why not."

Lenny just looked at him.

"Look, what do you have me on?" asked Tim.

"Like I said, being a despicable life form," answered Lenny. He then leaned over to Tim. "If you want to be real technical, then petty thief, aiding a fugitive, and, oh yeah, attempted and actual homicide."

"I can't tell you where he is," said Tim.

"Oh yeah?" asked Lenny. He gave a threatening smile and Tim cringed in fear. Lenny then left the room.

Lenny entered the evidence locker. He looked at a collection of items on a tray on the shelf. He then looked up at the officer in charge. "Is this the stuff they took off the guy I brought in?" Lenny asked.

"Yeah, I heard that you collared . . . Hey," the officer said.

Lenny had been looking through the items and found a cell phone in a plastic bag. He had picked it up and was leaving.

"You have to sign that out," said the officer.

"I'll be right back."

What am I doing? Lenny wondered. He took the cell phone out of the bag as he came to a door leading to the squad room.

Lenny flipped the phone open and brought up its memory. He went through the recent calls. *Mr. Mindful's number has got to be in here. This brand of phone is usually disposable and he probably has one too, but maybe we can track him through the cell towers.*

Lenny looked at the row of numbers and saw a familiar one. After feeling nothing, powerful emotions came up in him once again.

He peeked out into the squad room and pressed the redial button on the phone.

Detective Turner's phone rang and he answered it. "What do you want? I told you not to call me here."

Lenny stood there saying nothing. "Hello?" asked Detective Turner.

Lenny went through the door and across the squad room.

Lenny went up to Detective Turner, who looked up at him. "Yes?" he asked.

Lenny just looked at him and held up the phone. A brief look of fear flashed in Detective Turner's eyes.

Lenny grabbed Turner by his shirt and pulled him out from behind his desk. "You," Lenny cried. Emotions raged within him.

The other detectives rushed over to Lenny and Detective Turner as they struggled.

"You," Lenny cried. "It was you!"

"What's going on?" demanded Lieutenant Finn. Some of the detectives pulled Lenny off Detective Turner.

"He's been in contact with one of Mr. Mindful's goons," Lenny said. He showed him the phone.

Finn took the phone. "These are serious accusations," he said. He looked through the numbers.

"You've been talking with a known fugitive, the guy who tried to blow a building full of people up," said Lenny. "Did you help? How long? What kind of cop . . ."

Detective Turner suddenly became angry. "A good one," he cried. "Not that anyone noticed. It's all Lenny, Lenny, Lenny! No matter how many leads and suspects I gather, or how much work I do, it's Lenny who's getting invited to parties or who's heading to the top! I don't exist!"

"Is that what this is about?" asked Lenny. "Is that why you sold out everything you're supposed to believe in? You're pathetic."

"Me?" demanded Detective Turner. He started to charge at him, but some of the other detectives held him back. "You're the spoiled brat who gets all the attention and rewards while doing nothing. You're nothing! You never earned any of it. I'm ten times the detective you are! Ten times!"

"Traitor," cried Lenny. The detectives near him readied themselves to grab him, but he made no move toward Detective Turner.

Turner struggled with the detectives. "Ahh!" he cried. "It's not fair!"

"Enough," Finn said. He looked at the detectives holding Turner. "Take him to interrogation room four," he ordered. They dragged him away as he struggled.

Lenny walked away. *I should've seen it,* he thought. *I'm a detective. Or do I need Maria's visions for everything?*

Lenny reached his desk and leaned on it. He struggled with all the emotions going through him. *Gets all the awards and does none of the work. Maybe Jon's not the only one who broke the rules.*

Lenny felt a rise of anger. *No, this is Mr. Mindful's fault, all of it, and he's going to pay!* He darted off.

Lenny entered the room where Tim was being held. He looked up at Lenny. "You're going to tell me everything," Lenny said.

About an hour later, Ken and Josh were sitting around a table. "I don't like this," said Ken. "Tim should've been back an hour ago."

Suddenly, something flew through the gap between two boards covering a window. There was simultaneously a loud bang and a bright flash. *Flash bang grenade,* thought Ken. He covered his ears.

The two men saw blurred shapes race around them as S.W.A.T. team members came crashing through two windows and the front door. They rushed in and forced the men onto the floor.

"All . . . , " began one of the team members. Lenny darted past him and went across the room. "Sir, you've got to wait for us to give the all-clear on the other rooms." Lenny continued to go deeper into the building.

After searching a few rooms he came to a room at the end of the hallway. He went in and found Mr. Mindful sitting behind a desk.

"Don't move," ordered Lenny.

"Ordering me around like a common criminal," Mr. Mindful said. "I would think that you knew better. What are you going to do? Put me in a cage again?"

Lenny seethed with anger. "You attacked a defenseless girl," he said. "Why?"

"Because, as we both know, she was the real reason I was brought down," answered Mr. Mindful. "She was like all the rest, so high and mighty. They have always tried to make me behave, to put me in a box. They tried to contain me? I'm the smartest person in any room, and I choose to use those smarts to become one of the greatest criminals this world has ever seen. But I didn't get a good enough start in my career and it's her fault. I was supposed to be making my mark on history."

Mr. Mindful took a breath. "She was like all the rest. Just like my parents. They would always say, 'You must be mindful of others.' Well, guess what, I am Mr. Mindful. Soon, despite everything, I'll be making my mark on this world."

Lenny felt his anger boil in him. "You think she tried to contain you?" he asked. "Just wait until you see what I'm going to do."

Several members of the S.W.A.T. entered the room. "You're under arrest, you piece of garbage," Lenny said.

"I don't think so," Mr. Mindful said. He pressed a button underneath his desk.

A part of the wall behind Mr. Mindful flipped open, revealing a square of metal. Embedded in the metal was a digital clock counting down from thirty.

Lenny looked at it for a moment. *Oh no,* he thought. "Everyone get out of here." He and the others started to leave.

Lenny stopped and looked back. Mr. Mindful was going through a hidden door that was next to the timer.

"We've got to go," cried an officer. He grabbed Lenny and they left the room.

The last three, Lenny and two officers, left the building. It erupted in a ball of fire. The roar of the explosion filled their ears and made it difficult to think. The force of the blast sent them down to the ground.

In a moment, Lenny looked up at the burning building with a scowl on his face.

An hour later, Maria was lying a hospital bed. Lois came into the room. *I've got to tell her,* she thought.

"Honey," she said. "It's your father. He has . . ."

She could not go on. She erupted in tears and leaned over the bed.

Maria reached up and held her. They cried together.

BOOK 11

The Secrets
of the Cricket

Chapter 1

Maria woke up, got out of bed, and then got ready for the day.

She went to the bathroom and cleaned herself up. Maria pulled her hair back and then looked herself over in the mirror. She looked at the scar on her left cheek and ran a finger over it, vaguely remembering flying glass hitting her face during the accident.

Maria went downstairs. Lois was sitting at the kitchen table. "Hi," she said.

"Hi," Maria said. She got a bowl of cereal and sat down.

Lois looked at her. "Are you sure you're ready to go back to school?"

"Yeah," Maria answered. They ate in silence.

Later, Maria walked down a hallway in her school. The sights around her were familiar yet were not. She thought she saw people looking at her, but she was not sure.

Later that day, Maria entered her English class. She knew the other students were looking at her. Her teacher welcomed her back, smiling. As she talked, Maria saw her eyes dart momentarily to the scar on her face. The way the teacher acted was pleasant in a way Maria did not like.

Maria went through the next several classes blocking out everything that had happened to her. Her scar seemed to be a magnet for people's eyes.

At lunch, Maria got her food and started to sit down. As she was about to get a seat, she saw several students looking at her. After a moment, she left the cafeteria and went to the library.

At the end of the day, Maria was at her locker getting a few of her things.

There was a large, dark room. On the walls were red posters with a green symbol on them. A group of men in green, hooded robes stood in the room. They surrounded a pedestal with a statue of a cricket on it. Something fell down toward the center of the room. A man rushed over to the pedestal. 120 Baker Lane, March 20, 4:03 p.m.

Again, thought Maria. She did not know what she was feeling. She ducked into a bathroom.

Maria stood there doing nothing. She let out a sigh of anger and then frustration and then defeat. *It didn't help me,* she thought. Maria remembered the face of the man who had darted to the pedestal. *He was as old as Dad.*

Maria put her face in her hands. She felt a wave of emotion but fought it. After a few breaths she took out her cell phone and dialed Lenny.

Lenny sat in his apartment. On the coffee table before him were news clippings and files of cases he had worked on.

They all think I'm some genius detective. I let a teenager do the work for me and then she wound up in the sights of some lunatic.

Lenny felt anger rise up in him, but then he sighed and looked off to the side.

His cell phone rang. *Lieutenant? I'm not coming back to work. Not now and maybe not never.*

He looked at the caller ID. *Maria,* he thought. *I should probably add some more minutes to the phone.* "Hello?"

"Hi," Maria said. She told him what she had seen.

Again, Lenny thought. "Okay, I'll check it out. How are you doing?"

"Fine."

"Are you sure?"

"I'm fine."

Lenny went over to his computer and did a search for the address Maria had given him. A few links came up, including one for something called the Order of the Cricket. He clicked on the link.

A few minutes later, Maria came home. "How was school?" asked Lois.

"Fine," answered Maria. She went upstairs.

Maria went into her room and started to do some punching exercises. She had started to study karate after she had been kidnapped on a case.

It's just one thing after another, Maria thought.

Her punches into the air were more forceful as her anger rose. Her body felt the force of the blows as she struck with all her might. She struck out savagely one last time. "Ahh!" she cried.

Maria stood there breathing heavily. After a few minutes she began to calm down.

Her cell phone vibrated and she pushed down her emotions before she answered it.

"I've found what we're looking for," said Lenny.

"What is it?"

"There's a secret society called the Order of the Cricket. I found them online."

"A secret society with a website?"

"Yeah, strange, huh?" Lenny's tone was almost humorous. "They apparently believe in this bunch of mojo, like 'the music of the cricket is all around us' and 'if one learns to recognize the music, then one can go on to his true destiny.' They have pictures of their 'sacred cricket statue,' which seems like the thing you described. The address you gave me is their Great Hall, their meeting place. I'm going to do some more research and then I'll go down tomorrow."

"I'm coming too," said Maria.

"That's not necessary."

"I'm coming."

"It could be dangerous," Lenny said.

"That thing that's going to happen won't happen for a couple of days," Maria said. "Besides, I've been in danger before."

Lenny felt a pang of guilt. "You can't go."

"It's my vision."

"It's my case." *Even though I'm not sure I'm still on the job.*

"I'm going," said Maria. "One way or another."

Lenny sighed. "Fine." I'll pick you up tomorrow."

"Is it ready?" asked one man of another. He looked around nervously.

"Yeah," said the other man. "It's going to happen."

"It's time for some changes," said the first man.

School let out the next day. Maria left the building. *That was a little better,* she thought.

"Hey, Maria," said Jen. "You want me to walk home with you?"

"No, I'm fine," answered Maria. *She takes an interest now?* She walked away.

A few minutes later, Lenny's car pulled up. As Maria got in, she felt comforted by the familiar sights she saw. "How're you doing?" she asked.

"Fine," answered Lenny. "If we're going to do this, then you're waiting in the car while I go."

Maria thought for a moment. "Fine."

A few minutes, Lenny went up to the order's Great Hall.

A man with a thick, black mustache answered the door. "May I help you?" he asked.

"I'm here to ask some questions," said Lenny. He tried to sound uncertain. "I'm thinking of joining."

"Come in," the man said. "There's someone you need to meet."

The man led Lenny inside. Maria watched from the car, and after they went in, she got out.

Maria went around the building and came up to a sign that read "Order of the Cricket." There was also the symbol she had seen on the posters in her vision, which she then realized was a silhouette of a cricket.

Maria went up to a window and looked inside. The room was empty. She looked around and saw that there was no one about so she rolled up her jacket sleeves and pushed the window open. She climbed into the room.

Looking around, she saw no sign of anyone. She closed the window and went up to the door.

Peeking out of the doorway, she saw no one. Maria slowly went out to the hallway.

Lenny sat in a room. A man with brown hair came in and sat in the chair in front of him. "So, Mr. Highbridge, I hear you want to join our order," said the man.

"Yes, I've been lost for a long time. Maybe you can help me not to be lost anymore," said Lenny.

"Yes, we try to provide guidance to those who feel lost in this confusing world," said the man. "I don't know if anyone told you but my name's Claude Mayfield. I run this order. It's small, but the way of the cricket is a powerful philosophy. It can help you, and it will change your life."

"The way of the cricket will change your life," Maria heard a voice say. She peeked through a crack in the doorway to see a younger man talking with a much older one.

"It is a powerful philosophy," said the older man.

"I got that, Joseph," said the younger man.

"The music of the cricket is playing around us," Joseph said. "We simply must learn to listen for it so that it can change our lives. The sound of it is said to be beautiful and no one may ever truly understand it all, but we must try."

"How do you hear the music?" asked the younger man.

"Ted, you simply let it in," answered Joseph. "We're surrounded by it but can't hear it because we live in a society that floods our ears and minds with a bunch of meaningless noise. Once one calms one's mind it will come flooding in. People usually can't make it out at first, but once they filter out the noise and find the music, it will change their lives and their paths will become clear."

"So, what the order looks for in new members is the ability to let the music in?" asked Ted.

Maria suddenly heard a noise. She turned to see a shadow moving on the wall beyond a corner. *Someone's coming.*

Maria went to the other end of the hall. She heard footsteps approach and tried numerous doors. One opened and she went in.

Maria stood by the door and waited a few moments before the noises passed. Once they did, she looked around for a window, but there was not one.

A few moments later, Maria darted out of the room. She went around a corner and came to another hallway. She went down it, looking for an exit. Maria then heard talking and believed the sound was getting closer.

Maria placed her hands on a wall and placed a foot on the opposite wall. She moved her hands, one after the other, toward the ceiling, and her feet joined in. She was soon near the ceiling.

She looked down and saw two men going down the hall beneath her. Maria tried to be as still as she could be. They soon turned a corner and were gone.

Maria stayed there for a few minutes more just in case they came back. She felt the strain on her arms and legs. *Keep it together,* she told herself. *You can do this.* A few seconds later she dropped to the floor.

She darted around a corner and found a window. She opened it and climbed out.

Maria was waiting for Lenny in the car. "How did it go?" she asked.

"Fine," answered Lenny. He got in. "I used an old undercover alias, Carl Highbridge,"

"Any idea why whatever it was was falling?" asked Maria.

"It could be an accident," said Lenny.

"Maybe, but I don't usually get visions of accidents."

"Hmmph." Lenny looked at Maria. "Maria, do you think it's time to tell your mother about, well, everything?"

"No," answered Maria. "It would just complicate things even more."

"It's just that when I saw her in that emergency room, she needed answers for what was happening to her," said Lenny.

"I'm not telling her." Her tone was forceful. "This isn't the right time."

Lenny sighed. "Okay."

As they drove off into the distance, a figure was watching from a window of the Great Hall.

Chapter 2

Maria sat at the table having dinner with her mother. Neither of them said anything.

After several minutes, Maria spoke. "Excuse me," she said. Lois just nodded slightly. Maria got up and left the room.

Maria got into her room. She sighed and then went over to her bed.

Let in the music, huh, Maria wondered. She took a deep breath and then closed her eyes as she visualized a cricket playing music with its hind legs. She played the music in her mind and visualized it coming into her.

Suddenly, something flashed through her mind. It was like when she had a vision. She quickly opened her eyes and looked around. *No way,* she thought.

She closed her eyes and visualized the music again, this time more intensely.

Images once again flowed through her mind, though she could not make out any of them. Her mind flashed back to what Joseph had said, and then she returned to the music.

"Hi, honey," said Joseph.

"Hi, sweetie," said an old woman. She was sitting across from the door Joseph had come through. "Breakfast is on the table," she said. 21 Pine Lane, March 28, 8:09 a.m.

Whoa, thought Maria. *That actually worked. I actually made a vision come. If I had this when . . .*

Maria just lay there. After a moment she got up and got ready for her shower.

The next morning, Maria got up and got ready for school. As she finished getting dressed, her cell phone vibrated. "Yeah?"

"I'm going to check out a lead today," said Lenny. "I'm afraid I'm going to be out for most of the day so I won't be able to call you, but please try to call me if you get a vision, okay?"

"Sure."

She doesn't need to get involved, Lenny thought.

Later that day, Lenny stood in the Great Hall wearing a green robe. A man named Thomas noticed that he was eyeing what they placed on him. "These are our ceremonial robes," he said.

"Right," said Lenny. He adjusted the robe on his body.

Claude stepped into the middle of the room. "Brothers, we gather here to welcome a new member into our fold. Like so many, he is lost and we can only hope that the way of the cricket can guide him to his true path."

Claude gestured with a hand and Lenny stepped before him. "On your knees, please," Claude said. Lenny kneeled. "Oh, Great Cricket, please play your music so this one can hear it. May he hear it and inspire others to hear it too. May he find his true path and may the confusion of this world fall away. May he be a brother to us. Rise, Brother Carl Highbridge."

Lenny rose. "Brother Carl Highbridge," said everyone else in the room.

Claude extended his hand, which Lenny shook. "Carl, go meet with the others," he said.

Lenny went over to one of the groups that had formed as everyone split off and began to talk. "Hi," he said.

"Welcome to the club," said one of the men in the group.

I can use this meet-and-greet to get some information. Lenny thought. "Club," he said. "That sounds a bit different from what Brother Claude was going on about."

"Don't let 'Brother' Claude fool you," said the man. "To most of us this is just a way to get together, though he's a true believer." The man's eyes went over to the side. "Speaking of which."

Claude went over to a pedestal that was in the middle in the room. On it was a sacred-cricket statue. He bowed his head solemnly.

"That's our 'sacred statue,'" said the man. "Apparently it's been here since the founding of the order. Personally, I'm more into the rec room and the once-a-week barbecued ribs than that rock."

"Don't let him catch you saying that," said the other man.

Another man came over to them. "Hey, guys," he said. "Making the new guy feel welcome?"

"Sure, Jerry," said the first man.

"Jerry Jones," said the man. He offered Lenny his hand, which he took.

"Carl Highbridge," said Lenny.

"So, what do you think of our little club?" asked Jerry.

"It's nice," answered Lenny. "It's just a little out there."

"Yeah, some of us can be a little out there," said Jerry.

"Like our esteemed leader," said the first man.

"He means well," said Jerry. "He just wants this place to be something that helps people find their way. We all do. It's why we founded this place. It's just that there's more than one way to do that."

"Anyone acting strange or suspicious?" asked Lenny.

Jerry looked at him for a moment. "Well, there are those two guys over there." He turned and pointed at the two men talking to each other.

"Leo and George?" asked the first man. "They're harmless."

"Yeah, but they're always going off together and talking in secret like they're planning something," said Jerry.

Could be worth looking into, Lenny thought.

After the meeting Lenny followed Leo and George in his car. They had gotten into a car and driven to a trailer park, and then they went into one of the smaller trailers.

Lenny crept around the bushes as they went inside. He darted across the yard and went up toward a window. "We've got everything planned," said Leo

"Everything all set?" asked George.

"Like I said, everything's all planned."

"Yeah, but everything could go off plan."

"Don't worry."

"I do worry," said George. "This needs to go accordingly."

"I'll make sure it does," said a third voice.

There's a third guy, thought Lenny. *They're definitely planning something. It could be connected to what Maria saw.*

Lenny had trouble hearing what they said next. *Had they turned on the , T.V.?* he wondered. He strained to hear them.

What am I going to do? Lenny wondered. *I could follow one of them when he leaves, but that leaves possibly two unaccounted for. Maybe I could run off and get a tracking device for the cars they drove here. I could probably make it back before they left. It's not actually by the book, but no one seems to follow the rules anymore . . . especially me.*

Suddenly, the door opened. Lenny darted to a bush in the front yard.

"See you guys tomorrow," said George. Luke and the other man left.

"Don't worry about the election," said Luke. "By this time next week you'll be leader."

"I better be," said George.

They're talking about that election I heard about for leader of the order, thought Lenny. *Are they going to make that thing fall because of it?*

Lenny watched as the two men went to their cars and drove off. George went back inside, and a few minutes later Lenny went over to his car and left.

The next day, Lenny got dressed. Someone called him, but he let the answering machine get it. "You've reached the phone of Lenny Hipar," played the message. "Please leave a message and I'll get back to you."

There was a beep and then the voice of Lieutenant Steve Finn. "Hey, Lenny," he said. "I just want to let you know that you can take as much time as you need. We're all in shock by what your partner did, giving info to that nut job. Heaven knows why he had those people run off the road. I'll call to let you know what happens to him. Anyway, call me and let me know what you're doing. You have my number."

What am I doing? wondered Lenny. *Also, what am I going to do about Maria?* He sighed. *I don't even know that I'm coming back. It's not like I'm a real detective. All those cases I "cracked" were really Maria's doing.*

Lenny sat down and put his face in his hands. *I used her,* he thought. *I used her and she got hurt. No more. At most now, she's a consultant.* Lenny got his jacket and went out.

Lenny went into the Great Hall. He saw that there was no one in the lobby and decided to go into the Ceremonial Chamber, where most of the order's major activities took place.

Lenny saw that the members were gathered in the center of the room. ". . . may the confusion of this world fall away," said Claude. "May she be a sister to us."

A new member? wondered Lenny. He maneuvered his way through the crowd.

"Arise, Sara Lowes," said Claude. The young woman before him rose and turned around. It was Maria.

Chapter 3

"We've been planning on inducting sisters into our order for some time now," said Claude. He placed his hands on Maria's shoulders. "We had planned to do so a few months from now, but when this young woman came to us and described how she longed for her way, we knew she was a perfect fit for us and had to bring her in immediately. Despite the fact that she is young, we knew her heart truly longed to hear the cricket's music," said Claude. "Please welcome Sister Sara Lowe."

"Welcome, Sister Sara Lowe," said everyone else. Lenny joined in to avoid suspicion.

"Now, go meet your brothers," said Claude. He withdrew from her.

Lenny came up to her. "What's going on?" he whispered.

"Can't we talk about this later?" Maria whispered back.

George went up to them. "I wanted to be the first to welcome you, but apparently someone has beaten me to it," he said.

"Yeah, he's very friendly," said Maria.

They talked for a few moments and George left them. As he left, Maria saw Tim eyeing her.

Lenny then noticed the absence of a scar on Maria's cheek. "What happened to your face?" he asked.

"I used some of Mom's makeup to cover it up," answered Maria. "I didn't want to draw too much attention." She then went off and met with several other members.

After the meeting, Maria and Lenny left the Great Hall and got into his car. He had parked some distance away, but they still looked around to see if anyone had followed them. They got in and drove off.

"I can't believe no one told me about your introduction," said Lenny.

"Apparently, I impressed them so much that they wanted to get me in right away," said Maria. "Their leader, Claude, was the guy I saw in my vision with the thing falling toward him."

"You have a lot to explain."

Maria looked up at him. "Okay," she said. "When you first went in, I sneaked inside. I heard two of those guys talk about their beliefs. After I got home, I thought about 'drawing the music of the cricket' to me, and I found out that it works. I could make visions come to me by visualizing music coming into my mind or something. I had a vision of one of the guys I listened to. Then later I had some of people I know, including you. It was nothing major—I just saw you get inducted. I went over to your place while you were out and used the key you gave me to get in. I found the tape from the wire you wore to the ceremony and listened to it to prepare myself."

The wire I "borrowed," and now she can make the visions happen, Lenny thought. *Great—she's now even more deeply into this.* He turned around a curve and Maria kept talking. "This morning I went to Claude and told him I was confused by this world and that this confusion was everywhere and so forth. I used what I knew about their beliefs to make myself seem like a perfect candidate. They seemed to love me."

"Maria, you shouldn't have done that," said Lenny.

"Me? What about you? You decided you were going to do everything by yourself. I thought we were a team."

"Not anymore. Now I'm the cop and you're the consultant."

"Huh? Since when?"

Lenny was silent for a moment. "Since it happened," he said.

"What?" asked Maria. "That happened to me and you're . . . you can't!"

"It happened because I used you," said Lenny. "You're staying home. If you get a vision, call me."

Lenny stopped at a stop sign not far away from Maria's home. "No way," she cried. "No way after what happened, after what I lost, can you use that and keep me at home!"

"I'm doing that because I care about you. I'm going to keep you safe."

"I don't need you to keep me safe, you overprotective dork. I can do that myself."

"It hasn't worked so far," Lenny said.

Maria looked at him. She unbuckled her seat belt and got out of the car. "Hey, we're not at the Drop-off point yet," Lenny said.

Maria did not even turn around. "I'll walk."

Lenny watched her until she out of sight and then drove home.

Later that day, Maria sat on her bed and took a deep breath. *Here it goes,* she thought. She focused on Tim as she let the "music" in as she had done before.

"This is Jean," said Tim.
Claude shook the young woman's hand.
"She would be perfect for our order," said Tim.
"You're not just saying that because she's your girlfriend?" asked Claude.
He smiled as he asked. 120 Baker Lane, April 2, 3:56 p.m.

Maria opened her eyes. *That was . . . nothing,* she thought. She closed her eyes again.

After dinner Lenny dialed the number of Roger, a member of the order. "Hi," Lenny said.

"Can I help you?" asked Roger.

"I was talking with one of the guys and they said something was going to happen in a few days," Lenny said. "Any idea what that might be?"

"Oh yeah," said Roger. "The anniversary of the order's founding is coming up and we're doing something to celebrate. There will be a few sacred rituals and then food and fun."

"Sounds good."

"Yeah, it's going to happen in two days."

"Thanks," Lenny said. *In two days. That's the date of Maria's vision.*

Joseph stood before Claude in his office. "I would be perfect for the job," Joseph said. "I've planned events before, and I have some wonderful ideas about the anniversary celebration."

"I don't know," said Claude. 120 Baker Lane, March 26 4:40 p.m.

This might take some time, Maria thought. She closed her eyes again.

Two days later, Lenny approached the Great Hall. George was standing in front of the building. "Carl," George said. "How are you doing?"

"Fine," Lenny answered. "So, today is the big day, huh?"

"Yeah, it's our last big event before the election of our new leader," said George.

The election that you want to rig, Lenny thought. "Ready?" he asked.

"Yeah, I was just waiting to make an entrance," said George. They walked inside. "You know, if Claude can pull off a good celebration, then he's a shoo-in for next term as leader."

Lenny looked around the chamber. Not much was different despite the occasion. As he was looking around, he noticed something overhead. Hanging over the statue was a much larger figure of a cricket.

Chapter 4

That's what Maria saw in her vision, Lenny thought.

George noticed him looking at it. "Like it?" he asked. "A couple of the guys made it for the celebration. It's papier-mâché or something. Claude doesn't really do a lot of decorating at these things because 'it's what's in our hearts, not what's around us that makes a occasion special,' but he allowed it."

"Nice," Lenny said.

"Excuse me," said George. He went over to talk with Luke and another man.

Lenny looked around and replayed what Maria told him was going to happen. *I've got to keep everyone away from that pedestal. It's going to happen sometime around four, right? That still leaves me a few minutes. I should've staked out this place, but they opened it to the majority of the members only a few minutes ago.*

Lenny waited as he watched the members' numbers grow. He tried to hide his nervous energy as he smiled while greeting the other members. His eyes never fully left the pedestal.

"It's almost time," Claude said.

Lenny's heart raced and he checked his watch; it was 4:01. *It's almost time.* His eyes shifted back to the statue.

Claude went over to the pedestal. *Uh oh,* Lenny thought.

"If we can now begin," Claude said.

Lenny darted to Claude's side. "There's someone who wants to speak to you in the back," he whispered.

Claude looked at Lenny. "Okay," he said. He went to the back of the small crowd that had formed. People quietly chatted with each other as he went.

"What's going on?" asked one man.

"Did you hear that something was going to happen?" asked another.

When Lenny saw that Claude had reached the back of the crowd, he shot a look overhead at the figure and then rushed to the pedestal. He grabbed the statue and then darted out from beneath the figure.

"He's got the statue," someone said.

"Everyone stay calm," said Lenny. He held up a hand. "I'm police and we have a situation here."

Muttering filled the room.

Suddenly there was a snapping noise and the figure fell downward. The room was filled with a loud crash as the figure hit the pedestal, knocking it over and breaking into pieces.

People all over the room cried out. "What's the meaning of this?" someone asked.

"Did you cut the rope?" asked Roger's voice.

"Yeah, I frayed it so it'll take a while to break," answered the voice of Lou, another member.

Maria stepped into the front of the crowd, holding a tape recorder that was playing.

"Good. You're sure that it'll smash the statue?" asked Roger's voice.

"As heavy as it is, yeah," answered Lou's.

The crowd started speaking all at once. Roger darted from it and toward the door. Lenny put down the statue and ran in front of him.

Roger threw a punch, which Lenny dodged. He tried to grab Roger, but he pulled away. Roger threw another punch, but Lenny dodged it and then grabbed his arm and pulled him toward him. He put Roger in a headlock. As Roger kicked and struggled, Lenny forced him to the ground.

Lou ran out of the crowd toward them, but Maria darted in front of him. The crowd pulled back as people yelled out.

Lou threw a punch, which Maria blocked. She then grabbed his arm and flipped him onto the floor. She stepped onto his back, pressing her weight into him. Maria held Lou roughly by the hair with one hand as she raised the other in a fist.

Claude had picked up the statue as Lenny and Roger fought. After Maria had subdued Lou, he spoke. "What's going on here? Are you really a police officer?"

"Police detective, really, and for what's really going on here, let's ask Roger," Lenny answered.

Roger struggled for a moment and then stopped. "It wasn't personal," he said. "Once that stupid statue was destroyed, then things would change. We wouldn't have to go through rituals or listen to any more stuff about the cricket's music. It would just be about a bunch of guys hanging out. That's why most of us joined. Isn't that right, my 'brothers'?"

"What about the people who could've been hurt?" asked Lenny.

Roger was silent.

Lenny pulled him up and handed him over to Claude. "Do what you want with him, but I recommend you call the police," he said.

"Aren't you the police?" asked Claude.

Lenny looked at Maria. "Come on," he said. He and Maria left the room.

Together they went over to his car, took off their robes, and got in. Maria rolled up her robe in a ball and kept it on her lap while Lenny simply threw his in the backseat.

"We know who would've gotten hurt if that had happened," said Maria. "It would've been Claude, and all because he believed in the way of the cricket so much that he wanted to protect the statue."

They were silent for a moment.

"Okay, how did you do it?" asked Lenny.

"As I said, I can now make visions happen. I just checked all the members' futures until I saw Roger and Lou having that conversation a few minutes before the Great Hall opened. I sneaked in and recorded them."

And I thought having control over the visions was a bad thing, thought Lenny. "About what I said," he said.

"That's just going to take time to heal," said Maria. She unconsciously touched the makeup that hid her scar.

"Yeah," Lenny said. He was not sure what else to say.

"Just so you know, I can take care of myself," said Maria.

"Yeah, you can. You don't need me. You never did."

"What?"

"It's true. When I think of all the success I've had because of your visions . . ."

"Hey," said Maria. "Without you I wouldn't be able to do anything with them. When I first started, I had no idea what to do. You listened to me, and if it hadn't been for you, I wouldn't have been able to chase those robbers. You gave me courage when I was scared and saved my life more times than I can count, you really did. You always had my back."

Maria looked out the passenger's-side window. "You know, I think I actually blamed you for what happened, but it wasn't your fault. It was because of . . . him. I'm not saying that you're not a jerk, but you're my partner."

Lenny was silent for a moment. He arrived a block from Maria's house. She got out, holding the bundle of robes in her arm.

"I guess we just have to look forward to the future when our wounds will be healed," Lenny said. He made a face when he realized what he had said. "Sorry."

"It's okay," said Maria. She smiled and then closed the door and walked off.

Lenny drove away. Maria stopped at the corner and watched him as he went. *Look forward to the future,* she thought. Maria walked home.

BOOK 12

Race Against Time

Chapter 1

Maria woke up and got dressed. She got ready for what she thought would be an ordinary day.

Maria went into the bathroom to wash up and saw the scar on her left cheek as she had every morning since the accident. *Still there,* she thought. She looked at it for a moment and then pulled her eyes from the mirror. Maria washed up and went downstairs.

The kitchen where Maria usually found her mother making breakfast was empty.

"Mom?" she called. She looked around the kitchen and then, getting worried, searched the house. She could not find her. *Where is she?* she wondered.

Maria poured herself a bowl of cereal and tried to eat as she pushed her worry down. *I'm sure she'll come through the door any minute,* she told herself. She tried to eat as though everything were normal, but after a few moments she could not contain her worry anymore.

Maria put her spoon down and closed her eyes. She focused on her mother.

Lois pounded on the door. "Help," she cried. "Someone help me! I can't get out!" No one responded and Lois turned away from the door. April 2, 4:07 p.m.

Oh no, thought Maria. *Mom!* Her body was gripped in cold terror and she bolted up from her chair. *She's been kidnapped.*

Maria darted around the room. *I've got to call Lenny,* she thought. She dashed up to her room to get her cell phone.

"I'm glad you're okay," said Lieutenant Finn.

"Thank you, sir," said Lenny. He went over to his desk and sat down.

"What your partner did was deplorable," Steve Finn said. "His giving info to that crook obviously led to that man and his daughter being forced off the road, which led to his death. The D.A. said that once the nut's caught and he's tried for the homicide, Jon Turner will be named as accomplice along with all his other crimes. Don't worry—no one thinks you had anything to do with it. You're the guy who busted him, after all."

"I didn't think so, sir," said Lenny.

Finn left Lenny, whose cell phone rang. Lenny looked at the caller ID and recognized Maria's number. *Another vision?* he wondered. "Hello?"

"Lenny, you've got to come over," Maria said, and she explained what had happened.

"Don't worry," said Lenny. "I'll be right over."

Lenny got up and darted through the squad room. "Lenny, where are you going?" asked Lieutenant Finn.

"Sorry, sir, but I can't say," Lenny answered.

Maria was waiting in her living room. *This can't be happening,* she thought. *Not now.* There was a knock at the door and she let Lenny in.

"Did you find anything?" he asked.

"No, everything looks just the same as usual," she said. "There are no broken doors or windows, and her car keys are still here. I don't know what's happening." Maria tried to stay calm, but powerful emotions went through her. Her father's image flashed through her mind and she tried to block it out.

"You saw her in that vision, right?" asked Lenny. He was looking around.

"Yeah, but I couldn't get a location. That's never happened before."

"Don't worry" said Lenny. "It'll be all right." He continued to look around the room. "Can I look through your house?"

"Sure," answered Maria.

Lenny spent several minutes going through the house with Maria following him. Suddenly, the phone rang. "It could be someone who's wondering where she is," said Maria. "Like someone from work."

"We can't let anyone get too curious until we know what we're doing," said Lenny. "Besides, it's too early for a missing person's report."

"Maybe it's someone who knows where she is," Maria said. She raced through the house with Lenny following her. She reached the phone. "Hello?"

"Hello, my dear," said a familiar voice. *Mindful*, thought Maria. Powerful emotions went through her.

"You," she said. "It's you. You're behind this."

"Yes, I am," said Mr. Mindful. His tone was actually cheerful. "I have your mother."

Maria felt a surge of anger. She squeezed the phone, wanting to throw it. She willed herself to be steady. "Why are you doing this?" she asked, trying to be calm.

"Why do I do anything?" asked Mr. Mindful. "Because I want to. Because it fits my standing as a master criminal."

Maria clenched the phone and her teeth. She was so angry, she wanted to cry out. She stopped herself and took a deep breath. She looked at Lenny and mouthed the words *Mr. Mindful*.

Of course, thought Lenny. *He's the only one who knows about Maria and where she lives*. He took out his cell phone. "This is Detective Lenard Hipar," he said. "Badge number two two five zero seven eight five. I need a trace on a line calling a phone. The number is . . ."

"What stripe of cat loves water?" asked Mr. Mindful.

"What are you talking about?" demanded Maria. Mr. Mindful hung up.

"He's gone," said Maria.

"Cancel that," said Lenny into his cell phone.

Maria went over to the couch and put her face in her hands. Lenny went over and leaned toward her.

"Maria, I know that this is hard, but what did he say?"

"Just another one of his stupid riddles," answered Maria. "What stripe of cat loves water?"

Stripe? wondered Lenny. "Tigers have stripes," he said.

Maria thought for a moment and then went upstairs. Lenny followed her.

They entered her room. Maria went to her computer and brought up the search engine.

She did a search on tigers and thousands of links came up. She clicked on a link for an online encyclopedia. After reading for a few minutes she spoke. "Tigers like to swim," she said. "Apparently they're good at it."

"Yeah, but go back," said Lenny.

Maria went back to the list of links. At the direction of Lenny's pointer finger she clicked on one for the Paway Zoo.

An image of a tiger with some text below it came up on the screen. They read the text. "There's a new tiger at the zoo," said Maria. "They're having an event."

"Let's go," said Lenny.

Minutes later, they arrived at the zoo. Maria forced her way through the other visitors while Lenny was making his way through them more gently. "Excuse me," he said.

Maria came up to the gate. She could barely keep herself from running through it. Lenny came up and paid for two tickets. Maria darted inside just as Lenny had the tickets in hand.

Maria scanned the crowd, looking for any sign of her mother. She vaguely noticed that a man she passed looked at her scar, but she did not care. Lenny came up to her. "Where is she?" Maria asked.

"You know it won't be that simple," said Lenny. "Things with Mr. Mindful never are."

Maria approached a sign that gave directions to various exhibits. She saw an arrow pointed at the tiger exhibit and ran off with Lenny following.

They came to the exhibit. The tiger, named Slugger, was sitting on a platform of earth in front of a stone wall. In the wall was a cave with the inside shrouded in darkness. Beyond the platform of land was water. The edge where the tiger's area and the visitors' area met was raised several feet. There was also a railing.

Maria and Lenny scanned the exhibit. Lenny then scanned the surrounding crowds while Maria still focused on the exhibit.

"We're here," said Maria. "What do we do now?" After a few moments her eyes caught on something. "Look." She pointed at an odd shape in the grass.

Lenny went up against the railing. "I think you're right," he said. "There's definitely something there."

"I'm going to get it."

"Wait, tigers can slam a person with their paw with enough force to make it feel like being hit with a block of concrete," said Lenny. "I also read what you found online. There's also the teeth and claws."

Maria swung one leg around the railing. "I'm doing this," she said. She was quiet for a moment. "I can't lose another parent."

Lenny looked at her for a moment. "Okay," he said. "I'll lower you and pull you back up with my jacket, but you have to be quick and careful."

"Sure," said Maria. She swung the other leg around the railing. Lenny took off his jacket and Maria wrapped one of its arms around hers.

They looked at the single tiger present. Slugger was on the platform of land on the other end from the object, his rear end facing the railing.

"Go," Lenny whispered.

Maria went over the side as Lenny worked the jacket through his hands.

Maria walked backward on the raised wall. Occasionally she would steal glances toward Slugger. He was still preoccupied with some unknown thing in the tall grass.

Maria came a few feet from the water. "You're going to have to jump," whispered Lenny as loudly as he dared. He quickly looked around.

Maria unwrapped her arms and took a deep breath. She thought about all that had happened and jumped into the water with a soft splash.

The water reached Maria's stomach. She looked at the land portion of the habitat but could not see Slugger.

Maria waded toward the land portion as the strangeness of the situation dawned on her. *Just do it,* she thought. *Just focus on getting there and do it.*

Maria made it to the land portion and climbed up. Her heart raced as she looked around for Slugger. He was nowhere in sight. *He must've gone into the cave.*

She looked at Lenny, who was making frantic motions for her to hurry up.

Maria turned back and went over to where she had seen the object. It was blue, unlike the surrounding environment, so it was easy to find. Maria found it to be a large, blue envelope. She picked it up and put it in her back pocket.

Maria heard a growl and turned around. The tiger was facing her.

Chapter 2

Maria raced away as her heart rate shot up. She went over the edge of the land portion of the habitat, making a splash as she landed.

"Maria," cried Lenny.

The tiger went over the edge, making a loud splash as it landed behind her in the water.

Maria frantically moved through the water. She did not look back but allowed her terror to give her great energy.

She made it to the wall as she vaguely noted the sounds of the tiger gaining on her.

Maria jumped and her foot connected to the concrete just above the waterline. She pushed herself up and grabbed Lenny's jacket, which he had lowered. She grabbed it and he pulled her up as she ran up the wall.

As Maria came to the railing, she stopped and reached behind her. "Come on," said Lenny. He helped her over.

Maria pulled out the envelope. "I got it," she said.

"Hey, you," cried a voice. They turned to see a zookeeper coming at them.

"Go," said Lenny. They ran off.

They reached Lenny's car. Out of habit he had parked some distance away.

Maria was breathing rapidly. *That must be the craziest thing I've ever done*, she thought. She looked at the envelope. *I did it for her.*

They got inside the car and Maria opened the envelope. Inside was a piece of paper with writing on it. "At nine o'clock lightning struck the little boy," read Lenny. They sat there thinking.

"What does it mean?" asked Maria.

"I don't know," answered Lenny. He took out his cell phone and called another detective. "Paul, I need you to get on your computer."

"I'm on it," said Paul.

"Good. I need you to do a search on lightning strike, nine o'clock, and little boy," said Lenny.

"Okay," said Paul. "Any particular reason?"

"It's something I need," answered Lenny.

"Well, then, let me see," said Paul. He typed in the words and did the search. A few results came back. "There's a clock tower nearby, in Hedge Worth It was struck by lightning a few years ago. It was nine o'clock at night when it was struck, and there was a statue of a little boy in front of it."

"Thanks," said Lenny. He looked at Maria. "We've got a place." They drove off.

About a quarter of an hour later, they arrived in Hansfield. They passed a sign that read "Hedge Worth , Home of the Hedge Worth Roosters." A picture of a rooster was beneath the lettering.

I should be in school, thought Maria in a daze as the "real world" momentary seeped. She looked out the window. There were signs for businesses named Ticking Time Antiques and the Countdown Diner. There seemed to be more than a few souvenir shops as well. *The clock tower seems to be the main thing here,* thought Lenny.

They arrived at the clock tower, and as they got out, Maria saw the little boy statue a few feet away.

They went past it and into the lobby, where they saw a receptionist and a few people loitering around.

"Do you think we should take the tour?" asked Maria. She was looking at a sign that showed tour times.

"I don't think that'll help," said Lenny, "unless the tour goes to the very top." He was looking at a framed newspaper article and Maria joined him. The article talked about the lightning strike nearly twenty-five years ago and how it had hit the very top of the tower.

"We need a distraction," said Maria. She went to the center of the lobby. "There's a fire in the building," she cried.

The visitors looked around frantically. "I've got to call the fire department," said the receptionist. She reached for the phone on her desk, but Lenny stopped her.

"Madam, there's no time," he said. He flashed his badge and hoped he did it quickly enough so she did not see the number on it.

"Wait—how do you know about the fire?" asked the receptionist.

"There's no time to explain," said Lenny. He quickly led her halfway to the front door. The visitors had already left. As she followed them, Maria and Lenny went through a door that led to the stairs going up to the top.

There goes my career, thought Lenny. *Oh well.* They ran to the top. Maria thought about her mother and felt a burst of speed.

They reached the top. Before them was a door with a sign that read "Authorized Personnel Only."

"It's locked," said Maria.

"Stand back," said Lenny. He kicked out at where the lock met the doorframe. It went back a bit but did not open. Lenny slammed his body against it and pushed it, but it did not move.

"Together?" Maria asked. Lenny nodded. He stepped back and together they kicked out at the door. Their feet connected and the door flew open.

Maria fell forward to the ground. Lenny reached down to help her up, but she picked herself up and went off.

I'm going to be sore tomorrow, thought Lenny. He tried not to show his discomfort as he ran.

They went around the roof. "Where is it?" asked Maria.

"If you're asking about trouble, then it's right here," answered a voice.

Maria and Lenny turned around. There were three men standing before them. "The boss sent us here to make things interesting," said the man who had spoken.

Maria dropped into a fighting stance. Lenny looked around and saw a steeple that he had seen in a picture in the news article. He pointed. "There."

The three men charged at them. Lenny darted between them and Maria. "Go," he cried. "I'll hold them off."

Maria started to the steeple. One of the men, who was bald, tried to get past Lenny, but he grabbed him and swung him onto the roof.

Lenny turned to the brown-haired man who had spoken earlier and the man threw a punch at him. Lenny dodged it.

A blond man tried to tackle Lenny, but he dodged him. He charged at Lenny again, but Lenny kicked a leg out from beneath him. The man fell onto his stomach.

The brown-haired man used the momentary distraction to get close and started to throw a punch. Lenny turned around and grabbed his arm. He flipped the man onto the roof.

Maria came up to the steeple. She looked up and saw that there was another envelope attached to the top. She took a deep breath. *Come on,* she told herself, starting to climb up.

The brown-haired man got up and threw a punch at Lenny, who dodged it. The man threw two more, but Lenny kept dodging. Lenny grabbed the man's wrist and put him in a wristlock. He held the man in it for a moment and then shoved the man onto the roof.

The other two men got up and charged at Lenny. He grabbed the bald man and swung him into the blond man. They collided and fell down onto the roof.

Maria's heart raced as she climbed the steeple. *Come on,* she told herself. *Come on.* She thought about her mother and then her father. She felt a new determination and continued.

Don't look down, she told herself. Fear still grew in her, but she was almost to the top.

Lenny grabbed the brown-haired man and threw him on top of the other two. He threw himself onto the pile and tried to hold them down. The brown-haired man reached up and shoved him off.

Maria reached the top of the steeple. She grabbed the envelope and tried to pull it down, but it seemed to be secured with tape. After a few pulls she feared she was going to have to use both hands, which she did not want to do. Finally it came loose and she tucked it under her arm before starting to head down.

Her foot slipped and it swung through the air. Maria felt a jolt of fear go through her. She tightened her grip.

Maria managed to get bring her foot back onto the steeple. She was still for a moment. *You've got to go back down,* she told herself. *Lenny.* She finished climbing down.

Lenny backed away from the men. The brown-haired man grinned menacingly.

Maria jumped down onto the roof from the steeple. "I got it," she said. She was holding up the envelope.

"Let's go," said the brown-haired man. They darted away.

"Stop them," Maria cried.

Lenny tried to grab the blond man, but he shoved him away. The three men went down the stairway.

"They could know where my mom is," said Maria. She tried to run after them, but Lenny stopped her.

"This isn't the time," he said. "The fire department could be here at any moment and probably the police too."

Maria and Lenny went down the stairs. They had just gotten out when firefighters arrived. The three men were gone.

Chapter 3

Lenny and Maria drove away from the scene. Lenny kept an eye out to see if anyone was following them, but Maria kept her focus on the envelope. She quickly opened it and found a note inside. "In 1959 a female rooster laid an egg that looked like a baseball," read Maria. "She had to chase the blind mice from it."

She looked at Lenny. "What does that mean?"

Lenny thought about it. A few blocks later he pulled into a parking spot. "We have to keep going," said Maria.

"We have nowhere to go until we solve this riddle," said Lenny.

Lenny and Maria sat there thinking. *Roosters,* Lenny thought. *Roosters and baseball.* "I think I got it," he said.

"What?"

"The local baseball team is called the Hansfield Roosters. Remember the sign we passed as we were coming into town?"

"No," answered Maria. Lenny started the car and drove off.

They soon arrived at Lockye Stadium, home of the Hansfield Roosters. It was not the biggest stadium, but it was still impressive, especially for a town the size of Hansfield. As they passed the front gate, Lenny saw a sign that read "Hansfield Roosters, Founded in 1959."

They parked some distance away and ran up to the stadium. They came up to the front gate. It had a lock on it as well as a sign that said "Closed."

"What are we going to do?" asked Maria.

"Let's look around," answered Lenny. They went around the building.

They soon came to a side entrance, which Lenny tested. *Locked,* he thought. "How are we going to get in?" asked Maria.

"Give me a minute," said Lenny. He looked at the doorknob. "Well, it's not like we haven't broken the law already today."

"What?"

"Come on," said Lenny. He led her back to the car.

Lenny drove around and then parked in front of a hardware store. He made a hasty purchase in cash and then drove back.

Lenny and Maria went to the front gate. "Keep a lookout," Lenny said. Maria looked around as Lenny took out his new purchase, a pair of bolt cutters. He cut off the lock and opened the gate, and they went inside.

"You'd think there would be guards," said Maria.

"Just be thankful," said Lenny.

They went in and soon came to an opening that led to the seating area. Lenny stopped Maria and then put a finger to his lips.

Maria heard footsteps. *A guard?* Maria wondered. *We can't go back.*

A few anxious minutes later, the footsteps got fainter. Lenny peeked around a corner and then waved Maria to come. They darted to the hallway leading in the opposite direction from where the footsteps had come.

"Where are we going?" whispered Maria.

"I don't know," Lenny whispered back. "What about the part about the mice?"

Mice, thought Maria. *Blind mice. Cheese.* "Mice eat cheese," she whispered. "What about the food court?"

Lenny looked around. There was no one about, and he saw a sign pointing in the direction of the food court.

They arrived at the food court and Lenny tried the door. "Locked," he whispered.

"Could we try breaking the glass?"

"No—the guard could hear it."

"We've got to do something," whispered Maria. Her voice was rising as she spoke.

Lenny became worried. "Okay," he whispered. "We'll think of something. Just keep it down. Remember the guard."

Maria quickly looked around as Lenny looked through the window at the unused food court. *The whole place looks empty,* he thought. *They took all the equipment and chairs. Where are we supposed to find anything? It's just one big empty room.* "I don't think it's here," said Lenny.

"Then what does the riddle mean?"

"Blind mice," said Lenny. "Just like the nursery rhyme." Maria tried to remember the rhyme. *Three blind mice,* she thought. *Three blind mice.*

"Three," said Lenny. "It could be about the number three. If that's the case, then we should start at seat number three."

Maria darted off. "Maria, wait," Lenny whispered. He chased after her.

They came out to the seating area. Maria dashed down the steps as Lenny stopped and looked around. Then he followed her.

Moments later, Maria arrived at seat number three. She looked under it and found another envelope. She picked it up.

Lenny came up to her. "Stop," he said. "We've got to quit playing his game."

"Isn't that what we do?" asked Maria. "It's what we did the last couple of times."

"Well, this time I have a better idea."

"I can't not do this if it's the way to find her."

"Like I said, I have a better idea." Lenny put a hand on Maria's shoulder. "I need you to trust me."

"I do trust you," said Maria. "It's just that I lost my dad. I can't lose her."

"I know it's hard, but please, put any trust you have in me above that," said Lenny.

Maria was silent for a moment. "Of course," she said. "That's what partners do."

Partners, thought Lenny. He tried not to smile. "Let's get out of here." They left.

They drove away from the stadium. "Why don't you try to find Mr. Mindful with your visions?" asked Lenny.

Maria closed her eyes and focused on the man she knew only as Mr. Mindful.

Mr. Mindful sat in a darkened room. The man with brown hair came in. "Did you get it?" asked Mr. Mindful.

"Yeah," answered the man.
"Took you a long time to get back."
"There was a lot of traffic." April 2, 5:07 p.m.

"Still no address," said Maria. "Why?"

"Maybe it's an effect of the accident," said Lenny.

"But I've gotten addresses since then."

"Maybe it's a delayed reaction or maybe it's stress," said Lenny. "I don't know."

Maria put her face in her hands. "How do I make it stop?"

"I don't know," Lenny said again.

"Tell me this wasn't your idea."

"It wasn't," said Lenny. "I just wanted to try it."

Maria leaned back in her seat, closed her eyes, and then sighed.

Lenny looked at her. "You know, my father died a couple of years ago," he said. Maria looked at him, surprised. "He robbed a store when I was a kid and was chased by police. He tried to jump from one rooftop to another but fell to his death."

Maria was silent.

"He would say, look forward to the future when our wounds will be healed," said Lenny. He sighed.

"Is that why you joined the force?" Maria asked. "To make up for what he did?"

"No, I joined to make sure everything, including police work, runs smoothly and the way it's supposed to."

They were quiet for a moment. "I just wanted you to know that I know what it's like," Lenny said. They drove on.

Chapter 4

Maria and Lenny returned to Paway, the city where they lived. Once Lenny reached a deserted spot, he pulled over.

"What're you doing?" Maria asked.

"Getting some info," answered Lenny. He took out his cell phone. "Hi, Paul," he said. "I'm sorry to call you again, but I need some information on a Bob Polesky." A moment passed as Paul spoke on the other end. "What about his brother, Jeremy?" Lenny asked. "Is he still on parole?" Paul spoke some more. "Okay, thanks," said Lenny.

Lenny drove off. "I think we have a lead."

They arrived a short distance away from a small house. "Wait in the car," Lenny said. He got out and went over to the house.

Bob Polesky answered the door. "Hello, Bob," said Lenny.

"What do you want?"

"Is that how you treat an authority figure? I would figure with your history that you'd be more respectful."

"I'm out. I cut a deal and I'm out. It's not like I'm on parole."

"But your brother is."

"What does he have to do with this?"

"I need something, and if I don't get it, I'll call your brother's parole officer and have his parole violated."

"You can't."

"I can and I will if you don't do what I want."

"What is it?"

"I want to know where Mr. Mindful is."

"I can't tell you that because I don't know," Bob said. "I was arrested and I testified against him. Since then he's pulled jobs with other guys."

"Call him and tell him that you want to meet," said Lenny. "Tell him that you have something important to tell him."

"I haven't talked to him in ages," said Bob.

"You used to work for him. Find a way."

"He could come after me. He's probably angry enough with me for testifying against him."

"Don't worry about that," said Lenny. "I'll protect you. Besides, think of your brother. You want him in jail?"

Bob looked at him and closed the door.

Lenny went back to the car and told Maria what had happened. "You think he'll do it?" asked Maria.

"Let's hope so," said Lenny.

They watched the house. Maria's stomach growled. *I haven't eaten all day,* she thought. She looked at the house. *Not now,* she told herself.

"Thanks for helping me today," she said.

"No problem," said Lenny. "It's what partners do."

Minutes passed and finally a car pulled up in front of the house. Lenny started the car.

"He did it," said Maria. Bob came out and got into the car, which then drove off. Lenny followed them.

The car drove a zigzag pattern through town. Suddenly, it took a sharp left turn through a red light. "Hold on," said Lenny. He made his own sharp turn and Maria held on as they went. As they went around the curve, a car came extremely close. The sides of the two vehicles nearly touched, and Maria saw the face of a man who was riding in the other car.

They went past them and down a street. The car they were following was somewhat in the distance, but they could still see it.

Lenny kept a distance from it as he followed. "Shouldn't we be going faster?" asked Maria.

"We don't want them to see us," answered Lenny. Up ahead the car turned right. "It's not nearly as important to constantly see them as it is to know which way they turned." When he came up to the turn, he took it.

They came to a street with run-down houses on either end. The whole neighborhood seemed to be in disrepair. The car they were following pulled into a driveway and Lenny pulled into a driveway a few houses away.

"You think she's in there?" asked Maria.

"Possibly," answered Lenny. "We don't know for sure. Keep calm."

"Okay." Maria looked at the house and tried to fight the nervousness that was going through her. *Keep calm,* she told herself. Maria closed her eyes and did some breathing exercises she had learned in karate class. One moment passed followed by another.

Lois sat in the dark room. Where am I? *she wondered. She looked around, but all she saw was that she was in a plain, poorly lit room.*

Lois got up and walked around. After going around the room, she went back to the wall she'd been sitting against. She leaned against it and closed her eyes. "Maria," *Lois said. 26 Beaver Street, April 2, 2:54 p.m.*

Maria opened her eyes. "She's here," she said.

"How do you know?" asked Lenny.

"I know."

"It's back."

"It's back," Maria said. "I did some breathing exercises I learned in karate class to calm down like you told me to. I guess it was stress that was messing up my visions. It's been one stressful day."

"Wish we'd known that earlier," said Lenny. "Let's go." They got out of the car and went over to the house.

There was a man standing on the outer edge of the property who seemed to be standing guard.

Lenny pointed at himself and then at the man. He then pointed at Maria and pointed at the house, and then made a circular motion.

Maria nodded and started to go around the house.

Lenny watched her go and then turned his eyes to the man.

Lenny's cell phone rang and he answered it quickly, hoping no one had heard it. "Hello?" he asked quietly.

"Lenny, where are you?" asked Lieutenant Finn.

"I'm out following a lead," answered Lenny.

"On what case?"

"I can't say, sir."

"First, disappearing at the start of the day and now this cloak-and-dagger stuff," Finn said. "This is not good behavior for someone going places."

"I'm not going places," said Lenny. "I'm a cop and I'm chasing bad guys. I'm right where I need to be. So, whatever you've got planned for me, you can just keep it."

"What?"

"Got to go," said Lenny. He hung up and looked at his cell phone. *I must be crazy,* he thought.

The man turned to stare in the opposite direction and Lenny managed to sneak up behind him. Lenny threw a punch, but the man turned just in time to see it. He blocked it and kicked out at Lenny, who backed away.

"Hey," cried the man. "There's someone here!"

Lenny grabbed him and shoved him to the ground. "Quiet," he ordered. He placed a hand on his mouth. The man struggled with him and started to break free.

Lenny swung a fist and knocked the man unconscious. Lenny could see it was the man with brown hair. Lenny cuffed him and dragged him to the bushes. He then went inside.

Maria went through the bushes. "Hey," someone said. Maria looked up and saw that it was the bald man.

Maria swung a roundhouse kick, which the man blocked. He threw a punch, which Maria dodged. She sent a blow to his arm. He cringed in pain and Maria kicked him in his stomach. He doubled over, and she grabbed him and shoved him against the house. She did it again and again, and then let him fall to the ground.

The blond man came at her. Lenny threw a punch and he went down.

"Are you all right?" Lenny asked. "I heard the noise you two made."

"I'm fine," answered Maria. She went into the house. Lenny quickly cuffed the man and followed her.

Maria and Lenny went through the living room. They scanned the area.

"Congratulations," said Mr. Mindful. He stepped into view from a doorway.

Maria and Lenny quickly turned to face him. Maria ground her teeth. "Where's my mom?" she demanded.

"Around," answered Mr. Mindful. "What should be of concern to you is that your entrance here could not have gone unnoticed by a criminal mastermind. "

"Oh please," said Lenny. "We're all getting tired of the 'criminal mastermind' bit. You're just a loser who's read too many comics."

"Be quiet," ordered Mr. Mindful.

"Why me?" asked Maria. "Why did you ruin my life?"

"Because you're of that breed that tormented me all my life," answered Mr. Mindful. "Always trying to put me in a box. 'You must be mindful of others,' said my parents, teachers, so-called bosses, and all the shortsighted people who had gotten into my life. They were always trying to make me conform to their nice, neat standards. You were just the latest in a long line, and you had to pay. It's time the world conformed to my standards!"

"You killed my father," Maria cried. She assumed a fighting stance.

Lenny looked at her and then Mr. Mindful. "You take this guy," he said. "I'll find your mom." He darted through the room.

"Hey," cried Mr. Mindful. He started to go after Lenny, but Maria charged at him. She threw a kick at his leg. "Ahh!" he cried. He grabbed his leg. "That hurt."

"I'm just getting started," said Maria. She swung a punch at his chin that pushed his head back.

As he was stunned, Maria grabbed his wrist and put it in a lock, and then maneuvered his arm around his back. She pushed him across the room. He tried to struggle and stop her, but she kicked him in the shin. As he was distracted by the pain, she slammed him against a wall. She slammed him once, twice, three times. She kicked him in the leg again and there was an audible snap. "Ahh!" he cried.

Maria clenched her teeth as she felt something come out in her. She pulled him by the wrist she was holding. There was another snap. "My wrist" cried Mr. Mindful. "You crazy—"

Maria interrupted him with a punch.

He fell to the floor. He lay there, breathing heavily. Maria walked over to him. She stepped on his hand. "Ahh!" cried Mr. Mindful. "Stop!"

He swung a fist out, but Maria blocked it. He tried to claw at her, but she sent an open-handed blow to his chin. The back of his head hit the floor.

Maria put one foot on his chest. Images of her father went through her mind. She punched him in the face. She did so again and again. At first he tried to fight back, but then he could not. Maria did not stop, did not think about stopping. It was almost a mechanical series of actions fueled by rage.

Suddenly something inside Maria jerked. She stopped and held one fist up in the air. Mr. Mindful lay there unconscious. Blood was sprayed over his face like a red mustache.

"Oh my God," said Lois's voice.

Maria turned to see Lois standing by Lenny. Maria got off him. She looked over at her mother. Seeing her face incredibly strong emotions rose up in Maria. She ran up to her and they hugged each other. They remained in hugging for a few minutes. There was no noise except for Lois gently crying. Lenny coughed to get their attention. Lenny went over to check Mr. Mindful's pulse. "He's alive," he said. He looked around. "I don't see Bob. He must've taken off."

Maria got off him. Lenny took out his car keys and handed them to Maria. "Here, take my car," he said. "I'll find a way home."

"Wait, I know you," said Lois. "You were at the hospital the night my husband died. I didn't want to say anything, but you were on the news. What's going on?"

"Don't worry," said Lenny. "Everything will be all right."

Maria led Lois out of the house and to the car. She handed Lois the car keys. "Can you drive, Mom?" asked Maria. Lois nodded. They got in and drove off.

"I'm going to need some cars at twenty-six Beaver Street," said Lenny into his cell phone. "And maybe a bus."

Maria and Lois got home. Lois turned off the ignition and looked at Maria. "What's going on?" she asked. "What you did, that man. Why is everything . . ."

Maria looked at her mother's face. *It's just like Lenny said about her at the hospital,* she thought. She sat there for a moment and made a decision. She closed her eyes and focused. "Funny Time cereal, tonight on the evening news, so I've heard, Wonderman's adventures will continue," she said.

"What?" asked Lois. She was nearly hysterical.

"Let's go inside," said Maria.

Lois sat down on the couch. Maria picked up the TV remote and turned the TV on. "Funny Time cereal," said the voice of a cartoon box of cereal. It was a commercial. Lois had a look of surprise on her face and looked at Maria, who turned the channel.

"Tonight on the evening news . . . , " said the newscaster. Maria turned the channel.

"So I heard," said a woman to a man. Maria turned the channel.

"The adventures of Wonderman will continue," said the announcer of a cartoon show. Maria turned the TV off.

Maria sat down on the couch beside Lois. "Mom, we need to talk."